MW00849884

LOST IN OWL CREEK

Fresh start. New terror.

LOST
IN OWL CREEK

CAREN HAHN

Lost in Owl Creek by Caren Hahn

Published by Seventy-Second Press

www.carenhahn.com

Copyright © 2024 Caren Hahn

All rights reserved.

No part of this publication may be reproduced, distributed, or transmitted in any form or by any means, including photocopying, recording, or other electronic or mechanical methods, without the prior written permission of the publisher, except in the case of brief quotations embodied in critical reviews and certain other noncommercial uses permitted by United States of America copyright law and fair use.

Hardcover ISBN-13: 978-1-958609-11-8

Paperback ISBN-13: 978-1-958609-10-1

This is a work of fiction. Any references to historical events, real people, or real places are used fictitiously. Names, characters, places, and incidents either are the products of the author's imagination or are used fictitiously.

Cover design by Andrew Hahn.

Edited by Rachel Pickett of Polished Copy Editing Services.

Printed in the USA

In memory of Stephanie Condon, Rebecca Weston,
and all the other children who don't come home.

BOOKS BY CAREN HAHN

Find all of Caren
Hahn's work on
Amazon.com

CONTEMPORARY SUSPENSE:

This Side of Dark

What Comes After

THE OWL CREEK SERIES

Smoke over Owl Creek

Hunt at Owl Creek

Lost in Owl Creek

ROMANTIC FANTASY:

HATCHED

Hatched: Dragon Farmer

Hatched: Dragon Defender

Hatched: Dragon Speaker

THE WALLKEEPER TRILOGY

Burden of Power

Pain of Betrayal

Gleam of Crown

Visit carenhahn.com to receive a free
copy of *Charmed: Tales from
Quarantine and Other Short Fiction*.

TREATMENT OF SENSITIVE TOPICS

As a mother of six, I understand deeply the fear of losing a child. While most parents will never have to experience the horror of seeing their worst nightmare come true, I recognize that this topic may be unsettling for readers. As an author, I've attempted to treat the subject of child abduction sensitively and without gratuitous indulgence—while maintaining the necessary gravitas such a serious topic requires.

Lost in Owl Creek is low on graphic description and high on emotional resonance, but out of respect for any readers who are unsure about proceeding, you may find a list of some of the more triggering content on my website at https://carenhahn.com/books/lost-trigger-warnings. (Or use the QR code above.)

LOST IN OWL CREEK

OWL CREEK MYSTERIES BOOK 3

CAREN HAHN

SEVENTY-SECOND
PRESS

1

A THIN LAYER of frost glittered on the stone path leading up to the massive front door of the Fishers' sprawling brick home. Stained a deep walnut, the door's ornate woodwork served as an elegant backdrop for a giant cedar wreath hung over the etched glass window. Twinkling lights shone in a large picture window to the right of the entrance, hinting at a Christmas tree in its customary place of honor.

Abby's shoes, black Mary Janes with a flower motif stamped onto the strap, scraped against the paving stones as she darted ahead of Val to reach the door first.

"Hold on, wait for me." Anxiety made Val's tone sound strained. As much as she wanted this meeting—needed it, even—she was sick with dread and needed a moment to collect herself. Walking up this path was awakening memories she'd tried to bury for nearly a year. She felt numbness hardening around her and recognized it as a defense mechanism to being here, in this place. But she would power through.

She had to.

She and Abby had spent Christmas in Phoenix with Val's mother and sister Gina then caught a flight to Chicago the following day. Abby would spend the rest of the holiday break with her Grandma and Grandpa Fisher, but Val had something important she needed to do first.

Someone she needed to see.

Because the stately home sat at the end of a winding drive accessed through a security gate, there was no way to show up unannounced. Sure enough, as Abby reached for the doorbell, the front door opened.

Charles Fisher greeted his granddaughter with a wide smile.

"Grandpa!" Abby cried as he scooped her up into his arms.

Charles wore a pair of chinos and a navy cardigan over a button shirt without a tie, the most casual Val ever saw him. Even the Christmas holiday was a time to put your best foot forward when you were a Fisher.

Val had prepared accordingly, wearing a pencil skirt and heels despite the dusting of fresh snow on the upscale suburb of Chicago. She'd purchased a whole ensemble special for this occasion just so she wasn't wearing anything Jordan could recognize from their life together. Even though she'd bought everything at a discount store in Pineview, the clothes felt like an extravagance.

In the months since the Owl Creek bombings, she'd gone to work as an aide at the elementary school. The pay was barely enough for her and Abby to live on, especially now that she was registered to start taking classes at the community college in January. But this investment in her wardrobe had been necessary to assert whatever independence she could when she faced her husband.

"Good morning, Valerie," Charles said, setting Abby down and offering an arm for a half hug. "Can I take your coat?"

"Hi, Charles. Merry Christmas." She leaned into the hug, the familiar warmth of him putting her at ease. He smelled pleasantly of Old Spice, which always reminded Val of her own dad. She slipped out of her wool coat—the one garment she hadn't replaced—and handed it over.

"How was your flight?" Charles asked, a kind sparkle in his eyes. "Did you try the trick with the stickers?"

Val smiled. "She loved them, thank you. Which reminds me, I stuck a package in the outside pocket of her suitcase, so she can have them on the flight home."

A rhythmic clicking on the tile floor announced the approach of Jeanette Fisher and Heidi, her Cavalier King Charles Spaniel. Jeanette wore flowing slacks and a white cashmere sweater that Val suspected cost more than one of her public education paychecks.

"Valerie, Abby, do come in. So good to see you." Jeanette's tone was warm and welcoming, but it put Val immediately on edge. Jeanette knew what she was doing there, what she carried in her messenger bag. After all these months of trying to talk Val out of a divorce, had her mother-in-law finally accepted the inevitable?

It was hard to believe. But then, Val had never felt like she and Jeanette really understood each other. Charles, though, was a different story. Val had always felt genuine acceptance from him.

She followed Charles and Abby through a pillared archway and into the formal living room where the Christmas tree stood. It was tastefully decorated in gold and white, looking like something out of a magazine. Presents wrapped in shining paper with velvet bows sat beneath its spreading boughs.

"Wow!" Abby said, gazing up at the tree. "Look, Mom, it's way bigger than ours. It's even bigger than the one at the park!"

"It's beautiful," Val agreed, thinking of the large tree that sat at the center of Main Street at home.

"Who are these presents for?" Abby asked Jeanette.

Jeanette crouched down and fingered an embossed tag so Abby could read the name. "Why don't you see for yourself?"

Abby's eyes widened. "For me?"

"Some of them," Jeanette answered. Smile lines creased the corners of her eyes. "We decided we would wait for you to come before celebrating Christmas. What do you think of that?"

Abby looked hopefully at Val. "You mean, I get to have two Christmases?"

"That's very generous of you." Val hoped her smile looked more genuine than it felt.

"They're not all for her," Charles said, as if guessing

her thoughts, "but Jordan wanted to get her a few things."

"Of course." Val glanced around the room, half-expecting and half-fearing to see Jordan in the doorway.

"He's waiting for you in the library," Jeanette said, the light dimming from her eyes. "Unless you'd rather wait..."

"No, thank you. My flight leaves this afternoon, so I need to get on the road." Val's stomach flipped again like she was going to be sick. She hadn't eaten breakfast at the hotel for this exact reason. But this is why she was here, so she gripped her messenger bag and left Abby gleefully examining the presents and blissfully unaware of the gravity of what her mom was about to do.

The double doors to the library were closed, and the frosted glass disguised the interior. Val wondered if she should knock, but surely Jordan knew she was there. Was he as nervous to see her as she was to see him? Val paused and took a deep breath to calm her nerves. *You are a warrior,* she whispered on the exhale as she opened the door.

Shelves lining one wall were filled with books, framed photographs on small easels, and other mementos of the Fishers' forty years together. The carpet was plush beneath Val's feet as she stepped inside, the small click of the door latch announcing her arrival.

Jordan stood before a gas fireplace and turned as she entered. The snowy daylight, cool and stark, fell across his features.

Val's breath caught.

She'd imagined—and dreaded—this meeting so many

times in recent weeks, yet she still wasn't prepared for what it felt like to recognize him. Her whole body came alert in a way that said, *I know you.* She paused just inside the door, trying to push away the feeling of longing that welled up inside—a memory of touch and tenderness over the formative years that had defined Val's transformation into adulthood.

"Val."

One word. Her name. His thumbs were hooked in his front pockets, a posture as familiar as the timbre of his voice. His hands twitched and he folded his arms, then dropped them to his sides as if he wasn't sure what to do with them. He was dressed in jeans and a dusty blue sweater layered over a white shirt, a casual look that he still managed to make sophisticated.

"Come in," he said. "It's so good to see you. You look...amazing."

Somehow Val summoned the strength to step forward into the room. He reached for her like he wanted to touch her, but she shielded herself with the messenger bag and sidestepped to the nearest leather sofa. She sat on the edge of the cushion, unable to relax. The leather was cold against her bare legs.

"You look very much alive," she said. "Not exactly what I expected when you disappeared a year ago." She hadn't meant to say it, but the ache in her chest betrayed her and she couldn't hold it back. *Focus. He's not worth dredging up old pain.*

Jordan sat opposite her in a wingback armchair and leaned forward, his forearms on his knees. Just the way he moved was so familiar it stirred something inside of her. A knowing. A feeling of belonging. Still, there were some differences. He was thinner than she remembered and his sandy-colored hair was cut shorter than she'd ever seen it, making it look almost brown. His close beard didn't quite disguise the single dimple, and she found herself looking for it rather than looking into his eyes.

"It's too late to say I'm sorry," Jordan said. "I know that. But I am, Val, for what it's worth."

"Did that work on the prosecutors?"

He blinked. "I don't expect you to understand. What I did was unforgivable. But I hope you'll believe me when I say I really thought it would be best for you and Abby. I was trying to protect you, and I thought if I disappeared things would blow over faster." It sounded rehearsed, like a prepared speech, and she wondered how many times he'd imagined this meeting too.

But then, he'd kept his crimes a secret for years. If there was one thing he was skilled at, it was telling her things she wanted to hear.

Anger shot like heat up her spine. "You weren't thinking of us, you were only thinking of yourself. If you'd really wanted to protect us, you would have turned yourself in. What even happened to you?" A crack in her voice betrayed her emotion and she inwardly cursed herself for not holding it together.

Jordan sighed and looked out the window at the manicured lawn where snow lay as pristine as a postcard.

"I wish I could explain, but I can't."

In that moment, Val realized that for as much as she'd told herself it didn't matter, she *did* want an explanation. For him to deny her that felt like a final betrayal.

With effort, she pushed away all feeling behind the wall of numbness and turned to the matter at hand.

"Whatever, it doesn't matter now. I have the papers here." She opened her messenger bag and pulled out the sheaf of paperwork waiting for his signature. "The terms are what our lawyers discussed."

"I get relegated to the Disneyland Dad?" Jordan said dryly as he took the papers from her.

"Considering that you were Dead Dad until recently, I'd say this is an improvement."

The silence grew long as Jordan thumbed through the paperwork, occasionally pausing to examine something in more detail.

Val had a hard time breathing and offered a silent prayer that Marcene hadn't made any mistakes. Val had intended to let their lawyers handle all the communication, but Jordan had insisted on seeing her in person before signing the divorce papers. He'd conceded to all her demands, so this seemed one consideration she could give him. But the pressure she felt watching him examine all the forms made her wish she'd refused.

When Jordan reached the end, he paused and looked up at Val. "What is this?"

Val glanced at the sheet in his hand and mentally kicked herself. She'd meant to give the letter to Abby to deliver on her own. The last thing she wanted to do was make this meeting sentimental. "It's a letter Abby wrote to you last summer, before we knew you were still alive."

Jordan scanned the page, mouthing some of the words Abby had spelled phonetically with a smile tugging at his lips. His eyes widened when he finished. "There was a cougar on your parents' property?"

Val was immediately transported back to that summer day with Joel when they'd discovered Sam Howser's body on the hill behind the farmhouse. The terror she'd felt when the cougar threatened them. The way Joel had placed himself in front of her as a shield—an act which had awed her at the time and which she now understood to be so quintessentially Joel that she couldn't imagine him doing any less.

But she wasn't about to tell Jordan any of that, so she dismissed it with a simple, "Fish and Wildlife took care of it."

Jordan set aside the letter and settled back in his chair. "Thank you for making room for me in Abby's life. I know it can't be easy, but I appreciate it."

His gratitude took the edge off her stress.

"It's not what I wanted for her," Val said. "None of this is. But no matter how I feel about you, she has the right to make her own decisions about who her father is."

"I promise I'll be there for her," he said fervently. "She'll be able to count on me."

The ache in Val's heart grew. *I couldn't count on you*, she wanted to say. *Why should she?* But it was too late for that. She couldn't get those years back now. And she wouldn't even want to if given the chance. Not now that she knew what he was capable of.

Jordan signed the divorce papers with the same deliberateness he'd shown in reviewing them.

Val waited for a sense of relief to come as he finished the last one, but instead she just felt tired.

She bound them back in the folder and slipped it into her messenger bag.

"Thank you for coming to do this in person," he said. "It seems like two people should look each other in the eye when they end their marriage instead of doing it through strangers."

"Well, I'm glad it worked out," Val said brusquely, moving to stand.

He stood, too, and held out his arms. "May I...?"

She let him embrace her but held the messenger bag against her stomach and didn't return the affection. He smelled differently than she remembered, but the way his arms fit around her was so familiar she closed her eyes briefly, wondering how it had come to this.

He pulled back and held her at arm's length. "For what it's worth, I never stopped loving you. I knew I didn't deserve you, but I always loved you."

Val tried to muster a scathing response, but she could see the truth of it in his eyes.

"Sometimes love isn't enough," she said quietly.

He let her go but called to her before she reached the door.

"Val?"

She stopped and looked back, one hand on the doorknob.

"Is he good to you?" He didn't sound bitter. Only sad.

She didn't have to ask who Jordan was talking about.

"He is." She looked at the gas fireplace instead of making eye contact.

"That's good. I'm glad. You deserve the best." The pain in his voice made her throat tighten.

She wouldn't feel guilty for hurting him. She wouldn't feel guilty for moving on.

"Goodbye, Jordan," she said as she opened the door. But she looked back before she left and offered a last token of reconciliation. "Thank you."

2

RED and blue lights strobed across the yard, painting the residence with a sense of urgency as Joel parked his Charger behind a Yukon bearing the logo of the Wallace County Sheriff's Office. The long driveway leading to Leisa Greer's home was crowded with two county vehicles—three, now that Joel had arrived—hemming in a red Subaru, two minivans, and a truck. Two deputies moved around the yard, trying to herd a dozen or so people back to their vehicles.

The driveway was spongy underfoot as Joel stepped out of the car, a new one since their fleet had taken such a big loss in September's bombing. A detached garage sat off to the side of the property, its door open and exposing an array of furniture, tools, and plastic storage bins. A man stood inside, partially hidden in shadow. As Joel rounded the car, the man lifted a tarp that had been draped over something round and flat, possibly a decorative table or mirror.

"Noah!" Joel called, recognizing him.

The man raised his head and dropped the tarp.

"Come on out of there! We'll handle that."

Noah Proctor stepped out into the cold December light. Condensation gathered like dewdrops on his beard.

"I'm looking for KJ and Sophie. Leisa called me when she got home from work and found them missing." He was a little breathless, his voice tight with anxiety.

"I know you want to help, but we don't know what we're dealing with yet. Too many people getting involved could impede our efforts, tampering with the scene, you know?"

Noah looked abashed. "Sorry, Joel. We're all just trying to help. KJ's a sweet kid who would never run off on her own." He sniffed and looked away, tugging at his beard.

"I'll let you know if there's some way you can help. But for now, the best thing you can do is get out of the way." Joel knew Noah from the Volunteer Fire Department, but wasn't well acquainted with his sister, Leisa. Dispatch had informed him that not only was her daughter missing, so was the friend who had spent the night.

Hopefully that meant they were together somewhere, maybe doing something they shouldn't but not necessarily in danger. Best case scenario, this day would end with the girls embarrassed, the parents furious, and a lesson learned that would make all parties smarter.

That would be a good day.

The alternative...well, he wasn't ready to think about that yet.

Joel checked the time as he retrieved his kit from the trunk. Illinois was two hours ahead of Oregon, and he wondered if Val had already been to see the Fishers. Jordan's only request for signing the divorce papers had been for Val to deliver them in person, something Joel had opposed. But either guilt had made Val agree, or there was still a part of her that trusted her husband in spite of his history.

Soon to be ex-husband if all went well.

Joel closed the trunk with camera and gloves in hand and headed toward the house. Willis, a young deputy fresh out of the academy and still on probation, crossed the yard to intercept him. He'd recently been assigned to Owl Creek to help fill the gaps left after the bombing. Not a day went by that Joel didn't miss Larry and his years of experience with the community. Especially when working with deputies who looked barely old enough to shave.

Willis met Joel with a clipboard as he came up the cracked cement path.

"How's it looking?" Joel asked as he signed in his arrival time.

"No obvious signs of an intruder," Willis said. "Both moms are inside with Kim. Homeowner is Leisa Greer. Single, thirty-three. Daughter is KJ, and friend Sophie was spending the night, both twelve. Sophie's parents are Faye and Ralph McNamara. Faye came over as soon as Leisa called and so did half of Wallace County to help look for them."

Twelve. Too old to have accidentally wandered off. Too young to have gone far if they'd left in the middle of the night of their own volition. Unless they had help from an older friend with a car.

Joel scanned the surrounding area before going inside. Noah was now shepherding friends and family off the lawn and away from the garage. Joel shook his head at the thought of how the helpful friends and family had been polluting the scene for the past hour. Neighbors gathered on the other side of the wire fence in their pajamas, potential witnesses who would all need to be questioned.

The long driveway was set back from the county road and surrounded by trees. Against the base of the steep hill behind the house, Joel could just make out what looked like remnants of an old logging road. To his left was a weathered cedar fence that separated the property from that of Brett Rogers, a man whose obsession with collecting mannequins was matched only by his paradoxical need for privacy. Cameras and no-trespassing signs made it clear he didn't welcome visitors, but his scenes were a regular bid for attention. Sometimes they even included captions.

Joel wondered how a single mom of a twelve-year-old girl felt about living next door to Brett Rogers.

The little house was white and in need of a fresh coat of paint, but it didn't seem neglected. Instead, the windows looked to have been recently replaced and the roof was free of moss. The front door of the Greer home was open, an aluminum screen door the only protection against the late December chill.

Joel pulled on gloves as he stepped inside, entering into a breakfast nook area and kitchen with a living room on the left. The room was cool, and Joel suspected the pellet stove in the corner was the home's only source of heat. It sat dark and lifeless.

A woman in a plum-colored, puffy jacket perched on the couch with a mug in her hands. The scent of coffee was sharp in the air. She stood when Joel entered, an expression of expectation on her face. A middle-aged woman stood next to Kim, her brown hair pulled back into a ponytail, exposing gray roots. She wore a dark sweatshirt and jeans and was gesturing animatedly to Kim, but she stopped mid-sentence when she saw Joel.

"This is Joel Ramirez," Kim said by way of introduction. "He's a detective with the sheriff's office. Joel, this is Leisa Greer and Faye McNamara."

Leisa was the younger mom in the jacket and Faye wore the hoodie. They both moved to shake his hand, matching expressions of hope in their eyes. *Fix this*, they seemed to beg.

"You're KJ's mom?" Joel asked Leisa.

"Yes."

"Were you coming or going from work?" he asked, taking in the pink scrubs under her jacket.

"I just got home," Leisa said, then glanced at a clock hanging next to a mirror near the door. "Well, about an hour ago. Geez, how has it already been an hour?"

"Still no word from your daughter?"

"No. I keep calling. She's not answering or responding to my texts."

"Does Sophie have a phone?" Joel asked Faye.

The older woman shook her head. "We don't let our kids have cell phones until they're fifteen. We knew if

Sophie really needed to get a hold of me, she could use KJ's phone."

Joel could hear the regret in her voice. The what-ifs already mounting.

"What time did you leave for work last night?" he asked Leisa.

"It's a twelve-hour shift, seven to seven at the hospital in Pineview. So I left a little before six."

"Okay. We're going to take some pictures before we do anything else. Can you walk me through your movements from the time you got home this morning? Anything you touched or moved that you can remember?"

"Of course." Leisa nodded jerkily. "I got off work at seven. I had to stop for gas, so by the time I got home it was almost eight thirty."

"Where did you get gas?"

"At the Chevron near the freeway. I knew the girls had stayed up late and would probably still be asleep, so I tried to be quiet when I came in."

"You entered through the front door?"

Leisa shook her head. "The side door by the kitchen. It's closest to the driveway."

Joel took a step to the side until he could see through the kitchen. A white door with a square pane of glass sat in the corner next to a bank of green cupboards that were chipped and scraped with age.

"Was that door locked?"

"I think so?" She said it like a question. "I used my key, but I didn't check it first. But it should have been locked. I reminded KJ to lock up after I left. She knows better with me working these late shifts, but maybe she forgot." Leisa's eyes were rimmed red, and she clutched her phone so tightly her knuckles were white.

"What did you do after you came inside?"

Joel's gaze flitted to the light gray purse tipped over on a side table, a set of keys spilling out. Next to it sat a pile of mail topped with a holiday card resting on a green envelope addressed to "Leisa and KJ."

"I was going to go straight to bed, but I thought I'd check on them first and that's when I saw they were missing."

"So the first thing you did was check on the girls? You didn't check your phone or put down your purse—"

"No, sorry, I did put down my purse. And I had gotten a couple of texts while I was driving, so I stopped to answer them."

Joel made a note. That would be easy enough to verify. "Did you lock the door after you came in?"

"Yeah, but I unlocked it again when I couldn't find them in the house. I checked outside but couldn't find them anywhere. That's when I called Faye."

On his notepad, Joel sketched a rough diagram of the room with its single couch, rocking chair, and beanbag where a blanket had been draped as an afterthought, then penciled in the kitchen with its separate entrance.

"What time was it when you checked on the girls?"

"I'm not sure. Sometime after eight thirty. Maybe eight forty?"

Faye looked up from her phone. "You called me at 8:38," she said authoritatively.

Leisa seemed older than her thirty-three years, her

face tight with cold and fear. "Okay, so a little before that."

"Did anything else seem out of place? I see you're still wearing your coat. Is the stove usually turned off when you come home?"

Leisa looked down as if surprised. "I guess I didn't take it off. I don't run the stove during the night. Pellets are too expensive."

Joel looked down the hallway, dimly lit with a single fixture. "Who else lives here with you?"

"No one. It's just me and KJ."

"And KJ's father lives in the area?"

"He lives in Pineview."

"I'll need his name and address."

"Sure. Jimmy Greer. Let me get you his contact info."

While she thumbed through her phone, Joel asked, "Tell me about your relationship."

Leisa glanced at Faye. "It's fine, I guess. We get along okay for KJ's sake. Here's his phone number and address."

She handed over the phone for Joel to write down the details. Most people tried to portray their ex-relationships more amicably than they really were, especially when children were involved. Joel suspected if he'd asked Leisa's closest girlfriends to describe her relationship with Jimmy, they would have used very different language.

"Is there any chance he could have come and picked up KJ without telling you?"

"Doubt it," Leisa scoffed. "He wasn't that interested

in being a dad when we were married. I have to remind him about her birthday so he doesn't forget it, and half the time he cancels when it's his weekend to have her over."

"We'll send a deputy to talk with him just to make sure."

"When do we organize a search party?" Faye asked, looking at Kim. "We've got friends and family ready to come out as soon as you say the word."

"Thanks," Kim said. "Our county Search and Rescue team may need the extra hands."

"Can you tell me a little more about Sophie?" Joel asked. "Does she stay over a lot?"

"Maybe once a month," Faye responded.

Leisa nodded in agreement. "When I work the night shift, KJ feels better when she has a friend. Usually it's Sophie. They've been friends since first grade."

"Where is KJ's room?"

Leisa moved down the narrow hallway adorned with pictures of a toothy adolescent girl with light brown hair and freckles. Joel paused in front of a picture of a basketball team. Instead of official uniforms, they wore matching t-shirts. He recognized Howie Lambert, a local elementary school teacher who had coached both the boys and girls junior high basketball teams for years.

"Does Sophie play basketball too?"

Leisa pointed to a tall girl wearing glasses. "That's Sophie. Howie does an after-school basketball club in the spring for fifth and sixth graders. They both played last year." A look passed between her and Faye.

"Do you need a recent picture of the girls?" Faye

asked. "Should we be putting together posters to hang around town?"

Joel understood her eagerness to act, to feel like she had some control over a senseless situation. The moms had already decided it was a stranger abduction, but stranger abductions weren't as common as most parents feared. It was far more likely the girls left with someone they knew. Likely they even left willingly.

"We'll want pictures for sure. Do either of the girls have boyfriends?"

Faye looked at him like he'd asked her something vulgar. "They're twelve," she said flatly.

"How about friendships with older teens? Any friends or extended family members old enough to drive?"

"I've got six kids, Detective." Faye's tone made it clear she wasn't impressed with his line of questioning. "Sophie's my youngest, so yeah, she has family members old enough to drive. But they don't know where she is. They're all worried sick and so are their friends. None of them has any clue where they went."

She stopped short of telling him that he was wasting his time, but Joel heard it in her voice. He didn't argue with her about the number of twelve-year-olds he'd seen involved in dangerously adult activities. Instead, he looked at Leisa.

"KJ would never run off like that without telling me," Leisa insisted. "She was excited to have Sophie come over. They were going to watch a movie and make popcorn. She texted me last night to ask if they could make smoothies. Does that sound like a girl who would run off with older friends in the middle of the night?"

"When was that? The text about the smoothies."

Leisa pulled out her phone again. "7:22." Her lips were thin and white around the edges. "Then she called me at ten, but I couldn't answer. On my next break I texted her to see what she needed and she said 'never mind.' That was the last I heard from her."

"May I see?" Joel asked.

He took Leisa's phone and scanned through the texts.

KJ was listed under the name Katie-bug with a profile picture of a girl holding a half-eaten cone of turquoise ice cream. She was sticking out her tongue and it was colored with a bright blue stripe down the middle. At the time the picture was taken, she couldn't have been much older than Abby was now, and it gave Joel a jolt to imagine Abby disappearing from her home in the middle of the night.

The screen door whined and they all turned toward it as an older woman with soft white hair stepped inside. She looked vaguely familiar, but Joel couldn't think of why. Kim moved to intercept her.

"I'm sorry, ma'am, but you'll need to wait outside."

"Leisa?"

"I'm here, Mom."

As Leisa hurried toward the door, Joel continued down the hallway alone. A door at the end opened onto a small bathroom, and a short deputy with a thin goatee stood guard in the doorway to the bedroom on the left. He stepped aside to make room for Joel.

"Morning, Marcus."

"Hey, Joel. Didn't think you were working today. Aren't you out this week?"

"Not until tomorrow," Joel answered as he added the hallway and bedroom to his sketch, including the placement of the unmade single bed and the rumpled sleeping bag on the floor.

"Was the light already on or did you turn it on?" he asked.

"It was on when I got here. Mom probably turned it on when she was looking for the girls. Also, you'll want to see this."

Marcus shifted to indicate the bathroom doorway. The door was half closed, and when Marcus pushed it all the way open, it revealed two dark spots the color of dried blood on the floor near the door jamb. Weak daylight came in from a narrow privacy window above the shower. Joel crouched to take a better look, the skin of his back stretching painfully as he leaned over. It was still tender from where a thousand shards of glass had burrowed into his skin more than three months earlier when the sheriff substation had been bombed. Not all of the glass had been removed, and sometimes embedded pieces still rose to the surface and became acutely sore.

Even without a light, Joel could see a fine layer of dust on the bathroom floor, but the surface of the drops of blood looked clean. Dry, but glossy smooth. Recent, then.

Joel straightened. "Keep everyone out of here. I'll need to get pictures of this room after I finish the bedroom."

At times like this Joel wished the county had a dedicated crime scene processing unit. There had been talk about getting a team of evidence techs for a couple of years, but the bombing had put all that on hold as the agency worked to recover from the loss of essential personnel.

Joel moved to the nearest corner of the bedroom and held up the camera to get a view of the whole room, adjusting for the light coming in from the single window. A large poster of a Korean boy band hung on the wall near the bed, with photos and childish artwork scattered on either side. Ribbons, buttons, and a deflated mylar balloon that said "Happy Birthday" in shiny red letters filled in the gaps.

Joel moved methodically around the room, taking pictures from each corner. A bookshelf sat beneath the window with most of its books stacked haphazardly rather than filed in neat rows. Four books lay on the floor next to the bookshelf and two more were by the bed next to a long, narrow strip of frayed, blue fabric. Joel had spent enough time with Abby to know that the mess wasn't necessarily the sign of a struggle. It was just as likely evidence of a distracted child.

The closet had tracks for sliding doors, but there were no doors there now. Clothes hung from hangers in various stages of attention, from orderly to dangling by a hem. A laundry basket sat in the corner, with a collection of dirty socks and underwear scattered on the floor like they'd been victims of a half-hearted toss. Dirty laundry was good. That would make it easier for a search dog to pick up a scent than if KJ and her mom kept their laundry together.

Joel paused near the window. Outside, clouds hung heavy in a pewter sky and a fine mist drizzled over the patch of lawn. On Rogers's side of the cedar fence, a leafless tree stood, thick moss and a tangle of mistletoe clinging to its bare branches. A small box sat high in the tree and Joel made a note to follow up with Rogers about the possibility that something was picked up on his camera. Not that Brett had ever accommodated requests from law enforcement before, but maybe he would make an exception for two missing girls.

It was as Joel moved to the last corner that he noticed the alarm clock on the little bedside table was dark. He looked for the cord, wondering if it had been knocked loose from the nearest outlet during a scuffle. But there was no cord, only an empty port where the cord should have plugged into the back of the clock. More than that, a charging brick sat in the outlet, also empty of a cord.

Joel paused. Charge cords were easy to move around and misplace. But the cord from an alarm clock? That made less sense. However, it would make a suitable ligature if a kidnapper had come expecting to find one girl and needed to improvise when he found she had a friend.

Kim leaned into the room. "I've got a fingerprint kit if you're ready for us to get started."

With a distinct feeling of unease, Joel lowered his camera. "I'm going to call Cooper. I think we're going to need some help on this one."

3

JOEL LOOKED up as a familiar figure exited the newest SUV parked on the shoulder at the end of the Greers' driveway. Special Agent Stacy Porter from Eugene's FBI Resident Agency was a balding black man whose height and stern features had a way of commanding respect as soon as he entered a room. Joel knew that his intimidating appearance hid a warm and charismatic personality, but he'd only learned that after working with him on several cases. The first time he'd met him, Joel had felt uncomfortably out of his depth.

Now Stacy reached forward and shook his hand.

"How are you, Joel?" Stacy's breath clouded in the chill air between them. "Glad to see you all in one piece."

"Not as glad as I am. Thanks for coming down here so quickly."

"Of course. I know you're a bit short-handed, so we're happy to help. We've got a Victim Specialist on her way from Portland." Stacy turned as three other agents approached, a woman and two men. Joel shook hands with each of them, noting Rita Coleman's sharp eyes and firm handshake.

Joel led them to Lieutenant Cooper, who was smoking a little distance away. Neighbors stood in the yard next door, pajama pants peeking beneath blankets hugged around their shoulders. The lots here must have been at least five acres, maybe twenty if they ran all the way up the mountain. But the parcels were long and narrow, so the houses stood no more than fifty yards apart.

"What would you like from us?" Stacy asked Cooper.

"Anything and everything you can spare," Cooper said. "We're stretched thin as it is and have two detectives out on medical."

Stacy nodded. "It'll be a while before our Evidence Response Team can get here. You got a location where we can set up command?"

Cooper looked at Joel. "You know the area better than I do."

Joel had already made a few calls. "The Grange is just a few minutes away on the other side of town. Closer to the freeway, too." The Grange Hall was used for social events and as a polling station during elections. With a large room for assembling groups and a sprawling parking lot, it was an ideal fit.

"I'd like to talk to the mom," Agent Coleman said, stepping forward with hands buried deep in her jacket pockets. Her thick mane of springy locks was held back away from her face by a wide band, exposing a dramatic widow's peak. "Is she inside?"

"Both moms are, yeah," Joel said. "I was going to go talk to the neighbors, unless you want me to join you."

"It's all right." Coleman nodded to Agent Justin Wong and together they headed for the house.

Joel left Cooper and Porter working out logistics and headed toward the wire fence, skirting the free-standing garage. A man herded two teenage boys away as Joel approached, leaving two women standing alone in their absence. One was holding a lit cigarette, but the ash collecting on the end made Joel suspect she'd forgotten it was there.

The other wiped her hands on her fleece Santa-print pants.

"How's Leisa doing, Detective?" she asked. "Any clue where the girls have gone?"

He answered with a question of his own. "You knew they were missing?"

"Leisa called me first thing this morning. Poor thing. Must be going out of her mind with worry."

"Are you and Leisa close?"

"We look out for each other. Especially after Jimmy left. I always told her I'd lend a hand if she needs it."

"And your name..." Joel pulled out his notepad.

"Penny Standridge. Penelope."

"Who else lives here with you?" Joel's eyes flitted to the other woman holding the cigarette.

"I'm just visiting." She took a step back as if alarmed to be included.

"This is my sister, Tansy. She's up from California

for the holidays. My husband, Doug, is in the house with our two boys."

"How old are your sons?" Joel asked, thinking of the teenagers he'd seen.

"Logan is seventeen and Jacob is fourteen."

"Are they friends with KJ?"

Penny's gaze slid to the fence. "They used to play together when they were younger, especially Jacob and KJ. You know, back in elementary school before they were old enough to care if their friends were boys or girls. But that was years ago. Jacob is in high school now and Logan is getting ready to graduate."

"Does Logan have his own car?" Joel asked, looking over her shoulder at the cars lining the driveway. A white Toyota truck, a silver Dodge minivan, and a green Honda Civic.

"No. He usually drives the Honda but it's not his. Why?"

"Just standard questions. Were you all home together last night?"

"Yeah, mostly. Tansy and I were out shopping and came home at about nine."

"Did you notice anything out of the ordinary next door? Hear anything or see anything unusual?"

Penny shook her head. "It was dark when we got back. I do remember Leisa's Christmas lights were on, and I thought she had the night off. So I was surprised when she called this morning and said she'd been working."

"Why did you think she had the night off?"

"Her car was there in the driveway."

Joel paused. "Are you sure about the time?"

Penny looked at Tansy. "Pretty sure."

Tansy pulled a phone out of her back pocket. "I got a call from my friend as we were driving home. I could check the time on that...yep, 8:34. And we hadn't exited the freeway yet, so it would have been later than that when we got back."

"Did you get a good look at the car?" Joel asked. "What made you think it was Leisa's?"

Penny looked uncertain. "Well, it was dark, so I can't say for sure. It was a hatchback, though, and looked like hers."

"What color was it?"

"I thought red, but maybe not. It was dark. I just assumed it was Leisa's. I'm sorry, I don't know."

"You said it was a hatchback. Did it look like a wagon or could it have been smaller?"

A look of distress lined Penny's forehead. "I...I'm not sure. It wasn't as big as a minivan or one of those...what do you call it, one of those crossovers. But I didn't get a good look. I just thought it was Leisa's."

"Did you notice when it left?"

Penny shook her head. "I wasn't paying attention. I'm sorry, Detective."

"If you remember anything else, let me know." Joel handed her his card. "I'd like to talk to your husband and son too, to see if they saw or heard anything last night." He turned as a black Charger pulled up onto the shoulder. Vehicles were filling the shoulder up and down the county highway now.

"Sure, that's fine. If you want to come on inside, I'll make you a cup of coffee."

"Thank you. I'll just be a minute." Joel made his way down the driveway as Marnie Sanders got out of her vehicle.

She was wearing a bulky coat and jeans, reminding Joel she was supposed to have the day off.

"I'm sorry I couldn't get away sooner," she said. "I got the decorations passed off so all they have to do is follow the instructions, and if they can't do that, then it's a lost cause and she can decorate for her own stupid wedding. What can I do to help?"

"The neighbor says she saw a car in the driveway three hours after the mom says she left for work last night. I'm going to follow up with the rest of the family."

"All right, I'll check in with Cooper and see what he needs. Oh, and Joel?" Marnie looked back over her shoulder.

"Yeah?"

"Merry Christmas."

***

VAL'S LAYOVER in Salt Lake City gave her just enough time to buy an overpriced sandwich and find an empty seat at the gate where she could plug in her phone with twenty minutes left before boarding.

Sitting in SLC thinking of you, she texted Joel. *Only a few more hours and I'll be home!*

She unwrapped her sandwich while she waited for a response. After spending hours sitting on an airplane crowded with holiday travelers, it was hard to believe that it was only that morning she'd seen Jordan and said goodbye to Abby. The flight to Portland would be quick, but the long drive from the airport to Owl Creek meant she wouldn't be home until close to midnight.

The sun was setting in Salt Lake, casting a pink glow over the snow-covered mountains in the east and reflecting off skyscrapers clustered at their base. As the hours took her further away from Chicago, Val felt a loosening deep inside.

Could it really be over?

It had been almost a year since that day when she'd learned from federal agents the truth about her husband. The day she'd learned that he'd used his connections as the son of Senator Jeanette Fisher to steal millions of dollars through a scheme targeting older retirees on fixed incomes. That was the same day she thought he'd committed suicide, only to learn almost six months later that he'd lied about that too.

But now, his signature was on the documents that would allow her to be free of him.

Well, almost. There would always be Abby tethering them to each other. But Jordan had been surprisingly selfless about the whole thing, conceding to her demands and asking for very little in return. It was almost as if he, too, were anxious to get it over with. Considering that he was facing a likely prison sentence, maybe this was one battle he didn't want to fight.

Even with his cooperation it wouldn't be easy, having

to balance summer breaks and holidays around Abby's visits with Jordan and his parents. But that was so much better than Jeanette's insistence that Val stick it out and wait until after Jordan's trial to make any decisions about their marriage.

Now, she was going to be free.

To celebrate, Joel had scheduled time off so they could enjoy a holiday getaway of their own. He'd booked two nights at the historic Ellis Cove lighthouse on the Oregon coast. The renovated lightkeeper's home had been repurposed as a bed and breakfast offering a breath-taking view of the lighthouse and the vast expanse of ocean. Now that Val was almost home, the thought of being completely away from everything was finally starting to feel real. This was the first time they'd planned a trip for just the two of them, and she was more excited for it than she'd been to spend Christmas in Arizona with her family.

Her phone buzzed and she laid aside her half-eaten sandwich, feeling a heightened joy as she answered.

"If you're calling to get a hint about your Christmas present, you're wasting your time. I know your investigator tricks and they won't work on me."

Joel's chuckle sounded forced. "I wish. I've got some bad news, Val."

Val's smile faded. "Uh oh. What is it?"

Work. Of course it was work. It was always work. But he'd promised that he'd gotten the time off and no matter what happened, he wouldn't cancel on her.

"Two girls went missing last night. KJ Greer and Sophie McNamara."

"Oh no." Val's stomach turned over around the half-eaten sandwich. "What happened?" She knew KJ and Sophie. They were six graders at the elementary school. Even though Val worked more with the younger grades, everyone knew the large McNamara family. Sophie's mom worked at the school too and was as much a fixture in the community as the Christmas truck parade.

"It's too early to say, but we've got the FBI here and we're treating it like a stranger abduction."

Val swore softly. "Joel, that's terrible. Poor Faye. How are you doing?"

"Fine. Just trying to find these girls."

"I don't know why I asked. You wouldn't tell me if you were in too much pain anyway, would you?"

She sensed a smile in his voice. "'Too much' is totally relative. I'm fine, Val. But I'm afraid I'm going to have to postpone our trip."

Val tried to keep the disappointed sigh to herself, but she wasn't quite successful. "Of course."

"I'm so sorry. I really hate to do this, but we need all the manpower we can get. I can't leave when it's so critical."

Val steeled herself. "Don't worry about me. I'll get over it. We can go another time," she added, even though she knew how hard it had been to arrange this trip around work and Abby in the first place. "It'll be fine. You find those girls, Joel."

He didn't say, *We will.* He didn't even say, *We're trying.* Instead, his quiet, "We have to," haunted her as she hung up the phone.

4

Joel pocketed his phone and moved to the exterior door that opened from the Grange's kitchen to the parking lot. Lori Sumsion, the retired Home Ec teacher who now operated a little bakery on Main Street in Owl Creek—just around the corner from where the sheriff's substation used to be—was wheeling a cart of sandwiches and boxes of chips up the sidewalk.

"Can I help you with that?" Joel asked as he opened the door.

Lori looked up and her lined face relaxed into a smile. "Thank you, Mr. Ramirez." She had always addressed her students as Mr. and Ms. and remembered them no matter how many years had passed since they were in her class.

Joel lifted the cart over the lip of the threshold and maneuvered it onto the tile floor.

"There's ham, roast beef, turkey, and even a few gluten-free options in case anyone needs them," Lori said. "They're fresh, but don't let them sit out all night. Make sure they get refrigerated so no one gets sick. Those two boxes down below are cinnamon rolls. Better get one before they're gone."

"This is really generous of you." Joel helped her pile the sandwiches into pyramids on the serving counter. A large window opened up like a concession stand, and across the corridor the hum of deputies and FBI agents drifted from the large hall.

"Anything we can do to help," Lori said gravely, wiping her hands on her apron emblazoned with the bakery's logo. "We're all sick about it. Dean was out with the searchers today and plans to go back in the morning. Everyone's trying to help."

"That's really great. Tell Dean thanks if I don't see him."

"God bless you," Lori said as she headed toward the door. "And those poor girls."

Joel grabbed a sandwich even though he didn't feel much like eating. In their first briefing, Stacy had been clear that an investigation like this could push them all to the limits of their physical and mental endurance. If they didn't make small efforts to take care of themselves now, they could end up falling apart just when they were needed most.

So Joel took his sandwich and a water bottle as he headed back to the command post.

The Grange Hall was outfitted with rust-colored industrial carpet that dated itself as having been laid a generation or two earlier. It looked like it would last generations longer, the kind of carpet that would never wear out under countless potluck dinners, community dances, and Halloween parties. Now the room was laid out with long tables bearing telephones, computers, and large display monitors showing maps and cell phone towers in the surrounding area.

A large whiteboard on wheels had been pulled in and a hand-written list had been started to track the timeline of events as the investigation unfolded. A steady hum of overlapping conversations—some in person and others over the phone—added to the impression of controlled chaos. Labels on the tables indicated the different agencies who'd responded to help; FBI, State Police, Search and Rescue, and local firefighters among them.

"Joel!" Marnie Sanders spied him and waved him over. "You ready to go try the neighbor again?" She glanced at the unwrapped sandwich in his hand. "Let me grab one of those first. I'm starving."

"They're in the kitchen."

Joel went to his chair and picked up his jacket and bag. All day he'd been interviewing neighbors and friends of the Greers and McNamaras, while other deputies, FBI agents, and even some state troopers had been searching the hill and woods near the Greer residence. Brett Rogers hadn't opened his door to Joel when he'd knocked, and the sight of the camera in the tree near the fence itched at him. If Rogers had captured anything that could help their investigation, it would be just like him to keep it to himself. Surely he had to have seen the activity at the house all day. Any decent person would have been eager to help. But Brett Rogers was not decent.

Marnie returned a minute later with a partially unwrapped sandwich. "Your car or mine?" she asked as she chewed.

"I'll drive and then you can eat. I'm not that hungry."

"Thanks. This is good. Way better than Subway."

"Wait until you try her cinnamon rolls."

They signed out with the attending deputy and stepped out into a gentle evening rain. Lights from multiple news crews illuminated the west side of the Grange. Sheriff Larson stood under a tent with Porter and Cooper at his side, giving a press release to a gathering of reporters who wore waterproof jackets slick with rain. Media relations were vital in getting the word out. And word *was* getting out. The phones were ringing off the hook and two FBI analysts had been assigned to sort through leads to determine their level of credibility and then assign them in orders of priority to investigators.

Joel moved a stack of papers to the back to make room for Marnie in the passenger seat. They didn't usually pair up on assignments, but Marnie would have been his first pick for partners if he'd needed one.

She pulled out her phone as he drove and grimaced at the screen. "Looks like I'm surrounded by incompetents. How hard can it be to make a balloon arch? All they had to do was follow the instructions."

"When is the wedding?" Joel asked with a smile, not admitting that he would have no idea how to make a balloon arch, instructions or not.

"Two days." Marnie rubbed her temples and

moaned. "I told my sister this is the last time I'm helping her plan a wedding. 'Plan' as in, she expects me to do it all. If this marriage doesn't stick, I'm out for the next one. I tried to get her to simplify, but she got it into her head that a Christmas wedding has to be a certain way and apparently it's my job as the big sister to make it happen."

Joel followed the road into Owl Creek. The streets were inky dark under the steady rainfall. Even the streetlights on the main roads seemed to withdraw their light, and the park's illuminated fir tree and the tinsel holiday decorations lining Main Street looked almost garish by contrast.

"Wow. They're making progress," Marnie observed as they passed the site of the new Wallace Community Bank. The skeletal shell of a new structure—smaller and more modern than the old brick building—was visible in the watery orange light coming from a nearby streetlamp.

"Yeah. It's going up pretty fast." Joel didn't mention how he still felt displaced driving down Main without the familiar landmark of the old historic building. Or how many times he'd had to stop himself from turning at the City Hall intersection where the sheriff's substation had once stood. He couldn't remember anything about the bombing, but the pain in his back reminded him daily how lucky he was to be alive. Kathy and Brian hadn't been so lucky.

"How is Val doing?" Marnie asked. "She's working at the school now, right? Do you think she'll go back when the bank opens?"

"I don't know. The pay at the school isn't great, but she likes being on the same schedule as Abby."

"Is she still in Arizona? Oh wait, no…isn't this the weekend you were supposed to go to the coast?"

"Tomorrow. But I've already told her we'll have to cancel."

"Oh Joel, I'm sorry. You worked over Christmas and everything."

"It's fine. Everyone else has families. It's not a big deal."

"You have a family now, too."

Joel shot her a look out of the corner of his eye. Marnie's brown hair was pulled back into a ponytail making her profile look austere in the cool light from the car's glowing instrument panel.

"It's true," she insisted. "You've got to consider them now. I'm sure Val thinks she knows what she's getting into, but you can never know, not really. Not when you have a child. The stakes are always higher."

Joel wasn't sure what to say to that. As they took the county road out of town, he didn't bring the Charger up to speed because he knew he'd be slowing down soon. The Greers lived just before the first sharp bend where the road began its climb into the mountains. He noted the Christmas lights were on, as the neighbor Penny had mentioned. Did Leisa have them on a timer? Or had she turned them on as a beacon for her daughter? Calling her home through the dark.

Joel knew—they all knew—that if whoever took KJ and Sophie planned to kill them, it was probably already too late. But they were still operating under the hope that they would be found safe. They had no other choice.

He pulled into Brett Rogers's driveway, the dirt surface pitted with holes. Wedged between a rusted tool cabinet and a clothes dryer with the back panel missing was an old Ford truck in light green with walls made of wooden planks built onto the bed. The truck was half full of broken furniture, wet cardboard boxes sagging as they lost their shape, and two mannequins. The Charger's headlights briefly illuminated their pale figures, making them seem alive.

It was disconcerting to say the least.

Marnie looked out at the yard where more mannequins were posed on a glass-topped table, a rusted bed frame, a sunken bookcase, and a chair in front of an old computer. She shook her head.

"You know, I've seen a lot of strange things in this job, but this has got to be the weirdest."

"I don't know. I once responded to a welfare check on a house where the woman was hoarding her own urine and waste. Mannequins don't seem so bad after that."

Marnie shuddered. "I don't understand it."

"I wish Larry were here. Brett trusts him. No, that's a stretch. He tolerates him more than he does the rest of us."

"Larry's a hard guy not to like."

Larry's injuries in the bombing still had him in and out of hospitals with so many surgeries his abdomen resembled a patchwork quilt. Joel secretly worried he might never be fit to return to duty but refused to be the first to admit it out loud.

He got out of the car and pulled his jacket tighter around him as a frigid gust of wind blew the rain sideways. The path to the door wasn't lit, so he used a flashlight to guide their way around an old toilet and a tractor tire. A flash of movement caught his eye and he tensed, swinging the light to the left. A light shone back, and in an instant he realized it was his own reflection caught in a large mirror leaning haphazardly against a peeling armoire.

Over his shoulder, the mannequins stood like eerie sentinels watching his approach. He swept his light over them for good measure, trying to shake the feeling of being watched.

"This guy's gotta shine at Halloween," Marnie murmured behind him.

The slippery porch steps were cracked and covered in moss. Joel knew from previous visits that the doorbell didn't work, so he skipped it and knocked on the door. Neither he nor Marnie spoke as they waited to see if Brett would answer his door. It was hard to hear anything besides the quiet drizzle of rain.

Joel knocked again. "Brett Rogers?" he called. "It's the sheriff's office. We're here to ask you a few questions."

They waited for several long minutes. Without a warrant, all they could do was knock and wait. It was up to Brett whether or not to answer. The windows were covered with heavy drapes and no light was visible from outside.

"Mr. Rogers, we're here about some missing children. We think you might be able to help. You may have seen something that can help us find them."

At last the porch light turned on and the sound of a chain slipping out of its track was followed by the door opening.

Brett's face was shadowed and haggard, with deep pockets where his skin sagged on his cheekbones.

"I didn't have anything to do with those missing girls," he said. His voice was slippery and soft, making it hard to hear. It took half a beat for Joel to put the words together in his mind.

"We're not saying you did, Mr. Rogers, but we're hoping maybe you saw or heard something last night that could help us. We've questioned all your neighbors as well. It's standard procedure."

"Standard procedure," Brett scoffed. "That's what they say when they don't want you to know what they're really up to. Who are you?" His tone turned sharp as he spotted Marnie.

Marnie stepped forward and extended her shield. "Marion Sanders. Detective with the Wallace County Sheriff's Office."

He leered at her. "Ain't you supposed to wear a skirt and heels like them broads on TV?"

Marnie ignored him. "How well do you know your neighbors, Mr. Rogers? Leisa Greer and her daughter KJ."

His grin faded. "Don't know 'em at all. I keep to myself; they keep to themselves."

"Do you work, Mr. Rogers?"

"I'm on disability on account of my back."

"So you're home day and night? You probably see a lot of comings and goings at their place. Did you see anything last night?"

Brett pinched his lower lip. "I don't spy on my neighbors, if that's what you're implying."

Joel turned and pointed at the camera in the maple tree bordering the yard. "You do have quite the surveillance system set up, though, don't you? Mind if we take a look at your footage from last night? You might have caught something without meaning to. Something that will help us find these girls."

At this suggestion, Brett took a step backward.

"I don't have to give you nothing."

"You're absolutely right. But it would really help us out. Surely you want to help us find these girls. You wouldn't even have to share all the footage. You could just give us the footage for the one camera on the western side of your property, the one that borders the Greer property."

"That one don't even work no more," Rogers said dismissively. "I just keep it in the tree to deter trespassers."

"Do you get a lot of trespassers?" Marnie asked.

"I've had a few," Brett said. "Thieves trying to steal my stuff or kids trying to prank me."

"Maybe one of those trespassers had something to do with these girls disappearing," Marnie said. "Wouldn't it be great to help them get caught?"

Brett looked for half a second like he might consider

it, but then his expression hardened and he retreated further into the house.

"S'not my problem, detectives. Have a good night."

He closed the door and the porch light went dark.

"Pleasant guy," Marnie remarked.

"That was the nicest I've ever seen him," Joel said. "Having you here almost made him remember his manners."

"You believe what he said about that camera not working?" Marnie asked as they picked their way back to the car. The persistent rain accentuated the cold, sending it straight to Joel's bones.

"Not a bit. In fact, I'm betting he's either screwing with us to get us to waste our time on a warrant that will end up useless, or he's hiding something he really doesn't want us to see."

Marnie mulled this over. "I've got some questions for Leisa Greer. I have a hard time thinking she wouldn't have a few complaints with a neighbor like that. We might be able to get a warrant for those tapes after all."

"Detective?"

The woman's voice startled Joel and he searched the darkness near the road, raising his flashlight and one hand moving to his sidearm.

Penny Standridge stood there in her puffy jacket, cringing against the light.

"Mrs. Standridge, what are you doing out here?"

She would have had to walk along the county road which wasn't safe for pedestrians in broad daylight, let alone after dark.

"My son Logan remembered something about last

night. I didn't know if I should call the tip line or not and then I saw your car out here."

"What did Logan remember?" The teen had been interviewed by another deputy during the day, and Joel had heard that it hadn't amounted to much.

A car approached the sharp bend going too fast and swerved into the oncoming lane before correcting. Water sprayed in an arc toward the shoulder and Penny stepped further off the road.

"It's not safe to be walking out here," Joel observed.

"I walk on this road all the time," Penny said dismissively. "So, Logan came home today and said a deputy talked to him at work. He was kind of stressed about it, so he wasn't thinking very clearly. But later, he remembered something. When he took the trash cans out to the curb last night, he saw a light in Leisa's yard. Like, a flashlight."

"What time was this?" Joel asked, alert.

"He thinks maybe ten o'clock? I know it wasn't earlier because I was getting after him for not taking the trash out sooner. He promised he would do it before bed and I guess he did."

Joel exchanged a look with Marnie. "Is Logan home now? We'd like to talk to him about what he saw. We can give you a ride so you don't have to walk back."

Joel opened the back door of the Charger and let her in just as his personal phone buzzed in his pocket. It was Val. Feeling a twinge of guilt, he silenced the call. He was supposed to be in Portland right now, picking her up from the airport.

Marnie's words about stakes came back to him. Did

Val know what she was getting into dating someone in law enforcement? For that matter, did he know what he was getting into dating someone with a child? The answer to both questions was, of course not. But they were both committed to figuring it out, and so far she'd been understanding.

He just hoped she would forgive him for this one.

VAL SCROLLED through the news on her phone as she walked through the Portland airport. The iconic turquoise carpet looked the same as she remembered from her childhood, with intermittent specks of color passing underfoot as a backdrop to the Pineview Daily article illuminated on her screen. There were photos of Leisa's house surrounded by county vehicles and FBI agents in the yard. Somehow the photos made the whole situation seem devastatingly real, and she regretted her earlier disappointment about something so insignificant as a change in vacation plans.

She'd tried to call Joel as soon as she landed, but her call had gone straight to voicemail so she'd settled on a text instead.

Just landed. Hope you're doing okay.

He hadn't replied.

Now she was scouring Google for updates on the missing girls, but all the articles were at least six hours old. There was a video of Faye, Sophie's mom, being

47

questioned by Wesley Peters, a reporter for the local Channel Six news. But Val had put away her earbuds when the flight landed, so she'd have to watch it later. Whenever Val had a conversation with Faye McNamara, she was vaguely reminded of the White Rabbit from Alice in Wonderland. The older woman seemed to always be late to something and only half present. But she had a ready smile and a heart big enough to embrace everyone she met. She genuinely seemed to love her chaotic life, so to see her now with her face drawn with worry aged her about ten years.

Val's phone rang and she answered it lightning fast. "Hi."

"Hi. You made it?"

Just hearing his voice soothed her.

"Yeah. It was kind of a mess. I guess Seattle is fogged in so they're diverting a bunch of planes here and we had to circle for a while before we could land. But I'm here now."

"Good." Joel sounded tired, but sincere.

"How are things going there?" Val moved aside to make room for a motorized cart and settled into a seat at an empty gate. Her luggage could wait.

"Busy. I just wanted to say I'm sorry I couldn't answer before. It's a zoo around here."

He was drowned out by the sound of a train horn.

"Where are you?"

"We're at the Grange. They set up a command post here."

"Will I see you tonight? No pressure. I just...I miss you." It had been over a week since she and Abby left for

Arizona, the longest she and Joel had been apart in months.

Joel's sigh was almost a groan. "I don't know when I'll be able to get away. But I miss you, too. Sorry I can't be there with flowers and a luggage cart."

Val snorted a laugh. "A true romantic right there. That's okay. Nicole is waiting outside Baggage Claim."

"Tell her thanks from me. I've gotta go, but hey, at least we're in the same time zone now. Can't wait to see you."

"Me too. Love you."

"Love you too."

She hung up and looked out over the airport. It was busy with holiday travelers, families whose faces reflected eagerness for whatever lay ahead. Seeing loved ones, visiting warmer destinations, or maybe just getting to sleep in their own beds tonight. Val allowed herself to feel sorry for herself for just a moment. She'd be going home to a cold house and a cold bed, without even Abby there to keep her company.

But then she thought of KJ and Sophie's moms, how empty their homes must feel right now. How panicked they must be.

She pushed away her loneliness and stood.

It wasn't how she'd expected her night to go, but at least she knew her family was safe. There were worse ways to spend the night.

5

It was near midnight when the judge signed the search warrant for Brett Rogers's video footage. Cooper and Porter were working in tandem to coordinate the investigators on both the federal and county side, sending two agents with Joel and Marnie to serve the warrant.

Joel slipped on his vest, cringing at the weight against his back. Doctors had warned him that it might take years for all the glass to work its way out, so he would just have to get used to it. His shoulder mobility had been the most concerning. He'd worked hard in physical therapy, and even after passing his gun range test—allowing him to carry a weapon again—he wasn't satisfied. He'd been going to the range two or three times a week to practice, driven by a fierce determination to ensure he would never be outgunned in a fight.

Now he drew his duty weapon and followed Agents Wong and Coleman to Brett Rogers's front door. They waited in expectant silence, ears attuned to any noise carrying over the rain. Their breath streamed before them in ghostly clouds. Somewhere in the distance a dog barked.

Rogers didn't answer.

The FBI agents breached the door and stood to the side, sweeping over the entry with flashlights. It was filled with towering piles of books and newspapers that leaned so precariously a single brush-up would likely trigger an avalanche. A strong odor of rot and filth poured out of the house.

Coleman swore as she panned her light over the columns. "You're up, Ramirez."

Cooper had the idea that Joel and Rogers shared some kind of rapport, despite Joel's reminder that Rogers had targeted him and Val last fall. Not only had Rogers taunted them with an offensive tableau, but some of the mannequins had also shown up on each of their lawns. Cooper had shrugged this off.

"I'm not saying he likes you. But he might not hate you as much and that's almost as good."

"Brett Rogers!" Joel called now, his voice swallowed by the pillars of trash blocking their path. "This is Joel Ramirez from the Wallace County Sheriff's Office. We have a warrant to search this residence. Please come out now so we can do this peacefully."

All was quiet in the house.

"We have a K-9 unit and will send him in after you if you don't come out," Marnie called.

Joel raised an eyebrow.

She shrugged. "Sometimes it works."

Coleman stepped inside and fumbled for the light

switch, but the small fixture did little to illuminate the crowded space.

Joel's shoe squished against something soft as he crossed the threshold. Tension tightened his neck and shoulders. It was hard to shake the feeling that they were walking into a trap.

They followed a goat trail to a living room where at least a dozen old cabinet radios filled one half of the room. A sagging couch was covered in National Geographic magazines, and an overpowering smell like wet dog filled the air. Very little of the walls was visible, and the portions that were, climbed with mold.

Wong and Coleman continued further through the trails toward the back of the house.

"There's a fire," Wong said, turning back.

Joel's heart skipped a beat. A fire in this place would be a death trap, but Wong didn't sound panicked. He reached for his radio.

"It's outside," Coleman said, her eyes black in the low light. "Near the back door."

Marnie turned on her heel and moved back the way they'd come.

Joel followed, his flashlight in one hand and gun in the other.

Someone grunted behind him and the sound of cascading books made him turn. Wong was pressed against the wall, and both he and Coleman were cut off from the entrance.

"You all right?" Joel asked.

Wong swore fiercely. "We'll find a way out the back."

Joel breathed a sigh of relief as he exited the house.

Marnie's light was ahead, bobbing through the junkyard. Joel followed as quickly as he dared, scanning the ground for a clear path. She was on the other side of a boxy shape that looked like a hot tub, but he couldn't figure out how to get to her. The more he tried to pick his way through, the more the debris funneled him away from the house.

Mannequins stared at him with their blank faces, some mottled with age and lichen from exposure to the weather. Haunting shapes that rose out of the darkness at every turn.

Joel climbed over a stack of tires and brushed up against a tarp covering a shapeless mass. The tarp had collected rainwater where it sagged, and the movement sent the water running down his neck. He hissed involuntarily at the cold.

Marnie's voice came over the radio. "I hit a dead end," she said, her voice clouded with frustration. "I'm circling back."

"I'm still trying to find my way through."

Only a few minutes had passed, but that was too long. Joel's pulse raced with the urgency of getting to the flames in the back yard, the firearm in his hand slick with rain.

Finally he rounded a haphazard pile of cement blocks and found a trail to the back porch. Brett Rogers stood near a burn barrel, flames casting orange light across his long face. He glanced up and saw Joel approaching, then threw something into the barrel and raised his hands.

"I'm not armed! And you're trespassing!"

"Step away from the barrel!" Joel called out. "We've got a warrant to search your residence for any video footage from the past forty-eight hours."

Marnie appeared from behind a wall of blackberry bushes that had overgrown an old car. Brett's gaze darted to her. He didn't smile, exactly, but the corners of his mouth pulled in something like a sneer.

"Best of luck to you, then," he said as he backed away.

"What'd you do, Brett?" Joel demanded.

The acrid stench of melting plastic filled the air. Joel grabbed a plastic bucket half filled with rainwater and threw it over the fire in the barrel. The flames sizzled and a cloud of steam erupted.

"Mr. Rogers, you're going to need to come with us now," Marnie said, pulling out her cuffs.

"You can't pin those girls on me. I didn't have nothing to do with it."

The sliding glass door at the rear of the house opened and Wong and Coleman stepped out. Joel ignored Brett's protests and pointed his flashlight into the barrel. A pile of videocassette tapes lay at the bottom, some melted beyond recognition. A few still held their shapes, but whether the lab would be able to find something useful was another question. Whatever Brett was trying to hide, Joel prayed it would lead them closer to finding the girls.

THE SEARCH at Brett Rogers's house had to be performed in shifts in order to alleviate the strain on those executing it. Although the warrant was only for video footage—whether in tape form or digital storage—the chaotic state of the house was such that looking for items as small as an SD card was worse than looking for a needle in a haystack. Digging through his belongings didn't make Brett Rogers seem more human. If anything, Joel was even more disgusted by the man.

At 4:00 a.m., Cooper sent Joel home.

"Get some sleep. We're coordinating a larger effort with multiple agencies to help out at first light."

Joel removed his gloves and bunny suit gladly. He hadn't been home in almost twenty-four hours and he needed a shower after wading through the rot and decay of Rogers's life.

His body felt every one of those hours, but his mind buzzed. Logan Standridge said he'd seen what looked like a flashlight outside the Greer house sometime after 2200 hours. Leisa reported KJ had called her at 2216 but didn't leave a message. Was someone there at the house? If so, why hadn't KJ called 911?

Leisa had made a small choking noise when she'd learned about the blood spatters on the threshold to the bathroom. In that small noise, Joel had heard all the fear of a mother whose worst nightmare has come true.

Hours later, as he lay in bed tossing and turning, it was that sound that haunted him.

Eventually he slipped into a restless sleep where he revisited disconnected memories from the day. When he woke a few hours later, only the passage of time indicated that he'd slept. He certainly didn't feel rested. But his mind was already spinning, anxious to get back to the Grange and find out the latest in the investigation.

He picked up his phone and saw a text from Val.

Call me when you can. XX

Joel checked the clock, wondering if he dared take the time for a full conversation. Maybe it was better to send a short text.

Sorry, worked all night. Heading back in now. Maybe later?

I've got a better idea. Come over tonight?

Definitely better. I'll try.

He felt guilty as he put away his personal phone. He didn't want to make promises he couldn't keep, but he suspected he wouldn't get away any easier tonight.

When he got to the Grange, he headed straight to the coffee station. Cooper was there, looking surprised to see him.

"I thought I told you to go home," he said.

"I did. Now I'm back."

Cooper hesitated. "Well, I won't lie and say we don't need your help. The search is still going on at Brett Rogers's place, and now the media is camped out and getting in the way. And I still need someone to talk to Leisa's ex."

"I thought the ex-husband was questioned yesterday."

"Not the ex-husband. The ex-boyfriend. Leisa says they broke up last spring, and he didn't take it so well. Kept showing up unexpectedly at the house, that sort of thing. You want to go check him out or go back to the search?"

Joel shuddered thinking of Rogers's property. "What's the ex's name?"

Cooper grinned. "That's what I thought. Dale has the info. But I want you going home at six tonight. Porter insists we set up alternating shifts. This could go on for weeks, and we can't have you burning out by day three."

"Have you been home yet, sir?" Joel asked, raising one eyebrow.

A muscle ticked in Cooper's jaw. "Not yet."

"I didn't think so." Joel smiled wearily and went in search of Dale.

6

VAL SLIPPED on a heavy gray work coat. Joel had left it at the house the day he'd helped them cut their Christmas tree. It still smelled like him and she paused for a moment to breathe in his scent. Nicole had brought her home from the airport last night and it was great to see her friend, but more than anything she'd been hoping to see Joel.

He hadn't come.

His texts that morning had been short and distracted, and in them she recognized an intense focus on work even as he tried to be available. It was a hard line to walk and she didn't want to make it more challenging by being needy. So she tried not to feel sorry for herself as she faced the frigid cold of a late December morning.

Warming an old farmhouse—whose sole heat source was a cast iron wood stove on the ground floor—made her feel like she'd stepped back in time to the days of the early pioneer settlers. It took her all day to get the drafty old house up to a comfortable temperature, and then it cooled down so fast at night that she had to start the process over again the next morning. Being gone for more than a week meant the house was colder than ever. Not quite cold enough for Val to miss the Arizona heat, but close.

A kindling box sat on the porch near the front door and Val felt a flush of gratitude when she saw it was filled with perfectly split, dry kindling. She was sure she hadn't filled it before she and Abby left for their trip. But she could picture Joel spending an evening after work making sure it was ready for her when she came home.

She no longer felt uncomfortable with these little acts of kindness. In the early days of their relationship, she'd been so worried about putting herself in anyone's debt that it had made her anxious to rely on Joel for anything. Now, as she gathered up the sticks in her arms —insulated from splinters by the thick cotton of his jacket—she marveled at how that had changed. She'd come to understand how important it was to him to be able to serve her, since there were so many other times his work commitments meant he couldn't show up for her the way she needed.

Most of the firewood was stacked against the side of the house where a sheltered overhang kept it out of the rain. But by November, Val had taken to keeping a small pile near the front door where it was easy to get to without leaving the safety of the porch. After the events of the past six months, she really didn't like going outside after dark.

Frost coated the lawn like a paintbrush whitewashing the world. Heavy fog obscured the surrounding hills and empty fields, and her new white crossover was almost indistinguishable in the driveway. Her breath plumed out before her, and when she stepped inside and shut the door, the interior didn't feel much warmer. The farmhouse had a lot of history, and she really did love it, but at times like this she thought longingly of modern insulation and HVAC systems.

Still, it was the home she'd grown up in and she had built hundreds of fires in that stove. She fell to the task like no time had passed, remembering without even thinking just where to place the damper and how to prop the door open so the air would draw properly when she lit the newspaper.

Within a few minutes the fire was blazing, promising toasty rooms to come, but for now Val kept Joel's coat on for warmth. She looked around the room, wondering how she was going to fill the hours now that their trip had been canceled.

The Christmas tree sat in the corner of the living room near the window, its branches drooping a little as it gave up the fight against its inevitable demise. Getting out the decorations had been tough, reminding her of a decade of Christmases with Jordan. But the familiarity had been good for Abby, and her joy had lessened Val's pain.

Her phone buzzed and she reached for it hopefully. But it wasn't Joel. It was only her sister Gina, wishing her well on her weekend.

Change of plans, Val texted back. *A couple of girls went missing and Joel can't get away.*

She included a link to an article about the disappearance.

Gina responded right away.

That's awful. Isn't Leisa Sue's daughter?

Val hadn't realized that. Sue was the kindly school secretary who had worked at the elementary school for as long as Val could remember. That would make KJ her granddaughter.

Is she? I don't know Leisa, but I know Sophie's mom. She works at the school and has something like half a dozen kids. I can never keep them straight.

Oh yeah. I was a counselor on Outdoor Ed with the oldest McNamara. They all look the same. Blond and blue-eyed. Nice family.

Three dots indicated she was typing again, and soon Gina's text was followed by another.

I'm sorry you can't go to the coast. The lighthouse sounded absolutely dreamy.

It's fine. Can't really complain when there are two kids missing, you know?

Val felt a little better by the time she finished her conversation with Gina. She might be facing a long weekend alone, but if giving up a romantic weekend meant it was more likely the girls would be found, she'd do it willingly.

She looked again at the sad Christmas tree and went to the small office down the hall where she'd stashed the box of decorations. The needles of the tree had taken on a brittle quality as it dried, and by the time she was finished packing away each decoration her hands were covered in abrasions. She lifted the dead tree out of the stand and dragged it to the outer door, leaving a trail of sweet-smelling needles and a forgotten half-eaten candy cane in its wake. By the time she got the carpet vacuumed and the chair moved back into place, the room looked bigger, but also sadder somehow.

Val checked the clock. There was still a lot of daytime to kill. She looked around at the surrounding walls covered in caramel-colored paneling. How much would it brighten the space if she painted it white? The house had been on the market for two months now, but showings had been few and far between with lackluster feedback. Maybe a little cosmetic improvement would help. And with three days of no work and no Abby—and no romantic getaway—staying busy was a must to keep the self pity away.

She needed a project.

Val grabbed her purse and keys and headed to town. On days like this she missed having an attached garage. Her car didn't start blowing warm air until she crossed the bridge into the town of Owl Creek. The river below was swollen with recent rain, the water high and churning a muddy brown as dark as Abby's favorite hot chocolate. Val's eyes drifted toward City Hall as they always did. Behind it lay the shallow crater where the second of two bombs had been detonated, seriously injuring Joel last September. She still had mixed feelings whenever she thought of that day. Gratitude that Joel had survived, but also guilt that their lives had resumed a semblance of normality while others had buried loved ones. Two deputies and five bystanders had been killed, and some survivors, like Larry, still faced a long road of medical challenges ahead.

How close she'd come to losing Joel sobered her every time, and she tried to shake off a feeling of gloom as persistent as the low clouds blanketing the hills as she pulled into the hardware store parking lot. Red tinsel garland hung from the store windows, with decorative balls hanging from hooks in the center. What had seemed festive when it first appeared at Thanksgiving now gave off a tired air, as if the joy of the season had leaked out and left only pretense.

A bell rang above the door as Val entered, and the smell of popcorn made her stomach turn. The strong odor repelled her, but Abby loved it. The popcorn machine made the hardware store her favorite stop in town, and Val couldn't help but admire the clever marketing to give unwilling tagalongs an extra incentive to visit. Her goal was always to finish her shopping before Abby ran out of popcorn, and she'd gotten very familiar with the store in recent months as she'd made small repairs on the old Victorian farmhouse.

Now, however, she was alone and could take her time looking at paint swatches and considering colors for the main room. The radio station out of Pineview still played Christmas music through the overhead speakers, and it seemed unusually loud in the empty store. Should she go with a warmer white or would it look dingy over time? But if she picked a white that was too cool would it feel institutional? Would better lighting help with that? Her mind was drifting to wonder what it would take to add some can lights to brighten the space when a female voice interrupted her thoughts.

"Want me to mix up anything for you?"

Aubrey was an older teen who sported large gauged earlobes and heavy eyeliner with false lashes, her lips and nails painted black. Before Val could answer, the bell rang, announcing that someone else had entered the store.

"Oh, hold on," Aubrey said. "I'll be right back."

A man dressed in the brown of a UPS delivery driver had entered the store and was looking expectantly toward the empty check-out counter.

Val tuned out Aubrey's cheerful greeting and placed two swatches side by side on the counter, making a decision to go with the warmer of the two. It was gray enough outside; she didn't want to bring the cool temperatures indoors too. Her pocket buzzed and she pulled out her phone, casting another glance toward the front of the store where Aubrey and the UPS driver had disappeared. Shouldn't they have another employee working today?

The text was from Nicole. She'd been a godsend

during those first weeks after the bombing and had turned into a trusted friend in the months since.

Can't wait to hear about your trip! I've always wanted to stay at the Ellis Cove lighthouse. You'll have to tell me all about it! Well...just surface level stuff. Please no gritty details.

She ended with a winking emoji that brought a smile to Val's lips even as she sighed. How many more people would she have to tell about her canceled plans?

Trip's on hold while those girls are missing. This is what I'm doing instead. Wanna help?

She snapped a picture of the wall of paint chips and sent it over.

Her phone buzzed again, but it wasn't a text from Nicole.

Val did a double-take. She couldn't help it. Seeing her dead husband's name—correction, soon to be *ex*-husband—was a little unsettling.

Hey V. Abby wants to know if you packed her purple elephant. She thinks you did but I can't find him anywhere.

Before Val could respond, he added, *Him? Her? What kind of a name is Shoe Shoe anyway?*

The tone was light and casual and so unexpectedly

normal, that Val couldn't think of how to respond. Was this going to be the new way of things?

The speaker overhead cut out for a mid-day news report.

"The search for two missing Owl Creek children continues today as investigators conducted a search at a neighboring residence. The home is said to belong to Brett Rogers, a truck driver and former marine. Authorities haven't said what they're looking for, but neighbors call Rogers a recluse best known for creating yard displays with an eclectic collection of mannequins."

Val snorted. *Eclectic* was one word for it. It sickened her to think Rogers might have had anything to do with KJ and Sophie's disappearance, but it wasn't a surprise. As far as she was concerned, he was capable of just about anything.

Aubrey was finally returning, so Val typed a hasty response to Jordan's text.

Abby left ZuZu in AZ. Gina's mailing him ASAP.

Feeling a little guilty for her brevity, she hit send and slipped her phone back in her pocket. Let Jordan think what he wanted. She didn't owe him an explanation.

"Sorry about the wait," Aubrey said, flustered. She brushed at a loose strand of hair that had escaped her twin braids.

"It's fine," Val lied. "Are you all on your own today?"

"I'm not supposed to be," Aubrey grumbled as she picked up the paint chip. "The guy who's supposed to be working with me called in sick. Something's going around, I guess. What sheen do you want?"

Val considered the half-eaten candy cane she'd picked out of the carpet an hour earlier. "Better do semigloss."

Aubrey prepped the paint and, as it was shaking in the mixer, excused herself to go ring up another customer. With a jolt, Val recognized the waiting couple. Maddie Gottschalk had been one of the survivors of the Wallace County Bank bombing. Unlike Val, she had stayed on at the bank, working at their Salmon Ridge location until the Owl Creek branch could be rebuilt. Maddie's husband caught Val watching and murmured something to Maddie. Val couldn't remember his name. Brian? Byron? No, Bryson. She'd only met him once and had found him a little too friendly for comfort.

Maddie looked over and met Val's gaze. Val offered a half smile and Maddie raised a hand in greeting. Her smile didn't reach her eyes, though, and she looked relieved when Aubrey handed over their plastic bag of purchased items. There had been a tension between them ever since Val had moved back to Owl Creek, and since the bombing, any part of their childhood friendship was gone for good. Maddie didn't look back as she tucked her receipt away, but her husband shot Val an apologetic look as they headed to the door.

7

"Could you fit through that bathroom window, do you think?" Marnie grabbed the nearest chair and rolled it over to the table where Joel was writing down an address on his notepad.

He didn't have to ask her what she was talking about. The frosted window Joel had seen above the shower in the Greer bathroom was wide but not very tall. When a thorough search of the exterior of the Greer residence revealed a bent screen and fresh scratches against the windowsill, Leisa had explained—her fingers trembling around a cigarette—that the fan in the bathroom didn't work and they frequently cracked the window after showering to clear the air.

"I think I could get through it," Joel answered, "but I'd probably make a lot of noise. He must have taken his time in order to not alert the girls."

"Unless they were heavy sleepers. My eight-year-old can sleep through anything, even a blaring fire alarm."

Indentations in the ground beneath the window suggested a match with the ladder that had been found resting against the detached garage. Depending on his height, their suspect couldn't have weighed more than about one hundred eighty pounds or he never would have fit through the window. It was presumed that he exited with the girls through the door, locking it behind him. That much contact with so many areas of the house should have left a treasure trove of DNA evidence for the FBI lab, but even expedited requests were painfully slow when the clock was ticking.

Even more compelling was the long strip of fabric that had been found half buried in mud on the mountain behind the Greers' home. They were awaiting confirmation from the lab, but it appeared to be similar to the narrow length of blue flannel found in KJ's bedroom, suggesting that whoever had taken them was familiar with the property and knew that he could access it from the old logging road.

"It might not be a coincidence that he picked that window, especially if he knew their habits. Which brings us back to Lyle Merritt." Joel gestured to the picture of Leisa's ex-boyfriend displayed on his computer screen. "I have an address for his previous girlfriend. Leisa said they were off and on again for years, so she might know where he is. You want to come?"

"Sure." Marnie tossed her coffee into the nearest trash can and grabbed her coat.

Joel couldn't help but think of Abby and how he would feel if she'd disappeared out of her home in the middle of the night. Even if he and Val were no longer together, he would have to have a heart of stone not to reach out. Yet Leisa hadn't heard a word from her ex.

He passed the large, wheeled whiteboard as he headed to the door. The blank spaces were filling out with hand-written notes as new information came in. But two items were conspicuous in their lack of concrete details: the light Logan Standridge had seen in the yard, and the car Penny had seen parked at the house.

While the search at Brett Rogers's home continued, volunteers combed the mountain behind the Greer home for the third day in a row. Joel's primary objective—together with investigators from state, federal, and local agencies—was to chip away at the growing list of subjects needing interviews, attempting to piece together the events of the days leading up to the disappearance. Every location they visited, every person Leisa or KJ spoke to in person or online, every phone conversation or social media interaction—it all needed to be documented and sifted through to ferret out what might be relevant.

In the meantime, leads were coming in at a staggering rate as word of the missing girls spread across the country. Most weren't very credible, but everything had to be considered and there was no way the team of investigators could keep up without extra support.

Clouds hung heavy over the hills as Joel drove out of town along the river. It was a winding road with blind corners at almost every curve, and he found himself tensing as they passed the spot where Val had been run off the road last September. He had no recollection of the bombing, but he remembered that night all too well. The memory of her car in the river still haunted his thoughts.

The turnoff for the residence they were looking for was marked by a mailbox and a red plastic box for the county newspaper—The Pineview Daily—mounted to a support framed around an old wagon wheel. The dirt road climbed a steep, heavily-forested hill that grew murky with mist as they neared the low-lying clouds. Aggressive blackberry bushes encroached on the road from either side, and Joel drove slowly, mindful of the tight switchbacks.

At the end of the road sat a two-story house built against the slope. The driveway led them to the upper story with a wide deck while the lower story opened out onto an overgrown lawn fenced with chicken wire. A child's plastic push toy sat near the basement door. A blue Pontiac Firebird waited in the driveway, the engine ticking like it had only recently been shut off. That was a good sign.

"I'll keep an eye on the car," Marnie said as she got out of the Charger.

Joel nodded and followed the deck around to the front door, his shoes clipping dully against the wooden planks. All was quiet in the house, and in the light rain even the normal sounds of birds were stilled. A squirrel bounded along the deck's railing, then climbed effort-lessly down the corner post to disappear below.

Curtains covered the dark windows. Joel pushed the doorbell, and when he couldn't hear it ring inside, he knocked.

The curtain nearest the door fluttered, but the door didn't open.

Joel knocked again.

The sound of a door slamming somewhere at the back of the house pulled his attention and he jogged back the way he'd come.

A scrawny figure stood in the driveway with her hands up, staring with wide eyes at Marnie.

"We're not going to hurt you," Joel said, raising his hands in a placating gesture. Indeed, Marnie hadn't even shifted her stance from casually leaning against her wheel well, her hands shoved into the pockets of her coat. But judging by the girl's expression, she might as well have drawn her weapon.

Joel stepped cautiously toward the girl and her gaze darted to him and then to the Pontiac.

"You're not in trouble," he said. "We just have a few questions about Lyle Merritt. Do you know where he is?"

The girl shook her head and lowered her hands. Joel guessed she was about sixteen or seventeen. She was wearing denim overalls over a pink crop top and heavy boots. A silver stud pierced her pink nose. No coat in spite of the December chill.

"My name is Joel and this is Marnie. We work for the Wallace County Sheriff's Office. What's your name?"

"Shyla."

"Is this your car?" He gestured to the Pontiac.

"It's my mom's."

"Can we get your mom's phone number?"

She raised her chin a fraction of an inch. "Why? She done something wrong?"

"We're looking for Lyle Merritt and we understand your mom is a friend of his. We're hoping she'll help us find him."

"She don't owe you nothing."

Joel shot a look at Marnie. The girl had gone from spooked to sassy in a matter of seconds. He preferred spooked.

"We think she'll want to help us," Marnie said. "We need to talk to Lyle Merritt about KJ Greer."

Something flickered in the teen's eyes at the name. "I haven't seen Lyle in a long time. He was hanging around a bit, but my mom kicked him out last summer after she caught him with his hand in the babysitter's pants."

Joel thought of the plastic toys he'd seen in the yard. "Your mom has other kids?"

Her glare was scalding. "No. Missy is my daughter."

Her haughty tone dared him to judge her.

"So Lyle lived here with you and your mom?"

She shrugged. "He slept on the couch mostly."

"When did he move out?"

"Right after graduation, I guess."

He hoped for her sake it was her own graduation. "Early June?"

"Yeah."

"Shyla," Marnie said gently. "Is Missy Lyle's daughter?"

She recoiled, tugging at the piercing in her nose. "No, gross! He's like forty years old or something."

"So why are you trying to protect him?"

"I'm not trying to protect him. I don't care about him at all. But I don't know where he is."

"Do you know if he has a job?"

"Last I knew he was working at a repair shop. I don't know where."

Joel noted this down. "Can I get your mom's number? She might remember what it's called."

"Fat chance. I'm not stupid."

Marnie's expression didn't change, but Joel knew her well enough to sense her impatience.

"Did the babysitter file a police report?"

Joel already knew she hadn't or it would have come up in his initial search for Lyle Merritt.

Shyla frowned. "I don't know, why?"

"If she was underage, Lyle could get in big trouble, even if it was consensual," Marnie said. "And your mom could get in trouble for not reporting it." She looked pointedly at Joel. "Do you remember any sexual assault cases in May or June?"

Joel frowned as if in thought. "Now that you mention it, there might have been a case involving a babysitter."

Shyla took a step forward, arms folded against her midriff. "That little slut. Did she tell you she was under-age? She's older than I am! Don't believe anything she says."

"I'm sure if we could talk to your mom, we'll get it all sorted out."

Shyla's shoulders twitched. "Fine. He's her problem anyway." She pulled out her phone and read off the number while Joel wrote it down. "Can I go now? I'm late to pick up Missy."

Joel stepped aside so she could back out the Pontiac.

Marnie grimaced as they got back in the car. "Lyle sounds like a real piece of work."

"Leisa doesn't seem like the kind of woman who would put up with someone like that. How long did you say they dated?"

"Too long according to Leisa," Marnie said with a twist in her lips. "Still, she said that Lyle and KJ got along well. And I know what you're thinking, that plenty of moms don't realize the people they trust around their children are the ones they should be protecting them against."

"And their babysitters, apparently."

Marnie grimaced. "This is why I won't let my fourteen-year-old babysit for people I haven't vetted. We need to find that babysitter and hear her side of the story."

Joel nodded as he finished jotting down notes of their brief interaction with Shyla. They were one step closer to finding Lyle Merritt, but the real question was whether that would bring them any closer to finding the missing girls.

———

VAL FROWNED at the freshly painted living room wall. "If you give a mouse a cookie..."

"What's that?" Nicole looked up from where she was pouring more paint into a disposable tray. She wore stained sweats and her hair was pulled back in a blue bandana, the ends of her red curls speckled with white.

"You know the kids' book, *If You Give a Mouse a Cookie?*" Val explained. "I feel like that's what we've gotten ourselves into. Now that the walls look so fresh and clean, I've got to freshen up the trim. Then all the new paint makes the carpet look disgusting. But even if my mom could afford to replace it—which she can't—then I'd want to update the light fixtures and do something about that ugly dark brown brick." She gestured to the hearth where the wood stove was doing its best to warm the room in spite of cracked windows letting in an icy draft for ventilation.

Nicole took a step back to take in the room. "It never stops, does it? But just the paint alone is making a big difference. Even if you can't replace the carpet now, the whole space feels so much brighter."

"Bright is good." Val's eyes wandered to the windows where a persistent drizzle hung over the outside world.

"Have you had any showings over the holidays?" Nicole asked, rolling her brush through the creamy paint and leaving ripples of white against the tray.

"No. We got everything cleaned up so the realtor could show it while Abby and I were in Arizona, but apparently things are slow this time of year."

"It'll pick up in January, I'm sure," Nicole said cheerfully.

Val wasn't so sure. Although homes were moving at a brisk pace in most of the country, the housing market in Owl Creek was always a step or two—or twenty —behind.

Val's phone chimed and she reached for it. There was a text from Jordan with a picture of Abby sitting on an ornate plastic horse. Val immediately recognized the carousel; it was the main attraction at a local park that they'd frequented as a family when they'd lived in Chicago. The expression on Abby's face told her Abby remembered it too. She was beaming, her green eyes sparkling with wonder as she gripped the golden pole with fuzzy mittens Val didn't recognize.

Jordan's accompanying message included a heart and the words,

Enjoying our last day together. Thanks so much for this.

Val felt a hitch in her chest. She started to type, *I didn't realize house arrest included carousels,* then stopped. It sounded peevish, and she didn't want bitterness to color every interaction between them. But she couldn't help feeling a little jealous. Her special outings with Abby usually fell between free and really, really cheap.

"What is it?" Nicole asked.

"Jordan." Val put her phone away without responding to the text. "He has my new phone number and just texted me a picture of Abby."

"Oh. Does that...bother you?"

"I don't know. I'm glad to know how she's doing. But it's really strange to get texts from him. Like, are we supposed to be friends now?" She didn't mention the heart. What did Jordan mean by it? Was it intended toward her or as an expression of affection for Abby?

Nicole gave a half smile as she loaded her roller brush with more paint. "At least he's trying. My ex just disappeared without a backwards glance. Of course, he'd never had trouble finding new friends, if you catch my drift."

"Neat."

"Yeah, I was just grateful we didn't have kids together so I could wash my hands of him and be done with it. It was hard on Ella, but she got over it and I learned an important lesson." Nicole's daughter was from her first marriage to a kindly man who had been killed in a logging accident when Ella was only three. As near as Val could tell, no one she'd been with since had measured up to her first love.

"I wish I could wash my hands of Jordan so easily," Val said. But she thought about Abby's glowing joy in the photo, and how much happier she'd been since having Jordan back in her life, and realized she didn't mean it.

Nicole ran the roller brush in V-shaped strokes across the wall. "Do you think you'll stay in Owl Creek when the house sells? Or would you consider going back to Chicago?"

"No, we won't go back. But I don't know if I want to stay in Owl Creek forever either. Maybe we'll look for something in Pineview. There are more jobs there and it's closer to the college."

"You're still planning on taking classes?"

"I start in two weeks." Val smiled to hide her nervousness.

She picked up an angled brush to work on cutting in around the window. It was tedious work, but she didn't trust it to anyone else, so while Nicole focused on the large areas that had the most impact, Val stuck with the frustrating detail work to make sure that any flaws were her own.

"How about Joel?" Nicole asked after a few minutes. "How long before they build a new substation here in town?"

"I don't know." The unpainted paneling was cool against Val's cheek as she leaned against it to get a better view of the line of paint she was tracing along the edge of the window trim. She was grateful for the excuse not to look at Nicole, recognizing the unasked question behind her words. How serious was her relationship with Joel? How might it change if she moved away? Was it serious enough to stay? But Val focused instead on the here and now. "It's a pain for him to drive all the way to Pineview for work. It was nice when he was just in town."

"He doesn't now, though, right? They're headquartered at the Grange."

"Right. Yeah."

They painted in silence, Val's thoughts drifting to the search for KJ and Sophie. She wondered how their mothers were holding up and whether she should reach out to Faye McNamara. Could she do it in a way that wouldn't be awkward?

Nicole's thoughts had clearly gone the same direction when she said a few minutes later, "I just don't understand why they don't have any suspects. How could two girls go missing in the middle of the night without any clue who might have taken them?"

Val murmured in agreement.

"I was talking to Leisa yesterday," Nicole continued,

"and she said Brett Rogers is a person of interest in the case."

"Not surprising," Val said. "Makes sense they would look at him."

"Even if he didn't do it, he's got to have an idea who did. All those cameras he's got on the property? He has to have seen something. But Meg says he's a brick wall when it comes to working with police." Nicole's sister was married to Larry, another deputy with the Sheriff's Office. She was so connected in the community that she knew more about most things going on than Val ever did.

"Why would you need those cameras unless you had something to hide?" Val replied. "It's too bad Leisa didn't have some kind of security system. That's the first thing I would do if I had to leave Abby home alone overnight. Not that I'm saying this is Leisa's fault," she hurried to add, realizing how it sounded.

"She had a phone, I think. You'd think that would have been enough."

Val didn't reply, knowing Nicole's daughter had a smartphone and—as near as Val could tell—access to every form of social media Val had heard of and then some. She couldn't imagine letting Abby own a phone so young. She and Jordan had always said she wouldn't have a phone until she was old enough to drive. But Val might reconsider if she were in Leisa's shoes, having to leave her daughter alone for long hours while she worked nights.

One thing Val had learned quickly as a single mom is that what she aspired to and what was possible were often vastly different things. She thought of how much her life had changed and all the ways she worried that she was failing Abby.

This is why she'd invited Nicole over. It wasn't good for her to be alone, thinking in circles and questioning every decision over the past year. Now that Jordan had established contact again, it felt like she was navigating a minefield while blindfolded.

Val stopped working again.

"Here's the thing," she said, one hand on her hip and gesturing with the paint brush. "I know Jordan is trying to stay on good terms, and I appreciate it. Really I do. But it almost feels like he's trying too hard. Like...I don't know, shouldn't he be a little upset with me? But no, he's all accommodating and generous and sending heart emojis and—"

"Wait, what?" Nicole straightened.

Val's face warmed. "He probably didn't mean anything by it. I don't know." She showed Nicole Jordan's text. "But that's the thing, I don't know what he means."

Nicole's eyebrows drew together. "That is not okay. You've gotta set some boundaries with him. No flirting, no hearts, nada."

Hearing Nicole's strong reaction made Val oddly defensive. "He might not have meant it that way. He was talking about Abby, so it was probably about her."

"I don't care if he's talking about his mother. He's not allowed to send hearts to his Ex. Wife." Nicole punctuated each word with a shake of her roller brush.

"All right. Point taken." Val chuckled. "I guess I'll

have to tell him, 'Stop being so nice. It triggers my Spidey senses.'"

Nicole grinned. "That's a good start."

Val went back to her painting, wondering if it would take as long to figure out how to *be* divorced as it had to *get* divorced in the first place.

8

It was early Friday morning when Joel reached the small engine repair shop in Salmon Creek where Lyle Merritt was reported to work. Marnie was off for her sister's wedding, so he'd arranged for Willis to meet him there, but there was no sign of the deputy's SUV when Joel arrived. He parked down the street to wait.

The repair shop consisted of a bright blue garage next to a private residence. A riding lawn mower was parked outside and the single bay door was open, but the interior was shadowed and difficult to see. Joel kept his engine running to maintain heat in the car's cabin while he waited. If he sat too long he was going to get drowsy. Too many late nights were catching up to him. But it was day four since the abduction and there were more leads than they had the manpower to follow up on.

Sightings of the girls were coming in from all over the country, including outside a strip mall in Florida and a movie theater in Dallas. But the reality was that it was more likely they were taken by someone who knew one of the families well. They probably hadn't even left Wallace County.

As Joel watched, a tall man in coveralls exited the garage and lit up a cigarette. Joel took a picture for good measure, then glanced in his rearview mirror as Willis pulled up behind him in his Yukon. Joel shut off the engine and joined the deputy as he got out of his vehicle.

"I hate that road," Willis said. "My kid always gets carsick. Last time we came up here he barfed all over the back of my head, just spewed it right out."

"Thanks for that visual." The cold bit at Joel's cheeks and he zipped up his coat.

"Is that him?" Willis asked, looking toward the garage.

"I can't tell. The build seems right from his DMV record."

The man smoking had a long beard and hair tucked behind his ears. He looked up as they approached and dropped the butt of his cigarette to the pavement, grinding it beneath his boot.

"What can I do for you, officers?"

"We're looking for Lyle Merritt," Joel said. "I understand he works here."

"Sure. Lyle!" he called in the direction of the garage.

"Yeah?" A man with a close-shaved beard poked his head out the open bay door. He made eye contact with Joel and recognition made his expression go slack. Then he spun around and disappeared. The clatter of something heavy falling to the floor followed.

Willis swore and hitched up his belt. "I hate it when they do that."

"Is there another exit?" Joel called as he ran toward the garage.

The man with the cigarette gaped. "Uh, yeah, there's a door out back."

Willis ran inside while Joel circled around the outside of the building. He heard a slamming door before he rounded the back and saw a figure tearing across the patchy lot behind the garage. Lyle leaped over a short fence into the yard of a private residence.

Joel chased after him, knowing he was faster than Willis with all his gear, but he wasn't back to full running shape since his recovery. His lungs burned, and his jacket felt too hot, but he managed to keep Lyle in his sight. He didn't appear armed, but his loose-fitting gray coveralls could have easily hidden a weapon. And even if he wasn't armed now, that could change quickly depending on who lived in the nearby houses.

Following Lyle into the neighbor's yard, Joel could make out Willis's labored breathing in the still winter morning as he radioed for backup. Joel cut through the yard just in time to see Lyle disappear around the corner of the house. He was closing on him.

The side yard was empty when he got there, and he sprinted down the narrow gravel path, pausing to open the vinyl gate.

Just as he pushed it open, the gate slammed back from the other side, wrenching Joel's wrist. He bit back a cry of pain as footsteps sounded on the other side, gravel scattering in their wake.

Inwardly cursing himself, Joel pushed the gate— cautiously this time—and it swung without obstruction, opening onto a view of a man in coveralls disappearing across the street and into a stand of trees.

Joel scanned the street and called Willis. His chest heaved from running.

"I'm on tenth heading north. He's headed into the woods."

"Copy that. I'm circling around to the high school. That'll give me eyes on the other side."

"Backup?"

"Soon."

"Send a couple of units to tenth in case he doubles back."

Joel didn't often get caught in a foot chase since leaving patrol, and at times like this he didn't miss it one bit. He ran across the road and into the woods, searching wide for any sign of Lyle. The towering evergreens filtered daylight, and fallen trees and limbs overgrown by a carpet of moss made the footing treacherous. More careful now since the gate mishap, Joel stepped over ferns and gnarled roots erupting from the earth, moving as fast as he dared. Hidden twigs snapped under his feet. His knee ached, reminding him of his recent injuries, and he limped a little to keep some of the weight off.

Lyle could be hiding anywhere. They'd have to flush him out with more deputies. Maybe even bring in air support. A narrow foot trail appeared and Joel followed it, picking up his pace. Distant sirens grew louder and stopped. Backup was close.

Sudden movement caught Joel's eye. A leafless vine

maple shuddering. It was a slight thing, but the air was still. At the base of the shrub lay a fallen log, shaggy with moss and ferns growing out of the bark. Joel moved toward it, eyes on the ground.

There.

A bit of gray fabric was visible under the long fronds of a fern.

Joel drew his sidearm quietly, grateful it was his left wrist aching and not his right. As he stepped toward the far end of the log, a twig snapped under his foot. Lyle Merritt jumped to his feet, looking around wildly.

"Hands where I can see them, Mr. Merritt," Joel said, raising his gun.

Lyle swore and raised his hands. "I didn't do it. I didn't take those girls."

"Which girls would that be?"

"KJ and her friend. I swear I had nothing to do with it."

"Then why run away?"

"Because I knew what you'd think. But I swear they were alive when I saw them."

Joel narrowed his eyes. "When did you see them?" He didn't dare approach because the uneven ground would require taking his eyes off Lyle. The tables could turn too fast if he lost the upper hand. He would just have to wait for backup.

"I talked to KJ, that's all. I didn't even go in the house."

"You were there that night?"

"Yes, but I left as soon as she told me Leisa wasn't

home. I swear I didn't have anything to do with them going missing."

A bead of sweat ran down Joel's back. "Let's go to the station and talk about it there."

He looked over Lyle's shoulder to where Willis and two other uniformed deputies were approaching from the edge of the woods. Lyle whirled around and feinted as if to run.

"Don't do it, Lyle. We've got you surrounded. This will go a lot easier if you cooperate."

"I didn't do anything." His voice cracked and he looked for a second like he wanted to lunge at Joel.

"I believe you," Joel said, but he didn't lower his sidearm. "Come in peaceably and we'll get it all worked out. Hands on your head, Lyle."

Reluctantly, Lyle raised his hands. Willis grabbed Lyle's arm from behind and handcuffed him. Joel breathed a sigh of relief and holstered his weapon. His wrist throbbed.

"You gonna read me my Miranda rights?" Lyle sneered. "Nothing counts if you don't read me my rights."

"Don't you have those memorized by now?" Willis asked.

Lyle's cussing filled the air as Willis led him out of the forest.

Joel headed back to his car, grateful that Willis would deal with Lyle. He needed an ice pack for his wrist, and it was going to be a long drive back down the mountain. Long enough to develop a strategy for getting Lyle to confess what he'd done the night KJ disappeared.

JOEL PLACED a notebook and coffee mug on the table in the interrogation room at the Pineview station and angled the chair with the back to the door.

"All right, bring him in."

When Lyle entered the room, he chose the chair Joel's props subtly encouraged him to choose, the one that would allow the cameras to view him most clearly. Joel sat at an angle, trying to make his posture non-threatening. That could easily change if he needed it to, but for now he wanted to earn Lyle's trust.

"Before we get started, do you need anything?" Joel asked. "Coffee? Water? A sandwich? I think we've got some cinnamon rolls left. Just don't tell anyone."

Lyle shook his head. "No thanks."

"You sure? You've gotta be hungry. Or at least thirsty."

"Maybe some water would be good."

"Sure thing. Give me a second."

Joel left the room and closed the door behind him. Lieutenant Cooper waited outside.

"He's got two vehicles registered in his name, but neither of them fit the description the neighbor gave."

"Maybe he borrowed a car?"

"Maybe. Agent Wong is talking to Leisa again, trying to find out the nature of his relationship with KJ. Coleman will be watching and prepared for the next round of questioning when you're ready."

Joel nodded. Interrogations like this could take hours.

He grabbed a water bottle and returned to the room where Lyle waited, fidgeting nervously with his phone.

"Sorry that took so long. They didn't have any in the refrigerator. I hope you don't mind room temperature."

"That's all right." Lyle unscrewed the cap and drank half the water before returning the lid with trembling fingers. "So, do you have some questions for me or what?"

"Nothing really formal. I just want to have a chat about what happened the night KJ and Sophie disappeared. Let me get this recorder set up; there we go. It's easier than taking notes the whole time. Now how about you start with where you were when you saw them. Tell me your side of the story."

"Well, it was at Leisa's house. I stopped by for a few minutes and KJ answered the door. When I found out Leisa wasn't home, I left."

Joel nodded encouragingly. He copied Lyle's posture, folding his arms and leaning back in the chair. He kept his tone relaxed. Folksy, even. "That's good. I need you to try and remember any details you can. What time was it? What was KJ wearing? Anything you can think of would be really helpful."

Lyle nodded, his shoulders softening. "Let's see, it was probably about six-thirty. I'd gotten off work and drove straight there. It was dark so I couldn't see what KJ was wearing. A sweatshirt, I think."

"Were there lights on inside the house?"

"Sure, yeah. The lights were on."

"So you knocked on which door?"

"The kitchen door. No one uses the front door except Amazon."

"Tell me what happened next."

Lyle seemed a little calmer now. "KJ answered the door and I asked if her mom was home. She said no, so I left."

Joel waited.

Lyle shifted.

"I didn't try to go inside or anything. I just wanted to talk to Leisa, but she wasn't answering her phone. I thought I'd try and catch her at home."

"While she was working?"

"I didn't know she was working night shifts."

"That makes sense." Joel nodded. Lyle's right hand had moved to his jaw, and Joel copied the movement, a subtle technique that worked at the subconscious level to help earn the subject's trust. "What else can you tell me about KJ from that night? How did her mood seem?"

Lyle shrugged. "Fine, I guess. Nothing out of the ordinary."

"And what's ordinary for her?"

"I don't know. She's a nice kid. Friendly."

"What about Sophie? Did you see her there that night?"

Lyle folded his arms and slouched in the chair, his legs stretching out under the table. "Nah. Like I said, as soon as I found out Leisa wasn't there, I left."

"And it was dark?" Joel verified. "No porch light or anything on outside?"

"Yeah, nothing like that."

"But you think she was wearing a sweatshirt. What color was it?"

"Pink? Yeah, pink."

"Can you remember exactly what you said?"

"I just said, 'Hey, is your mom home?' And she was like, 'No, she's working.' And that was that. I wished her a happy New Year and then I left."

"What was it you wanted to talk to Leisa about?"

"Nothing important. Just saying hi. Maybe see if she had plans for New Year's."

"So you and Leisa are on good terms?"

Lyle leaned forward, placing his elbows on the table. "Pretty good. We were never that serious, more friends really. It just wasn't the right time for us. But yeah, we get along."

Joel moved to reflect Lyle's posture and pitched his voice lower. It felt almost secretive. "You know she's been really upset about this whole thing."

"I'll bet. KJ's a great kid. I can't believe anyone would do this. Poor Leisa. I wanted to help—I heard they needed volunteers for the search—but I had to work. I've been thinking about them all week, though."

"It's been pretty rough. Losing your only child? It's like someone's ripped her heart out."

"Oh man." Lyle rubbed his nose and sniffed.

Joel leaned back and crossed his right leg over his left. Within a few seconds, Lyle copied the posture. *That's it.*

"Can I ask you something, Lyle?" Joel asked, keeping his tone like two friends sitting over a couple of beers.

"Sure." Lyle's expression was open.

"How did KJ feel about you dating her mom?"

The change in questioning made Lyle pause. "She was fine, I guess."

"You guys got along?"

"Yeah."

"You and KJ close?"

"I guess you could say that. She's a good kid. Easy to like."

"How close were you? Was she affectionate? Give you hugs and stuff?" Joel thought of how easily Abby had accepted Joel into her life, trusting him without hesitation.

"Sometimes."

"Did you two ever spend time alone? Kind of like daddy-daughter time?"

"Sure. I mean, not a lot. But yeah, sometimes I'd pick her up from school and we'd go get an ice cream cone or something."

"Did she ever sit on your lap or snuggle with you?"

Lyle started. "No. She was too big for that. That would have been...weird."

"Was there anything you felt like you had to hide from Leisa? Did you ever touch KJ or make her touch you in a way that would have upset her mom?"

Lyle recoiled so fast his chair creaked under his weight. "What are you insinuating, Detective? You think I abused her? Molested her? No way. That's not the kind of man I am."

"What kind of man are you?"

"The kind who keeps his hands to himself and leaves little girls alone."

"Is that what Candi Jensen would say?"

At the mention of the babysitter's name, Lyle's face turned red. "That's different. Candi Jensen is a grown woman. She's like, twenty-five, and it was only the once. The baby had gone to bed and Candi was bored and came onto me. I swear, she wasn't even my type."

Lyle's lies were racking up so fast, Joel could hardly keep track of them all. Candi was only nineteen, and according to Shyla's mom they'd had a thing going for about a month before she caught them together.

Joel backed off. "All right. Let's go back to the night KJ disappeared. You came to the house at about six-thirty to see Leisa. KJ came to the door and let you in—"

"No, I didn't go inside."

"Okay, so when you saw her, she was wearing a green sweatshirt but you couldn't see much else because it was too dark since they hadn't turned on the porch light. You asked if Leisa was home and then wished KJ a Happy New Year and that was it. You left and went...where?"

Lyle raked a hand through his hair. "Uh, I think I just went home. Yeah. I went home after that."

"Okay. So you got home at...what time?"

"I don't know. Probably seven."

"Great. This is really helpful. Let's take a quick break. I'm going to go get a cup of coffee. Do you want one?"

"Do you know how much longer this will take?"

"A bit more. Thanks for your patience. Oh, hold on." Joel made a show of glancing over his notes. "KJ's sweatshirt. Remind me, was it pink or green?"

Lyle blinked rapidly. "What did I say before? It was hard to see. It might've been green. Yeah, that's it."

"Interesting." Joel's tone turned serious. "Because not only was the porch light on that night, the Christmas lights were on too. Leisa has them on a timer and they were on before she left for work. The neighbor verified seeing the house lit up."

Lyle's cheeks reddened. "Well, I was tired, I wasn't paying attention."

"Leisa also says that she told you to stop coming around the house. That she changed her number because you wouldn't leave her alone."

"Wha—? No way," Lyle scoffed. "She never said—"

"Look, I know you're holding back. Maybe you're embarrassed, maybe you're scared, but if you ever cared about Leisa and KJ, then cut the crap and tell me the truth. What were you really doing that night? What happened when KJ answered the door? Because we have two missing girls and you may have been the last person to see them alive."

Lyle's eyes darted to the door, but he'd have to get through Joel first. Joel could see him considering his options. Flee, double down on the lying, or break down and tell the truth. When he crumpled in his chair with a sob, Joel knew which one he'd chosen.

It took him a minute to regain his composure. Joel sat quietly, perfectly calm on the outside despite his impatience.

When Lyle gasped and rubbed his eyes, Joel handed him a tissue for his nose.

"What happened that night, Lyle?" he asked gently.

Lyle shook his head. "I don't know. I wish I did. But I had these painkillers, see, and I guess I took too much because it's all a blur. I never should have gone there. I just wanted to talk to Leisa but she told me I wasn't allowed to be around KJ like that. I knew she'd be mad. KJ didn't let me in, though, I swear. I didn't even know there was another girl until I saw it on the news. And then I was worried about what Leisa would say if she found out I'd been there so I couldn't say anything. But I swear I didn't have nothing to do with those girls going missing. I would remember that. Wouldn't I?"

"Can anyone corroborate what time you got home?"

"I'm staying with a buddy of mine. He was home all night."

Joel pushed the notepad toward Lyle. "I'll need his name and address. And we're going to need to search your vehicle and your residence. Will you give us permission or do we need to get a warrant?"

Lyle cringed. "I didn't do anything to them, I swear."

"We can confirm that a lot faster if you give us permission to do the search."

Lyle slumped in his chair. "Fine. Do what you need to do."

"You're doing the right thing. Let me go get you that coffee."

Joel checked the time as he left the interrogation room. Lyle had folded pretty quick, but there was still a lot more ground to cover. Lyle seemed to genuinely believe he didn't have anything to do with the missing girls, but Joel had seen people do crazy things when they were under the influence.

"Nice work." Agent Rita Coleman was waiting for him.

"It's a start."

"Porter's assembling a team right now and Anderson is working on an affidavit for the judge in case he changes his mind. Do you need a break or are you okay to keep at it?"

"I'm good. As long as he's not asking for a lawyer, I want to get whatever I can while he trusts me."

"Sounds good." Coleman allowed herself a small smile. "This is good work, Detective."

Joel nodded, accepting the compliment but knowing it wouldn't be worth much if it didn't lead them to the girls.

9

Abby knelt backward on the couch, looking out the window at the yard. "I think it's snowing!"

"Is it?" Val bent to peer out the window, resting one hand on Abby's small back. "Hmm, I don't see anything." The clouds were parting, offering a rare glimpse of a pale winter sky as twilight descended.

"I did. Tiny snowflakes floating in the sky." Abby wiggled her fingers to demonstrate. "Do you think we'll get as much snow as Grandma and Grandpa Fisher?"

"Probably not. The forecast doesn't show any, but you never know."

"I hope it snows all day and all night and then they have to cancel school on Monday!"

Owl Creek didn't typically get much snow, so even a light dusting could put everything on hold as drivers avoided the icy roads.

"I thought you liked school."

"I do, but I like snow days better. Dad says he wants to take me skiing someday."

A flicker of jealousy soured Val's smile. She tried to think of something positive to say. "Your dad does love skiing. So do Grandma and Grandpa Fisher. In fact, they used to have a cabin in the mountains in Utah where they went skiing every winter."

"Really?" Abby brushed her hair from her face as she turned to look at Val. "Did you go?"

"Once," Val answered, "but I'm not much of a skier so your dad and I stopped going after you were born. I don't know if they even own it anymore." She stroked Abby's curls, following the curve of her little round head. "Have you unpacked your suitcase yet? I need to wash your clothes or you won't have anything clean to wear on Monday."

A sheepish look flashed across Abby's face. "Not yet. I keep forgetting."

"Go get your laundry basket now while you're thinking about it."

Abby pushed her way off the couch and headed for the stairs as Val's phone buzzed.

I'm leaving now. Do you need me to pick anything up at the store?

She relaxed. Until that moment she'd feared Joel would have to cancel. It seemed too good to be true that he would finally get an evening off.

No. If I forgot anything we'll go without. I just want to see you.

Same. It was followed by a heart emoji.

Feeling a lightness in her chest, Val returned to the kitchen where she'd been laying out a charcuterie board and fruit tray. She'd picked up Abby from the airport the night before and her chatter filling the house had been wonderfully comforting after a quiet and lonely week. But Val was also hoping for some time alone with Joel without Abby playing chaperone. Fortunately Abby's sleep schedule was still on Central time, so Val was hoping for an early night.

It was full dark when Val went out to the porch for more firewood. The sky over the distant hills was filled with an array of brilliant stars, the Milky Way forming a band of light that took her breath away. She couldn't linger to admire them, though, because she was instantly chilled through. Without a blanket of clouds overhead, temperatures had plummeted; it would be a bitterly cold night.

As Val loaded her arms with a few split logs, she was interrupted by the growl of an approaching engine and tires on the dirt road. She straightened in time to see Joel's truck approaching. She cradled the wood in her arms, smile blooming while she waited for him to park.

He must have stopped at home first because he was wearing jeans and looked freshly shaved.

"Hi," she said as he came up the porch steps, her heart skipping when he smiled. Though they talked every day, she hadn't seen him since she'd left for Arizona almost two weeks earlier.

"I was wondering where my jacket was."

"Oh, yeah." She glanced down at the work coat. "You left it here. What—"

She cut off as he took the wood from her arms and set it on the porch floor.

"I need to stoke the fire," she complained with a smile.

"Come here." He pulled her to him.

"But I'll get you all dirty."

"I don't care." He enfolded her in his arms and she relaxed against his chest, feeling the weight of his chin on her head. It felt as if something deep inside her was attuned to him, and now that he was here at last, that piece of her thrummed contentedly.

"You okay?" she asked when the silence stretched long.

He didn't answer.

She pulled back to look at him. The shadows under his eyes. The weight in his gaze.

"Joel?"

"I'm okay now." He leaned in to kiss her, and his kiss was soft and restrained. It was over too quickly. He released her and bent to pick up the firewood. "I could really use a drink."

Val's stomach tightened. "Joel, you know—"

"Sorry." He winced. "That wasn't...don't listen to me. I'd rather be here with you."

"I did get sparkling cider," she said lightly.

"That'll be perfect. Just being with you is perfect."

Val reached for the door and pushed away the shame welling up in her belly. He *did* look like he could use a drink, but he wouldn't drink with her. One of the early boundaries she'd had to set in their relationship included no alcohol. After Jordan's betrayal, she'd turned to drinking to numb the pain, and it had quickly spiraled into a need that drowned out all else. Even Abby. When she'd moved back to Owl Creek, she'd given it up for good.

Joel had been supportive, and she knew forgetting now was a sign of how badly the week had gone.

"What happened?" Val asked, holding open the screen door for him. A black brace peeked out from the hem of his coat sleeve.

"It's my wrist. I did something stupid chasing a subject yesterday."

Val looked him over for other injuries. "Did you catch him?"

"Yes, but it didn't do much good. It turned out to be a dead end. He has an alibi for the whole night and there was no evidence to support pursuing him further."

"Was it Brett Rogers?"

Joel shook his head. "Someone else."

Val felt a flicker of disappointment. "I heard the mannequin house was searched. Seems like he would be the obvious choice."

"He's an odd duck for sure."

Joel wasn't supposed to talk about an ongoing case and Val didn't push him even though questions crowded so thick on her tongue it was hard not to spit them out.

"Well, we don't have to think about that now. I'm

just glad you're here. You're staying the night?" she asked hopefully.

"If you'll have me."

Always, she wanted to say, but worried it would send the wrong message. There were times—so many times—she wanted to take their relationship to the next level. To broach the subject of a permanent living situation. She'd even thought about bringing it up on their trip. But she always held back, her concerns for Abby putting her own needs on hold. She'd never dated as a single mom before, and they hadn't been together that long. If something went wrong, she didn't want Abby's heart broken any more than it already would be.

"Whoa." Joel paused in the entrance to the living room. "It looks good."

"Thanks. The paint makes a big difference, doesn't it?"

"It does. So much brighter."

"Abby, look who's here!" Val called up the stairs.

An answering thump on the upper floor was followed by little feet running down the stairs.

"Joel!" Abby cried as she ran into the living room. "You're here! Happy New Year! Mom says I can stay up until midnight and we're going to eat snacks all night."

"You're going to stay up until midnight?" He raised an eyebrow at Val.

"We'll see," Val said. "She's still on Chicago time, so it might be tough."

"But I'm going to try really hard," Abby said. "Do you want to see what my dad gave me for Christmas?"

Abby pulled Joel toward the old entertainment

center where a new gaming console sat. Joel looked at Val with surprise.

Val wrinkled her nose. Before, Jordan had always been just as committed to avoiding video games as she had. Apparently that had changed. She tried not to worry about what it meant for the future.

Disneyland Dad indeed.

While Abby described in detail her favorite game, the oven timer in the kitchen chimed and Val went to check on the bacon-wrapped dates. Before she could get there, Abby darted past.

"Just a minute, I have to go to the bathroom," she called over her shoulder.

Joel followed Val into the kitchen. "Do you need help with anything?" he asked.

"So, as I was saying," Abby's voice called from down the hall. "When you get into the room with the pirate flag and the treasure chest—"

Joel snorted a laugh and called back, "Why don't you finish using the bathroom first?"

"Abigail!" Val fought a laugh as she hurried to the bathroom. The door was wide open and Abby was sitting on the toilet, her pants down around her ankles. Val reached for the knob to pull the door closed. "You're going to be eight this year. Let's practice some privacy, okay?"

"But Mom, I'm trying to tell Joel about the trap that's hidden in the treasure chest."

"I know. But when Joel's here and you're using the bathroom, you need to keep the door closed. You can finish your story later."

By the time Val got back to the kitchen, Joel had turned off the oven and removed the dates. They sizzled on the baking sheet, filling the room with the aroma of salty bacon.

"Sorry about that. I don't think about it when it's just the two of us."

He started placing the dates on paper towels to drain the bacon grease. "Ah, to be so innocent and naive. I guess it's a sign she's feeling comfortable with me around though. That's good, right?"

"Yeah, definitely." But Val's heart squeezed at the words. Abby's eagerness made Val nervous. She couldn't predict the future with Joel. If there came a day when he was no longer in their lives, how would Abby cope? It made Val feel selfish to be pursuing a relationship when Abby was so vulnerable.

But as she watched Joel move around the kitchen as comfortably as if it were his own, she knew that wasn't fair. He brought a sense of security to their lives that made her a better person. A better mom. And the things they'd been through together made their history seem a lot deeper than only six months.

"Do you have a plate you want me to use for these?" He glanced at her and a smile caught the corner of his mouth. "What's that look for?"

"Oh, nothing." She busied herself looking in a lower cupboard for a platter.

"Tell me. What were you thinking about?"

"I just..." She found the platter and stood, hesitating over the words. "We're good together, right? You and me."

"Sure. Yeah, I think so. Why?"

"I think so too. I just...I'm glad you're here."

She slipped an arm around his waist and as he leaned in to kiss her, she reached for a date. Joel snatched her wrist before she could pull it away and she drew a quick breath of surprise.

He laughed. "Your diversion tactics need a little work."

He released her wrist and she grinned.

"Is that an invitation?"

She raised up on her toes and kissed him long and deep. When she pulled away, his dark eyes were bright and at last seemed to have shaken the earlier weight.

"You know, Abby is still on Chicago time," Val said. "It wouldn't be hard to convince her midnight has come early..."

"Abby who?" His dark eyes glimmered as he leaned closer.

Before he could kiss her, Abby's voice broke in. "Whew! I'm back," she announced as she made a beeline for the chips. "Mom, are you making muddy buddies?"

Val pulled away from Joel. "I was waiting for you. I thought you said you wanted to make them."

Muddy buddies had been a New Year's Eve tradition in Val's childhood, and she'd continued it into adulthood. Jordan had always teased her for it, complaining that cereal wasn't a dessert to be served in civilized company, but Abby loved the treat and insisted.

It was strange now to reflect on how she'd spent the holiday a year ago. Val and Jordan had gone to a party thrown by some friends, people she wasn't even in contact with anymore. After word had gotten out about Jordan's fraud, their friends had been quick to cut ties. That New Year's Eve party was the last time she'd seen most of them.

The past year had been the hardest of her life, and she wasn't one bit sorry to say goodbye to it.

Now here she was in Owl Creek, waiting for the official word that her divorce was final, with a man she'd never thought she'd have a chance with. And she couldn't be happier.

VAL WAS A GENIUS. Joel had expected Abby to crash early, but she was fueled with chips and fruit and muddy buddies and showed no sign of slowing down. So Val quietly changed the clocks in the living room and kitchen and they counted down to midnight two hours early.

In spite of firm rules about Abby not having liquids past seven o'clock so she didn't wet the bed, Val poured Abby a quarter cup of sparkling cider.

"It's only laundry," she muttered to Joel with a rueful smile as she clinked her glass with his. "Happy New Year."

Abby's eyes were bright and her cheeks were rosy from the heat coming off the wood stove. Joel was reminded of the picture he'd seen of KJ when she was about that age and it pained him. He held Abby tightly when she hugged him goodnight.

While Val settled Abby upstairs, Joel turned off the overhead light so the room was lit by the glow from the glass-fronted wood stove. He pulled out his phone and connected it to the Bluetooth speaker on the bookshelf. He'd planned to share this playlist with Val on their trip, but this would do just as well.

When he heard her footsteps on the stairs, he pressed play and slipped his phone into his pocket. She paused in the doorway as the familiar guitar chords from Keith Urban's "Making Memories of Us" filled the room.

Her eyes filled with something like awe.

"You remember?" Joel asked.

"Yes, but I didn't think you would."

Joel reached for her hands and pulled her to him as the gentle tune brought back the memory of that Homecoming night their senior year. He slipped his hands around her waist, and she wrapped hers around his neck. In the dim light it was easy to think of nothing except the gentle curve of her hips as they swayed to the music.

"I think that's the last time we danced," she said with a coy smile. "I was so nervous, I thought for sure you'd hear my heart pounding. Lacey only let you dance with me then because you had to. She shot daggers at me the whole time."

"I just wanted to go home," Joel murmured. "Remember how badly we lost? Most of the team skipped it, but I had to be there."

"I'm glad you went or I would have looked really stupid dancing by myself. The Homecoming queen who lost her king."

"Dancing with you was the best part of the night."

Val scoffed. "Whatever."

"It's true," he insisted. "That should have told me something, but I was too stupid to realize it."

"We were both too young to know what we were doing. It's good we had a chance to grow up first. I just can't believe you remembered what song we danced to that night."

"That was Lacey's fault," Joel admitted. "You know how popular it was? She was trying to make it be 'our song,' but it came on the radio once and I wasn't thinking and mentioned dancing with you. She was furious. She wouldn't listen to it after that and changed the station if it ever came on. So I couldn't have forgotten if I'd tried. It became almost a guilty pleasure that I'd listen to by myself."

"Well, you can indulge in that guilty pleasure with me any time you want." Val's hands on the back of his neck pulled him closer.

"Really?"

He kissed her and the music swelled, filling him with sentiment and desire. She fit in his arms as if they were made for each other. His lips traced her jaw to her ear, and she stripped off her bulky scarf, giving him easier access to her neck, her clavicle, the hollow at the base of her throat. They weren't moving with the music anymore, following a rhythm of their own. She breathed faster as she fumbled with the buttons of his shirt.

Suddenly the song cut out, replaced with a ring tone. He sighed.

"Who's calling you this late on New Year's Eve?" Val moaned. But the look in her eyes told him she already knew.

"Give me a sec."

He was already in motion as he answered, walking down the hall to the office across from the bathroom. If Cooper was calling Joel on his personal phone, he had a good reason for it.

Cooper's clipped words were like a douse of cold water. "We got something back from the lab. Most of the video footage from Brett Rogers was destroyed in the fire, but not all of it. There's something I want you to see. You're only a few minutes away, right?"

"Uh, yeah. Not too far."

"Good. See you soon."

Cooper hung up and Joel closed his eyes to give himself one second of disappointment. Then he packed it away and went to get his jacket.

He found Val in the kitchen, rinsing and stacking the dirty dishes. His guilt intensified. Not only was he leaving her after she'd worked so hard to make it a nice evening, he wouldn't even be there to help her clean up. She turned, her eyes skimming over his jacket.

"You had the night off." It wasn't quite an accusation, but close.

"Something's come up," he said apologetically. "I'll come back if I can."

Val looked at the microwave clock. The altered time read 1:09 a.m., which meant it was actually 11:09 p.m. So much for ringing in the new year together.

"I know I shouldn't complain," she said, her voice tight. "But I hate this."

"I know." He gave her a lingering kiss goodbye, but his mind was already moving ahead to what had been found on the tapes they'd rescued from Brett's burn barrel.

THE GRANGE WAS STILL HUMMING in spite of the late hour. Porter's rotating shifts meant that the work of following up on leads didn't stop when the sun went down. Cooper motioned him over to a computer with a wide monitor where an FBI agent was sitting.

"Thanks for coming in, Joel. Porter's guys have been combing through the cassettes that you salvaged, and we may have found what Brett Rogers was trying to conceal."

The footage that appeared on the screen was a close-up of a window with the blinds partly opened. Joel recognized the open closet.

"KJ's bedroom," he observed.

"Yep."

Joel frowned. "The camera I saw was too high up in the tree to get an angle like this. This is too...deliberate."

"Right. Like it was specifically set up to film through her blinds."

The FBI agent scrubbed the timeline to little effect, then stopped and let it play. KJ had entered the bedroom with a towel wrapped around her body and another towel wrapped in a turban around her head. She was moving jerkily and it took Joel a bit to catch that her mouth was moving. She'd just taken a shower and was singing and dancing in her bedroom as she got dressed.

Joel could almost hear Abby's voice in his head. She

loved to sing to herself in the bathroom, a completely unconscious expression of childlike joy. He felt a surge of protectiveness toward KJ, especially when she dropped the towel to the floor. Her body carried the softness of prepubescence, and anger toward Brett Rogers crackled in his chest. He pushed it away out of habit, knowing there would be time to feel that later. Right now he needed to focus. Think, not feel.

There was a tremor in the camera and the focus shifted from the girl dressing for bed to the blind slats themselves.

"What was that?" Joel asked.

"The auto-focus gets confused for a bit. But it comes back after a while. Pull up a chair and Allen will take you through everything. Rogers wasn't at his house tonight when Coleman and Miller went to pick him up, and I want to know exactly what we're dealing with by the time we find him."

"Sure. " Joel checked the time as he settled into a hard plastic chair. It was a few minutes past midnight.

Happy freaking New Year.

10

Sunday morning dawned with a thick fog that turned the world into a blank white sheet outside the farmhouse windows. The snowfall Abby had hoped for never materialized, but a heavy frost had almost the same effect. The surrounding hills were completely obscured by fog, except for the shadowy forms of fir trees and cedars emerging like the ranks of a slender army as Val drove down Alderbrook Lane to the county road. Her new car was a mid-size SUV, and what had initially felt like an extravagance now seemed like a necessity as she navigated the ruts on the dirt road.

Abby sat in the back seat, the heels of her black Mary Jane's clicking together as her feet dangled above the floor.

"I see Bigfoot!" she exclaimed, pointing out the window.

Val looked in spite of herself. "There in the fog?"

"Yeah, he was standing next to a tree."

"Wow. You must have really good eyes. All I see is fog."

Abby had been obsessed with Bigfoot for months—drawing pictures and making up stories about his family who lived in the woods with him.

The county highway was quiet on this first day of the new year, and a heavy stillness lay over the town as Val drove into Owl Creek.

"Why don't we go to church?" Abby asked. "We used to go with Daddy."

Val looked in the rearview mirror.

Abby's hair was pulled into tight pigtails tied with blue ribbons. Her favorite plastic hair clips with sparkling purple unicorns kept the wisps out of her face. For now, anyway.

"Do you want to go to church?"

Abby shrugged. "Emily and Kara do. I'm the only one in my class who doesn't go."

Val doubted that, but didn't say so. "When I was your age I went with my mom and dad to the church over by the high school. The one with the big white cross on the front."

"The yellow one?"

"Yeah, that's it. That might be where Emily and Kara go. We could try it sometime if you want. But not today because we're going to a different church."

"The one for the missing girls?"

"Yes, that one."

After a pause, Abby said, "Their families must miss them a lot."

Val pondered this, thinking about those months after

Jordan had disappeared when they'd presumed him dead. These weren't just idle words. Abby had been forced to reckon with grief a lot younger than most.

"I'm sure they do. That's why we're going, so their families know that we care about them. Maybe that will help them feel a little bit better."

Val had stopped attending church in Chicago after news broke about Jordan's crimes. It was easier to stay away than to risk seeing judgment in people's eyes. Pity, anger, morbid curiosity, disgust. When she first came back to Owl Creek, she assumed she would face the same treatment. But she didn't feel that way anymore. Maybe it was time to go back. Maybe she needed it as much as Abby.

Today wasn't about worship, though. The church the Greer and McNamara families attended was holding a special service. Word had gotten around that the community was invited to come show support for the families of the missing girls.

On every utility pole lining Main Street were photos of KJ and Sophie, their bright smiles a contrast to the stark yellow MISSING across the top. Some of the poles had bright pink ribbons tied around them—slashes of color that hung limply in the morning air. At the little park across from Stan's Market, another memorial of sorts had been hastily erected near the town's Christmas tree, featuring large posters of the girls with a tip line asking for any information. Despite being laminated, rain had seeped through and warped Sophie McNamara's face, giving the poster an air of neglect and abandonment that made Val uneasy.

The Church of Christ sat across from the Post Office, a block down from where the new bank was under construction. Val still tensed whenever she drove past it, just a slight reminder from her body that it hadn't forgotten what she'd been through. The church parking lot was nearly full, and cars were lining up on the street. A fully loaded logging truck took up more than half the road and Val carefully eased her way around it to swing in behind a white minivan. She hadn't been in the old brick building in years, but she distinctly remembered as a child attending a community Christmas party, complete with a musty-smelling Santa.

Now she and Abby were ushered inside by an older man in a sport coat, his buttoned shirt straining over his belly. They followed the line of congregants through the foyer to the back of the chapel. Wooden pews were filling quickly, and Val happened to catch Nicole's profile before her view was blocked by a passing family.

"Let's see if there's room by Nicole," she whispered to Abby, detouring around the back of the room where an elderly woman with a walker was moving slowly toward the front.

Nicole turned and caught her eye, then smiled and slid closer to her daughter, making room for Val and Abby on the bench.

"I'm glad you could make it," she whispered as Val sat next to her.

"Of course. Thanks for telling me."

Nicole's daughter Ella sat stony-faced next to her mom. Nicole had explained that Ella had worked with the sixth graders as a high school counselor on their week-long research trip in the fall. She knew KJ and Sophie well.

Soft organ music played through the chapel, reverberating against the vaulted ceiling. Val spied the McNamara family sitting on the front row. Faye's hair was pulled back into its characteristic ponytail, but it looked limp and unwashed. Sophie was the youngest of six or seven kids; Val wasn't sure exactly. She couldn't tell how many of the teenagers and young adults sitting on the bench with Faye were her children, but there was a staggered array of heights, and the hair colors ranged from blond to auburn.

Val's heart constricted as she watched Faye, imagining what she must be going through. Instinctively, she reached out a hand to pull Abby closer.

Abby looked up and smiled, then leaned her head against Val's chest for a hug.

"I didn't know Joel was going to be here," Nicole said.

Val followed her gaze to the back of the room where Joel was standing with Marnie Sanders.

"I didn't know either." She was still disappointed that he hadn't been able to come back last night, but sitting there in the church with Faye in her sight, she chided herself for complaining.

"Should we scoot over and let him squeeze in? We can make room," Nicole offered.

"Nah, it's okay. He's working." She caught his eye and gave a small smile.

"Scoping out the suspects?" Nicole's tone was darkly

suggestive. "I heard they questioned Howie Lambert yesterday."

Val's smile faded. "I'm sure they're questioning a lot of people."

She looked around the room at the families filling the pews. Could one of the men sitting next to his wife be the man who kidnapped KJ and Sophie? Did someone in that room know where they were? Was someone in that chapel a child rapist? Or a murderer?

It was a grim thought but Val couldn't shake it. For as small as Owl Creek was, there were a lot of people she didn't know. Of those she did, she couldn't guess what they were capable of.

The pastor began the proceedings with a hymn and a prayer for the McNamara and Greer families. He waxed thoughtful and reflective about KJ's life, but Sophie's life seemed to be overshadowed by talk of her siblings and parents, giving Val the distinct impression that being the youngest in a large family meant Sophie was known more as part of a collective than as an individual.

After the pastor concluded his remarks, Sheriff Larson came to the pulpit and the feeling in the room shifted. A silence fell that amplified the scuff of his shoes against the polished floor.

"Thank you for sharing part of your Sunday with us," the sheriff began. He looked grayer than the last time Val had seen him, and she wondered if some days he regretted seeking reelection last fall. After word had gotten out about his political rival's involvement with a group that had been distantly connected to the Owl Creek bombers, Larson's reelection had been assured.

But now, he looked like he would have preferred retirement.

"Our thoughts and prayers go out to the Greer and McNamara families. As you know, our investigators, together with a team from the FBI, have been working tirelessly to find KJ and Sophie."

His voice echoed against the rafters and he gripped the edges of the pulpit like he held a personal grudge against it.

"I can't overstate how much we need the help of regular citizens like you. As you may have heard from the media, we're looking for a red hatchback that was seen at the Greer residence on the night of December twenty-sixth. If you know anything about who that visitor to the Greer residence was, please share it. Incidents like this rarely take place without someone knowing something about it. Maybe you've seen something in the past week that seemed out of place. Maybe you've heard something that stood out in your mind. Talk to one of our deputies about it, even if it seems unimportant. You never know when it might be the piece we need to find both of these girls and bring them home. Thank you."

Val leaned over to Nicole. "Does that mean they don't have any real suspects? I thought they were looking at Brett Rogers."

Nicole shrugged. "Maybe they don't have enough to charge him yet."

The hard wooden bench was becoming a nuisance against Val's spine. She shifted and looked back to find Joel, but he and Marnie were both gone. She wondered if they'd found whatever they'd come for.

JOEL CHECKED the time as he entered the hardware store. It was near closing time on Sunday evening and he was supposed to be headed home. Pressure was increasing to find Brett Rogers and bring him in for questioning. Joel had been to the nearby Moon Apartments looking for Brett's nephew, but the unit was dark and no one had answered. A neighbor said the nephew had moved out two months back.

Before heading back to the Grange, Joel had stopped by the hardware store in an effort to continue fleshing out the movements of the victims in the last twenty-four hours before they disappeared.

A teenager looked up from the cash register, her hair twisted into two messy knobs behind her ears. She wore heavy eye makeup in shades of black and called to him in thinly disguised annoyance, "Just so you know, we're closing in about five minutes."

Joel produced his shield and her charcoal lips parted in surprise.

"Is your manager in? I need to ask a few questions."

"Christian? Sure, let me get him."

The store was empty, and Joel could hear their whispered conversation as the cashier returned, the sibilants sliding over each other in urgent haste.

"How can I help you?" Christian was a short white man in his early forties whose red polo shirt strained across his broad shoulders.

Joel shook his hand. "I have questions about a customer who visited this store on the morning of

December twenty-sixth. Would you be able to verify when she was here?"

"Sure. Let's go back to the office and I'll see what I can do."

Joel followed him past rows of paint cans and drill bits to a small flight of wooden stairs that led to a box at the top, like a sentry on a tower. The construction likely dated back to before the days of CCTV because large windows built into the two walls looked out over the hardware store. Now, a monitor in the small office showed a rotating view from three cameras—one behind the till, one outside with a view of the outdoor equipment, and another positioned at the back of the store.

Christian removed a stack of files from a chair against the wall and gestured to Joel to sit while he settled behind the desk and typed his password into the computer.

"Let's see, what date was that again?"

"December twenty-sixth. Leisa Greer is her name."

Christian's hands paused. "Greer? As in KJ Greer?"

"It's her mother. I'm checking up on a few details from the day KJ disappeared. Do you have record of when she was here last?"

"Do you have a phone number for her? It's easier to search our database that way."

Joel gave him Leisa's number and waited as Christian typed it in.

"Let's see, she has a rewards account with us so I should be able to tell you...yep, she completed her purchase at 10:14 a.m."

"Who was working that day? They might remember her and her daughter."

Christian clicked over to another application and scrolled through a calendar.

"Hmm, it looks like Nathan and Aubrey were working that shift. Aubrey's out front now, but Nathan called in sick. He came down with a fierce stomach bug after Christmas and has been out all week."

Joel noted it down. "What can you tell me about Nathan?"

Christian fidgeted with a pen. "Oh, not much. He's worked here about a year. Divorced, I think. Has a couple of kids."

"Can I get his phone number?"

Christian shared Nathan's contact information and called Aubrey to the office.

"I turned off the 'open' sign," Aubrey said. "Still need to close out the register."

"That's fine," Christian said. "Detective Ramirez has a few questions for you about Leisa Greer. KJ Greer's mom."

"The missing girl?"

Joel produced a picture of Leisa and KJ. "Christian tells me you were working the morning of December twenty-sixth. Do you remember seeing them that day?"

Aubrey leaned closer to examine the photo. "Yeah. Poor thing. I remember them because the store was dead. Oh, sorry." She looked abashed, her cheeks turning red. "I probably shouldn't say that. I didn't mean to be insensitive...it's just a saying, you know? We had maybe three people come in all day; I don't know why we were even open."

"Anything stand out to you from their visit?"

"The girl was wearing a cute panda hat, you know, with eyes on the forehead? I was cleaning the popcorn machine and saw them come in and said, 'Oh, cute hat!' and she smiled." Aubrey's words carried the weight of someone who'd been reviewing the moment over and over in her mind. "Her mom was looking for plumbing so I pointed her to aisle eight, and that was that."

"Anything strike you about her mood? Either one of them?"

"No. The mom seemed a little stressed, I guess. I mean, it's the day after Christmas and she's buying plumbing supplies. That's never a good sign, right? But Nathan was checking, so you probably want to talk to him. He might remember more. He's a pretty chatty guy."

"Anything else you need, Detective?" Christian asked.

"Let me know if Nathan makes it in tomorrow and I'll stop by. If you remember anything else about that day, give me a call."

Joel handed them both a business card and excused himself as the interior lights of the store dimmed. So far Leisa's story of her movements that day were checking out, not that he'd expected otherwise. But with the list of tasks growing faster than they could check them off, every bit of progress mattered.

The service earlier that day had been a unique opportunity to get many residents of Owl Creek together in one room. There had been a few faces he'd particularly watched for. KJ's father, Jimmy Greer. Her basketball coach, Howie Lambert. The Standridges and the neighbors who lived across the road from the Greers. Then there had been those who caught his attention by trying to insert themselves into the Greer or McNamara inner circles, while others kept their distance. Lyle Merritt was there, but he stayed on the opposite side of the room and, as far as Joel saw, never approached Leisa. It seemed that most of the community had come out for the service, and it had been standing room only all the way to the exit doors.

The one face he hadn't seen was Brett Rogers.

11

THE LIGHT above the shop turned the world outside a sickly orange while Val sat at the kitchen table, a mug of tea steeping in front of her and her phone in hand. The fog had intensified overnight, diffusing the shop light so that the whole world glowed. Val was trying to limit how much time she spent reading up on the kidnapping, knowing full well that, though media played a vital role in keeping the public informed, they never knew as much as people thought they did. But she kept being drawn back to her news feed, as if the latest report could give meaning to such a senseless nightmare.

> The Wallace County Sheriff's Office is looking for Brett Rogers, the neighbor of Katie Jean Greer, otherwise known as KJ who, together with her friend, Sophie McNamara, went missing the night of December twenty-sixth. Brett Rogers is considered a person of interest in the case and was last seen at his

home on December twenty-seventh. Rogers has a reputation for being a recluse, with a collection of mannequins displayed in his yard. Some in the area find it to be a harmless hobby. Others are less generous.

"What kind of person puts scenes like that on display?" asks Owl Creek resident, Cheryl Harper. "It's disgusting."

Rogers couldn't be reached for comment, but in an interview from 2012 in local paper *The Pineview Daily,* he claimed to have over one thousand mannequins. Rogers began his collection shortly after moving to the area in 2004.

Val couldn't stop the feeling of bitter anger that swelled inside as she thought about the man who had used his mannequins to make lewd jokes about her and Joel. He'd even directed a subtle threat toward Abby. Val's stomach turned as she looked at the archived photo of Rogers standing in front of his house with a flock of mannequins behind him.

A soft tread in the hallway made her switch off her phone. Abby shuffled into the kitchen bundled in a blanket.

"Hey, Gabby-girl. How'd you sleep?"

"Not good. It was so cold I didn't get any sleep at all."

"It got really cold, didn't it?" Val murmured in sympathy. "Let's put another blanket on your bed tonight. There's a fire going in the living room, so grab your school clothes and you can dress in there while I get started on some oatmeal."

That was another habit she would have to curb someday if Joel became a permanent fixture in their home. As it was, he typically only stayed over on weekends, so there was no harm in using the living room as a dressing room on cold school mornings.

Growing up, Val had never fully appreciated how much of her mother's time must have been spent tending to the fire during the day so that by the time they got home from school it had warmed the downstairs well.

Feeling grossly irresponsible, she turned on the oven in the kitchen, letting it heat up to four hundred degrees before shutting it off and opening the door, enjoying the blast of warmth as she prepared the oatmeal. Her mind wandered over the day ahead, skipping to lunchroom duty and reading groups with the first grade classes, then on to the field trip the following day with Abby's grade. They were going to the hatchery located upriver in conjunction with a classroom project raising salmon to release into the wild later in the spring.

As Val considered what she would need to bring on the field trip—wet wipes, sanitizer, an extra lunch in case a child forgot one—she realized the date and stopped. Checked the calendar.

Had she miscounted the weeks?

No, looking back at her tracking app, she hadn't miscounted. She was supposed to have started her period the week before. It might not be a big deal, especially since her periods weren't exactly like clockwork. But, what if...?

Val rubbed at her eyes, feeling a stirring in her chest. She and Jordan had always planned to have another child. In fact, they'd been trying for about six months before he'd disappeared. Abby was going to be eight in April and Val had always hoped to give her a sibling sooner rather than later.

But now, as a single mom living paycheck to paycheck and preparing to start classes at the community college an hour away, she couldn't think of a worse time to have a baby. She and Joel were usually so careful...

Shame washed over her and she tried to ignore it. Worrying about it wouldn't fix anything. Besides, this might just be a weird month.

Still, as she added cinnamon and brown sugar to the oatmeal, a part of her couldn't help but wonder what Joel would think if she were pregnant. What would it be like to have a baby with him? What kind of a father would he be?

The thought warmed her. Joel was so good with Abby, more patient than she was sometimes. Still, their relationship was new enough that she couldn't guess what a baby might do. It would accelerate some decisions, that was certain.

Decisions she wasn't ready to make.

Decisions she was pretty sure Joel wasn't ready to make either.

"Guess what, Mom," Abby said, interrupting Val's spiraling thoughts. She walked into the kitchen while pulling on a sweatshirt with rhinestones and a koala bear. "I saw Bigfoot."

"Again?" Val asked. "Where?"

"Upstairs in my room."

"No, I mean, where was Bigfoot?"

"Outside on the hill."

Val's insides chilled. This was twice Abby claimed to have seen Bigfoot near their house. What if there really was someone out there? With thoughts of KJ and Sophie on her mind, she leaned over the sink to look out the kitchen window.

"Where on the hill did you see him?"

"He was behind the trampoline."

"He was in our yard?" Val couldn't keep the concern from her voice.

"Not in our yard," Abby said, as if Val were stupid for misinterpreting. "He was in the forest behind the trampoline."

The diffused shop light didn't reach the edges of the yard. Still, maybe Abby's view from upstairs had been different.

"How do you know it was Bigfoot?"

"Mom. I know what Bigfoot looks like," Abby said dismissively.

"Can you describe him to me?"

"He's tall and all covered in hair and doesn't wear clothes."

"And that's who you saw this morning?"

"Mmhmm." Abby took her bowl of oatmeal to the table.

Her matter-of-fact attitude reassured Val. She was pretty sure that if Abby had actually seen someone in the yard—covered in hair notwithstanding—she would have been spooked. They'd had a prowler on their property over the summer and Abby had been nervous about him for weeks.

It was much easier to pretend a Sasquatch was lurking in the woods than a human intruder. Abby had probably just seen the shape of a tree trunk through the blanket of fog. But still, Val made a mental note to take some time to check the footage from the security cameras she and Joel had installed a few months back. Though, as she looked out the window one last time, she realized that in all this fog a camera would be useless.

Val calmed her nerves by focusing on routine. "Today's a counseling day so I've packed you an extra snack."

Abby nodded as she finished off her bowl of cereal. "Can I have a piece of toast?"

Val checked the clock. "We have a few minutes. Put your shoes on while it's in the toaster."

Val's phone buzzed as Abby slid off her chair. It was a text from Joel.

> *I'm sorry about last night. I got in late and needed to do laundry and ended up crashing hard on the couch.*

A sympathetic smile pulled at the corner of Val's mouth.

> *Don't apologize for doing your job. I figured something must have come up. How are things going?*

Val tried to keep things general but she was itching to know what he knew.

He responded with one word.

Rough.

Val frowned.

Take care of yourself, okay? I'm worried about you.

Abby's toast popped up just as she walked in the room.

"Just in time!" Val announced brightly, sensing that this would be the nature of things on this first day back to school since the holiday break. The adults keeping up a cheery facade in order to avoid upsetting the students at the school while also trying not to minimize any stress and fear the children might be feeling. It would be a tough balancing act and she felt a surge of sympathy for KJ and Sophie's teacher.

As they drove toward town, Val watched Abby in the back seat. She peered through the fog, watching for the Greer house where toys, flowers, and signs had been laid like religious offerings against the fence. Abby didn't talk about the missing girls much, and Val could only guess what was going on in her head.

But she always looked for the house.

It was Brett Rogers's house that grabbed Val's attention, though. County sheriff vehicles and black unmarked SUVs were parked on the shoulder. Val strained to see any sign of Brett being hauled out in handcuffs, but it was too dark in the pre-dawn light and the only shapes she saw were mannequins. If they were searching his residence again, that was a good sign. It was surely only a matter of time before he was arrested. As far as Val was concerned, it was a long time coming.

JOEL EYED the chairs in the briefing room and decided to remain standing. As uncomfortable as the metal folding chairs were, he was so tired he wasn't sure he would be able to stay awake. Not a great way to start the day, and the sooner the caffeine kicked in from the coffee he was holding, the better.

"Good morning, folks," Cooper said, greeting the handful of deputies gathered in the room. "We're a small group this morning because of the teams conducting a search at the residence of Brett Rogers. We've also got four storage units rented under his name to go through. This will be a massive effort and we're coordinating with other agencies to lend a hand."

Joel exchanged a look with Marnie. The expression on her face told him she didn't want to go back any more than he did.

"In the meantime," Cooper continued, "Brett Rogers's whereabouts are still unknown. Bringing him in is our top priority. We've added some names to our list of acquaintances—former colleagues and extended family in the area who might know where he is. Anything else you were doing needs to be shelved until we find him."

The room held an undercurrent of urgency, and it cleared quickly when they were dismissed a few minutes later.

"I was going to follow up with more of Leisa's

extended family today, but I guess that can wait," Marnie said as they walked down the hall toward the command room.

"I swear I recognized her mom from somewhere, but I don't—"

The entrance door swung open and Joel and Marnie turned reflexively. But it wasn't a deputy or FBI agent reporting back from an assignment. Instead, an elderly woman wearing a stocking cap and heavy parka stood clutching a green reusable shopping bag.

"Can we help you?" Marnie asked.

The woman bumped the door behind her. Her mouth moved but no sound came out.

"Are you looking for someone?" Marnie's voice was pleasant, but her eyes sharpened.

"I'm here." The woman's voice was thick with uncleared mucus.

Marnie took a few steps forward and Joel followed, hanging back to avoid making the stranger any more nervous than she already was.

"Are you trying to report a tip? We aren't open to the public, but you can call the tip line to make a report."

The woman barely came up to Marnie's shoulder. Her eyes flitted to Joel and back to Marnie and she looked like she might bolt. Then she cleared her throat and announced, "I'm here to turn myself in."

12

DEBBIE THOMPSON's hands were thin and covered in age spots, the knuckles swollen with arthritis. She folded them and placed them gently on the table, reminding Joel of the thin bones of a bird. She looked askance at the recorder Joel placed in the center of the table.

"This will help us make sure we don't miss anything in our reports," Marnie said. "Now, can you repeat your name for the record?"

As Marnie went through the preliminaries, Joel watched Debbie Thompson's hands. They hadn't stopped trembling since she'd placed them on the table, and Joel wasn't sure if it was caused by nerves or a neurological condition.

"Now, Debbie—can I call you Debbie?" Marnie asked.

"Debbie's just fine."

"Thank you for coming in, Debbie. Can you explain what brought you here today?"

"It's like I told you already, y'all have been looking for me and I'm here to turn myself in." Her voice quavered.

"What makes you think we've been looking for you?" Marnie asked. Her voice was kind and her expression was carefully non-threatening.

"It's my car you've been searching for," Debbie said. "I didn't know it because I wasn't at the service on Sunday, and I don't get TV out at my place ever since they moved to the digital antennas. It wasn't until Sharon Hardy called me that I knew. So here I am."

"What kind of car do you drive?"

"It's a Ford Explorer. Red. I needed something that could clear the road better than my minivan."

"And were you at the Greer residence the night of December twenty-sixth?"

"Yes. They were last on my rounds so it was pretty late. Almost nine o'clock."

"What sort of rounds is that?" Joel asked.

"My cheer cards." Debbie glanced at Joel uneasily before returning her gaze to Marnie. "I make holiday cards for the widows and single moms in our church. I would have delivered them before Christmas, but I was feeling a little under the weather, so I delivered them the day after. There was something going around, you know? Knocked my neighbor flat out for almost a week."

"That's very thoughtful of you," Marnie said. "You do this every Christmas?"

That would be easy enough to verify with other women in the church.

"Not just Christmas. Every holiday. Halloween,

Mother's Day, Fourth of July. I've been doing it since my husband died almost ten years back." The corners of her mouth turned up in a smile.

"And you hand deliver each one yourself? That's ambitious." Marnie looked impressed.

Suddenly Joel remembered that morning at the Greer residence. A Christmas card made on green cardstock with flecks of gold had been resting on the counter near Leisa's purse.

"Can you describe the card for me?" he asked. "Do you remember which one you gave to the Greers?"

Debbie's mouth sagged again. "I don't. I'm sorry, Detective. I make them all differently."

"But you would recognize it if you saw it?"

"Absolutely."

"Did you see KJ that night when you dropped off the card?" Marnie asked.

"I did. She answered the door, but only a crack. She's usually so friendly when I see her at church. But that night she seemed nervous and closed the door before I could even wish her a Merry Christmas."

"And that struck you as odd?"

"Well, I don't know. After all, it was late and her mom's car was gone. I asked if Leisa was working and she said yes and took the card and thanked me."

"Did you see if anyone was with her?"

Debbie shook her head. "There were lights on in the house and I think I heard the TV. But I assumed she was alone. And then..." She paused, her eyes dropping to her trembling hands.

"Yes?" Marnie prompted.

"I smelled cigarette smoke. Leisa doesn't smoke so I assumed it was one of the neighbors.

"Did you see anyone?" Joel asked.

"No. It was cold and dark and I wanted to get home. They were my last stop."

"Could you tell which direction the smoke was coming from?"

"I'm sorry. I wasn't paying attention."

Debbie didn't have anything else useful to add, so they wrapped up their questioning and Marnie stopped the recorder and showed her to the door.

"Poor thing. Trying to do a good deed and thinks she's going to be arrested for it."

Joel smiled. "Last time I checked, gas was more expensive than a postage stamp."

"I think it's great she has a purpose for her later years."

"Interesting that Lyle claimed KJ was friendly and warm when he stopped by, but Debbie said she seemed nervous and wouldn't open the door all the way."

"If I were a twelve-year-old girl home alone and Lyle Merritt showed up on my doorstep, I would be nervous to open the door to anyone else too."

"Which begs the question, whose cigarette smoke did Debbie smell that night?"

Marnie tapped her notebook against her leg. "We'll need to talk to the Standridges next door again and find out if anyone was out smoking that night. But you know who else smokes?"

"Brett Rogers." Joel nodded. Had Brett been watching Debbie Thompson, waiting for her to leave?

Marnie grimaced. "It seems like every round of questioning invariably leads us back to him. The sooner we find him, the better."

AFTER TWO HOURS of cafeteria lunch duty, Val was finally able to take a quick lunch break of her own. The teacher break room was empty, a shocking contrast to the noise and chaos of the lunchroom. Val didn't mind monitoring the cafeteria—she was one of the few aides who could say that—and enjoyed getting to know the kids of all age groups. Unlike some of the adult staff who expected the kids to eat in near silence, Val figured a healthy amount of energy and enthusiasm was a good sign, so she was a lot more relaxed than some of her colleagues. But it was still nice to take a few minutes to give her ringing ears a break.

While she picked at her food, she thumbed through her texts. Gina had sent her a picture of her oldest son on a rock climbing wall, his Arizona-standard shorts and t-shirt a contrast to the gray of the Oregon winter.

Val's response was brief and distracted because Jordan's name was showing up with three unread texts and her stomach clenched as she wondered what he wanted.

Would you be opposed to me getting Abby a phone for her birthday?

I know we always said we would wait, but it would be nice for her to be able to call or text whenever she wants.

Not that you aren't doing a great job letting her call me. Thank you for that. I just think it might be easier on you both this way.

It was a simple enough request but triggered a cascade of mixed emotions in Val.

No, she didn't want Abby to have a phone. She was too young and Val wasn't ready to take on the demands of internet safety with a seven-year-old. But it *was* annoying to have to surrender her phone to Abby any time she wanted to talk to her dad. Sometimes Val would put him off when he wanted to call, planning to do it later when it was more convenient, then feel guilty if she forgot.

She also didn't want Jordan having unlimited access to Abby. The current arrangement meant Val could supervise their interactions, something she would lose if Abby had her own phone. On the other hand, the way he said "we" sparked something in her, a feeling of teamwork and trust. He was asking for her collaboration the same as he had when they'd been married. Like he was prepared to treat her as a partner, not an adversary. Could she do the same for him?

Then again, maybe that was the point. Maybe this was part of a larger campaign to earn her trust and undermine her in some way. Maybe this was the start of a slippery slope that would end with Val powerless against Jordan's machinations.

Or maybe he was just a dad who missed his little girl.

Val restarted her reply three times before committing.

Hmm, that's a big ask. Give me a chance to think about it?

Jordan's response came in seconds.

Of course. We've got lots of time. I'd cover the bill so you don't have to worry about that. Thanks for not shutting me down.

His gratitude made her uncomfortable. It felt too much like he was begging, which made her feel like she was being stingy.

Before she could respond, Jennifer Kennick came into the room looking a little breathless.

"Hi Val!" The sixth grade teacher made a beeline for the counter where two boxes of donuts were sitting next to a pile of napkins.

"Do you need help?" Val asked.

"Yes, please. There's a jug of lemonade in the fridge and cups in the cupboard. It's Mara's birthday today. Poor thing. She's been having a rough day. Her mom brought these in as a surprise and I want to have it all set up when they come back from the library."

Val didn't need to ask why; she often saw Mara playing with Sophie and KJ at recess. She found the lemonade and cups and asked, "And how are *you* doing?"

Jennifer shook her head as she stacked the boxes, then paused with them balanced on her hip. "It's tough. The worst thing is seeing how it impacts the kids. I took a few minutes to gather everyone in a circle and asked them to share what they were feeling. At first, they talked about KJ and Sophie. But then Leo shared about his cousin who was killed in a drunk driving accident and Gillian talked about their home being broken into last year and how her mom still leaves the hall light on for her at night."

Val tsked in sympathy. "That's awful."

Jennifer nodded. "It's like all this has reawakened their own trauma. Then Kai started talking about sex trafficking and I had to put an end to that before the other kids got freaked out. It's a different world for these kids today and I don't know how we're supposed to keep them safe."

Val couldn't think of anything to say to that, except that Jordan's request seemed less and less like a good idea. With a package of cups in one hand and a jug of lemonade in the other, she followed Jennifer down the corridor to her classroom. Along the way, they passed Howie Lambert's fifth grade classroom. The sound of deep voices drew her attention to the open door.

Standing together at the front of the room were Howie and Bryson Gottschalk, Maddie's husband. They both wore matching dark expressions on their faces.

Jennifer followed her gaze and stopped in the doorway. "Bryson, hello."

"Hi, Jenn." His eyes flickered in recognition when he spotted Val. "How are you holding up?"

Jennifer shrugged. "Doing my best. What brings you here?"

"Just thought I'd stop by on my lunch break, see how things are going."

Something about that didn't sit right with Val but she couldn't think of why. The juice jug was digging into her fingers, and she shifted it in her grip.

"We're all feeling pretty helpless here," Howie said.

Jennifer noticed Val shifting her load and roused herself. "Well, we've got a birthday to set up for. Good to see you."

Val waited until they'd made it to Jennifer's classroom and out of earshot before asking, "How do you know Bryson?"

Jennifer set the box of donuts on a table next to a stack of graded papers.

"He volunteers with the basketball club. It's not an official sport, just a club Howie runs in the spring for fifth and sixth graders. He gets a good turn out. We see Bryson quite a bit then."

Val didn't point out that it wasn't spring yet. Nor did she mention the niggling thing bothering her. She didn't know Bryson well, but she was pretty sure from her time working with Maddie that he worked in Pineview. Working an hour away meant there would be no stopping by on a lunch break for a simple chat.

JOEL PULLED off the road onto the grassy shoulder across the street from a rambler with wooden shutters flanking the main window. Light leaked out beneath bent mini blinds, the color and brightness shifting in the patterns of a television set. The only streetlights on this road were at the intersections, and shadows clung to the edge of the yard where trees and a hedge of arborvitae divided the property from the neighbor's. A carport was just wide enough for two vehicles, but only one sat there now—a Chevy Impala that appeared a light sand color in the light emanating from a small window overlooking the carport.

He called in the license plate before he got out of the car. It was registered to a Bobbie Jones, age sixty-six, with an address outside of town. Either Nathan Weiss had bought, borrowed, or stolen Jones's vehicle, or the address was outdated and Joel was in the wrong spot.

Joel gave the Chevy a long look as he passed it on his way to the front door. Mud was packed into the rear wheels' tread, a common occurrence this time of year. The low murmur of the TV hummed in the night air as he passed the window.

He rang the doorbell and heavy footsteps sounded inside. The porch light flicked on, making it momentarily hard to see the man who opened the door while Joel's eyes adjusted. He had a medium build and wore semi-rimless glasses and a goatee. He coughed into his sleeve, a wet, crackling sound.

"Sorry about that," he said as he straightened. "Still trying to get over this cough."

"Are you Nathan Weiss?" Joel produced his shield.

Nathan nodded, his Adam's apple pronounced as he stared. "What can I do for you, officer?"

"I'm Joel Ramirez with the sheriff's office and I have some questions about KJ Greer. May I come inside?"

"Who's that?"

Joel produced a MISSING flier. "You must have seen her picture around town."

"Oh yeah, right. The missing girl. I don't know anything about that."

"We understand that you may have been one of the last people to see KJ on the day she disappeared. Do you remember her coming into the hardware store with her mom on December the twenty-sixth?" When he hesitated, Joel added, "You were working with Aubrey that day."

"I really couldn't say. A lot of people come through that store around Christmas time. I might recognize her mom, but I don't pay a lot of attention to the kids. They're just there for the popcorn, you know?"

Joel pulled up a picture of Leisa and KJ together to show Weiss.

He glanced at it, then stifled another cough. "Hmm, yeah, I think I recognize her. What'd you say her name was again?"

"Leisa Greer. This is her daughter, KJ, who went missing the night of the twenty-sixth."

"Man, that really sucks. I don't remember KJ, but Leisa looks familiar."

"What can you tell me about her visit the day after Christmas?"

Nathan raised his eyebrows and his mouth twisted in

amusement. "Honestly? Absolutely nothing. I've been sick all week and am only now starting to feel like I can think straight. If you say they were there, I believe you. But I would talk to Aubrey about it because I wouldn't even trust myself to remember what I had for breakfast."

"Do you have company, Mr. Weiss?"

"What?" He looked genuinely baffled. "No, I'm home alone."

"That Impala under the carport, is that yours?"

His expression cleared. "Ah, no, it's my mom's. My Jeep is having starter trouble and she loaned me her car until I get it out of the shop."

"Do you smoke, Mr. Weiss?"

He folded his arms in a defensive posture. "Sure. Now and then."

"What kind of cigarettes do you smoke?"

"Oh...Camel mostly." Weiss shifted a little, withdrawing minutely back into the house. "I don't see what any of this has to do with that missing girl. Yes, I worked the day after Christmas, but I didn't know her. And I'd rather not pay to heat the outside, you know?"

"I'm happy to come in and wrap up these questions. It'll just—" Joel offered, but Weiss didn't let him finish.

"I don't think so. Trust me, you really don't want to catch this. But thanks for stopping by. If I remember anything, I'll let you know."

And with that, he closed the door.

13

THE YELLOW SCHOOL bus looked like a bright beacon against the earthy gray-greens of the dense forest. Oak and maple interspersed with the firs and pines, their leafless branches furry with moss. As Abby's class lined up to get on the bus, Val stood at the back of the line with a garbage bag, checking to make sure none of the students brought any trash from lunch that would inevitably end up on the floor of the bus.

"You dropped your hat, Laurel," she warned.

The second grader's beanie was too small and kept riding up her head until it popped off, tumbling to the ground. This wasn't the first time, and the pink and white stripes were stained with dirt.

Val cringed as a boy in canvas shoes sank in mud almost to his ankle. The students had been cautioned to dress warmly and wear rubber boots for their tour of the hatchery, but in spite of multiple letters home, not all of them were prepared.

"Chandler, go wipe your shoes off before you get on the bus. And please try to stay out of the mud?"

Taylor Newman, Abby's mild-mannered teacher, stood at the doorway to the bus, counting heads as the students climbed on.

Two arms wrapped around Val's waist and squeezed, and she turned to find a curly blond head buried in her side.

"Hey girlie," Val said, lifting her elbows to keep the trash bag away from Abby's face. "Did you have a good time?"

"Yeah, but I'm cold. I can't wait to get back on the bus."

Abby's friend, Emily, stood nearby, her cheeks pink with cold. "My favorite part was seeing the fish eggs," she said.

"Gross." Abby wrinkled her nose. "They were disgusting and smelled weird."

"What was your favorite part?" Val asked, looking back at the bus. It was a mystery of the universe why it took so long to load elementary students onto a school bus.

"I liked feeding the salmon."

"That was cool, wasn't it?"

"They were trout, not salmon," Emily corrected.

"Oh, right." Abby shifted impatiently. "I think I need to go to the bathroom."

Val suppressed a sigh. They were all supposed to have used the bathroom during lunch, but young children couldn't count on their bladders cooperating with an adult's timeline. And she knew better than to think

Abby would survive a bumpy ride back to the school with bladder—and dignity—intact.

"Emily, will you be Abby's buddy? You know where it is, right?"

"Sure." "Yep!" Both girls responded at the same time and started toward the outbuilding where the single bathroom was located. Abby paused and turned back, slipping her backpack from her shoulders.

"Could you hold my backpack?"

Val nodded, slinging it up onto one shoulder, the strap stiff and scratchy.

The gap in the line closed behind the girls, and Val greeted the next students. "Do you have anything that needs to be thrown away? We don't want to leave any litter behind. Throw it away now before bringing it on the bus."

A squawk near the bus drew her attention, and she turned to see Caleb Foster standing on the steps of the bus, his face red and his expression urgent. Ms. Newman was shaking her head and gesturing toward the bus. Caleb seemed to move through life from one crisis to another, but he was a sweet boy and Val approached to see what she could do to help.

"Hey Caleb, what's the matter?"

Taylor Newman flashed her a look of gratitude. "Caleb, step down and tell Ms. Rockwell what's going on. Maybe she can help you. Yep, come on off the bus; there you go. We need to get everyone else on."

"But don't leave me," Caleb begged, eyes wide.

"They won't go without us, don't worry," Val said, setting down the garbage bag so she could direct him away from the other kids. "They just need to get everyone else on the bus. So, what's up?"

She crouched down so she could look him in the eye.

"I think I dropped my pencil when we were feeding the fish. I stuck it in my notebook but now it's gone." His voice was high and tight.

"Oh, that's too bad. But we can get you another pencil when we get to the school."

He shook his head vehemently. "I have to find it. My grandpa gave it to me."

The tears pooling in his eyes tugged at Val's heartstrings. She was pretty sure someone in Caleb's family was incarcerated. It might even be this same grandpa. Pencil or not, she couldn't very well shrug it off.

"Tell you what, let's walk back over to the pools and if you keep a close eye on the ground, you might see it."

She took Caleb by the hand. It was dry and felt sandy like he hadn't washed all day. But she held on tight as they walked back to the hatchery office.

Jeff, the employee who had given them their tour, was talking to the other second grade teacher, Gloria Campbell. They turned as Val approached.

"I'm sorry, but this young man has lost something very important and we're wondering if we can go check back at the pools."

"Uh oh, what did you lose, Caleb?" Mrs. Campbell said in the abrasive way she had that made everything sound like a challenge.

"My pencil," he murmured.

The two adults looked at Val as if she'd been hoodwinked, but she held their gaze steadily.

"It's a special pencil, and I told him I would help him look for it."

Jeff softened first. "That's quite all right. Come with me; I'll take you."

Val didn't relinquish Caleb's hand. She wasn't about to release this boy to the care of a stranger, no matter how kind and energetic he'd been during their tour.

They followed Jeff back out the door and across a metal walkway that spanned the rushing water of the Owl Creek river as it tumbled over a steep spillway. The dull reverberation of their boots against the metal was drowned out by the water. A fine spray clouded the air beneath their feet.

Val smiled and squeezed Caleb's hand reassuringly.

The area around the trout pools was thick with muck and Val was grateful for her own rubber boots.

"There it is!" Caleb announced, running over to a large rock and stooping beside it. He held up a cheap mechanical pencil in triumph.

Val chuckled. "Good thing your eyes are better than mine. I never would have seen it. Come on, let's head back to the bus."

"Glad you found it!" Jeff called as they turned back.

"Thanks!" Caleb cried, his grin bright with relief.

When they returned to the bus, the line of students was gone and the diesel engine rumbled in counterpoint to the noise of the waterfall. The bus driver gave Caleb a long-suffering look and Val offered an appreciative smile but was met with cold weariness.

The bus was filled with the din of excited children

fueled with lunch and happy to be paired up with friends discussing the day's adventures

"Find your seats," Gloria Campbell called over the chatter as Val edged past her to her own seat. "We need to do a count before we go." Mrs. Campbell made her way slowly down the aisle, counting heads until she came to the back of the bus. "Forty-two," she announced with satisfaction.

But as the bus driver closed the door, Emily piped up.

"Mrs. Campbell, Abigail isn't back."

Val shifted to kneel backward on her seat where she could get a better view over the seats, looking for Emily. Abby wasn't in the seat beside her.

"Back from where?" Gloria barked.

"From the bathroom."

"Abigail Fisher, where are you?" Gloria called, her eyes sweeping over the seats. "I counted forty-two."

"It was Connor's fault!" a high-pitched voice said. "He crawled under his seat so you counted him twice."

"Connor Gardner!" Gloria Campbell's voice shot out like a whip. "Is this true?"

Val didn't wait to hear her lecture. "I'll go find her," she said to the bus driver, clambering back down the bus steps as the door opened again.

Poor Abby. She would be embarrassed to find the whole bus waiting on her while she was in the bathroom. Val expected to see her running from the direction of the outbuilding where the restroom was located, but the only person she saw was Jeff.

"Did you lose another pencil?"

"No, just my daughter," Val said with an apologetic smile. "She's in the restroom."

Jeff frowned. "There's no one in the restroom. I just checked to make sure before you drove away."

Val faltered. "Are you sure? She said she was going to use the restroom."

"You can check for yourself, but there's no one there."

Val kept her smile pasted to her face but picked up her pace as she followed Jeff to the building that served as part shed and part public restroom. The door to the restroom was on the side that faced the forest, a heavy metal thing that squealed when she opened it.

The single restroom was empty, its concrete floor bare from wall to wall.

Val stepped back and let the door close, puzzled.

"You want me to look around?" Jeff asked.

"Yes, please. I'll go check the bus again." Val sounded unconcerned, but an uneasiness was growing in her mind. Where else could Abby have gone? She was probably fine, Val knew. There would be an explanation and Mrs. Campbell would be annoyed and Abby would be embarrassed and Val would be glad she hadn't freaked out.

Crossing the gravel lot back to the bus, she offered a silent prayer that Abby had managed to somehow slip past her and was sitting in her seat getting a talking-to by Mrs. Campbell.

But when she climbed back on the bus, both teachers were waiting expectantly.

"Any luck?" Taylor Newman asked.

"No. Emily, I thought you were her buddy." Val tried to keep the accusation from her voice, but she needed information. Why had Emily left Abby?

"I was, but then Mrs. Campbell said it was time to go so I thought I had to come."

Gloria sighed. "The point of a buddy is so that no one's left alone."

Val felt pulled in two. A part of her wanted to go up and down the bus and see for herself that Abby wasn't there, ducking to check under every seat, but another part wanted to leave the bus and search the hatchery. Had Abby gone into the shed? Had she, like Caleb, lost something and gone to look for it? What if she'd wandered to other parts of the hatchery where they didn't have safety rails? What if she'd fallen in the river?

The thought made Val woozy. The volume of water pounding over the spillway would mean certain death for a little seven-year-old.

"I'll check with Jeff. Maybe they found her."

She left the bus and headed back toward the hatchery. Jeff and another employee were talking near the office.

"What's her name, ma'am?" Jeff asked.

"Abby. Abigail. She's wearing a white coat and rubber boots with watermelons on them."

"I've got Kurt and Pam looking downstream. Does she often wander off?"

"No," Val said quickly. But then she hesitated. Abby had gotten in a strange man's car last summer and gone to his house to look at kittens. Val couldn't say for sure what she would or wouldn't do. "But she's only seven. She doesn't always think things through."

Jeff nodded. "Well, we've never lost a child yet, so I'm sure we'll find her."

Val appreciated his confidence and clung to it like a feather in a maelstrom. She thought back to Abby leaving to go to the restroom. Her attention had been caught before Abby had reached the building. How much time had passed? She checked her phone. Twenty minutes? Thirty?

That's too long, a voice in her mind warned. Something must have happened. Something bad.

Now she was in real danger of freaking out. Val gulped down the feeling of terror rising in her throat as she looked back over the edge of the spillway. Further downstream, the river swept along with a quick, shallow current, but here it was tumultuous and violent. She strained to see any sign of Abby, dreading finding anything to indicate her little girl had fallen.

"Valerie?" Taylor Newman approached with Abby's backpack and Val's bag in hand. "I'm really sorry, but we need to get the bus back to the school or the students will miss their rides home."

"Oh, of course." Val took the bags, but her mind was reeling. "Are you sure she's not on the bus?"

Taylor shook her head. "I'll stay until we find her. Gloria will take care of my class. Have you called the police?"

"No. I'm sure she's around here somewhere." Val didn't want to admit the truth. Calling 911 felt like an escalation. Somehow, in her desperate mind, she believed if she didn't call, then it wouldn't be serious. It would be a silly story about how Abby got distracted and missed the bus and everyone worried, and they would all laugh about it later.

This was stupid. Making a phone call wouldn't make it more or less real.

Val pulled out her phone but stopped as Jeff emerged from the forest near the edge of the outbuilding. His fists were clenched and his posture suggested purpose.

When he reached Val, he held out his hand. In his palm was a little plastic hair clip with a sparkling purple unicorn.

"Do you recognize this?"

"That's Abby's," Val said breathlessly.

"I found it in the forest, about twenty yards from the restroom. I'm sorry, ma'am, but I think we need to call the police."

14

JOEL'S THOUGHTS spun in circles as he raced up the narrow mountain road to the hatchery. They were spread so thin working the Greer-McNamara case that Val had reached him before dispatch. He'd been on his way to Pineview to follow a lead in their search for Brett Rogers but had immediately reversed direction, flipping on lights and siren and stomping on the gas.

Abby was missing.

The sweet little spitfire who beamed at him whenever he saw her, who alternated between lighting up every room and sucking the air out of it with her demands for attention.

Missing.

Joel noted the low-level adrenaline coursing through him, more effective than any stimulant at giving him focus and making him alert. He had to be careful. Focus was good. Being distracted by emotion wasn't.

He parked behind a black SUV and saw another just

ahead. There were benefits to having the FBI so close working on the Greer-McNamara case. A roar of rushing water greeted him as he stepped out of the car. The hatchery office was a one-story wooden structure painted a light brown. He spotted Kim coming out of the forest to the north.

"Kim!" He jogged to meet her and she waited for him to catch up.

"Val's in the office with the school teacher," Kim said. "Agent Porter's here too. He offered and we weren't about to turn down help."

"Has Search and Rescue been called?"

"They're on their way."

Joel left her and headed to the office. The sound of the river subsided as he stepped inside.

Val was standing at a bank of windows looking out over the river, her back to the door. A backpack hung from her hands, and Joel felt a pang as he recognized it.

Stacy Porter was deep in conversation with a man whose mustache matched the brown of his shirt and a woman who didn't look old enough to be Abby's school teacher.

Joel approached Val and placed a hand on her arm, sliding it along the nylon of her jacket.

She turned and met his eyes, and for a brief instant he saw pure, naked fear. She was no stranger to pain, he knew that. But still, he was unprepared for the agony in her eyes.

She blinked and it was gone. "You came," she said simply.

"How are you doing?"

Her shrug was almost imperceptible. "They're bringing in dogs to look for her. She had a sweatshirt in her backpack from yesterday. They're hoping to use it to catch her scent."

"That's good. What happened? How did she get away from the group?"

"She went to use the bathroom while they were boarding the bus. You know how she is...waits too long to go and then it's an emergency. I got caught up helping another student and just assumed she'd boarded with the other kids. It wasn't until we were ready to leave that I realized she hadn't made it on. I should have checked sooner. By then it had been a good twenty minutes."

"It's not your fault," Joel said automatically. "You couldn't have guessed she would wander into the forest."

"Did she wander off?" It was almost a whisper, but it was fierce and intent. "Why would she? She knew we were leaving. What if the same person who kidnapped KJ and Sophie took Abby?"

Joel reached for her hands. They were clenched around the backpack loop, and he loosened her fingers to better grasp them in his own, setting the backpack on the floor.

"Don't go to the worst case scenario. There's no reason to think this is connected. Abby probably just saw a squirrel or something and chased it into the forest."

"But why didn't she find her way back? There was a giant yellow bus parked right there. It's not exactly something you miss. Not to mention she could have followed the noise of the water." Val shook her head. "This isn't making me feel better, Joel. I need you to take this seriously."

"Of course I'm taking it seriously. We'll do everything we can to find her. But it's too early to assume the worst."

"Joel." Stacy's warm voice came from across the room.

"I'll be back." Joel kissed her temple before he left.

"That was Jeff O'Hara," Stacy said when Joel joined him, nodding to the man with the mustache as he left the building. "He says they have CCTV on the water, the office, and the supply building. But the restroom is on the back side, out of range of the cameras."

"We'll need to talk to the children, see if anyone saw or heard anything."

"Their teacher says they will have all gone home to their families for the day. But she's working on getting us a class list. This is the same little girl who had threats made against her a few months ago, right?"

Joel nodded. "Her father is Jordan Fisher, so we thought it might have been retaliation, but it wasn't." At least, not retaliation against Jordan. The threat had been against Joel all along.

Stacy considered this. "Senator Fisher's granddaughter?"

Joel nodded.

Stacy swore. Pitching his voice lower, he said, "I'm going to talk to Sheriff Larson about bringing in another team. Once word gets out another girl has gone missing in this town, and this time it's a senator's granddaughter,

DOJ is really going to be feeling the pressure. We want to get ahead of this."

"Sounds good to me. Anything to find her and bring her home safe."

"But Joel," Stacy's dark eyes were serious, "you shouldn't be here. You know how it goes. Besides, you're already burning the candle at both ends with this Greer-McNamara case. Be with her mom. Help her hold herself together. That's where you'll do the most good."

Joel opened his mouth to protest, then stopped. Stacy was right. Joel knew he was right. So instead he said, "Anything you find, anything at all, I want to know about it."

The sound of a barking dog drifted from outside, announcing the arrival of the SAR team.

"The cavalry's here. Ms. Rockwell," Stacy said as he crossed the room, "can I see that backpack of your daughter's?"

Val left her post at the window to hand over Abby's backpack.

"If they don't find her..." Her voice trailed off as she watched Stacy exit the building, as if her thought was too awful to finish.

Joel knew the comforting thing to do was say, "They will," with all the weight of his law enforcement experience behind the claim. But he couldn't promise something like that. And in the silence that followed, as he stepped away from Val to go join the search, he felt a gap between them that was more pronounced than mere physical distance.

Outside, Stacy was organizing the agents, deputies,

and hatchery employees into a spoke pattern to search the surrounding area.

"We've only got a couple hours of daylight left," Stacy reminded the group. "There's a flag marking where the barrette was found that Mom identifies as belonging to the child. She's wearing a white coat and blue jeans, with pink rain boots that have watermelons on them."

Into Joel's mind flashed an image of Abby as if he'd seen her that morning. He could picture the white coat that Val regretted every time she noticed dirt staining the sleeves. He knew exactly where the watermelon boots would have been kept in the hallway near the front door.

Marnie sidled up next to him.

"You okay?" she asked.

He shrugged, keeping his eyes on Stacy as he finished his instructions. He felt Marnie watching him but ignored her. He wasn't ready to talk about what he was thinking. What he was feeling. What he was fearing. He'd only known Abby for about six months, but he couldn't imagine even her own father feeling more protective toward the little girl than he did in that moment.

VAL STOOD outside the hatchery office watching the yellow police tape twisting in a breeze she couldn't feel. Her mind felt stuck, replaying the day's events. Wondering how things had come to this. Nothing about the beginning of the day had suggested she would end it standing here in the cold when the sun set, watching investigators and Search and Rescue volunteers look for Abby.

Shouldn't the universe have given her a sign that this was the day her life would change? Shouldn't her mom senses have kicked in, warning her that something was wrong when Abby left to go to the bathroom?

Jeff offered her a cup of coffee in a disposable cup, and Val sipped it automatically, barely registering the bitter flavor. She kept waiting for that moment when someone would shout and there would be a flurry of activity and Joel would emerge from the forest carrying Abby in his arms. Safe. Val would shower her with kisses and tend to whatever scrapes or twisted ankle or minor injury had caused her to get lost in the woods, listening to her story about tripping in a hole and losing her way. She would be hungry and cold and would want to go home and take a nice hot bath. Val and Joel would take her home and dote on her the rest of the evening.

Instead, Val waited.

The shout never came.

"Do you need a ride home, Ms. Rockwell?" a woman asked.

Val was slow to respond, having to pull herself from the dream state where she was wrapping Abby in a soft blanket. She blinked to focus on the newcomer, a short woman with angular glasses framing kind eyes.

"I'm Gretchen Smith," she said, extending her hand. "I'm so sorry about your little girl. I'm here to help make sure you have everything you need. Can I start by offering you a ride home?"

"No thanks. I'm not leaving until they find her."

Gretchen nodded as if she expected this. "I understand."

Val tensed, waiting for her to point out the obvious, that they might not find her for hours. It might take all night, if they ever found her at all. But Gretchen didn't say any of that. Instead, she asked if she could get Val water or a fresh cup of coffee while she waited.

Val realized she was still holding the cup of coffee Jeff had given her, but it had turned cold. "Some water would be fine," she said because she didn't know what else to say to this helpful person who didn't seem to want to leave her side.

The parking lot was full of cars from the sheriff's office, personal trucks from the county Search and Rescue team, and black SUVs with government plates. A part of Val knew that with this effort and manpower, they would have found Abby by now if she'd been close to the hatchery.

A Channel Six news van had come and gone a little while ago. Val had gone inside while they were there—she had no desire to be caught on camera—but for once she was actually glad to see them. Getting the word out early could make a difference in a case like this.

A case.

It shouldn't be a case. It was just a second grade field trip.

Movement near the trees made her heart speed up when she recognized Joel stepping through the dense foliage. He was stopped by a black woman in an FBI jacket, and his expression was serious as they conferred together. Then he turned his gaze to Val and she felt a hitch in her chest.

She strode across the parking lot to meet him. "What is it? What did you find?"

He paused as if he didn't know how to find the words. "One of the searchers found a zip tie. We'll bag it and send it to the lab, and we're bringing in air support to get an aerial view of the terrain."

"A zip tie? What does that mean?"

She read the worry in his eyes, but his tone was calm and professional. "Kidnappers will sometimes use zip ties to subdue a victim."

Val felt as if the wind had been knocked out of her. She swayed and grabbed Joel's arm. "You're sure? It's not just something a maintenance guy dropped out of his pocket?"

"It could be. It absolutely could be."

But...she felt the word as clearly as if he'd said it.

Val swore, the hitch in her chest painfully sharp. "How did this happen, Joel? I was right there. There was a bus full of children not thirty yards away. No one heard or saw anything. Who could have done this?"

"Everyone will be questioned. Students, teachers, employees here at the hatchery. District personnel who knew about the field trip. Transportation employees who scheduled the busing. Everyone. It's going to take time, and you've got to be patient."

"Patient! When my daughter's missing? She could be halfway to California by now!" Anger was good. It helped her feel strong.

"They know what they're doing. You've got to trust them."

Val narrowed her eyes. "What do you mean, 'them?' Where will you be?"

Joel sighed and looked back at the woods. "I'm going to take you home. You need to get some rest and it's going to be dark soon."

"Joel." Her voice cracked on his name. "I can't leave her. She's out there somewhere. How can I leave?"

"There's nothing you can do here. It just makes one more thing for us to worry about. One more complication to work around."

"I'm her mother, not a complication!" Val hissed.

"That's not what I mean." His dark eyes softened. "Please, Val. Come home. Let them do their job. There's nothing more for you to do here. But if they need you, they'll know how to get a hold of you. You'll know everything I know."

"You promise? You won't keep anything from me?"

"Of course. As long as it doesn't jeopardize the integrity of the investigation, I promise."

Val let him lead her to the car, but she kept her eyes on the trees, willing Abby to materialize, a flash of light against the deep green. But there was only shadow.

15

THE BANDANA in Abby's mouth was wet with spit and she wished for a glass of water. But the man who had tied the bandana and put the pillowcase over her head hadn't offered her any water, and she didn't think he would hear her if she asked. She could tell she was in the trunk of a car. Or maybe the back of a truck. She couldn't see well through the black pillowcase, but he'd lifted her up pretty high to get there.

She never should have followed him into the forest. She'd promised Mom she would never go with a stranger again after Paul took her to look at the new kitties and Mom had gotten so scared she'd called the police. But Abby hadn't known he was going to take her into the forest and then pick her up and clamp a hand around her mouth so tight she was afraid she would never breathe again.

He wasn't a nice man; she knew that now. But he had seemed so friendly when she'd seen him earlier by the river. He'd crouched beside her and showed her a neat trick with a blade of grass, blowing on it to make it sing. Emily and Kara had tried it too, and they'd laughed about it until they'd heard Mrs. Newman calling them back over to join the rest of the group. Then the man had gone away and she hadn't thought about him again.

When Abby saw him waiting near the trees as she came out of the restroom and he motioned to her with excitement, she hadn't hesitated.

"Come look at the bunny rabbit," he'd said with a gleam in his dark eyes. His eyebrows were bushy like those big black and orange caterpillars that she and her friends captured during recess.

Now Abby wished she'd listened to her mom.

Her wrists were tied together with something that pinched her skin so sharp it must have been a wire. But her feet were free. She had tried to kick him when he picked her up but had just kicked off one of her boots instead. He'd held her tight and whispered in her ear, "I'm not going to hurt you. It's going to be okay, but you have to be still. If you make any noise I'm going to hurt you and then I'm going to hurt your mom, too. Do you want me to hurt your mom?"

Abby had stopped struggling then and listened. She'd shaken her head. She didn't want this bad man to hurt Mom.

"Good. Then you be a good girl and I'll leave your mom alone."

That's when Abby knew he was a really bad man.

JOEL TOOK Val to the school to pick up her car as night fell over Owl Creek, Agent Coleman following behind in her own vehicle. The streetlamps were coming on as they drove into town, and every utility pole and business sported posters with KJ Greer and Sophie McNamara's faces.

Val watched the posters pass in silence, cocooned in her anxiety. Joel searched for something reassuring to say, but his mind was full of details from the Greer-McNamara case, trying to answer the questions pressing on everyone's minds. Had Abby been abducted? And if so, was it connected to KJ and Sophie's case? Was she specifically targeted? Or was she simply in the wrong place at the wrong time?

A few months earlier, Abby had been targeted by Hannah Quinton seeking revenge on Joel. Could someone else have the same thing in mind?

Or was it related to Jordan? Typically, the non-custodial parent would be the first one deputies looked at. Jordan was under house arrest at his parents' home, so it would be a nonissue to verify his whereabouts.

Thinking of it now, Joel said, "Investigators will want to question Jordan."

"Ugh. I forgot about Jordan. Of course, he should know." Val's gaze flitted to Joel and away again. "But I don't...how can I tell him? 'Remember how you just agreed for me to have full custody of our daughter because I'm such a responsible parent? Guess what. I lost her.'"

"Hey." Joel reached for her knee. "This isn't your

fault. We don't know what happened. You can't blame yourself."

Val shook her head. "It's my job. I'm her mother and I was. Right. There." She enunciated her words bitterly.

They arrived at the school where Val's car was one of only two vehicles in the lot. The other was a green pickup truck parked in the light coming from the entrance.

Howie Lambert got out of the truck as Val exited the car. Three girls in shorts and sweatshirts approached the entrance—two holding basketballs and the third dribbling hers as they opened the front door.

"Not in the halls," Howie warned, his raised voice coming muffled through the car window. The girl dribbling the ball picked it up and held it as she went inside.

Howie turned to Val and said something, but Joel couldn't catch it. Val shook her head and didn't make eye contact as she got in her own car. Word was getting out about Abby and would travel faster on the heels of KJ and Sophie's disappearance. Three girls missing from the same town a week apart? And the third was the granddaughter of Senator Jeanette Fisher?

Val would need to brace herself for a media storm unlike anything she'd seen yet.

Joel followed her home, considering the media strategy they might use. Connecting the cases in the public's mind might be problematic if it turned out they weren't related. But there would be no way to stop the public speculation. And it would certainly keep KJ and Sophie in the public eye if they were attached to the granddaughter of a senator.

By the time Joel pulled up at the farmhouse, he'd gone into full investigator mode. Seeing Val get out of the car, he experienced a slight jolt when the back door didn't open and Abby didn't jump out.

Val didn't wait for him, instead pulling out her phone and making a call as she made her way up the porch steps to the door. Joel waited for Coleman. From the snatches of one-sided conversation he could hear, he guessed Val was calling her sister, Gina.

Coleman was joined by Gretchen Smith, the FBI's Victim Specialist that Joel had met a few days earlier when visiting the Greer residence.

Smith looked over the old farmhouse appraisingly. "What a lovely home."

Coleman, too, looked it over with a critical eye, and Joel could see the investigator surveying it with a very different intent.

"Come on in," Joel said. "Valerie's on the phone, but she'll join us in a minute."

"That's fine; no rush."

He showed them into the living room and set about building a fire. He wasn't used to being on this end of things. He wanted to jump into action, to start collecting and analyzing evidence. When tires sounded on the gravel driveway outside, he looked out the window eagerly. It was another FBI vehicle, this one blocking the road behind the first. Joel brought in chairs from the kitchen for additional seating for the agents. He stoked the fire, building it up so that it roared behind the glass doors. Then he found he'd run out of things to do.

It was enough to drive him crazy.

Val 's heart pounded as she dialed Jordan's number. Maybe he wouldn't answer and she could put this off a little longer. But she knew it wasn't fair to him and would only prolong her agony.

"Hi, Val. What's up?" Jordan sounded relaxed and cheerful.

"Uh, I have something to tell you. And it's going to be hard."

"Okaaay. It sounds like bad news."

"It's really bad. The worst." Val's throat closed. It was harder to tell Jordan than it had been to tell Gina.

"What is it?" His voice sharpened with concern. "Did something happen? Is Abby okay?"

"No." Val pushed it out through the sob she was holding back. "She's not okay. She's missing."

There was a beat of silence on the other end.

"What happened?"

Somehow relating the events made it easier for Val to get control again and the burning in her eyes and throat receded. She pulled off her coat and wrapped herself in the fleece blanket that sat on the end of the bed, curling up in the chair in the corner.

"If only I could travel!" Jordan exhaled in frustration. "I need to be there with you, not stuck in this house and my handful of approved destinations within a five mile radius."

There was a heavy pause and then he amended, "Okay, I know the alternative is being locked up in a cell right now. Thanks for not pointing it out."

"It did cross my mind," Val said dryly.

"You know me, I've never been good at standing on the sidelines. What can I do?"

"Investigators will want to talk to you. They'll want to see if there could be any connection to someone seeking revenge against you." Val tried not to let her own bitterness leak through. Jordan hadn't blamed her for losing Abby. It was only fair she not blame him either.

"Of course. Anything I can do to help. How about media? Not me, of course. No one wants to feel sorry for me right now; they're too busy hating me. But my parents would do it in a heartbeat. How about reward money?"

"I really don't know." Val's head spun. She hadn't been thinking past the state forest surrounding the hatchery. Jordan was already thinking coast-to-coast. "I'll ask Joel. He'll know what they're planning."

There was another pause.

"Okay, sure. Ask Joel." Jordan sounded guarded but like he was trying really hard not to be. "How are you, Val? Really?"

The kindness in his voice threatened to undo her again.

"I can't think about myself right now, Jordan. I'm going to need to go. I'll talk to you later."

"I hope so. I'd rather hear directly from you, not just through some media specialist or police department assistant."

"I'll do what I can," Val said, marveling that she was willingly planning on talking to him again.

When she hung up, she went to the bathroom and started the shower running so it would warm the room with steam before she had to undress. The welcome scent of freshly kindled woodsmoke drifted from downstairs.

In the bathroom, Val spied the plastic bag with the unopened pregnancy test in it and felt sick. There was no way she could think about that now. When a knock sounded at the door, she grabbed the bag and tossed it in the cupboard under the sink before opening the door to Joel.

"There are a couple of agents here to see us."

Ice crept through Val's heart. "Why?"

"They just want to ask some questions."

His calm demeanor was more reassuring than his words.

"You would tell me if it was bad news, right? You wouldn't make me hear it from a stranger?"

"Of course not. If you want, go ahead and shower. I can talk to them first."

"No, it's okay. I'll come now." Val went to the tap and shut it off. As she turned around, she noticed an edge of the plastic shopping bag had caught and was hanging out the cupboard door. A reminder that she could put off the pregnancy question for now, but eventually she would have to face it.

IT WAS surreal for Joel to sit in Val's living room waiting to be questioned by agents Coleman and Wong just as Leisa Greer and Faye McNamara had done only last week. He offered Val his hand and she clung to it with both of her own. Gretchen Smith, the Victim Specialist, sat on her other side.

"They're here to help," she'd said to Val with a smile as Coleman and Wong performed a cursory search of the house. "Remember that. But if they get to be annoying and you decide you need your space, just say the word and I'll tell them to back off."

Val had grimaced. "It's fine. They can burn the place to the ground, I don't care, if it helps them find Abby."

Now her eyes were fierce and bored into Coleman's as the FBI agent spoke.

"Ms. Rockwell, you need to know that we are treating this as a stranger abduction," Rita began. "There's always a chance that we're wrong and your little girl just wandered away in the woods, but there's enough evidence to suggest she didn't leave of her own will, and classifying it as a stranger abduction will allow us to divert more resources sooner."

"I know about the zip ties," Val said. "What else?"

"Jeff O'Hara says he saw someone in the woods near the hatchery yesterday. It's public land, so he wasn't trespassing, but we haven't yet identified who it was."

"What did he look like?"

"White, maybe six feet, medium build. Brown hair and beard. O'Hara says he was dressed for the weather and might have simply been a hunter scouting the terrain. But there's a chance he also might have witnessed something that pertains to this investigation."

The stove chimed like a gong as it expanded in the heat.

Justin Wong shifted in the hard wooden chair.

"What can you tell us about Abby? What's her personality like? How about her interests?"

"Well..." Val seemed at a loss for words. Joel understood why. How do you describe a little fireball like Abby in a way that does her justice? "She's friendly and loves people. Almost too friendly."

"Can you explain what you mean?" Rita Coleman asked.

"To be honest, it makes me uncomfortable how quickly she accepts others. Even before she could talk she would stare at complete strangers until she got their attention, just so she could wave when they noticed her. She's always been that way. She assumes everyone loves her, and they can't help it. They always do."

"Last summer she went to a stranger's house to see his new kittens without Val's permission," Joel interjected, gently adding more current information.

"Do you think it's possible someone could have lured her away from the group?"

Val looked down at her hands gripping Joel's. She was rubbing his thumb with her own, her skin pale against his. "I wish I could say no. I've tried to teach her, especially after that incident. But no matter what I do, she doesn't seem to understand."

There was a slight note of defensiveness to her tone. No, not defensiveness. Desperation.

"Have you had anyone show undue attention toward Abby recently? A teacher at school or church? A friend or neighbor?"

Val looked up. "There was...this might be nothing,

but yesterday before school she thought she saw Bigfoot in the yard."

Joel straightened. "What? You didn't tell me."

"I haven't had the chance. Besides, it was foggy and I couldn't see anything. It might have just been her imagination. You know how she is."

"She likes to pretend?" Wong asked.

"She's obsessed with Bigfoot. She saw him the day before that...on Sunday on our way to the church."

Coleman and Wong exchanged a look.

"Obviously she wasn't actually seeing Bigfoot," Val insisted. "I was going to review the security footage but she had an appointment in Pineview after school and last night we were busy getting everything ready for the field trip."

"I can get you the footage," Joel volunteered before they asked.

Coleman nodded. "And how long have you two been together?"

"Three months," Joel said at the same time Val said, "About five months."

Val's eyes snapped to his and she looked embarrassed. "Sorry, I was counting since August. But you're counting since...after the bombing..."

"I lost a bit of time while I was recovering in the hospital," Joel explained to Wong and Coleman. "August is good too."

"So not very long," Coleman said.

Val made a noise like she was going to object.

"We've known each other since we were kids, though," Joel said. He knew this was part of an interview, to sift out the irrelevant from the relevant, but he was starting to feel a little impatient himself, wanting to cut to the chase.

"Have you heard of any Bigfoot sightings before?" Wong asked Joel directly.

"Not here at the house. Abby's always looking for him everywhere we go, but I didn't know she'd claimed to see him here."

Joel avoided looking at Val. He felt flat-footed that he didn't know this important detail, but the only person to be annoyed with was himself. He simply hadn't been around.

Coleman leaned forward and rested her elbows on her knees. "We'd like to post someone outside the house, if it's okay with you. We'd want to do that anyway, but considering who your daughter's grandmother is, we need to make sure there isn't an additional threat against you."

"Me?" Val blinked in surprise.

"It's a necessary precaution. If this is an act against Senator Fisher, there's a possibility the whole family could be targeted."

Joel sensed Val's objection rising, but she swallowed it back down. "As long as you aren't wasting resources that need to be used looking for Abby," she acquiesced.

"Of course. We won't get in your way. And we'd like to monitor your phone activity in case you receive any threats or ransom communications."

Val balked a little at this, but only for half a second. "Okay, sure. Whatever you need."

"Thank you. Now, if you don't mind, we're going to

need to talk to you both separately. Ramirez, is there a place we can talk in private?"

"Sure." Joel stood. "There's a room just down the hall."

Val stood with him and he could see the anxiety in her eyes. The worst times of her life had involved federal agents questioning her.

He leaned in close, catching a whiff of her scented skin products. "It's all right," he murmured. "This is totally normal. They're here to help. I'll be right back."

Gretchen Smith took his seat as he left, and Joel heard her ask Val about the house as he led Wong down the hall. That was good. Get her talking about something safe, help her relax.

Joel stepped into the little office across from the bathroom. It had once served as Mary Rockwell's sewing room. Built-in cupboards lined one wall, and on the opposite side an old bulletin board was mounted above a heavy metal desk. Val's laptop sat there now, and the bulletin board was filled with Abby's drawings.

He stepped forward and pointed to one. "That's Bigfoot."

Agent Wong peered at it. "These others too? She does have a fascination, doesn't she? Any chance Bigfoot is code for someone? Someone who has been showing her extra attention but didn't want her mom to know?"

"You mean grooming her." A part of Joel rejected the thought. He would know, wouldn't he? But he chided himself, knowing he sounded like every parent whose child hides something from them. "Of course there's a chance. But I haven't seen any red flags, and Val is very...

vigilant." He almost said *over-protective* but caught himself. "They've had a hard time of it the past year and Abby's safety always comes first."

"Would you say she's a good mother, then?"

"Absolutely. Abby's her world. She'll sacrifice anything for her." *Even me.* It stung to realize it was still true, but he knew it was. Val had given him up once before, and he still didn't feel completely confident that she wouldn't drop him again if she thought it was best for Abby. It made him suddenly sad, but he wasn't going to unpack that now. The sooner they finished this questioning, the sooner the agents could move on to the next step in their investigation.

Seven hours and counting.

16

ABBY DIDN'T REALIZE she'd fallen asleep until she woke up and the car had stopped. For a brief second, she thought it had all been a bad dream—the man in the forest and the car taking her away—but the sharp pain in her wrists and the thick bandana in her mouth reminded her that it was all too real.

Confusion gave way to fear. She was tired of being brave. She just wanted to go home and see Mom. Who was this bad man and why had he kidnapped her?

There was a hissing sound like the back lift gate of a car opening, and Abby stiffened. The man must have come back. When he spoke, he had the same happy voice he'd used when he'd told her to come look at the bunny rabbit.

"Okay, Abby. You've been such a good girl. Are you hungry? Do you need a snack?"

Abby was too scared to be hungry. She shook her head. What she really needed was to go to the bathroom.

"How about water? Are you thirsty?"

Abby nodded. Her throat hurt from being so dry.

"Good. I'm going to take good care of you, you'll see. I'm going to take the hood off and then I'll get you a drink of water. But it's really important that you don't scream or make any noise, because if you do I'm going to go find your mom and make her bleed, and it'll be your fault. You don't want me to do that, do you?" His voice was still cheerful in spite of the threat.

Abby shook her head.

"Good. Good girl."

The pillowcase was slipped from Abby's head and she blinked. It was dark outside and the bad man was colored red from the lights at the back of the car. He had a beard and curly hair. Under his jacket, Abby saw a shirt that the other workers at the hatchery wore. He reached to untie her bandana and she caught a scent of something salty.

"Okay, here's a little bit of water. Let me help you since it'll be hard with your hands tied."

He propped the water bottle against her lips. She swallowed eagerly, but it was awkward and the water spilled down her chin.

When he pulled it away, she said, "I have to go to the bathroom."

The man looked around and frowned. They were surrounded by forest, and in the distance she could see headlights passing through the trees, marking a road. But no one seemed to be on the dirt road where they were.

"Can you hold it a bit longer?"

"I have to go bad."

The bad man swore under his breath. "Let me get your other boot. Do you know how to go in the woods?"

Abby nodded. "My mom helps me." A big lump formed in her throat. Was Mom okay? Had this bad man already done something to hurt her? Would Abby ever see her again?

Without warning, hot tears dribbled out of her eyes.

The man sighed. "Okay, Abby. Here's the thing. There's somewhere we're supposed to be and if we don't get there in time, then bad things will happen. So I need you to work with me here. If I let your hands free, can you pee in the woods or not?"

Abby nodded and wiped at her eyes with her arm.

The bad man awkwardly shoved her rubber boot onto her foot—the one she'd kicked off in the struggle—then pulled a knife out of his back pocket. Abby caught sight of a gun sitting at his hip as his coat moved.

"Are you going to shoot me?" she asked in a small voice.

"Not if you do exactly what I tell you," the bad man said. He cut the sharp wire around her wrists. It wasn't metal after all, but plastic. She sighed as her wrists came free and she inspected them for cuts.

"That hurts a lot," she accused.

"Pee. Now."

Abby looked into the dark trees. She didn't have a flashlight and the shadows looked full of wild things.

"What are you looking at? Right here, come on. We've got to go."

"Here?" Abby looked up at the bad man in horror.

"I'm not supposed to go to the bathroom in front of anyone."

The bad man opened his mouth like he was going to say something but changed his mind. After a pause, he smiled. "I know this is all probably kind of scary. But I have a special surprise for you when all this is over. You're going to love it."

Abby frowned suspiciously. "I just want to go home."

"Tell you what. If you can be a good girl and do everything I tell you, I'll take you home."

"Really?" Hope felt as light as a butterfly in her chest. She clung to it.

"I promise. So you go pee right now and do whatever else I say and I promise I'll take you home."

Abby walked cautiously around to the other side of the car where she could have a little privacy. She didn't know what the bad man wanted from her, but she would do anything if it meant going back home.

AFTER THE FBI AGENTS LEFT, Val retreated upstairs, and Joel went to the kitchen to make up a light dinner. It was so late, and he was pretty sure she hadn't eaten since lunch. Val never liked to eat when she was stressed, but he'd learned that was the most dangerous time for her to skip meals. If he could have food ready and easily accessible, she'd be more likely to eat it.

Marnie called just as he was draining the pasta.

"Is this a bad time?"

"It's fine. What's going on?"

"I just wanted to check on you. How are you holding up?"

Fine was the automatic response that came to mind, but his mouth couldn't form the word. He wasn't fine, but he couldn't think about how he was feeling when there was Val to consider. Taking care of her gave him something to do, a way to keep his own torment at bay.

"I'm trying to figure out if there's a connection between Abby and the other girls."

It wasn't a real answer, but it kept the conversation on safe ground. Joel rinsed the pasta and shook the colander for good measure before leaving it in the sink to drain. He leaned against the counter, staring at the drawings pinned to the fridge with magnets. Two of them were of Bigfoot, his head impossibly small compared to his long body.

"Join the club. Anything come to mind?" Marnie asked.

"Not yet. Abby's abduction was bold. Risky, even. Taken in broad daylight with two classes of second graders nearby? He'd planned for it at that exact location. KJ and Sophie, on the other hand, were taken at night by someone who only had strips of cloth to tie them up, and had to improvise with charge cords. It doesn't feel the same, but what are the odds that there would be two cases so close together?"

The more his brain worked on puzzling it out, the less he had to think about what might be happening to Abby right now.

"That's what Porter says, too. The FBI is taking over the Greer-McNamara case and they're bringing in a whole boatload of agents from Portland, D.C., Chicago, you name it. I'm sure Cooper will talk to you about it, but you don't need to come in tomorrow."

Joel grimaced at the thought. "Did Cooper say I'm off the case?"

"Not in so many words."

"Good. We still haven't found Brett Rogers. I'm going in."

Marnie didn't argue. After a pause, she changed the subject. "I had an interesting conversation with Faye McNamara today. Apparently she wasn't going to let Sophie do the basketball club in the spring. Something about a run-in she had with Howie Lambert last year. She thought his assistant coach was too familiar with the girls, giving them rides home from practice, that sort of thing. She expressed her concerns to Lambert and said he didn't take them seriously. When she found out Gottschalk was assisting again this year, she decided—"

"Hold on. Who's that?"

"The assistant coach?"

"Yeah."

"Bryson Gottschalk. You know him?"

Joel rubbed at the stubble on his chin. "I do. Played football against him in high school. His wife and I go way back."

Marnie paused a beat. "Lambert was already questioned and he never mentioned Gottschalk or the fact that Faye issued a complaint. I only mention it now because...any chance Gottschalk has had dealings with Abby?"

Now it was Joel's turn to pause as he considered the

question. "Not that I know of. Val and Maddie worked together at the bank, but they aren't that close." *Anymore,* he didn't add. In high school, Val would have called Maddie her best friend, but the relationship hadn't rekindled with Val's return to Owl Creek.

"Well, it was a shot in the dark but I thought I'd ask. I'll keep you posted if anything else comes up."

Patience was one of the most important characteristics needed for investigative work. But now, as Joel looked at those childish drawings of Bigfoot, waiting felt like torture.

"I'd better go, Marnie. Thanks for the call."

"Sure. We're all praying Abby comes home."

Joel hung up the phone and busied himself whisking up a white sauce and turning over Marnie's words in his mind.

"What was that about?" Val came into the kitchen wearing sweats and a long-sleeved t-shirt, her wet hair hanging in waves past her shoulders.

"Marnie was sharing some developments with a lead in the other case. The sauce is almost done and then pasta will be ready."

Val shrugged. "Do you need to go into work?"

"Not tonight. Don't worry about me. How are you?"

Val's face twisted and she stepped toward him with her arms outstretched, slipping her hands around his waist. Joel flipped off the burner and slid the pot to a cold one before leaning against the counter and pulling her close.

She clung to him for a long moment before speaking. "I can't do this, Joel. She's all I have. I know the statistics.

If whoever took her plans on killing her, she's probably already dead. I can't live with that."

Joel wished he'd never told her that in most child abductions that occurred with an intent to murder the child, the victim was dead in six hours.

"A statistic is just that. It isn't a guarantee. Abby needs you to have hope."

Val shuddered and nodded, then pulled away. "I feel bad keeping you from looking for KJ and Sophie. Gina offered to come stay with me for a few days."

"That's nice of her." Joel was more relieved than he wanted to let on. He loved Val and he didn't want her to feel abandoned. But he needed to be doing something. With Abby missing he felt an even greater urgency to find KJ and Sophie, as if finding them would improve Abby's chances.

He dished up the pasta while Val rinsed greens for a salad. When the water in the sink ran long, he glanced over and saw her staring. A bright pink plastic plate sat in the sink with a matching cup, likely left over from breakfast.

"Val?"

She blinked and looked up. "Sorry. Here you go. I'm not hungry."

And with that, she left Joel with two plates of food and no appetite.

17

IT WAS dark when the car stopped, rocking Abby awake. Her neck was stiff and she felt colder than she could ever remember being in her life. The bad man had given her a sweatshirt to wear over her coat, but it smelled funny so she had taken it off and was using it as a pillow. When he opened the door, a blast of icy air greeted her. Little snowflakes drifted in the glow of the car's brake lights.

They were in the parking lot of a motel like the kind Abby had stayed in with her mom when they moved to Oregon, only then it had been summer and the asphalt was so hot her shoes stuck to it. Mom had been worried all night—peeking out the curtain every time she heard noises outside—and had made Abby wear flip-flops even in the shower. They'd both been glad to leave in the morning.

Now the bad man was looking around at the other cars in the parking lot with the same kind of nervousness. He gestured to Abby impatiently.

"Why aren't you wearing the sweatshirt? You're going to freeze."

Abby didn't answer as she crawled out of the car and dropped to the ground. A layer of snow had accumulated on the pavement.

"Where are we?" she asked, reading the yellow sign that said MOTEL followed by a long word that started with V-A-C. Was it "vacation?"

"Not where we're supposed to be," the bad man muttered. "Hurry, we've got to get inside."

He jammed the sweatshirt over Abby's head without unzipping it, and it was big enough that it made it over her head with only a little tugging. She yipped as the zipper pulled her hair.

"Shut-up!" the bad man hissed, glancing toward the motel office. It sat like a little house at the corner of the parking lot.

Abby glared at the bad man. "You're not supposed to say that word."

"Come on." He pulled her roughly toward a line of red doors, but when the key wouldn't work one-handed, he had to let go of her in order to jiggle the lock with his other hand.

Abby looked back at the little house. Could she run across the parking lot and reach it in time before he caught her? She backed away a half step, but he'd already opened the door and was pushing her inside.

"That hurts," Abby complained.

The bad man slapped Abby's cheek so fast she didn't see it coming. She dropped to the floor, her whole face stinging and hot tears pooling in her eyes.

"Look, kid. I was told not to hurt you and there's a bonus for me if I don't. But I was also told that in exigent circumstances I can use more extreme measures. Do you know what that means?"

Abby curled into a ball on the stained carpet and shook her head.

"It means that if I decide I need to tape your mouth shut or tie you up again, I can. It even means I don't have to feed you if I don't want to. Is that what you want?"

Abby shook her head. She wanted him to stop talking. She wanted him to go away and she wanted to take off this dirty, stinky sweatshirt and she wanted to see Mom again. A sob passed through her like a tremor.

"Good," the bad man said. "Then stop crying and do what I say. This wasn't part of the plan but they've closed Highway Twenty so we don't have a choice until this storm passes."

Abby couldn't stop the tears now that they'd started. She buried her face in her arms, hoping he wouldn't hit her again. But he was leaving the room, the outer door closing behind him.

Suddenly Abby remembered seeing a telephone on the table next to a TV. It was an old-fashioned kind of phone—the kind that had a twirly wire on the end—but it might still work.

The thought broke through her tears and she scrambled to her feet, wiping her eyes and nose on her sleeve.

She picked up the receiver and looked at the buttons, then realized she didn't know what Mom's phone number was.

As she stared hopelessly, wishing she knew which

buttons to press, the door opened and the bad man came in carrying a duffel bag.

When he saw her holding the phone, he swore and dropped the bag. He reached her in two swift strides and pulled the phone out of her hand, then slammed it down, yanked the cord from the base, and dropped it behind the cupboard.

Shakily, he ran a hand through his curly brown hair and said a bunch of words Abby didn't know but that she guessed Mom wouldn't like at all. She backed as far away as she could until she bumped into the wall. She didn't want him to hit her again.

But he wasn't watching her. Instead, he looked around the room, taking in the two beds and the dark paneling. He looked at it the same way Mom had looked at the other motel.

The blankets had colorful zigzag patterns like Abby had seen in Arizona when she visited her cousins for Christmas. It smelled bad, like someone had been smoking cigarettes. Her throat was already feeling scratchy.

The bad man's gaze darted around the room like he was trying to find something. Or make a decision. Finally, he opened the bag and withdrew a long plastic string. It wasn't until he got close that Abby realized what it was.

"No, don't do it." She turned her body and tried to hide her wrists.

"Shut-up and hold still."

"But I have to go potty. Please don't tie me up again."

He wavered and glanced toward the bathroom.

"Fine, but go quick."

Abby used the bathroom as quickly as she could, not wanting him to get mad at her. There wasn't a soap pump, and she fumbled with the wrapped bar of soap. By the time she picked the paper apart to get to the soap, she could hear the bad man talking in the other room.

He must have been close to the door because she heard his voice over the running water, but she couldn't understand what he was saying. The only voice she heard was his, followed by gaps of silence.

When she opened the door, he was standing right there. He slipped his phone into his pocket and smiled.

"All right, you ready for bed?" He sounded nice again instead of angry.

Abby shrank against the doorframe. She knew now that he wasn't nice no matter how much he pretended.

"I don't have my jammies or my toothbrush."

A look of annoyance flickered in his eyes.

"You'll just have to go without tonight. But I'll get you some later, I promise. When you get your surprise."

Abby was starting to think the surprise was a lie. She sidled past him and went to the bed closest to the bathroom. The one that didn't have his duffel bag on it.

He seemed to have forgotten about tying her up, so she didn't want to remind him. She pulled away the scratchy blanket but couldn't figure out if she was supposed to get under the sheet or not too. Mom usually helped her with the extra sheets on motel beds.

She climbed into bed with her rubber watermelon boots on.

"Aren't you gonna take your boots off?" the bad man said.

Abby ignored him. If she were going to escape, she needed to have her boots.

Because while she was in the bathroom she had remembered something important. She didn't know Mom's phone number but if she called 911, the police would answer. Maybe it would even be Joel.

The man had unplugged the phone on the table, but if she could find the cord, maybe she could plug it back in. When the man was asleep, she would sneak to the phone and call 911. But how could she tell the police where she was without waking the man? She imagined Joel answering the phone. He would know it was her. She would just have to whisper, "This is Abby," and he would send all his police friends to the motel.

Just thinking about it made her feel hopeful. She would pretend to go to sleep so the bad man wouldn't know she was still awake, and then as soon as he went to sleep she would get up and call Joel.

But faking sleep meant closing her eyes, and the bad man wasn't as tired as she thought because he wasn't going to bed. There was only one chair in the small room and he moved it to block the door and sat there, typing on his phone.

Was he going to stay there all night? Maybe bad men didn't need to sleep. Abby squeezed her eyes shut and tried to pretend she was sleeping. At first it was hard because she didn't feel tired and the lamp on the table was too bright. Her rainboots were really uncomfortable too, and she tossed and turned, trying to find a position that didn't bother her. Every so often, she squinted one eyelid open.

The bad man was still awake, the light of his phone shining on his face.

Abby yawned, reminding herself that she couldn't go to sleep if she were going to escape. But after a while, her thoughts turned slippery and started forming disjointed dreams of Joel coming to save her until eventually she couldn't think any thoughts at all.

Val didn't sleep. She sat in the living room with her phone in hand and plugged into a charger in case someone called with word that Abby had been found. Or a ransom demand had been issued.

Gretchen Smith had said she would return in the morning to give her an update, and Val had been stricken to realize the FBI didn't think they would find Abby before morning.

Joel stayed at her side all night, but he left before dawn the next morning. For the first time, Val thought she might really and truly hate his job.

"I'll be back tonight," he said as he kissed her goodbye.

She leaned into him, loath to be left behind. "I wish I could go with you. I wouldn't get in the way; I just want to know what's going on."

"You will. Use Gretchen; she's here to help. She'll keep you in the loop, and you'll know what I know."

"It's been sixteen hours since she disappeared." Val searched his dark eyes, making him meet her own.

There was a flash of something in his eyes. A hint of regret or fear. But it was gone in an instant.

"You can't think like that. There are always those cases that defy the odds."

"How about KJ and Sophie? It's been a week, Joel. What are their odds?"

His shoulders stiffened and he released her. "That's why I have to go. I'll see you tonight." The old farmhouse shuddered as he closed the front door behind him.

Watching out the window as he made his way to his car in the pool of orange light cast by the light over the shop, Val checked the time. It was five in the morning and Joel hadn't slept. She wanted to call him back, to tell him they could continue the investigation without him. That he needed his rest so he didn't burn out. But she knew he wouldn't listen.

It was too early to call Arizona, but she needed to talk to her sister. She needed to talk to someone. Gretchen Smith? She seemed nice enough, but she was basically a stranger and Val needed to talk to someone she trusted. Instead, she went to the kitchen to start some coffee.

Val preferred to get her news online but had subscribed to the *Pineview Daily* as soon as the weather turned cold to provide a steady supply of newspaper to use as fire starter. Someone had brought the paper up from the box at the end of the drive, and it lay on her kitchen table under a small pile of bills and promotional fliers. The main headline was about the Pineview High

School boys' basketball team sweeping a tournament over the weekend.

A smaller article next to it caught her eye. "Another girl goes missing in Owl Creek."

Val snatched up the paper, sliding the mail onto the table. The article was short and sparse on detail, which wasn't surprising. It was impressive that they'd managed to include anything at all. They must have rushed it in at the last minute for it to have gone out with yesterday's afternoon paper.

There was talk of the field trip, but no mention of the hair clip or the search party. In fact, the overall tone was that it was likely a tragic accident, and the rest of the article was devoted to a recap of KJ and Sophie's abduction.

Something that Val couldn't identify pushed her to search in the desk drawer for a pair of scissors, and she carefully cut the article from the paper. She laid it on the desk, smoothing the crease that carved it in two, willing the words to mean more than a sidenote in the larger story of the other missing girls. The article didn't even name Abby or include a photograph.

Val could fix that.

She found the packet of Abby's school photos in the top drawer of the desk and cut out a 3x5 image. Abby had a little wrinkle in her nose, as if the photographer had said something to make her laugh and she'd been trying to hold it in. Her eyes were bright and her blond curls—which had been tamed before she left the house— had the loose look of an exuberant recess.

Above the desk hung a bulletin board where Abby's

artwork hung. Val hesitated. She didn't want to disturb Abby's drawings, but she was filled with purpose. This was important.

Val gently removed Abby's drawings of Bigfoot and placed them in a manila file folder. Then she selected a pink plastic tack and pinned the article and the photo next to it. It felt like the beginning of something, like she was marking a moment that would forever define her life. And she knew that it was too late for the what-ifs. This wasn't just a bad dream that she could hope to wake from. It was there in black and white, recorded for all of history.

Val had someone precious and she lost her.

She stood like that for a long time, reading the scant words until she practically had them memorized. Then she stoked the fire to keep the chill at bay and went to the kitchen to start some tea. It felt robotic, this fidelity to habit and routine. If it hadn't been for the sickening dread that dragged on her like gravity's pull, she could almost imagine that Abby was upstairs sleeping and would soon wake and stumble down the stairs while rubbing sleep from her eyes. But the only sound was the low thrum of the fire in the stove and the occasional pop of the house's joints flexing as they warmed.

The first hint of a lightening in the sky had appeared through the kitchen window when a knock on the door startled Val. She checked the time and was surprised to discover it was already after seven.

Don't get your hopes up, an inner voice warned, but she couldn't stop the jolt of anticipation that coursed through her like adrenaline. When she opened the door, though, there was no FBI agent on her porch. Instead, Nicole stood there with a bag of groceries in hand.

"Hi," was her only greeting as she stepped inside. If she noticed how Val's face fell, she didn't show it. "You've got quite the set-up out there," she said over her shoulder as she headed for the kitchen.

"I do?" Val went to the living room and looked out the window. A little distance down the driveway a black RV the size of a luxury bus was dimly visible in the pre-dawn light. It was parked on an old overgrown road that accessed the opposite field, within view of the house without blocking the road.

Had the FBI been there all night? Immediately Val was reminded of the media camping out after Jordan's supposed death. *It's okay, these are the good guys,* she tried to remind herself. But it still made her skin crawl.

She returned to the kitchen where Nicole was unloading items—a package of giant cinnamon rolls from Lori's Bakery in town, a small bunch of bananas, and a carton of eggs. Nicole then found a bowl and started cracking eggs one-handed while simultaneously digging out salt and herbs from Val's cupboard.

"Don't you have to be at work?" Val asked.

"Not today, I don't. I called in. So anything you need, I'm here."

Val felt a spark of gratitude breaking through the numbness of disappointment. "I don't even know what I need. But thank you."

Nicole looked back at Val over her shoulder. "I know it's not the same, but I remember when Gabe died how I stopped caring about anything. I took care of Ella because I had to, but I forgot to take care of myself. Meg was a lifesaver then, and I was lucky to have her close. But your sister is in Arizona, right? So as long as it's okay with you, I'll be your substitute sister for a bit."

"Thanks." Val couldn't quite manage a smile, but she mimicked the motion and hoped it was enough.

With Nicole working in the kitchen, Val felt a stirring call to action. She pushed away the heavy weight behind her eyes and stoked the fire again, then went upstairs to start a load of laundry. She paused at the door to Abby's room. The bed was rumpled and dirty socks made a trail to the laundry hamper. Bits of paper sprinkled on the rug were leftover from cutting snowflakes to tape to her window. A necklace made of dyed macaroni noodles was looped on the handle of a dresser drawer.

Ordinarily Val would straighten the bed and sweep up the soiled laundry without a second thought, but now she hesitated. The unthinkable question of, "What if this is the last time Abby will throw her socks on the floor and leave her pants inside out in a jumble on the floor?" kept her paralyzed on the threshold.

Val knew it was superstitious and maybe a little unhealthy, but a weight of portent hung heavy in the air. If she could somehow summon Abby's return by keeping everything just as she had left it yesterday morning when she went to school, then Val wouldn't disturb even a single thread.

She closed the bedroom door and returned to the kitchen where she was greeted with the savory smell of scrambled eggs. Val's stomach turned. She knew Nicole meant well, but she couldn't imagine trying to eat anything right now. The microwave chimed and Nicole withdrew a cinnamon roll, freshly warmed with icing dripping down the side.

"Sorry it's not homemade. I gave up baking years ago," Nicole said as she spooned the eggs onto a plate next to the cinnamon roll.

"It looks great," Val lied, trying to disguise her revulsion. Did Nicole have any idea how many calories that one cinnamon roll had? She mentally calculated the number of broken egg shells resting in the carton and figured the percentage of eggs Nicole had dished up for her. That would be almost another three hundred with the melted cheese sprinkled over the top. But Val took the plate and thanked Nicole.

"Did you get any sleep?" Nicole asked as she settled across from her with her own plate.

Val picked at the eggs, moving them around her plate. "Not really."

"If you want, I can—"

A knock at the front door brought Val out of her chair.

"Do you want me to get it?" Nicole offered, but Val was already down the hall and almost to the door.

This time it *was* Gretchen Smith. Agent Rita Coleman was at her side. Val welcomed them inside, examining Coleman's face for any sign of news, but her expression was inscrutable.

"Good morning, Valerie," Gretchen greeted. "How did your night go?"

Val ignored the question. She wanted information,

not chit-chat. Nicole appeared in the kitchen doorway and Val motioned for her to join them in the living room.

"This is my friend, Nicole," she said by way of introduction. She and Nicole sat on the couch while Gretchen and Rita took the kitchen chairs that had been left there overnight.

"What's your last name?" Rita Coleman asked, pulling out a little notepad.

While Nicole shared her details, Val couldn't wait any longer to ask her question.

"Is there any word about Abby?"

"It's been a busy night," Gretchen said. "They've brought in aerial support and are coordinating with other agencies to search the area. Media outlets have been notified and Senator Fisher is planning a press conference at eleven o'clock Central time to help get the word out."

"Are you worried the extra attention will waste your time with false leads?"

"We have a system for prioritizing leads," Rita explained, "and we'll bring in more analysts if we have to. Chances are someone saw something, they just don't realize that what they saw was important. We'll gladly process ten thousand leads that go nowhere if it means finding one that leads us to Abby."

Val picked at a hole in her jeans, combing through the frayed strands with her fingernail. "Do you think her disappearance is connected to whoever took KJ and Sophie?"

Rita's lips tightened briefly. Her dark eyes held an intensity Val found a little intimidating, but mostly reassuring. She wanted every investigator looking for Abby to be intense about it.

"We're keeping all options open at this point. The FBI is taking over the investigation into the Greer-McNamara case to be sure."

"I told you Brett Rogers threatened Abby. Are you looking into him? He's KJ's next door neighbor."

"I can assure you we are looking very seriously at Brett Rogers, in addition to others. There is a forest road about half a mile from the hatchery that the perpetrator may have used. We're canvassing all residents along the river to see if anyone may have seen something."

Val nodded. "I know Brett Rogers owns a truck, but I'm not sure it runs. He may have another vehicle."

"We've got all that information," Rita said smoothly. "The best thing you can do is stay here and keep your phone on you at all times. Keep it charged. Don't leave it downstairs if you need to go upstairs. Take it into the bathroom with you when you shower, that sort of thing. Answer all calls that come in, whether or not you recognize the number."

Val nodded soberly. As much as she hated the thought of Abby being kidnapped as part of a ransom plot, there was a small part of her that wished the phone would ring just so she would know once and for all. So her thoughts wouldn't spiral in a million different directions with fears of Brett Rogers or cougars or escaped felons hiding in the woods.

"Do you have family support in the area?" Gretchen asked. "Anyone who can be here with you?"

"Tomorrow my sister is flying in from Arizona to stay with me for a few days."

"And I'll be here as much as Val needs me," Nicole volunteered.

Val glanced at her gratefully. The truth was, knowing the RV was parked outside and FBI agents would be coming and going made her stress simmer at a higher temperature. Over the past year, she'd come to value privacy in a whole new way. Being in danger of losing it now stirred a familiar panic.

She would take Nicole's company over that of a fed any day.

When Gretchen and Rita left, Val went straight to the kitchen and began gathering plates.

"Don't. I'll get them," Nicole protested, following behind.

"I need to do something. I'll go crazy otherwise."

"But you haven't finished eating."

"It's fine. I'm not very hungry."

In truth, the emptiness in her stomach was comforting. Val knew she shouldn't enjoy it so much, that it was a sign she was headed for a relapse. The shame made it feel like a guilty pleasure, like an old friend she hadn't seen in years. At a time when everything else in her life was completely outside her control, she welcomed it.

18

"Joel."

A hand on his shoulder made Joel stir. Stacy Porter slid a chair over and sat beside him, his heavy brow furrowed with concern. Ashamed, Joel realized he'd been staring at the computer screen for several minutes without taking anything in, his thoughts drifting to Abby.

"Don't take this the wrong way," Stacy began, his voice low, "but you should really go home. We can manage all right and we're doing everything we can to find your little girl."

Joel's chest tightened at the word *your*.

"I'm all right," he said. "We still haven't found Brett Rogers, and no one knows him as well as I do. You need me."

It was his ace card, but he played it shamelessly. With the FBI heading up both investigations now, it was the only way to arguably stay involved. The FBI presence had increased tenfold overnight and more were arriving by the hour. The wheeled whiteboard sat abandoned in a corner, making room for even more equipment and personnel than before.

Apparently the life of a Senator's granddaughter was more valuable to the Department of Justice than two girls from run-of-the-mill Owl Creek families. It would have bothered Joel except for the fact that Abby was the one they were looking for, so the overwhelming presence was comforting. And if KJ and Sophie benefited from it too, all the better.

The trick for Joel was how to stay involved. He shouldn't work Abby's case; he knew that. He couldn't risk anything that would potentially weaken a future court case. But he could certainly keep looking for the other girls, and what he'd said about Brett Rogers was true.

Stacy knew it, too. "I don't disagree with that. But you're no good to us if you reach a breaking point."

"I'm fine," Joel repeated, pointedly turning his attention back to the screen.

Stacy hesitated, then patted Joel again as he stood, his heavy hand sending a dull throb through Joel's injured shoulder. He hadn't done his PT exercises since the girls went missing and his shoulder was in danger of tightening up. He hadn't been to the shooting range either, something he would need to correct as soon as he had a free afternoon.

Joel rubbed the grit out of his eyes from the sleepless night. He was bone weary, but that wasn't why he couldn't concentrate. He felt pulled in too many directions, and as much as he was worried about Val, he would be climbing the walls if he took the day off. There was still so much work to do. So many leads to follow. The girls had been seen by a trucker just outside of Reno. They'd been glimpsed coming out of a movie theater in Pineview. KJ had been spotted at a rest stop south of Portland, and Sophie had been seen in an alley behind a second-hand clothing store on the coast.

A disturbance on the other side of the room made him look up. Stacy was slipping on his coat and Marnie was jogging toward him.

"Willis is requesting backup. He thinks he found Brett Rogers."

It was at times like this that Joel appreciated the V8 engine in the county-issued Charger as it powered over the mountain passes with a low growl. Pineview was sixty minutes away for a typical citizen obeying the speed limit. Joel made it in under forty.

The residence was a single-wide trailer that sat at the end of a cul-de-sac in a trailer park. As Joel neared the trailer park, he cut the siren and slowed his speed. The road was blocked by a barricade, and cars from Pineview PD joined the county vehicles lining the street. Considering Rogers's feelings toward law enforcement, Porter and Cooper had decided to let the local agency bring him in. They didn't want to escalate things with a visible FBI presence, but Joel knew they would be standing by and ready to jump in if needed.

He strapped on his vest and moved to join Cooper

who was standing at his car talking on the phone. His radio crackled with call signs from dispatch and responding units.

"Stay close," Cooper ordered. "I want you and Sanders on the arrest team." He turned back to his call. "You got that phone number yet, Clyde? Good man. Send it over."

Cooper hung up the phone and handed it to Joel. "I want you to make the call."

Joel was tempted to object, to remind Cooper that Rogers had never shown Joel anything except contempt, but his words to Stacy were too fresh. This was his ticket to stay working the investigation.

As if Cooper guessed his thoughts, he added, "I'd ask Larry if he were here, but he's not. You're the closest thing to a friendly face we've got. We've secured the perimeter and evacuated the units on either side. Find out if he's alone, and if you can, convince him to give himself up."

Joel took the phone and kept Cooper's car between him and the trailer. The chain-link fence was short, no more than three feet tall, and sagged in spots. The grass had the gray look of midwinter and the only ornament was a kid's plastic slide. All was quiet on the cul-de-sac, but Joel knew that deputies would have surrounded the lot, anticipating all possible escape routes if Rogers made a run for it.

It was up to Joel to make sure they didn't need any of those contingencies. That Rogers gave himself up peacefully.

No pressure, Ramirez.

Joel dialed the phone number Cooper gave him and waited.

It rang twice before being picked up.

A child's voice answered and Joel's stomach dropped. There was a kid inside?

"Hewo?" A very young kid, judging by his speech.

"Hello," Joel said, his prepared preamble suddenly gone out the window. "My name is Joel, what's your name?"

"Caden."

"Hi Caden. Do you live in the house with the Santa wreath and Christmas lights on the roof?"

"Yes. Do you want to talk to my dad?"

"Sure. Yeah, I would like to talk to your dad. Is he home?"

"No."

"Is anyone at home with you? Your mom or anyone else?"

"Only my dad's friend. Do you want to talk to him?"

"Yes, please. I would very much like to talk to him."

"Okay." There was a rustling sound as the child moved through the house, breathing into the phone as he walked. Then a gruff voice sounded in the background and the line went dead.

Joel dialed again but there was no answer.

"There's a child in the home," he said to Cooper as he tried again. "Young, his name is Caden."

Cooper muttered a curse. "We've got to get that child out of there." He reached for a bull horn and Joel edged away as he turned it on.

"Brett Rogers, this is Lieutenant Greg Cooper of the

Wallace County Sheriff's Office. We know you've taken refuge in the residence of Bill Osborn. We don't want anyone to get hurt. We just want to talk to you. One of my detectives is going to call you. You know him; it's Joel Ramirez. Please answer the phone when he calls, Mr. Rogers. He's calling right now."

Cooper nodded to Joel and he hit the redial. How did Cooper think he was supposed to convince Brett to turn himself in? Every interaction they'd had ended with Brett essentially giving him the bird.

The phone rang and for a second Joel thought Brett wouldn't answer. But then it picked up.

"Hewo?" It was Caden again. His voice sounded different now. Scared.

"Hi Caden. It's me again, Joel. Is your dad's friend there with you?"

"He says he doesn't want to talk to you."

"Okay, here's what I want you to do, Caden. Can you put the phone down and come outside? Right now. Just walk out the front door."

There was a pause. "It's cold outside," Caden protested.

"That's all right. We've got blankets out here. We'll make sure you're warm."

"I don't know..." Caden was interrupted by a voice in the background. Joel couldn't make out what they were saying, but he heard Caden's higher voice mingled with an older man's lower pitch.

"He doesn't want me to leave. He says I should stay here. That's what my dad would want."

"I think more than anything, your dad wants you to

209

be safe. We can keep you safe, but only if you come outside. Can you look outside the window? Do you see all these police cars?"

Caden grunted as he moved and Joel imagined Abby climbing on the couch to look out the front window. Joel waved toward the house.

"Do you see me?"

Movement fluttered in the living room window and Joel spied a small hand waving back.

"I see you. Do you see me?"

"Yes, I do. If you come outside now, we can meet for real. I'll help keep you safe."

There was a long pause.

"He wants to know what you want to talk to him about."

"Tell him that we just have some questions for him. We think he can help us find a bad guy."

Another pause.

"He says you think he's the bad guy."

"I didn't say that," Joel said. "Caden, can you tell me if your dad has any guns?"

"I don't know."

"Does your dad's friend have any guns that you can see?"

"No, I don't think so."

"Good. That's really good. You're being such a good helper. Can you tell me what he's doing right now?"

"He's smoking a cigarette in the kitchen—"

Caden cut off and Brett's rough voice came on the line.

"That's enough, Ramirez. We're done talking to you."

"Brett, wait. We don't want anyone to get hurt. Let the boy go."

"I'm not keepin' him here. You think this is some sort of hostage situation?"

"Let him go and then we can talk about it."

"No, see, I know what you're trying to do. But you don't got no right to come into someone else's home looking for me. So Caden and I are going to stay right here."

He sounded agitated, like he could barely hold still. Joel relaxed his grammar to reflect Brett's speech.

"We just wanna talk to you, that's it. If you come out peaceable, we'll make sure you and Caden are both safe."

"This is a witch hunt. You've got some vendetta against me after your girlfriend got all twisted up about those mannequins. You're hiding behind your badge to punish me. But I don't answer to you for what I do on my own property."

"Nah, it's nothing like that. It's your right to express yourself how you want. Sure, I didn't like you winding up my girlfriend, but I was just looking out for her. We do that, right? We look out for the people we love." Despite the frigid January air, Joel was beginning to feel heated under his coat.

Brett didn't respond.

"Now, I know you appreciate your privacy and don't like us gettin' involved with your business. And I can respect that. But I also know you don't want anyone to get hurt. That's not the kind of man you are. Leisa Greer

211

is just trying to find her daughter. Maybe you saw something that night without knowing it. And if you didn't, that's okay too. We have a whole list of people we've been talking to; all your neighbors, friends and family of the Greers. The sooner we can talk to you and cross you off our list, the sooner we can get back to finding these girls."

"Why'd you bring in the SWAT team, then?"

"This ain't the SWAT team." Joel's gaze flitted to Cooper who held up ten fingers. Ten minutes before SWAT arrived. "We're just making sure everyone's safe. Including you. Why don't you start by sending Caden out. You'll see, we'll keep him safe."

Brett's voice became muffled and Joel listened intently as Caden's voice replied, but he couldn't catch the exchange.

"I'm not sending the kid," Brett finally said to Joel. "This is his home and he shouldn't have to leave."

"Okay, that makes sense. How 'bout you come out so we can talk to you?"

"I've done too much talking as it is. Leave me alone."

"You know we can't do that, Brett. We saw the videos, did you know that?"

There was a pause on the other end of the line.

"You tried to destroy them, but it didn't work. There's some stuff on there you didn't want us to see, isn't there?"

Silence. But the line hadn't disconnected. Brett wanted to hear more.

"It doesn't look too good, I have to admit. But I've been doing this job long enough to know that things aren't always what they seem. I'll bet you have a good reason for what you've been doing. I want to hear that reason. I want to clear up any misunderstandings once and for all so we aren't wasting any more time chasing after you when we need to find these missing girls."

"It ain't what it looks like." Brett's voice trembled. "That's why I had to destroy those videos. I knew you'd get the wrong idea."

"Sure. That makes perfect sense. I want to hear all about it, but to be honest, Brett, I'm freezing my butt off out here. Couldn't we do this in a warm room with a cup of coffee? Come on out now and we'll have that chat and clear everything up."

There was a little hiccup of sound and the line went dead.

"What did he say?" Cooper asked. "Is he coming out?"

Joel shook his head. "I don't know, but I think I made some headway. He's scared, but I think he knows—"

Before he could finish, the trailer's front door opened a crack. Deputies shouldered rifles in a heightened state of alert. The interior of the trailer was dark compared to the cold wintry light outside. Joel stared intently as the crack grew and finally a shape appeared.

It was Brett Rogers, looking small and grandfatherly as he stepped onto the porch dressed in an old knitted sweater, his hands raised timidly.

Joel stepped forward, Marnie and two other deputies on his heels.

"Hey, Brett, that's good. Keep your hands up, just like that."

Brett scanned the street beyond the cul-de-sac, blinking rapidly. When he spotted the deputies with their rifles, he shrank back as if to escape inside.

"Don't worry about all that," Joel said quickly, slowing his approach. "No one's gonna hurt you, I promise."

"I ain't armed," he insisted.

"Okay. That's good." In his peripheral vision, Joel noted two deputies coming from the back of the house. Brett hadn't seen them yet. Joel tried to keep his attention on him. "Come on down the steps. No one's gonna hurt you."

Brett stepped cautiously down the stairs and a deputy grabbed him from behind.

"What—let go, I'm not armed!" Brett protested as the deputy slapped cuffs on him and patted him down.

"Brett Rogers," Joel said, stepping forward. "You have the right to remain silent."

Brett spit out a vile curse. His pale cheeks were pink in the cold. "I knew I couldn't trust you, Ramirez. Get your hands off me you filthy, border-jumping Mexican. You don't got no right to do this. I didn't do nothing wrong."

"Anything you say can and will be used against you in a court of law," Joel continued, ignoring him. He grabbed Brett by the shoulder and led him to a waiting car, Marnie on his other side. Her expression was hard, but he recognized the intent gleam in her eye. The hope that they were finally going to get some answers.

19

"Missing girl's neighbor arrested," the headline seemed to shout. Nicole had left to pick up her daughter after school, and Val had been scanning the news online all afternoon, unable to focus on anything through a heavy brain fog that she knew was partly from lack of sleep but mostly from fear. Seeing the headline gave her a grim sense of satisfaction. But also anger. Had Brett Rogers taken Abby too? How had he known about the field trip? It didn't make sense, but she couldn't begin to understand a person like that.

Val sent Joel a text.

Just heard the news. Good work. If Rogers took Abby, I swear I'm smashing every single one of his creepy mannequins.

He didn't respond, and she wondered if he was involved in interrogating Rogers or if they would have someone else do it. She knew interrogations could last hours. It could be later tonight or even tomorrow before they were finished.

While Val waited, she got out her laptop. All the local news outlets were carrying the story, and it was only a matter of time before it went national. She printed anything she could find and pinned it on the bulletin board after highlighting or circling any details that caught her eye. She'd already gone through the newspapers from the past week, looking for articles about KJ and Sophie.

She thought about the evidence boards she'd seen on TV.

"I've never in my life used a ball of string to solve a case," Joel had scoffed once while watching a crime drama. As much as she loved him, he could really ruin her favorite shows sometimes.

Looking at her collection of articles and pictures, she tried to think of how he said he used his whiteboard. It was all about the timeline, trying to figure out the order of events leading up to the crime.

Val didn't have a whiteboard, but she had a blank wall—a wall she planned on painting eventually. So she grabbed a red Sharpie and began writing the dates directly on the wall. Now that she had a purpose, she scoured the articles with more intent.

She started with December 26, the night of KJ and Sophie's abduction. Then she worked backwards, trying to pinpoint who had been to the house and who the police were questioning.

Once she'd gleaned all she could from the news articles, she moved forward in time to January 3 when Abby disappeared. Then she filled in the space as best she could with details of the field trip and preparations leading up to it. By the time she'd exhausted all her available resources, the wall was a mess of red writing and scribbled cross-outs. She stepped back and waited for some kind of pattern to jump out at her. Some sort of clue to bring everything together.

If she were in a television show, this would be the moment when the answer was revealed.

But this wasn't TV. And the words, for all their violence of red on white, were just words. They didn't tell her anything she didn't already know.

***

"HE'S ASKING FOR YOU."

Joel looked up from the computer where he'd been writing up his report on the arrest of Brett Rogers.

Marnie looked weary. She and Agent Wong had been questioning Brett all afternoon, and Joel had stayed at the sheriff's station in Pineview in case he was needed.

"Why?"

Marnie shrugged. "He won't say. He just says he wants to talk to you. I don't think he likes Wong much. And, you know, I'm a woman." She smirked in disdain.

Joel closed out the report and reached for his bag. It was nearly 6:00 p.m. and he could really use one of Lori's sandwiches right about now. But they were back at the Grange. Instead, he grabbed a donut from the counter next to the coffee.

Wong met him in the hallway near the interrogation room. "Rogers is still claiming not to have anything to do with the girls' disappearance. We even showed him still shots of the video of KJ's bedroom but he won't budge."

"Do you know why he wants to talk to me?"

Wong shook his head. "You got through to him before. Maybe you can get through to him again."

Joel had never noticed how rodent-like Brett's features looked until now seeing him under the glaring fluorescent lights of the interrogation room. His receding chin was covered in a layer of gray stubble, and his elongated nose came to an exaggerated point.

"Evening," Joel said, placing the donut on the table before Brett. As yet he had rejected a lawyer, which surprised Joel. But maybe he mistrusted lawyers as much as he mistrusted law enforcement.

Brett eyed the donut. "That for me?"

"If you want it. To be honest you'd be doing me a favor. I never could resist a good donut and I've had more than I need this past week."

Brett kept his eye on the donut as if considering, but he didn't reach for it.

Joel sat diagonally across the table from him, positioning himself to look as non-threatening as possible. If Brett wanted to talk, the best thing Joel could do was avoid putting him on the defensive.

The silence stretched long and awkward between them. Brett fidgeted in his chair, but Joel was still. He had long since learned the value of not being first to speak.

Finally Brett opened his mouth, closed it again, then flitted his gaze to Joel's.

"Do you remember it?"

Joel hesitated, unsure of the question. "Remember what?"

"The bombing."

As if in answer, the skin on Joel's back prickled.

"Not really."

Brett nodded as if he'd expected that answer. "Mine happened in Laos. But I remember it. Micky was hit first and it shredded his leg like it was made of cardboard. A piece of shrapnel hit me right in the head."

He turned around and pulled up his limp salt-and-pepper hair at the base of his skull. Joel could make out an aberration in the way it lay. A scar of a long war in a forgotten time.

"I didn't realize I'd been hit until Sarge starts yelling and grabbing me and then I see all this blood on his face and I realize it's mine. But it didn't hurt. Ain't that weird?"

"Hmm." Joel grunted.

"We lost three of our unit that day. Field surgeon thought I was gonna be the fourth, but my Nancy always said my head was harder than rock." His eyes took on a wistful sheen and he trailed off.

Joel didn't know what Brett's point was, but if he was talking, Joel would play along. "I've still got glass in my back," he said. "Dozens of shards embedded under the surface of the skin. Sometimes they rise to the surface and I have to ask Val—my girlfriend—to squeeze them out for me."

Brett watched him soberly. "It hurt?"

"Yeah. Shoulder still aches sometimes and I can't run as much on my knee as I used to."

"You're young. It'll come back," Brett said comfortingly. "Is Larry still in the hospital?"

"He is. The blast tore up his insides pretty good. Turns out they're actually necessary for survival."

Brett grunted. "Eugene?"

"Portland, actually."

Brett swore. "I never thought I'd see anything like that here in Owl Creek."

Joel leaned forward and put his elbows on the table. "We've got some families hurting again, Brett. The families of those lost girls."

Brett's mouth hardened. "I didn't have nothing to do with that, just like I told you before."

"Why did you want to destroy the tapes?"

Brett fixed a dark eye on him. "You know why. You'd already come asking for them and I told you no. I figured it was only a matter of time before you came and stole them from me."

"And you knew what we'd find when we did."

Brett nodded. "It looks bad, but you're wrong. I wasn't spying on KJ. I'm no pedophile."

"Your record isn't exactly clean though, is it?"

Brett scoffed. "Get your facts straight. It was a consensual relationship with a woman who understood the value of her company."

"You'd call an eighteen-year-old girl a woman?"

"She said she was twenty-four. And eighteen still doesn't make me a pedophile."

Joel didn't reply. He let the words sit, leaving the silence for Brett to fill.

Brett leaned forward. "Remember that big windstorm we had back in October? Knocked down a bunch of trees? Willard across the street had one fall on his car."

Joel nodded.

"It knocked the camera loose. When I found it, it had fallen on the freezer there under the tree. I left it there until I could get a new mounting bracket and didn't realize it was pointed right at the girl's window until it had been there for a couple of weeks."

"You don't check your cameras more often than that?"

"Nah. It's more about the show than anything. Trying to keep thieves and pranksters away. I was going to record over it but it hadn't come up in the rotation." Brett had lost the hard edge he usually had when talking to Joel.

"Why not tell us this before? You might have caught the kidnapper breaking into the Greer home, you realize."

Brett ran a hand through his stringy hair. "I wish I did, but I didn't. After I found out the girl was missing, I watched the footage from that night. There was only them two girls and no one else."

Joel straightened and reached for his note pad. "Your camera caught the girls on tape the night they disappeared?"

"It wasn't anything helpful. Just the girls in the yard wrapped in blankets. If there'd been anything else I would have turned it over to you, I swear it."

"What were they doing?"

"They'd come over to the fence like they were playing a game of chicken, daring each other to touch it like it was gonna shock 'em or something. They ran back to the house, but one of 'em stumbled and fell, and the other had to help her inside because she was limping like she'd twisted her ankle or something."

Joel thought of the blood on the bathroom floor. "Did you notice if she had shoes on?"

Brett paused and looked up at the ceiling, thinking. "I can't remember for sure. It was a cold night, but kids do dumb things sometimes, don't they?"

"What time was this that they were outside in the yard?"

"A few minutes before ten o'clock."

"You know, it would be really great if we could see this video for ourselves."

Brett shrank in his chair. "I know. I was a stubborn old fool. But I put it in the barrel with the rest."

"You're a smoker, aren't you?" Joel asked.

"A bit."

"Do you make it a habit to take your smoke breaks outside?"

"Not a habit, no. Sometimes in the summer I'll watch the sunset from my porch, but this time of year it's too cold."

"So you weren't smoking outside that night?"

"No."

"Do you have any way of corroborating your story about the camera?"

"I've got a receipt for the new mount," Brett said. "If

I can go back to my house, I know right where it is. And the camera was a bit dinged up from the fall."

"We can have an agent take you back there."

"With all due respect, Ramirez, these feds, they're not like you. You got class. You and Larry both. I don't want nobody else on my property."

"I'm not sure that's possible," Joel said, thinking of the search that had taken place all day while Rogers was in custody.

"Fine. Bring the woman, then. But if my story checks out, I'll be free to go?"

"We'll need to verify your movements that night. But yeah," Joel couldn't believe he was saying the words, "if your story checks out, you'll be free to go."

It was close to midnight when Val heard Joel coming up the stairs. The sound was so welcome after long hours of solitude trying to keep herself occupied that she almost ached with relief. Gretchen Smith had come over twice to check on her and had offered to stay, but Val had felt more anxious when she was there. Every time she went into the living room and saw the hulking shadow of the FBI trailer at the top of the lane, she had to remind herself that they weren't voyeurs looking for a news story. They were looking out for her and trying to find Abby.

But her muscles still tightened as if the vehicle was a threat.

She'd spent the evening moving boxes from the spare bedroom down to the office. Gina was flying in the next day and Val needed to make room for an air mattress so she had somewhere to sleep. Setting her up in Abby's bed was out of the question.

She turned her back to the makeshift guest room and looked Joel over as he approached. The dim light from the bedroom reflected in his eyes. He looked weary and burdened.

"I'm getting this room ready for Gina. She's coming tomorrow."

"That's good." He pulled her into his arms. "How are you?"

"I feel like I'm on the edge of a nervous breakdown." She closed her eyes for just a moment, taking in his warmth, before pulling away and searching his face. "How did things go with Brett Rogers? Any news?"

Joel sighed. "Not what we'd hoped."

"What does that mean?"

"It means he didn't have anything to do with the missing girls."

Val paused a beat. The words didn't make sense. "How do you know? How can you say for sure?"

"We followed the evidence. At this time, we're not considering him a suspect."

Disappointment rippled through her chest. Val hadn't realized how much she'd hoped that Brett Rogers would lead them to Abby until a handful of words tore that hope away from her.

"So what does that mean? Do you have any other suspects?"

"We're following every lead we get."

She recoiled, an ugly doubt creeping into her mind before she could stop it. What if he screwed this up?

Ashamed at her disloyalty, she tried to bury it. Joel was good at his job. Besides that, he wasn't working alone. The FBI, state police; there were more agencies than just the county sheriff's office working to find Abby.

Still, a voice whispered in her mind, *what if they aren't as good as you think? What if this becomes one of those cases where the investigation is riddled with mistakes and years later someone does an exposé on the three girls who never came home because of investigator incompetence?*

It was a horrible thought, and she bit back the words, flicking off the light to the spare bedroom and heading down the hall to her room.

"Val?" Joel followed her. "You're upset."

Val swiveled to face him, folding her arms. "What if you're wrong? What if it's been Brett Rogers this whole time, right under your noses?"

Joel sighed and ran a hand through his hair. "There are dozens of men and women pouring heart and soul into this case with decades of experience behind them. They know their stuff. I know it's hard for you to trust anyone but yourself. You don't even trust me half the time—"

"Yes I do," she scoffed. "Of course I trust you. Look around." She gestured to his clothes hanging in the closet and the extra pillow on the bed.

He arched an eyebrow. "And when was the last time you let me babysit Abby for you? Or how about the fact that you won't even let me pack her a lunch if you're running late? When it comes to Abby, you still keep me at a distance, and I'm beginning to think your trust issues go so deep that I'll never be able to prove myself to you."

The pain in his dark eyes stilled the protest rising in her throat. She wanted to deny it, but he was right. Suddenly she realized that she'd made a horrible mistake. In trying to protect Abby—to keep her from becoming too attached to Joel in case they broke up—she'd pushed him away. Again.

"I'm sorry," she said quietly. "You're right. But it isn't that I don't trust you. It's that I want to do what's best for Abby, and I don't always know what that is."

He shook his head as if it didn't matter. "My point is, I know you want it to be Brett Rogers. I know you hate him, and I'm not saying he isn't capable of it. But the evidence just doesn't support it. He's not the guy."

She felt a tightening inside, a resistance to his claim. But she didn't want to argue with him, not tonight. So instead she turned and went to the window, closing the curtains against the night.

Over her shoulder, she asked, "Did you hear that searchers found tire tracks on a logging road about half a mile from the hatchery?"

It was an olive branch of sorts, and he took it.

"That's good."

"Yeah, except that you say there's little chance it'll help them find the vehicle. Mostly it'll help with a conviction if they ever find who took her."

Joel gave a weary smile as he keyed open the gun safe that sat by the bed, placing his service weapon and his personal gun inside. "Sometimes I talk too much."

"Never. I wish I knew everything you know. I wish I could be out there searching for Abby instead of waiting for the next briefing."

"Gretchen's keeping you updated, though?"

"Yes, and she says I can call her anytime. But what am I going to say? 'Have you found her yet? How about now?'"

"Come on, let's get some sleep." He took her hand and pulled her toward the bed.

It was a sign of his exhaustion that he didn't follow up his invitation with a suggestion for something more.

It was a sign of her own that she didn't mention it.

But as she pulled back the blankets on the bed, she thought about what Joel had said about trust. She thought of the boxes she'd moved into the office and her crude timeline written in marker on the wall.

She hoped she'd remembered to lock the office door.

20

VAL CHECKED her phone approximately a hundred times while she waited for Gina to arrive. When a call came in from an unknown number, she barely registered that it had a local prefix before she answered and held it to her ear.

"Hello?" Her limbs tingled with a sudden rush of adrenalin.

"Is this Ms. Rockwell?" A man's voice. Young and strong.

"Yes?"

"Ms. Rockwell, this is Wesley Peters from the Channel Six news—"

Val deflated so fast she was left trembling. She grabbed a nearby kitchen chair and collapsed onto it. It took her a few seconds to realize he was still talking.

"My daughter's missing and you're calling to ask me for an interview?" An ugly feeling crawled from her middle to her throat until she thought she would choke on it.

He paused. "As I said, Ms. Rockwell, I'm really very sorry. This must be absolutely devastating and I don't want to add to your pain. But in cases like these the media can be a powerful tool. You know about Elizabeth Smart, right?"

Val clenched a fist, trying to think of a suitable way of telling him off. The FBI had a media liaison, but of course Peters would bypass them and go straight to her. He didn't give her enough time to collect her thoughts, rushing ahead to get to his point.

"Do you know how they found her? It's because people recognized Brian David Mitchell when they saw him on the streets of Salt Lake City. Her family kept her story alive in the media so that people wouldn't forget. So that they would still be looking. And when Mitchell brought her back to Salt Lake, all that hard work and media publicity paid off."

Val's indignant protest died. She didn't want to listen, but she couldn't quell the hope that begged for more.

"There was a narrow window of time when Elizabeth Smart was walking the streets of Salt Lake City in plain sight with her kidnappers. A tiny sliver when she had a chance of being rescued before Mitchell planned to take her into the mountains and disappear for good. And in that brief window, people noticed and did something about it. But first they had to be informed so they knew what to look for, and that's where I come in."

Val licked her lips and finally spoke.

"I wouldn't even know what to say."

Wesley's tone gentled. "That's all right. We can talk about it and make a plan. Will you consider it?"

"I...I'll think about it."

Val's head seemed too heavy and she held it in her hands, her bent elbows braced against the table.

"That's all I ask, Ms. Rockwell. Just think about it. This is my personal number and you can reach me anytime. If there's anything I can do for you, just let me know."

It was only after she hung up that Val wondered what sort of access Wesley Peters had to information that she didn't. News archives, certainly. Police reports? Court records? Val didn't know how to begin gathering information like that. But surely Peters would.

An idea was forming in her mind as she went into the office and looked critically at her wall of notes. She was beginning to think of it as her "war room," and the news articles had spilled over from the bulletin board to be taped to the wall.

On the left, she had two columns—a list of suspects in the Greer case and a list of suspects in Abby's disappearance. The list for KJ and Sophie was long, but Abby's was painfully short. There was the new hire at the hatchery who had a criminal history, but it was all misdemeanor stuff and nothing involving children. Then there was one line that just said, "People who hate Jordan." Gretchen assured her the FBI was looking into all of Jordan's victims, but hadn't identified any likely suspects.

Val agreed. Whoever took Abby knew about the field

trip, which limited likely perpetrators to people close to home. The third name was Brett Rogers, and she couldn't bring herself to cross it out, no matter what Joel said. She wondered if Rogers was free yet. Would they have someone watching him? Or were they stretched too thin for that kind of surveillance?

When a knock sounded on the outside door, Val returned the marker and locked the office door behind her.

Gina opened the front door just as Val entered the hallway.

"Val!" She beamed and dropped her bags, slamming the front door with a bang.

Gina was a little shorter than Val and her hair was a whiter blond, whether from the Arizona sun or Arizona standards of beauty, Val wasn't sure. It was tucked under a stocking cap and she wore a thick parka.

"Are you going skiing?" Val asked with a little laugh.

"It's absolutely frigid outside!" Gina complained. "Are you getting your weather from the Arctic?"

"Maybe it'll warm up now that you're here." Val embraced her sister, enjoying the familiar feeling of comfort as she leaned in.

"It's less than two weeks since I saw you last. I could get used to this," Gina said. Then she stopped, her smile fading. "I mean, obviously for better reasons. How are you holding up?"

"I'm still in one piece," Val said lightly, patting her body as if taking stock. "You can put your bags in your old room, but I've only got an air mattress in there for now, sorry."

"Wow, you painted the paneling." Gina stopped at the bottom of the stairs and took in the living room. A host of excuses rose to Val's lips—it was cheaper than a complete remodel, she'd researched it first to find the right look—but then Gina added, "It looks nice. Good choice."

Val relaxed and led her sister upstairs. "The hot water has been tetchy lately, so you might have to run it for a while before you shower, especially if you're the first one to use it in the morning."

It was amazing how just having Gina there and talking about something as simple as the hot water heater soothed some of the spiky edges of Val's soul. As they passed Abby's room, the thought crept unbidden into her mind, *This is how you'll survive if Abby doesn't come home.*

Val staggered slightly, winded. Gina didn't notice, having paused to look in Abby's room, hesitating at the doorway as if it were a sacred space she wasn't allowed to enter. Her eyes traced the rumpled bedding, the dirty socks, the books scattered on the floor near the bean bag. Without looking at Val, she reached for her hand.

"They'll find her, Val," she said fiercely.

Val didn't speak. She didn't want to admit what had just crossed her mind. She didn't want to contradict Gina's hope with sobering statistics and likely outcomes. It had been forty-eight hours since Val last saw Abby, and while Gretchen was checking in regularly, sometimes accompanied by Special Agent Coleman who briefed her on their search efforts, the end result could always be summed up in three words.

We don't know.

JOEL STEPPED into the office at the elementary school and suddenly realized why he'd vaguely recognized Leisa Greer's mother when she'd arrived at the house the day KJ disappeared. She was the school secretary, sitting behind the desk with her reading glasses perched on her nose as she typed on the computer, a telephone receiver pinned against her shoulder. She glanced up as he entered, a slight nod registering his arrival.

He had his shield waiting when she hung up the phone.

"Detective Ramirez," Sue said kindly, removing her glasses and standing in order to shake his hand. "How is Valerie doing?"

Joel felt a subtle jolt, like missing a step at the end of a staircase. He hadn't come prepared to answer personal questions but realized now he should have expected it. The school community was tight. Of course she would know of his connection to Val and Abby.

"She's hanging in there," he said noncommittally. And then, because this visit suddenly felt more personal than he'd planned, he followed it up with, "How are you doing?"

Sue glanced away as if it would be easier to say the words if avoiding eye contact. "Trying to stay optimistic. We're all praying for KJ and Sophie. And now Abby too."

"Thank you. I'm actually here to see Howie Lambert. Can you tell me when he has a free period?"

"Sure." She blinked away the redness in her eyes and sat at her computer. In less than ten seconds she had pulled up his schedule. "His class should be transitioning soon to go to PE. Would you like me to call him down here?"

"It's all right, I'll go to his classroom."

Sue reached for a clipboard. "Before you go..." She handed him a visitor sign-in sheet with a list of names, times in and out, and classrooms visited.

Joel glanced up before writing his name. "How long do you keep these sign-in sheets?"

"We start fresh every morning. The old ones get shredded."

Joel's hope dimmed. "So you wouldn't have anything from earlier this week?"

"Afraid not." Sue's expression was sad, as if she could guess what he was thinking. "But I know everyone who comes in and out of this school, and I can promise you that no stranger has been in this week asking after Abby."

Joel nodded but didn't say what he was thinking. It was very likely that whoever took Abby wasn't a stranger. It may have even been a staff member or someone else connected with the school. Someone who wouldn't attract suspicion.

He took the sticker she offered him—with the word VISITOR printed in whimsical letters—and stuck it on his jacket as he went to the fifth and sixth grade wing. The comforting smell of food wafted from the cafeteria and he passed a class of little kids walking in single file with their arms folded tightly and their cheeks bulging out like pufferfish. Their young teacher was walking backward, modeling the action with a finger to her lips. When she turned and saw Joel, her cheeks collapsed and she blushed, but she didn't miss a beat as she herded her students through the door to the cafeteria.

He would have to remember to ask Val if mimicking pufferfish was standard practice in school these days.

The door to Howie Lambert's classroom was open when Joel arrived, but the room was empty. The central feature was a large model of the solar system made with what appeared to be inflatable beach balls hanging from the ceiling. Posters with motivational sayings dotted the walls, featuring space themes and popular sci-fi movies— some Joel recognized and others he didn't. The individual desks were littered with glue and scissors and bits of colored construction paper, as if the class had been taken by surprise when it was time to leave for PE. The chaos tugged at Joel, reminding him of Abby sitting in the middle of Val's living room floor cutting strips of paper for a Christmas chain.

Maybe this had been a bad idea. This was twice he'd been ambushed by thoughts of Abby since coming to the school. He was supposed to be focused on KJ and Sophie, not grieving.

When Howie arrived, a look of alarm crossed his face as he spotted Joel, then it relaxed into recognition.

"It's Joel, right?" he asked, offering his hand.

Joel smiled. "You remember me?"

"Sure do. How's your sister? I don't see her around much."

"She's good. She's up in Portland and doesn't make it down very often. Kids keep her busy."

"They'll do that." Howie smiled, the corners of his mustache lifting. His trim figure and straight posture suggested that, in spite of his age, he took fitness seriously. "What can I do for you?"

"I understand you've started a basketball club for the fifth and sixth graders."

Howie kept his tone light, but Joel didn't miss the slight pulling away, almost imperceptible. A wall coming up that he was trying to pretend didn't exist.

"We're in our fourth year now. It was Hansen's idea. Do you know Mick Hansen? He's been coaching at the high school since...eleven? Twelve? After Rigby left."

"You say starting the club was his idea?" Joel opened his notepad and Howie folded his arms.

"What is it you're after? I need to prep for my next period and it would go a lot faster if you just cut to the chase. I already talked to the other deputy about all this."

Joel kept his posture relaxed and open. "A few more questions have come up that I think you can help me with. Besides Mick Hansen, who else helps out with the club?"

"Hansen pops in from time to time. My unofficial assistant is Bryson Gottschalk."

"Unofficial?"

"He volunteers. The district can't afford to pay him, but he loves it. It's good to have the extra pair of hands." An undercurrent of defensiveness made the words sound hard. As if he noticed that himself, Howie uncrossed his arms. "Look, I really do need to wrap this up. Bryson is a good guy. Sometimes he...comes on a little strong for some people."

Joel kept his face impassive and his eyes on his notepad. "What do you mean by that?"

"A couple of the parents..." Howie folded his arms again. "He's a big kid at heart. But sometimes, you know, you have a protective mom or dad who thinks he should be a bit more restrained."

"Can you give me an idea of some of the things that bother parents?"

"He can get kind of physical with the kids. Not in a bad way, just wrestling, rough-housing, that sort of thing. We had a couple of complaints, so now he leaves those kids alone."

"Including Sophie McNamara?"

Howie's impeccable posture straightened even more. "Is that what this is about? Why didn't you just say so?"

Joel leveled his gaze and held it for a long moment until he was sure he had Howie's attention. "It's curious that in your initial statement there's no mention that Faye McNamara complained about Bryson's attention to her daughter."

Howie's complexion was decidedly rosier than it had been when the conversation started. "I didn't want to give anyone the wrong idea. I'm telling you, Bryson is just a kid at heart. He wouldn't do anything to hurt any of those girls."

"Is that what you told Faye when she complained?"

"Not in so many words, no. I talked to Bryson and he left Sophie alone after that."

"The district requires a background check on its volunteers, right?"

Howie shifted uneasily. "Yeah, of course." But something about the way he said it made it sound like he was reciting a script.

"I'm sure it wouldn't be hard to verify with the district office," Joel said pointedly.

Howie blanched. "Okay, I know I wasn't supposed to let him help without doing a background check, but we both kept forgetting. It's not like either one of us was trying to do anything underhanded. It's just one of those things. But I swear this season I'm going to make sure it gets done before we start."

"Is that why you didn't tell investigators about Faye's complaint against Bryson? Because you didn't want anyone to know you violated district protocols?"

"It's not that. It's...look, this really isn't any of my business. You'll have to talk to Bryson about it."

"You're the coach. You're the one who allowed him access to the kids. I want to hear from you what was going on."

"It's nothing like that, I swear it." Howie lowered his voice and glanced at the door. He was clearly rattled. "I didn't want to say anything because I'm sure this doesn't have anything to do with KJ and Sophie. But there was one time about six months ago when Bryson was going through a rough patch with his wife and he asked me to hold on to a laptop and hard drive for him."

"Is that right?" Joel paused and looked up. "Why would he do that?"

"I don't know. He was having a hard time and needed some help and it didn't hurt me any so I helped out.

"What was on it?"

"Couldn't say. It wasn't any of my business. He's a real techy kind of guy, so I assume he just wanted to make sure he didn't lose anything important if his wife kicked him out."

"How long was the laptop in your possession?"

"A few weeks, I think. They worked things out, though. He picked it up and we never talked about it again. I didn't say anything because I didn't want investigators to get the wrong idea and go down some rabbit hole that could end up embarrassing a good man."

"I see." Joel snapped his notebook closed, his disgust at Howie's violation of safety protocols heightened by the fact that it wasn't that long ago he'd been a kid who looked up to Coach Lambert. He kept his indignation in check as he handed over his business card with instructions to call if there was anything else Howie was keeping from him.

As he walked down the hallway toward the office to check out, he thought of all the withering things he would have liked to say to Howie. Maybe he'd better let someone else question Bryson.

Sue wasn't in the office when he signed out. He peeled off the visitor sticker from his jacket as he pushed through the door into a drizzly January rain. It took him a few minutes to finish up his notes, so he sat in his car

239

with the engine running and the defrost clearing the windshield.

The only warning he had that someone was approaching was a brief movement in his side mirror before they rapped hard on the glass of his door.

Joel's hand instinctively moved to his hip where his firearm rested. It took him a heartbeat to realize the face peering into the window was one he recognized. Suzie Fryer's face was pinched with cold, the tip of her nose red.

His interactions with her had never been pleasant. As she gestured to roll down the window, he braced himself for some complaint or verbal assault.

"Detective Ramirez," she began, her breath forming a cloud. She wore an oversized coat that swallowed her small frame. "I just wanted to say that I heard about your little girl and I wanted to say I'm sorry. I hope you find her soon. And...and I hope she's all right."

She turned and walked away, hugging herself against the cold, before Joel could muster a reply. He watched her disappear around the corner, marveling at how after almost ten years in this career, people could still surprise him. And wishing he'd thought to tell her thanks.

21

VAL BRAKED to ease around a big depression that spanned nearly the full width of the road.

"I don't think I've been on this road since I was a little girl," Gina said from the passenger seat.

There were so many logging roads in the mountains surrounding Owl Creek that Val didn't know them all. Her dad had favored this one for Sunday afternoon drives during her childhood years. An old clearcut area sat a couple miles up the mountain and offered a sweeping view of the winding river and the town of Owl Creek nestled in the valley.

"Thanks for not thinking this is a stupid idea," Val said as she shifted into a lower gear to give the car more power on the incline.

"We're taking a drive, that's all. Just like you told that FBI agent. What's wrong with that?" Gina gave her a sidelong glance. "Here's the thing, you need to get out of your house and out of your head. If it just so happens you brought binoculars to get a good look at Brett Rogers's property, I'm not going to stop you."

Val appreciated Gina's spin, but she knew it was a stupid idea. The fact that she would be mortified if Joel found out was proof enough of that.

To add to her feeling that she was doing something wrong, her pulse hadn't quite stabilized after seeing the black SUV parked at the bottom of the lane, which had started following them after she passed. Soon afterward, Gretchen Smith had called asking if Val needed a ride anywhere or if she'd mind some agents tagging along. Val had told her not to bother, that she just needed some fresh air. The vehicle following them had dropped out of sight, but she wasn't convinced they weren't still back there somewhere.

She continued up the mountain anyway, following the rutted road with tight corners that slowed her further. After about ten minutes, Val worried that she'd missed a turnoff or that the reforested area had grown so much over the years that she didn't recognize it. The cold rain was unrelenting and she had her car's heat on full blast for Gina's sake. Firs and pines towered overhead, but deciduous trees in the lower understory were leafless, their buds just beginning to swell. By late spring the forest would be lush and form a thick screen on either side of the road, but now it gave a skeletal feeling, matching the gloom of the weather.

At last they rounded a bend and the forest suddenly fell away, the valley opening up on their left. Val braked hard and pulled onto the shoulder. The view was just as she remembered, though the distant hills were shrouded in clouds.

Gina sighed and pulled up her hood. "I guess this is the part where we get out."

"You don't have to. You can stay in the car."

"No way. I'm here for you, remember?"

It was a small thing, a casual statement tossed out as Gina unlocked her seatbelt, but it gave Val a stirring of warmth in spite of the wintry day.

She reached for the binoculars that sat on the back seat and locked the car as she left, even though it was likely they wouldn't see another person.

She really hoped they wouldn't see another person.

The reforested clearcut was growing vigorously, not yet mature enough to block the view, but tall enough that Val climbed atop a wide stump to find a better vantage point. She could clearly make out the county highway that ran out of town and the sharp bend where Brett Rogers placed his mannequin scenes for maximum exposure to the viewing public. Peering through her binoculars, she adjusted the focus so she could zoom in on the property. A creeping sensation in her mind warned that she shouldn't be spying on the man, but she ignored it.

She was doing it for Abby.

She would do anything for Abby.

It was hard to believe, but the back yard of the Rogers property was packed full of even more junk than the front, and from this angle she could barely make out the corner of a sliding glass door in the rear of the house. A set of vertical blinds was smashed against the door and she imagined the interior looking similar to the yard.

She shuddered at the thought of Abby being kept prisoner in a place like that. Joel said they'd searched the residence, but all that junk could hide a thousand secrets. Hidden closets or walled up rooms could be disguised by so much furniture and piles of crap that investigators wouldn't even realize that one room's dimensions didn't fit the layout of the house.

Her imagination had been very busy of late, and if she could imagine it, she knew that someone somewhere was capable of doing it.

"How does it look?" Gina sniffed beside her.

"Looks like a public safety nightmare. How does anyone live like that?"

"Do you see anything...suspicious?"

Val lowered the binoculars. Despite her hooded jacket, her face was wet, and damp soaked into her jeans below her knees where she'd waded through the brush.

"There's no sign saying, 'I've got three girls held captive here,' if that's what you mean. Honestly, I don't even know what I'm looking for."

"Can I look?"

Val handed the lenses over and stepped down from the stump so Gina could take her place.

Gina adjusted the focus, her voice drifting above Val's head. "I listened to a podcast once where a guy had secretly dug a tunnel under his house that spanned all the way across several neighbors' yards. True story."

"Why?"

"I don't remember. But part of it collapsed, which is how they discovered it. Just think of all the places you could hide a secret entrance with so much stuff everywhere. Authorities could search the house all they want and not find anything if the entrance was in that old Volkswagen, for example."

"True, but I don't know if that would be possible here. You forget about our high water table. There's a reason we can't have basements, remember?"

But the image of an underground tunnel took her fears to a whole new level. What if Abby were being kept underground? What if the roof collapsed and became her tomb?

Val pulled her gaze away from the valley and scanned the hillside behind her, trying to ground herself in her surroundings to push away the image of Abby being buried alive.

Inhale. Cold air biting her lungs.

Exhale. Warm air misting past her lips.

A pale smudge against the winter-weary forest drew her eye. She peered at it, barely noticing Gina handing the binoculars over and leaning on her shoulder for support as she hopped off the stump. Val raised the binoculars to her eyes, finding the bit of color that didn't belong.

"What are you doing?" Gina asked.

"Checking something. There's something up there in the bushes."

"Probably someone's trash. Maybe a hunter took a dump and didn't bury the toilet paper all the way."

But Val knew it was too big to be a scrap of toilet paper. She focused the lenses and her body responded before her mind acknowledged what she was seeing. Her pulse accelerated and a tightness seized her chest.

"What is it?" Gina asked.

Val started moving before her mind fully realized it, carving a path back to the road through the rain-soaked bushes, blackberry vines snagging at her clothes.

"Val?" Gina called behind her.

"Just a second."

Val reached the car and crossed the road, then started climbing the opposite slope, binoculars forgotten in her hand. The hill was steep where it had been carved away to make room for the road, and some of the bank still didn't have much vegetation even after all these years. She stooped a little and reached for ridged sword fern and trailing English ivy to keep her moving forward.

Her heart pounded, a sick feeling swirling in her gut. Maybe it was trash like Gina said. Maybe it was clothing discarded by a couple of teens up to no good. Maybe when she moved aside the spiny leaves of the Oregon grape obscuring her view from below she wasn't going to find—

But no.

The fear that had gripped her proved what her brain had suspected all along.

The body of a girl.

A face she knew well.

THE LOGGING ROAD was so crowded with vehicles, Joel had to park behind a black SUV with government plates and walk a quarter mile up the steeply graded road before reaching the clearcut viewpoint.

Val had called him directly after dialing 911. The strident panic in her voice made him fear the worst. The truth wasn't that much better.

Val's white crossover was hemmed in by deputy vehicles and the medical examiner's truck, a white plume of exhaust coming from the tailpipe indicated she was keeping warm inside.

He glanced at the view of the valley as he approached the car. What had Val been doing up here on a day like this when visibility was so poor? Rain distorted the glass of the driver's side door, and the inside was faintly fogged over, making it hard to see Val's face. She jumped a little when he knocked on the window, then threw open the door so fast it almost grazed his knee.

"Finally." She hugged him tightly, burying her face in his chest.

"I came as soon as I could." He looked over her head to the hillside where at least a dozen shapes were moving among the brush. A canopy had been erected to keep the icy rain off the body while the FBI processed the scene.

"I thought it was Abby." Val's voice was muffled against his coat.

"I know."

It was an inadequate response to the terror of your worst fears being realized. The relief when they weren't. The gnawing dread of still not knowing. The horror that someone else's nightmare had become reality.

Gina exited the car from the passenger side and circled around to join them. "Hey," she said in a somber greeting. It had been years since Joel had seen Val's little sister and he took in the passage of time in a glance. Her gaze, too, seemed to be measuring him.

Val pulled away, tucking a tendril of hair behind her ears. "Marnie took our statements, but we can't leave yet. We're boxed in."

"What were you doing up here?" Joel asked, his eyes drawn back to the tent.

Val exhaled in a rush. "Don't be mad, okay?"

Joel's gaze snapped back to Val. "Why?"

"I wanted to get a look at Brett Rogers's place."

"Val, I already told you—"

"I know what you said. But I just needed to see it for myself."

Joel sighed. "Well, it may have been a stupid reason to be up here, but I'm glad you found her. Who knows how long it would have been before someone else discovered the body."

Val nodded, her lips pressed together like she didn't trust herself to speak.

"It's pretty awful," Gina said.

"Ramirez!"

Joel looked up to see Cooper motioning him over. He squeezed Val's elbow and left her to thread his way through the crowd of vehicles to the slope on the other side of the road. Cooper looked haggard in the fading daylight, his chin lined with graying stubble and deep shadows under his eyes.

"Do her parents know?" Joel asked.

"Not yet." Cooper led the way up the slope to the tent. "Watch it. One of the ladies got sick."

Joel stepped around the area he indicated, feeling a

pang of sympathy as he thought of either Val or Gina so sickened by the discovery that they'd vomited into the brush.

Joel knew immediately the decedent was Sophie McNamara, recognizing her from photos in spite of the livor mortis on one side of her face making her skin appear mottled and bruised. She was dressed in fleece pajama pants dotted with candy canes and a knit top with a faded saying that was so covered in filth Joel couldn't read it. She didn't wear a coat or shoes, and her bare feet were coated with dirt.

Agent Coleman joined them, her expression grim.

"Is this public land or private?" she asked.

Cooper looked at Joel.

"Where we're at now is public, but there are private parcels lower down."

She nodded. "Saw those coming up. We're organizing a canvass of the residences. We might luck out and catch someone with video footage of a vehicle. She can't have been here long."

Sophie lay on her side as if the killer had wanted to make it look like she was sleeping. There were no obvious signs of trauma, but her pajama sleeves didn't cover all the way to her wrists, and her arms were scratched and bruised. Her nails looked dirty and ragged. A red welt formed a ring around her right ankle.

Marnie was standing a little ways off and Joel made his way over to stand beside her. She looked down at Sophie's body with a mixture of anger and sympathy.

"Her shoes were missing," she said.

Joel looked at the soles of Sophie's feet, black with

dirt. Where had she been that her feet had gotten so filthy?

Then he realized what Marnie meant. "They never turned up at the house?"

It had been a tedious exercise with Sophie's parents, trying to sort out which clothes Sophie had left at KJ's that night instead of during an earlier visit. There had been a pair of sneakers, but Faye McNamara had insisted they'd been left there earlier because Sophie had been missing them for weeks. All of the other shoes had belonged to KJ.

Joel voiced the obvious question. "So if she had them when she was abducted, why isn't she wearing them now?"

"Maybe her killer took them to prevent her from escaping."

Joel looked at the red mark around Sophie's ankle. It seemed to call to him like a message. Unbidden, the opening line of Abby's favorite movie came into his mind. *This is the story of how I died.* It was a tongue-in-cheek opener for a child's cartoon. But now, looking at Sophie's body, it felt macabre. The story of her murder would be written on her body and it would be up to the state forensic pathologists to decipher it.

She was curled into the fetal position, her head tucked in toward her chest, her bent elbows close to her body. She was so small in death, seeming younger than her twelve years. Her parents had said she was quiet and bookish, a hard worker who excelled at whatever she did. But lying on the forest floor, with ferns quivering nearby and flecks of moss clinging to her lips, she seemed diminished. Younger.

If only those lips could speak and tell them where she'd been. Who had taken her. And where they could find KJ.

22

When Val closed her eyes, all she could see was Sophie McNamara. The ghastly tint of her skin. The way small leaves and bits of dirt and moss crawled up her neck like insects.

So Val didn't try to sleep. She sat in the living room with a notebook and pen, wrapped in a blanket even though the room was comfortably warm. Her only company was the steady sound of rain, but even that quieted after a while.

Gretchen and Agent Coleman had followed them home once they were finally able to leave the mountain hillside where Sophie's body was found. Gretchen had shown only concern, but Rita's sympathy had been mixed with a fair bit of annoyance.

"For your own safety, please allow an agent to accompany you when you leave the property. Even if you're just going to the coffee shop, we'd feel better tagging along. It's no trouble, really."

Val had replied with a vague, "I'll keep that in mind." But she had no intention of going anywhere in public where she might see people she knew, let alone bringing a federal entourage. What would she say? How could she face their stricken expressions?

Now, as she poured out her thoughts onto the lined paper of a notebook, her fear of facing the community leaked into her narrative. She described her suspicions of Brett Rogers and named others who were equally suspicious for the opposite reason—being too kind and solicitous to her and Abby. She was so engrossed in the words flowing under her pen that she didn't realize Gina had come downstairs until she appeared in the doorway.

"Can't sleep either?" Gina folded her arms tight across her body.

"It was hard enough before, but now..."

Val shifted to make room for Gina on the couch. The lamplight suffused her sister's features with a gentle touch, softening them and reminding Val of when they were younger and stayed up late watching movies and sharing secrets after their parents had gone to bed. Back when their biggest concerns had been an upcoming history project or whether their latest crush acknowledged them in the halls at school.

"I can't stop thinking about that poor girl, but it's my Emma I see instead." Gina shuddered.

"That's why I'm writing it down," Val replied, closing her notebook. "It's a technique Joel taught me after the bombing. He said it helps when he's had to deal with something...intense. He writes it all out, everything that happened, and then when he runs out of things to say, he tears it up and throws it away. Or in my case, I'm going to burn it."

"Hmm. I'm not sure if that would be better or worse. I'm trying *not* to relive it."

Val shrugged. "Your brain has to deal with it some way. I can get you paper if you want to try it."

Gina ran a hand through her limp hair. "Would it help me sleep?"

"Maybe."

Gina heaved herself to her feet. "All right. Is there paper in the office?"

With a jolt, Val threw off her blanket. "It's all right, I'll get you some. The last of the boxes are in there until I can go through them, and everything is a mess."

To her relief, Gina sank back against the couch and didn't follow her down the hallway. Val slipped the key off the doorjamb—probably not a great place to keep it if she didn't want Gina to see her war room—and unlocked the office door. She quickly grabbed a few sheets of paper and a pen and locked the door again behind her.

"Thanks for coming with me today," Val said as she handed over the writing supplies. "I feel so bad that you had to see that, but I'm so glad I wasn't by myself."

"What else are sisters for if not to get PTSD together?"

"Better together than alone." Val settled back in with her blanket and her notebook. As silence filled the room she realized, with a surge of gratitude, that her flippant words just might be one of the truest things she'd ever said.

THE WRITING EXERCISE HELPED—AS did talking for another two hours after they burned their papers—and Val was able to sleep fitfully for a couple of hours with her bedside lamp on to keep away the darkness.

When she awoke, it was to find a layer of snow coating the grass outside and turning the burned trees on the hill behind the house into beautiful contrasts of white and black like a graphite sketch.

Her first unguarded thought was how excited Abby would be to wake up and discover the winter wonderland outside her window.

Immediately that was followed by overwhelming despair as her world shifted to accommodate her new reality. Like Atlas stumbling, Val felt a staggering within herself, trying not to lose her grip. Trying not to be crushed by the weight that felt even heavier after finding Sophie's body the day before.

It was only a couple of inches of snow, enough to cover the grass, but it meant school would be canceled as it would take time to clear the roads and bus drivers weren't equipped to drive in the snow. It should be a day of playing in the snow and drinking hot chocolate in front of the stove. Val imagined feeling a distant thump as Abby jumped out of bed and ran to Val's bedroom. Imagined hearing Abby's voice calling for her in excitement, telling her about the snow.

The house was still.

It was the stillness she couldn't escape. It lingered on the edges of her day and pressed on her at night. How could something that was so full—full of grief and fear and what-ifs—leave her feeling so gutted?

From down the hall, Val heard water running in the bathroom and was comforted by the noise, a reminder that she wasn't alone. Gina must be up.

Val went in search of a clean sweatshirt as she waited for the bathroom to be free, and when she opened her door, Gina was waiting for her.

"You have a scale," she said flatly.

Val cringed at the accusation.

"Yeah, I do." She ignored her sister and continued on her way to the bathroom.

"Val?"

"Lots of people have scales, Gina. It's not a big deal."

Gina followed her down the hall.

"That's not what you told me. You said it was important in your recovery not to have a scale. That was one of the rules you made for yourself. When did you get it?"

"I don't know. It was a long time ago." But that wasn't true. Val remembered exactly when she bought it, because Gina was right. It was one of the rules she'd followed religiously for years. But one day after the bombing—while Joel was still in the hospital and she'd been so worried about him, when she'd felt buried under the overwhelming stress of finding a new job, settling the insurance claim, and buying a new car—she'd found herself in Walmart staring at the scales. It was like her brain shut off and someone else took over, putting the scale in her cart, paying for it, and bringing it home.

Now she looked at it there in the bathroom, indicting her for her weakness.

Joel had never noticed, but why would he? There was so much she hadn't shared about that shameful part of herself.

As if Gina could read her mind, she asked, "Have you told Joel you're having a hard time? You said you would when we talked about it at Christmas."

"No, I told you I would tell him *if* I'm having a hard time. But this is nothing. It's just a scale."

Gina sighed and leaned against the wall. "Look, I know I wasn't any help the first time you were going through this. I was too young and too far away and I didn't know anything about...well, anything. But I'm here now. Tell me what you need and I'll help you. You need me to do the shopping? You need me to make meals and snacks and sit with you while we eat together? I can do that."

The suggestion ignited panic in Val's chest. "Honestly, Gina, I'm fine. You don't need to worry about me."

"Okay. When was the last time you ate? I mean a real meal with normal portion sizes."

"In case you forgot, my daughter is missing. It's a little hard to have an appetite when I can't think about anything else."

But Gina wouldn't be deterred. "So, yesterday? I didn't see you eat anything last night."

"Can you blame me?" Into Val's mind came a memory of Sophie lying in the woods and a wave of nausea accompanied it.

"How about before I came?"

"I made a grilled cheese sandwich and a salad yesterday

before you got here." It was technically true. She'd made the sandwich in an effort to keep herself on some sort of eating schedule, but hadn't been able to make herself swallow. It had ended up in the trash, along with her chewed bites.

She felt the compulsion to keep a food diary rising unchecked and knew that what Gina was saying was true. She was sliding, and it scared her.

Maybe having Gina come stay was a bad idea. Her sister watched her now with a wrinkle of concern creasing her brow.

"Please let me help you. That's why I'm here. I can't just watch you destroy your life. No matter what, you have to fight this. For Abby. For Joel. For me. We all love you and will do anything you need, but you have to tell me what's really going on."

"You really want to help?" Val asked.

"Of course."

"Then stop talking about it. Trust me when I say I'm fine. If there's anything for you to worry about, I promise I'll tell you."

She knew it was a lie and suspected Gina knew it too, but she closed the bathroom door on her sister before Gina could call her out on it. Val picked up the scale and stuck it in the cupboard, resting it on the bag that held the unopened pregnancy test.

JOEL HAD ATTENDED MANY AUTOPSIES, but Sophie McNamara's felt different. As he stood off to the side in the exam room of the State Medical Examiner's Office, watching the forensic pathologists prepare the room and start the recording, he tried not to imagine Abby on the table. Lifeless. Colorless.

It was excruciating. Without a clear suspect, the impotence he felt was overwhelming.

They completed a thorough exam before removing Sophie's clothing, then examined her internal organs to determine the cause of death. The pathologists worked carefully, verbally cataloging their observations while the minutes ticked away. They took fluid samples, weighed and measured her organs, and retrieved four hairs from her pajama pants, the fuzzy fleece trapping them like a magnet.

Fibers were recovered from the ligature mark around her right ankle, likely made by a thin rope or length of paracord. They also found pale blue fibers in the abrasions around her wrists.

Two hours later, Joel was on the phone with Cooper to share the preliminary findings.

"There were signs of sexual abuse, but he didn't kill her. She was dehydrated, and there was nothing substantial in her stomach. Taken with the signs of exposure, they think she was probably in those woods for, at most, two days."

Cooper muttered, "This weather isn't helping with the search. We didn't find any signs of vehicular access and the dogs lost the scent. "

"She had multiple lacerations on her feet, including one that looked like it came from a piece of glass, which fits Rogers's description of the girls' activity in the yard and the bit of glass recovered near the fence."

Every new piece added to the puzzle should have made Joel feel like they were getting closer to an answer. Instead, it felt like the whole thing had been polluted by another unrelated puzzle and he couldn't be sure that when any two pieces fit they even belonged to the same picture.

Sophie had been restrained, but somehow she'd managed to escape. Joel didn't think she'd been intentionally freed. Her captor had been too calculating in the abduction, careful not to leave fingerprints or anything beyond the strip of blue flannel. Joel didn't think he would have let Sophie go with so much of his own DNA evidence on her body.

Now Sophie's clothing was bagged and labeled and ready to enter as evidence, including blood stains on the lower leg of her pants. Cooper had already reached out to Porter to see about getting a DNA analysis done more quickly than what the state could provide, but it was still a waiting game with no guarantee that the FBI would come up with a match.

Joel stopped at a gas station before leaving Clackamas to pick up sunflower seeds and an energy drink to keep him awake after the sleepless night. Hours later found him jittery from the caffeine and his mouth shredded from sunflower shells. Sleet rattled like beads on the windshield as he left the Willamette Valley behind and started the climb through the mountains leading to Owl Creek. He barely noticed the miles slipping away, distracted as he was turning over recent events in his mind.

Forty-five minutes outside of Owl Creek, snow dusted the towering firs and gathered along the shoulder of the freeway. The energy drink was catching up to him, and Joel pulled over at a wooded rest stop. The parking lot was nearly empty; the only other vehicles two semi trucks and a minivan. He used the restroom quickly, eager to get back on the road. But as he headed back to his car, he stopped, arrested by a Have You Seen Me? poster pinned to a wooden information booth.

Abby.

It was jarring to see her smiling face and golden curls when his thoughts were full of child rapists and murderers. Again, he thought of the decedent on the exam table, but it wasn't Sophie he pictured there. It was Abby.

Joel felt suddenly cold, far colder than the January damp could explain. It was a bone-chilling cold that threatened he'd never be warm again. He hurried to his car and sank into the driver's seat. With shaking hands, he started the engine and leaned back against the head rest, trying to ease the feeling like a vise gripping his chest. The air blowing out of the vents was warm, but still the cold persisted.

His thoughts wouldn't coalesce into words, and he let them run wherever they would. Thoughts of Abby and Val, KJ and Sophie, the haunting grief of Faye McNamara, the urgency to find KJ, the intense fear of failure. He gave himself permission to feel whatever he was feeling, even when it threatened to tear out of this throat like a sob.

In the dim desolation of a highway rest stop, he buried his face in his hands, letting the anguish rip through him. Palpable as much as it was indefinable.

When the tension finally eased and he raised his head, he wiped his eyes and realized only a few minutes had passed. He felt purged but also weakened somehow, as if whatever it had taken from him cost him more than simply a burning throat and stinging eyes.

But he also felt like he could get back on the interstate and drive the rest of the way to Owl Creek. He knew he could face the next round of decisions to be made and evidence to be analyzed. And he knew that he could keep going, no matter how long it took to bring KJ home. Even if, like Sophie, it was just to give her a proper burial.

23

Buckle up. M&D are headed your way.

JORDAN'S TEXT roused Val from her stupor. She was still in bed, having laid down after her confrontation with Gina that morning. Gina had come in at one point and told her that she'd built a fire and asked Val to tend it while she went to the store for a few things. Val had told her she would be down in a few minutes, after she made a call to the community college to withdraw from her classes.

That was over two hours ago, and she still hadn't managed it.

When she saw Jordan's text, she realized how much time had passed. The fire was probably dead and Gina would be home soon.

She texted back, *They're coming here?*

They want to bring more attention to Abby's disap-
pearance and think it will help if they're in person.
They're offering a reward of 100K.

It was a sizable amount, but not what Val would have
expected, knowing how much they loved Abby. Before
she could respond, he added,

They wanted to do more but the FBI told them no.
Apparently offering too much brings out fortune-
seekers with false leads.

Do they need a place to stay? Val asked, though she
didn't think she could stand it if they wanted to stay
at the farmhouse.

No, don't worry about them. I just wanted you to be in
the loop. Sorry I can't be there too.

The thought of standing with Jordan in front of the
cameras made Val's insides twist with revulsion.

It's for the best, she texted. *Thanks for letting me*
know.

With phone in hand, Val found herself scrolling
through her texts and call history. She landed on the
number for Wesley Peters from the Channel Six news.
So far she'd avoided making a public statement, but if
Jeanette and Charles were coming to Owl Creek, she

couldn't stand by and let them speak for her. She wouldn't.

And if she were going to have to be in the public's eye anyway, maybe she could get something in return.

By the time Gina returned, bustling up the stairs with a package of toilet paper, Val was sitting on the top step, gazing out the landing window to where dense snow clouds gathered against distant hills.

"Hey, you got out of bed," Gina said cheerily, ignoring the fact that Val was still in her pajamas.

Val managed a meager smile. "You caught me. Jordan says his parents are coming. I figured I'd better make an attempt at looking respectable before they get here."

"I don't think anyone expects you to look respectable right now. But you might feel better if you take a little time to take care of yourself. By the time you get cleaned up, I'll have something for you to eat."

"You have the stuff I asked you to get?" Val asked.

The skin around Gina's eyes creased with worry, but she didn't say anything as she handed over a plastic bag.

Val knew the FBI was monitoring her phone. Could they also use it to listen in on her conversations in the house? She didn't know if that was possible, but she wasn't about to take chances.

She passed her smartphone to Gina who took it with her downstairs. In the meantime, Val went to the bathroom and closed the door. In the shopping bag she found a black flip phone encased in plastic. Gina hadn't liked it when she told her what she needed, but she'd come through for her as only a sister could.

While the phone charged, Val took the hottest shower the temperamental water heater could produce. She stood in the heavy stream of water, wishing it could drive away the images of Sophie in her mind. But the fickle hot water ended long before her memory of the previous day's events did.

After she dressed, the steam from her shower clouding the cold mirror with condensation, Val grabbed the flip phone and dialed Wesley's number before she could talk herself out of it.

"Peters," he answered brusquely on the second ring.

Val took a deep breath. "This is Valerie Rockwell."

"Oh." The shift in his voice was immediate. Gentler. Softer. But also more alert. "Ms. Rockwell, I'm so glad you called. Have you given any more thought to my suggestion?"

"I have, Mr. Peters."

"Please, call me Wesley. I'm glad to hear it. I want to do anything I can to help you find your daughter."

"Good. Because it turns out that I need your help after all."

THE STEAM in the bathroom had dissipated by the time Val hung up the phone. Wesley Peters had been eager to keep her talking, asking questions about how she was doing, if she had enough support, and eventually transitioning to the day Abby disappeared. She knew she shouldn't be talking to him, so she kept her comments restricted to emotion rather than fact, sidestepping whenever he tried to pin her down on details.

In return, she'd asked him a list of questions of her own. Similarities he saw between both abductions. Questions about who the investigators were interviewing in the Greer case and what he knew about them. Things Joel couldn't tell her even if she asked him.

Wesley had also kept things close to the vest, claiming that with the discovery of Sophie's body the day before he didn't have much time at the moment and would much rather sit down, face to face, over a cup of coffee. In spite of his obfuscation, Val had learned a few things. There was an ex-boyfriend who'd been brought in for questioning, a seventeen-year-old neighbor who seemed suspicious, and an incident that had taken place between Faye McNamara and a volunteer basketball coach Wesley supposedly couldn't remember. It wasn't much, but it was enough to whet her appetite, and she'd ended the call with a commitment to talk again.

Val dug through the bottom drawer of the cabinet, looking for her brush to blow dry her hair. Most of the flotsam and jetsam belonged to Abby. Child flossers in bright colors and animal shapes. A small tube of tooth-paste from a recent visit to the dentist, brightly colored with sparkles. Bandaids and bobby pins that spread no matter how much Val tried to contain them, all tangled with little blond hairs.

She stood there, forgetting what she'd been looking for. Riveted by the careless reminders of a life lost.

Without making a conscious decision, she reached under the sink and pulled out the grocery bag with the pregnancy test. Now, as she pulled the stick out of the box and reviewed the instructions, she thought how surreal it would be if she were pregnant. It would be the most irresponsible thing she'd ever done, even more irresponsible than when she'd gotten pregnant with Abby and dropped out of college before finishing her degree.

As she placed the stick on the back of the toilet to wait the requisite five minutes, she offered a silent prayer that it would remain a single line. A negative test.

She busied herself drying her hair, forcing herself not to look at the test until five minutes passed on her timer. As the hot air warmed the room, her mind slipped into thoughts of how her life would change if the test were positive. She would need to find an OB/GYN. She would need to tell Joel. Would he be excited? Or upset? Abby would be thrilled, Val knew. Especially if it were a girl. Maybe Joel would be excited too. They could think of a fun way to share the news with Abby after she came home.

By the time the five minutes passed, Val was envisioning Abby's beaming face and little arms squeezing her around the neck with childish glee, picturing her delight as each week Val shared how the embryo had grown, comparing it to familiar objects from an apple seed to a plum.

Val turned off the blow dryer, her hair still slightly damp. Heart pounding, she checked to see if her life was going to change forever.

The stick still only had one line. It was negative.

At the sight of that one line, something cracked inside her. She was relieved, yes, but somehow it looked like a cruel judgment.

You have no business bringing more children into the world, it seemed to say.

How could she mourn a baby that didn't exist? Why did she feel like her child had been taken from her again?

And yet, for reasons she couldn't understand, Val broke down for the first time since that afternoon at the hatchery. Shaking with sobs and covering her mouth to keep them silent, she collapsed onto the floor near the tub, her knees bent and head in her hands.

Gina found her there a few minutes later.

"Val?"

She glanced at the pregnancy stick on the toilet tank.

"Oh Val..."

Soon Gina was sliding down the wall to sit next to her, smelling of cooking onions as her arms encircled Val. Val leaned her head against her sister's shoulder and wiped at her face.

"This is so stupid. I don't want to be pregnant. But I feel..."

She couldn't finish the thought as her face crumpled with another round of fresh, burning tears.

"It's not stupid," Gina murmured. "It's okay. You've been trying to be so strong. It's too much for anyone to bear."

Val took a deep, shuddering breath.

"I just can't help thinking...I know it's dumb, but what if I'm being punished for losing Abby? What if I can't be trusted to be a mom to anyone?"

Gina rubbed Val's arm.

"Are you and Joel that serious? Were you trying to get pregnant?"

"No, just the opposite. I wouldn't do something so reckless. I feel like I'm barely getting my life together as it is."

"There you go, then. If you were trying not to get pregnant, and then you didn't get pregnant, how could that be a punishment?"

It made sense hearing it in Gina's words, but somehow it still felt like a condemnation.

"I just feel so...like it's my fault. I should have gone with her to the restroom. I shouldn't have taken Caleb to find his pencil without checking to make sure she was okay. I shouldn't have brought her to Owl Creek where children aren't safe in their own beds. I should have known. I should have felt that she needed me, that she was in trouble."

To her credit, Gina didn't argue with her. "I know you already know why none of those things are true. You're a smart woman, Val. Whatever happened to Abby was only one person's fault, and you know it wasn't yours."

Val's tailbone was starting to ache. She pulled herself to stand and reached for the roll of toilet paper to blow her nose. Gina stayed close, watching her with brown eyes lined with compassion.

Val gripped the sink and braced herself to speak the words she'd as yet refused to say out loud.

"What if they never find her?" she whispered. "How can I live with that?"

Gina took a deep breath. "You'll find a way."

Hot tears seeped from Val's eyes again, quiet things, not the wracking tempest of before.

"What if I can't?"

In answer, Gina wrapped her arms around her. Val returned the embrace, resting her cheek against the top of Gina's head. She felt soft and familiar and clung to Val like she was seeking comfort as much as offering it.

"You always find a way, Val. That's who you are."

―――――――

RAISED voices drifted from inside Leisa Greer's house as Joel and Marnie approached the front door. They exchanged a look before Joel rang the doorbell. He couldn't understand the words, but the voices sounded like a male and female. At the sound of the doorbell, the voices stilled. The snow was mostly gone now, except for a trapezoidal shape that outlined the northern shadow of the house stretching across the grass.

Noah Proctor answered the door, looking disheveled and agitated.

He stared for a beat before opening the storm door.

"Hey Joel. Come on in. Ms...?"

"Marion Sanders," Marnie said, offering her hand in greeting.

The smell of cigarettes filled the air, and a bowl on the table held a collection of cigarette butts.

Noah noticed Joel's gaze and frowned. "She quit smoking when she was pregnant with KJ. One more thing he took from her."

Leisa stood in the hallway as if she'd just come from the back. The pellet stove was running, a low rumble in the corner of the living room. Casserole dishes and plastic containers—empty and washed clean—sat stacked on the counter labeled with masking tape and names written in marker.

"I don't know why everyone keeps bringing food," Leisa complained. "I'm only one person. How much do they think I can eat? Now I have to return their containers to them like it's a friggin' church social."

"I'll do that." Noah's offer sounded accusatory. "I told you I could." He gathered the dishes into his arms, balancing the plastic on top of the glass. Joel stepped aside as he moved toward the door.

"Are you going, then?" Leisa asked.

Noah looked back, his gaze sweeping over Joel and Marnie as if he was holding back what he really wanted to say.

"Yeah. Cass and I will be back later."

"All right. Thanks."

The words were neutral enough, but Joel sensed an undercurrent of something strained. Hostile, even.

"How are you doing?" Marnie asked.

"Oh…" Leisa blew out a breath and shrugged. "To be honest, not too good. They told me about the autopsy results for Sophie. I guess…my brother thinks I should prepare myself for the worst. But I can't. I just can't give up hope yet."

"We aren't giving up hope either," Joel said. "We're doing everything we can to find her, I promise."

"I thought the FBI took over the case. I've had more agents coming in and out of here the past few days than all of last week combined."

"It's a collaborative effort," Marnie explained. "I

assure you we're still very much involved. Can we go over the events leading up to her disappearance one more time? Just to make sure we aren't missing anything. Any contact KJ might have made with someone out of the ordinary?"

"Honestly, the more we talk about it, the more I'm not sure about anything anymore. We had Christmas here, quiet. Just the two of us. I didn't work that night so we watched some TV and ate treats and she did her nails with a new UV light thing. You seen those?"

Joel shook his head but Marnie nodded. "When did school get out for the break?"

"The Monday before Christmas."

"What did she do during her days off?" Joel asked.

"Uh, she went to Sophie's one day, and Sophie came here. I took the girls Christmas shopping on Wednesday."

"Where did you go?"

"To the mall in Pineview."

"Were the girls with you the whole time?"

Leisa hesitated. "Yes, but...well, mostly. KJ wanted to do some shopping for me, so I went to Payless while they found my gift. I figured they would be fine if they stayed together."

Joel nodded. "And how long were they unsupervised?"

"It was only about thirty minutes. Maybe less."

"Do you know where they went during that time?" Marnie asked.

"Bath and Body. And I think they went to Claire's. But they only made purchases at Bath and Body. Oh, that's not true. There's a bookstore there; what's it called? Sophie mentioned that they went in there because there was a man doing a book signing all by himself. A local author or something. I forgot about that. Sophie—she's a big reader, you know—went and talked to him because she felt bad that no one was buying his book. I'm sorry, I don't remember his name. I don't even remember what the book was about. Maybe a memoir?"

"I'm sure the store manager will know. Is there anything else you did? Anywhere else you went?"

"Walmart. We grabbed lunch at Dairy Queen and then headed home. Oh, except my left turn signal was out so I stopped at the Auto Zone to pick up a new bulb before leaving. The one just across the street from Walmart."

"How about any suspicious phone calls over the past few weeks? Either directed at you or KJ."

"We've been over this so many times," she said with frustration. "No, there was nothing. I mean, I get those pharmacy texts; you know, the scams? But no calls. You guys checked KJ's phone and followed up with all those numbers, right?"

"How about social media?" Marnie asked. "Anyone contact you lately you don't know?"

Leisa scoffed. "That happens all the time. I'm really particular, though, and I tell KJ she can only follow people she knows in real life. You never know when the cute thirteen-year-old who likes Minecraft and basketball is actually a fifty-year-old pedophile. I looked through that list you gave me of her contacts and nothing looked suspicious. She's pretty good about blocking people she doesn't know, even if they seem nice. Like that guy at the hardware store."

"Which guy is that?" Joel glanced up from his notes.

"He works at the hardware store. Nice guy. Friendly. Can't remember his name. He followed us both on Instagram a while back but I told her to block him. I don't want her getting the idea that it's okay for men to seek her out on social media."

"I'd like to take a look if you don't mind," Joel said. "Did you give him your information to look you up?"

Leisa scanned through her phone and handed it over. "No, but you know how it is. You're connected to enough people in the area that they start feeding you suggestions of friends of friends thinking you know them too."

In her list of followers, another face caught his attention.

"You're friends with Bryson Gottschalk?"

"Of course. He and I graduated together from Salmon Ridge."

"He helped coach KJ in basketball, right? Did you ever have any concerns about how he interacted with the kids?"

"No, Bryson is great. He's like a big kid himself. I would never say this to Faye, but I felt like she was over-reacting about all that stuff last year with Sophie. KJ worried she wasn't going to let Sophie do the club this year, which seemed a little extreme."

Joel clicked on the profile for the hardware store employee. "The Reel Nate. You accepted his request?"

"Yeah. He's nice. Not bad looking either, if I'm

honest. But he doesn't post that often, and then it's just stories."

Joel looked over the account. There weren't any posts and none of the stories had been saved. His profile picture was too obscured to get a clear image of his face, but it might be enough for one of the other employees to verify whether or not it was Nathan Weiss. He had hundreds of followers and followed over a thousand people. For someone who wasn't that active on the platform, he didn't seem all that discriminating about who he connected with.

But it wasn't @the_reel_nate who lingered in Joel's thoughts as he and Marnie left the Greer residence. It was the fact that Leisa had described Bryson in the exact same way Howie Lambert had.

"A big kid," they'd both called him. Either they were uncannily attuned to each other to use the same language to justify the man's behavior, or they'd picked it up from Bryson himself. And in Joel's line of work, the only people who felt a need to reassure others that they were safe with children were those who were anything but.

When he and Marnie arrived at the Grange, the media presence had nearly doubled. Joel checked his watch. It was almost time for the evening briefing which marked the end of their shift. It wouldn't hurt to stay for a little while longer and catch the news conference.

He and Marnie filed into the classroom and found that most of the chairs were already full. They stood against the wall near the door, and while Joel waited for the briefing to start, he considered texting Val to see how she was doing. But asking about someone's emotional state after finding a dead girl in the woods wasn't exactly the kind of topic you could bring up over text.

The briefing began with preliminary autopsy results from Sophie McNamara. Joel listened with half an ear. None of the material was new to him. Until...

"Blood on her lower pant leg appears not to belong to Sophie."

The mood in the room shifted.

"We don't have a sample for KJ, but we do for Sophie. While the blood found in the bathroom matches Sophie, initial tests of blood found on the lower hem of her left pant leg do not appear to be a match."

"Is it KJ's?" someone asked from the back.

"We can't say. But it's presumed at this point that it either belongs to KJ or to the perpetrator."

The words settled in the room and Joel found himself wondering who would be the first one to say what they were all thinking. Even if KJ was alive when Sophie escaped, it was highly probable she was deceased now.

No one said the words. In this room full of seasoned investigators, they all knew KJ's odds of being found alive went down drastically as soon as the news reported that Sophie's body had been discovered. But no one was going to admit it out loud. Not until they had no other choice.

24

ABBY'S ARM had fallen asleep where she'd been using it as a pillow. She was back in the car again, in the hidden area beneath the plastic cover that unrolled to make a hiding place for her behind the seats. Once she'd tried to move it and peek out the back window while they were driving, thinking she might be able to catch the attention of another driver. But the bad man had seen what she was doing in the mirror and barked at her that if she didn't stay put he would shoot her mom in the head.

He said that a lot, and it was thinking of Mom that kept Abby from trying to run away from him in the parking lot. He said he had friends who knew where Abby lived, and in the days they'd been stuck in the motel during the snowstorm, he'd told her more times than she could count of the terrible things he would do to Mom if she tried to escape.

Abby was uncomfortable in her hiding place, but at least they were finally out of the motel. She'd spent two days with the bad man alternating between watching TV and talking on the phone with someone who made him use curse words and kick the chair after he hung up. Most of his conversations were complaining about the storm and saying that he couldn't do anything about the weather.

Whenever he'd needed to use the bathroom or leave to get food at the gas station on the corner, he'd used those hard plastic ties to tie her hands to the bed so she couldn't leave. By the second day, she'd begged him not to leave because her wrists had hurt so bad from being tied up. On the third day, the sun was shining and his mood improved. He watched road reports obsessively and announced that afternoon that the freeway had opened and they would be able to leave that night.

Abby knew he was happy about it because when she asked where they were going, he didn't snap at her. He just said, "You'll see. We're going to go get your surprise."

She was thirsty again, and hungry too. Her stomach seemed to be eating itself the way it was gurgling. Sometimes she had stabbing pains that made her hug herself until they passed. Almost worse than anything else was the boredom. Lying in the dark with nothing to do was getting really old. She tried singing her favorite songs, but that made her more thirsty. Then she tried closing her eyes and remembering her favorite movies, imagining them scene by scene. But after a while she realized she didn't remember them as well as she thought.

After driving so long that she fell asleep again, the car stopped. Abby recognized the sound of a gas pump filling up the tank, and she wondered how to tell the bad man that she needed to go potty. She squeezed her knees together when the car started again. She wouldn't be able to hold it for long. Would he be mad if she had an accident?

But they didn't drive very far before the car stopped again. This time, the hatchback opened and the black covering slid back a little ways. The bad man looked to either side nervously, as if worried someone would see them. They were at a gas station like she thought, parked in the back where there were no other cars. A couple of semi trucks were parked at the edge of the lot, but they were far away and Abby couldn't see the drivers. The snow was almost too bright to look at with the sun glaring overhead. The wind gusted, so cold it took her breath away.

"I have to go potty," Abby said, shielding her eyes.

"I figured. First let's get you inside. Put this hat on and let's take off your coat." He pulled a sweatshirt over her arms and shoved a baseball cap on her head. "You can't wear the boots anymore. Put on these sneakers instead."

They were too big; Abby could see that before she even put them on. They had laces, but Abby wasn't very good at tying her shoes. She didn't mention any of this, though. The bad man didn't care about things like that, and she still remembered how much it hurt when he'd hit her in the motel. She didn't want him to hit her again.

So she did her best to tie the shoelaces and stuffed her hands into the pocket of the stinky sweatshirt to keep them out of the cold.

"Remember, if anyone sees you or if you talk to anyone, you'll never see your mom again. But if you're a good girl and do what I say, your mom will be safe."

Abby nodded. He helped her down from the car and held her hand as they walked into the store. She didn't want to hold his hand, especially because he held hers too tight, but if there was a chance she could see Mom again, she would do whatever he said. She kept her eyes fixed on the floor so she didn't accidentally make eye contact with someone and attract attention, but the urge to look up and see if anyone had noticed her was so strong, it was like an itch that she had to scratch.

The bad man asked a worker for a key to the bathroom, and Abby felt a thrill of freedom when she realized it was a bathroom for only one person and he was going to let her go in by herself.

"I'll be right outside," he said, and the voice he used made it sound like he was trying to make her feel better, like he was a nice dad taking care of his daughter. But Abby knew better. She knew it was a warning.

Once inside, Abby took her time. Maybe if she took long enough, the bad man would get distracted and she could sneak out the door when he wasn't looking. She could run and find the worker and tell him to call the police. Maybe the worker was already calling the police right now. Maybe he had seen a picture of her like the pictures of KJ and Sophie and the police were already on their way.

But then Abby went to wash her hands and saw her reflection in the dirty mirror. Disappointment swept over her. Between the stinky sweatshirt that was too big and the dirty baseball cap, she didn't look anything like herself. Her hair drooped under the hat and even her eyes looked like someone else. She hadn't brushed her teeth in days and she scratched at dried food on her chin.

A knock at the door was followed by the bad man's voice saying, "You about done in there, sweetie?"

It made her feel sick to hear his voice in that nice way, but there was something about it that gave her hope. Maybe he really was going to bring her home. Maybe, if she did everything he said exactly right, if she didn't make any mistakes, he would change his mind about taking her so far away.

So she hurried and dried her hands and pulled open the heavy door.

The bad man wasn't alone. A mom was waiting with a little girl who was shifting back and forth with agitation.

"Sorry about that," the bad man said with a laugh.

"It's fine," the mom said. Her hair was pulled back in a braid and she wore a bulky sweatshirt that said Bend, Oregon in fancy letters against colorful mountains. Her gaze flickered over Abby, and there was a look of pity in her eyes as she gave her a second glance.

Abby stopped, willing the mom to say something, to recognize her, but her own daughter was hurrying into the bathroom and calling for her.

"All right, I'm coming," the mom said, and then the bathroom door closed and Abby was alone with the bad man.

"What took you so long?" he growled under his breath.

He grabbed her arm and she gasped.

"I went as fast as I could," she insisted.

"Shut-up," he hissed.

He glanced around the store and up at a black ball in the corner of the ceiling. Abby followed with her eyes but barely had time to wonder what the black ball was before he yanked her around to his other side, blocking it from view as he pulled her back out to the waiting car.

"You're going to want to hear this," Marnie said, coming to lean against the table where Joel was working. She was unflappable as a general rule, but the brightness in her eyes put him on alert. "Rita just got off the phone with a dad of one of the second graders who was on the field trip. His daughter, Kara, is a friend of Abby's, so she was one of the first ones questioned that day and didn't have much to say. It seems she's been talking more the past couple of days and mentioned a man who approached Abby's group earlier in the day. Well before Abby disappeared. She thought he was an employee, they all did, but her description doesn't match any of the employees who were working that day."

Joel straightened. "What did he do?"

"Nothing threatening, that's why she didn't think of it earlier. They had separated into groups in the forest upriver, so out of view of any cameras. He commented on their drawings, then showed them how to make a little whistle with a blade of grass."

"Did anyone else see him?"

"Another friend was there. We'll follow up with her, and I'm going to check with all the employees to see whether or not it was any of them."

"Thanks for telling me." A low heat of anticipation stirred in Joel's belly. Though relying on children as witnesses was always limiting, having more than one who saw the man might help them get a decent composition sketch.

"Uh oh." Marnie stood, looking toward the door. "Look who's here."

Joel, too, stood as the Fishers entered the room accompanied by Stacy Porter and a member of their security detail in a dark suit with the bulk of a sidearm at his hip. Jeanette Fisher, bulldog of the Senate, looked more petite than she appeared on television. Charles Fisher must have been the one to give Jordan his height. Val had only ever spoken highly of Charles. It was Jeanette who gave her the most heartburn, and as Joel saw the diminutive woman take command of the room he thought he understood why.

"Where's Detective Ramirez?" Jeannette said, scanning the room until her eyes landed on Joel.

"Good luck," Marnie murmured quietly as he stepped around the worktable.

Joel stood and reluctantly crossed the room to respond to her summons.

"Senator Fisher," he greeted, shaking her hand and then her husband's.

Jeanette looked him over with eyes that held sharp intelligence and critical judgment. "Mr. Ramirez, it's a pleasure to finally meet you. Abby speaks of you often."

The tension in her eyes made it fall short of being a compliment.

"It's good of you to come."

"Do you have children, Mr. Ramirez?"

"No, I don't."

Jeanette smiled with condescending sweetness. "A mother would do anything for her children. That's doubly true for grandmothers."

Joel wasn't sure what to say to this. Charles seemed to sense his discomfort and came to the rescue.

"Thank you for indulging us. We know it's a bit of a disruption and don't want to get in your way. We appreciate all that you're doing to find Abby and are here to help in any way we can."

"Yes," Jeanette agreed as she took her husband's arm. "We appreciate everything you've done for Val, too. She's had a hard year and it's lucky she's had you to help her get through."

Again the tone carried a barb and Joel felt unsure of what to say. He settled on, "We're lucky to have each other."

"How wonderful." Her smile was as false as her hair color.

"We'll let you get back to work," Charles said, gently easing Jeanette away. "Agent Porter wants to discuss our statement to the press."

Joel breathed easier as they left to follow Stacy to the briefing room.

Marnie raised an eyebrow when Joel rejoined her. "Well, I guess you aren't going on their Christmas list next year."

Joel smiled in spite of himself. "Is it that obvious?"

"You were great. Don't bother ingratiating yourself to people like that, they aren't worth it. Senator Fisher is going to be hard-pressed to make you out to be the villain in this whole thing when it's her son's fault he and Val split."

"I guess I owe him, then. Which is unfortunate because if I ever see him in person, I'd be seriously tempted to break his nose."

It was completely out of character and Marnie knew it, which is why she chuckled as she went back to her computer. "Now, *that* I'd like to see."

25

VAL WAS REMINDED of last summer's fire camp as she surveyed the sprawling complex that had taken over the Grange. Law enforcement vehicles ranging from county to federal, from marked vehicles to unmarked vans, filled the parking lot. Another giant RV was parked near the entrance, similar to the one on her property. Media vans clustered on the south side near a large canopy that had been constructed against the wall of the Grange. Val recognized the location where press releases were completed on at least a daily basis.

"How much does Joel know about your eating disorder?" Gina asked as she pulled into the dirt parking lot. A thin layer of gravel was embedded in the dirt, and the lot was pocked with potholes. Val had asked Gina to drive, feeling like she couldn't handle one more thing considering what she was about to do.

Her jaw tensed from Gina's question. "Can we not do this now? I'm already stressed enough as it is."

"I'm just wondering what you've told him. He's in the best position to help, but only if he knows what's going on. Have you told him anything?"

"Of course I've told him. But it's not his problem. It's my problem." Val couldn't put into words the rest of what she was thinking. Jordan had been instrumental in helping her through her recovery, but she didn't want to rely on Joel in the same way. The thought of expecting him to be attuned to her habits and patterns, of sharing the most shameful parts of herself, didn't sit well with her. She didn't want to be the broken one in this relationship.

"If you want him in your life, it's going to become his problem," Gina said.

Val cringed. She knew Gina didn't mean it to sound like a condemnation, but she felt it that way all the same. It was a reminder that this would be a part of her for the rest of her life. That anyone who wanted a relationship with Val would also be forced to have a relationship with Ed, the anthropomorphized ex who represented her eating disorder.

Gina pulled into a spot as far away from the other cars as possible and put the car into park.

"Believe it or not, Gina, this isn't helpful," Val said when the engine stilled. "I'm about to go stand in front of a bunch of cameras and tell the world about my daughter's abduction. This is pretty much the worst time to talk about eating disorders or my relationship with Joel or Jordan or any of that."

Gina frowned. "I didn't say anything about Jordan."

Val sighed and grabbed her purse. "Please. You came

for moral support. For now that means helping me be less stressed, not more."

Gina nodded. "You're right. I'm sorry. Can you promise we'll talk about it later, though? Maybe with Joel there?"

Val grimaced. "All right, that's fine. I'll let you know when I'm ready."

She knew by the look on her face that Gina suspected that Val would never be ready for a conversation like that. But her sister didn't call her bluff, so Val rewrapped her scarf and prepared to face the icy breeze awaiting them outside.

Val was grateful to have Gina there, she really was. She just wished she'd never confessed so much about her eating disorder so that Gina couldn't keep throwing it in her face. But as she crossed the parking lot with the media tent visible out of the corner of her eye, she knew she couldn't have done this alone.

Inside the Grange, they were met by a deputy who made them sign in with their names and the time. They followed the noise to the main hall and paused for a second to take in the scene. Men and women were visiting in groups, hunched over computers, or talking on the phone. Some were dressed in business dress, others in uniforms representing local agencies, while still others wore durable work clothes suited to searching rugged terrain. Val even spotted a table of phones manned by a couple of Owl Creek residents. The largest presence was from the FBI, with dozens of agents moving around the room. There was a steady hum of activity, and Val and Gina went unnoticed.

At last, she spotted Joel across the room talking to Special Agent Rita Coleman. Adjusting her purse strap on her shoulder, Val waited, unsure of what to do. She'd never felt intimidated going to the local sheriff substation, but this was different. There was no genial Kathy waiting to greet her and ask her about Abby. No deputies she knew by first name.

A deputy she didn't recognize was the first to approach. He was young, with dirty blond hair cut close.

"Can I help you, ma'am?" he asked.

"I'm here to see Joel Ramirez," she said, trying to sound confident that she belonged there.

As if on cue, Joel glanced toward the door. His frown cleared briefly as he spotted Val.

Val felt her own expression ease—not quite into a smile, but close. Conscious of the room full of Joel's colleagues, she kept her hands firmly at her sides as he approached.

"You made it," he said, glancing at Gina behind her. "Willis, will you notify Lieutenant Cooper that Ms. Rockwell has arrived?"

The deputy moved to the door where Val and Gina had just entered, and while they waited, Joel asked in a low voice, "You okay?"

He knew how much she hated being in the spotlight, how triggering it was to answer reporters' questions. She tried to muster a smile and a clever quip, but she couldn't think of anything to say. Everything felt so dry and lifeless inside her. So she simply nodded.

Soon Lieutenant Cooper entered with a man Val

recognized, Stacy Porter of the FBI. He shook Gina's hand before reaching for Val's.

"Ms. Rockwell, thank you for coming in. Joel's explained what a particularly big ask this is, and we all appreciate you making that sacrifice."

"Whatever helps find my daughter."

"We've got a little time, so let's go talk somewhere a little more private, shall we? Go over a few things before you go on camera."

Val followed him and Cooper to a smaller room off the hallway. It looked like it was being used as an interview room, with someone's forgotten coffee in a disposable cup and a ball point pen left behind on the table.

Joel and Gina sat on either side of Val, and she tried not to feel like she was being interrogated as Cooper and Agent Porter sat across from her. She'd been interviewed by them both once before, after the capture of bomber Hannah Quinton. It wasn't a comforting memory.

"By way of reminder, the purpose of this media appearance is to keep Abby's name and picture out there. To remind people that she has a family who loves her. You can do more good than you realize."

Val nodded. "That's why I'm here."

"I understand you have a prepared statement?"

Val took the paper out of the plastic folder. "It's already been looked over and approved. All I ask is that I don't have to answer questions."

Cooper and Porter exchanged a look and nodded.

"We've already made that clear," Cooper said. "Sheriff Larson is going to follow up with a few other details about the case, so that should make it simple enough for you to step away."

"What kind of details?"

"Nothing you don't already know. That we're looking into every possible connection with the disappearances of KJ Greer and Sophie McNamara, but so far they appear to be unrelated. That we've performed searches—"

"How can you say that with certainty?" Val blurted, surprising herself. "How do you know the same person who took the other girls didn't take Abby too?"

Joel shifted next to her.

"We're keeping all avenues of inquiry open, of course," Porter said. "But as yet there's nothing about the two incidents that appears to be connected."

"Aside from being only ten days apart and in the same community, you mean?" Val inwardly cringed at the sarcasm in her own voice. This isn't what she meant to say, but the words were coming anyway. She felt Joel's hand on her leg, a gentle pressure.

"The choice of ligatures, the ages of the children, the intent and planning that went into Abby's abduction compared to the other, the lack of connection between Abby and the other victims—"

"Couldn't they intentionally be trying to mislead you? Who's to say KJ and Sophie were the intended targets at all? Maybe it was Abby all along and the others were meant to throw you off track."

She felt herself flushing but didn't back down. She wanted reassurance that she couldn't refute, and so far she hadn't gotten it.

"You are very astute, Ms. Rockwell," Porter said, but she could tell he was just saying it to placate her. The thought made her more annoyed. "We're looking at both cases from all angles. If you have any reason you think they're related, or anything you haven't shared about either one of these cases, I'd urge you to share it now."

"Not really," she admitted. "I just have a hard time thinking they aren't related."

Porter's phone buzzed and he stood. "We still have a few minutes, so if you wouldn't mind waiting here until it's time, then we'll bring you out after everyone's assembled."

Val agreed and released a long breath after the two men left the room. She felt like water was slipping through her fingers. She didn't have anything concrete that would help them in the case. It was just desperate grasping at nothing.

"I'm sorry," she said before Joel could say anything. "I'm not trying to cause trouble."

"Of course not," Joel said. "You're asking important questions; there's nothing wrong with that." He squeezed her thigh and she felt an immediate sense of revulsion at feeling his fingers imprinting in her flesh.

The thought came like a well-remembered song, filling her head with the refrain. *You're too fat. No one will ever love you. If you had any self-control you wouldn't look like this.*

Maybe Gina was right. Maybe it was time to get some help.

Val glanced at her sister. Later, when they were

293

alone, she would try to find the courage to be honest with her.

"You're going to do great," Gina said with an encouraging smile. "Just pretend that you're telling me off instead of talking to the cameras."

Val managed a weak smile. Within a few minutes, Cooper returned to escort her outside.

They walked in silence down the corridor to a side door that opened onto the parking lot nearest the canopy. Jeanette and Charles Fisher were waiting by the door and Val paused to give them both a stiff hug in greeting. Then she followed them out the door, with Joel and Gina flanking her on either side.

As soon as they stepped outside, the attention in the tent shifted their direction. The canopy was full, with standing room only. Men and women holding cameras emblazoned with news logos stood toward the back. Wesley Peters was in the front row and he gave a small nod as Val caught his eye. Recognition? Reassurance?

She couldn't see well past the microphones and cameras. Not because there wasn't plenty of daylight, but because her vision felt blurred. She looked at her feet, but then remembered Gina's words and lifted her eyes to look out over the reporters. She lined up next to Joel behind the podium as Sheriff Larson stepped up to the microphone. Every camera was trained on him.

Joel's fingers gently brushed hers, hooking onto them where they hung at her side.

Val listened to Larson introducing her and swallowed to moisten her throat. Her palms were clammy and she blinked, trying to clear her vision.

She was vaguely aware that the sheriff had finished and was looking toward her, inviting her to the podium. Her legs obeyed without any direction from her, and she was there before she realized it, staring down at the computer-printed statement she'd written with Gretchen's help.

"Thank you for coming here today," Val began. She couldn't tell if the microphone was picking up her voice well. The vacant black camera lenses made her stomach clench. "I also want to thank the Wallace County Sheriff's Office, Search and Rescue, the many volunteers who've come out to help, and the various state and federal agencies who have been working tirelessly around the clock to find Abby."

As she said Abby's name, her voice hitched. She swallowed, but her throat felt like sandpaper.

"Abby is the light of my life. She's like a ray of sunshine for everyone she meets. Teachers, classmates, the postal carrier, everyone loves her. Maybe that's why so many people in this community have taken her loss so personally, feeling her absence as if it were their own daughter who went missing.

"What I'm asking is that each of you within the sound of my voice do the same. Consider yourself part of a broader community who have the power to help find Abby. Keep your eyes open. Pay attention. Please use the tip line to report anything suspicious, even if you aren't sure it's connected. Maybe you were traveling through the area on business. Maybe you have a family member or a coworker who has been acting suspiciously. Whatever it is, don't hesitate to report it.

I'm asking you as Abby's mom, help us bring her home."

By the time she finished, her hands were trembling. As she turned away, a voice shot out from the front row, "Mrs. Fisher, was Abby was taken in retribution for your husband's crimes?"

Val stiffened, but didn't look back as she returned to stand beside Joel. He hid his anger behind a mask of indifference, but Gina was clearly livid, her face reddening. Jeanette, however, looked pale.

"As a reminder, Brody, Ms. Rockwell isn't taking questions at this time," Sheriff Larson said firmly, returning to the microphone. "Senator Jeanette Fisher, Abby's grandmother, has an important announcement that she'd like to make."

"You did great," Gina whispered.

Joel reached for Val's hand. She took a breath but couldn't seem to get enough air in her lungs as Jeanette began talking about the reward money they were offering in exchange for information that would lead to Abby's return. Val felt a warmth of gratitude for their generosity, which brought its own conflicting feelings with it. Val hated being beholden to the Fishers, but she couldn't have managed such a reward herself. If it meant she was in their debt the rest of her life, it was a price she would gladly pay to bring Abby home.

26

VAL'S CAR wasn't parked in front of the farmhouse when Joel arrived later that night. He had stayed late to review the video of the FBI's interview with Bryson Gottschalk for a second time. Maddie had stated that he was home with her and their baby the night of the twenty-sixth, and both Leisa Greer and Faye McNamara had confirmed that he hadn't had any recent contact with the girls. That they knew of.

But there was something about the way he'd said, "I like all kids. There's no crime in that. I just have more fun with them than adults," that kept running through Joel's mind long after he left the Grange.

He had a key to the farmhouse and could let himself in, but with Gina staying there he decided to knock and wait for someone to answer. It was Gina who came to the door.

"Hey, Joel." She stood aside and let him pass. She wore a pair of plastic glasses and had her hair tied back in a bandana. There was a faint chemical scent on the air as if she'd been cleaning.

"Do you know where Val is?" he asked.

"She went for a drive. I don't think she knew you were coming over."

"I've got some work to do so I'll just hang out in the office if it's okay."

"Fine by me."

But the office door was locked. Val had never locked it before, and seeing it locked now immediately triggered suspicion. He checked the doorjamb first but there was no key.

"Do you know where I can find a key to the office?" he asked Gina.

"No, but I can unlock it for you. Hold on."

She went to the kitchen and returned with a long pick used for shelling walnuts. She crouched before the handle.

"This is how we'd do it when we were kids."

Joel could have picked the lock himself but it seemed less intrusive for Gina to do it. Less nosy, even though he was suddenly very curious about what was behind that door.

When Gina opened the door and flipped on the light, she gasped. The color drained from her face and a look of panic flashed in her eyes like she was considering blocking Joel from entering.

But it was too late. Joel stepped into the room and took in the ugly truth.

Red and black writing scrawled over the wall, and he quickly recognized what it was. Dates and times and details about all three girls and their disappearances. Printouts of articles and photographs were pinned to the bulletin board, taped to the wall, and scattered on the desk. Aside from the missing girls, the person featured most was Brett Rogers. Pictures of him, satellite images of his property, county property records.

"I didn't know she was doing this." Gina sounded defensive and apologetic at the same time. "She said she was storing boxes in here so I didn't bother to check."

Joel didn't answer. He followed the sprawling collection, both concerned and impressed. Had Val done all this herself or had she had help? Some of the articles were old, the kind of thing Carter would have uncovered for him back in the day. When he spotted a note about Sophie's mom complaining about the basketball coach, he knew she had to have an inside source.

Then he remembered Wesley Peters's smug expression when he'd seen Val earlier that day. Would she really turn to Wesley Peters over him? Even worse, had she been feeding Peters information? Joel's gut twisted with anger. It wasn't just that she'd stepped grossly out of line in performing her own vigilante-style surveillance of Brett Rogers. It was that she'd hidden her investigation from Joel.

If Val didn't trust him, what did that say about him? What did that mean for the future of their relationship?

Jaw clenched, he pulled up the locator app on his phone. It couldn't locate Val's phone immediately, but an hour ago it showed her on the logging road that led to the the overlook. The same place where she'd gone to spy on Brett Rogers.

Joel swore.

"What is it?" Gina asked.

"She went back to the overlook."

Gina's eyes widened. "I didn't know. She just said she was going for a drive."

"Why did you let her go?" Joel snapped. "This isn't good for her, Gina. She's got to give up this fixation."

Gina's eyes darkened. "She's a grown woman, Joel. Tell me how I'm supposed to stop her."

Joel grabbed his keys.

"This whole thing is killing her," Gina shot out as he went to the door. "While you're out interviewing suspects and following up on leads, she's sitting here watching her worst nightmare come true. Remember that when you decide to lecture her about how she shouldn't get involved."

Joel stopped, his hand on the doorknob. "I'm not going to lecture her," he said over his shoulder. "I just want her to be safe. I'm worried about her."

"Then how about spending some time with her? It's eating her up inside, Joel, and frankly, I'm scared what's going to happen after I leave tomorrow." Gina folded her arms and leaned against the wall. "She needs you, Joel. I know you're busy and I know you're trying to find KJ, but Val is slipping away and you don't even see it."

Joel released the doorknob and turned. "What do you mean?"

"Have you actually seen her eat anything in the past week? Not just fix a plate that sits there untouched, but actually eat?"

Joel faltered. "That's a pretty normal response for something like this, though."

"Sure, but Val isn't normal. She can't afford that kind of slide. She can't even risk owning a freaking scale. It's the beginning, and I'm scared. Last time she had support. She had a whole team of medical professionals and friends and even Jordan to pull her out. But who does she have here?"

"She has me, Gina. I'm not going to let her self-destruct."

Gina grimaced. "That's what we all say. But then we don't know when to intervene and by the time we try it's too late."

Joel gripped his keys. "Okay, I'll talk to her about it."

Gina didn't look convinced. "You're a good guy, Joel, and my sister really loves you. But you don't see that she's not as strong as she looks and I'm—"

A car door slammed outside and Gina cut off.

"I'll leave you to it," she said darkly.

She hurried up the stairs and Joel heard the spare room door close as he sensed a tread on the porch steps.

Val came in looking like she'd been swimming fully clothed. Her puffy coat was shiny and dripping with water. She paused to take off her muddy boots, dropping them outside on the porch.

"I saw your car," she said as she closed the door. "I didn't know you were coming over."

"Where've you been?" Despite his best efforts, his voice came out stern.

She looked past him to the open office door and her eyes widened.

"Oh...you weren't supposed to see that."

She stepped to the office and hastily turned off the light and shut the door.

"Clearly. Can you explain why the office looks like a scene from *A Beautiful Mind?*"

"It's not that bad. I just needed a way to organize my thoughts. I don't have a great big whiteboard, and I plan on painting in there so...I know it's stupid. But it's the best I can do." She passed him to go into the living room, where she stripped off her sodden coat and hung it over the fire irons to dry close to the heat radiating from the wood stove.

Some of Joel's anger retracted with her admission, and he followed her into the living room.

"Val, I'm sorry I haven't been here all week. I didn't mean to abandon you and I thought with your sister here that you would be looked after. I can take a few days off if that would help."

Val looked up from where she was warming her hands at the stove. Her messy bun was relaxed and long tendrils of wet hair clung to her neck.

"Why would you do that? How would that help?"

Joel was taken aback. "So I can be with you. Gina's going home tomorrow, right? That way you won't be left alone."

Val rolled her eyes. "You've been talking to Gina, haven't you? I'm fine. The thing I need you to do is find KJ and Abby. Sitting here and holding my hand won't make that happen. I need you to do your job."

There was an edge to her voice that stung.

"I *am* doing my job, Val. We all are."

"I didn't mean it like that. I just mean that what I really need is my daughter found. And I have no power to do that. I sit and wait and relive that day a thousand times and wonder if there's something I missed. Some clue I saw without realizing what I was seeing. Something that would help us find out who took her. But I can't go out and talk to people and look up criminal histories and collaborate with FBI forensics people and analyze lab results and whatever else you do. All I can do is sit at home and wait. And think. There's no point in you wasting your time the way I have to waste mine."

"Is that why you went up there tonight? Because you're bored?"

Her eyes sparked. "Not bored, Joel. Powerless. Completely impotent. What if the same person who took Sophie took Abby? What if it's Abby wandering around in those woods? I drove up and down that mountain long after dark wondering if I might find her."

"What about Wesley Peters?"

She drew back, surprised. "How do you know—"

Joel bit back a curse at having his suspicion confirmed, but just barely. "You do realize you could jeopardize this entire investigation by involving him, don't you? He isn't on your side. He'll say whatever it takes to get a good story."

"Yeah, I know. I'm not stupid." Val folded her arms, shifting her weight. She lowered her voice, but it was still fierce. "I haven't told him anything I shouldn't. But I need information about KJ's case too, and no one will give me any. You say the evidence absolved Brett Rogers,

303

but what evidence? How can you rule him out so completely?"

"Look, Val, I know it's hard, but you have to trust—"

"No you don't know. She's *my* daughter, not yours."

Joel felt it like a slap to the face. The room felt stuffy and close, the stove too warm.

Val caught herself and winced. "I'm sorry, I don't mean it like that. I know you love her too. But you can't know what it's like to have the one person you brought into the world ripped away from you without being able to do anything to get her back. I'm the *mom*. It's my job to fix things. To save her. To have the answers. But I'm completely useless. Who even am I without Abby?"

Her anguish was so raw that for a moment, words failed him. Instinctively, he reached for her, but she shrugged him off.

"I need to change," she muttered, moving toward the stairs.

Joel stood alone in the living room. With only the floor lamp and the fire burning behind the glass stove door for light, it had a cozy, intimate feel, softening the signs of age and decay from the threadbare carpet to the cracks in the ceiling plaster. Joel sank onto the couch, his head in his hands, trying to get a handle on his own emotions.

He was angry, but more than anything he was hurt and frustrated. And afraid. He didn't want to lose Val, and he knew this kind of thing could destroy relationships. He had to get this right. Somehow, he had to be what she needed even when he couldn't figure out what that was.

Val's words rang through his head as he waited for her to return downstairs. When the minutes stretched long, he went upstairs to find her.

Her bedroom door was ajar, and he could hear her talking in a quiet voice.

"Don't say that. He's doing the best he can."

At first he thought she was talking to Gina and he waited for a good time to interrupt, but when there was a long pause, he realized she must be on the phone.

"I'm not going to argue with you about this tonight. He's never let me down. Not even once."

Joel considered returning downstairs, but then Gina's door opened. He didn't want her to catch him listening outside Val's bedroom, so he moved down the hallway toward the bathroom as if that had been his destination all along, passing Gina on the way.

Just before he closed the bathroom door, he heard Val's voice again. She sounded angry now.

"Stop it, Jordan. Joel is nothing like you."

Hot jealousy crawled up the back of his neck. He was too tired to deal with this tonight. He needed sleep—if he could manage to get more than a couple of hours—and then they could talk about it in the morning. But all he could think about as he turned on the tap was what else Val was keeping from him.

Distracted, he fumbled with the toothpaste and ended up knocking over his bottle of aftershave. It skittered to the edge of the counter and fell, landing with a thunk in the plastic wastebasket.

With an annoyed sigh, Joel dug into the trash to retrieve it, then paused. A pregnancy stick lay at the bottom of the liner, the end capped. The window was face up, showing two solid lines, the edges smeared faintly.

There had only been once in the years he'd been married to Lacey when—two weeks after a vacation where she'd forgotten her birth control pills—she'd thought for a brief moment that she might be pregnant.

The same feeling of hopeful dread he'd felt then came back so strong now he felt winded by it.

Maybe the pregnancy test was Gina's. But if it wasn't...

Joel gripped the edge of the countertop and looked in the mirror. His eyes were bloodshot and the deep circles under them, together with his five o' clock shadow, made him look haggard and strained to the breaking point. He *felt* strained to the breaking point. If he had one more weight added to his shoulders, he would collapse.

And what a weight this would be.

A child of his own.

The thought should have thrilled him. But with recent memories of Sophie laying on the exam table—the abrasions on her ankles and wrists where she'd been bound, the bruises and lacerations on her thighs where she'd been attacked, the helplessness he'd felt as he dutifully noted her injuries to allow the investigation to proceed in advance of the official report—Joel couldn't feel anything except a sickening despair.

His thoughts turned to Val. How long had she known? Why hadn't she said anything?

But instead of being angry, he thought again about her driving up and down that logging road looking for

Abby. If the weight of a pregnancy was too great for him, how must *she* be feeling?

Immediately he knew what he had to do. No matter what, he would be the father he'd always wished his own dad had been. He'd seen Larry balance work with family life so he knew it was possible. It would be hard, but he would do whatever it took.

Removing his contacts and rubbing his gritty eyes, he returned to the bedroom.

Val's light was off, but he sensed she was still awake. When he crawled into bed and folded his body next to hers, she held very still.

"Sorry, my hands are cold," he apologized.

She didn't respond.

While he waited for his body heat to warm the cold sheets, he tried again. "You're talking to Jordan?"

Her answer was guarded. "A bit. He wants to know what's going on with the case. I figure he has a right."

"He doesn't have to go through you, though. Someone should be assigned to keep him posted."

"I don't mind. Usually, that is. Tonight he was in a mood. I think he's jealous of you."

Joel wished he could say he didn't feel jealous when he thought about Val talking to her ex-husband, but the truth was that he did. He wasn't about to admit it, though, not if it put him in the same camp as Jordan.

In the silence that followed, he felt sleep powering over him like a tide. He pushed it back so he could get the words out.

"Val? When were you going to tell me about the pregnancy test?"

He felt her sigh rather than heard it.

"I didn't want you to worry."

It wasn't really an answer to his question, but it expressed the burden she'd been carrying and he felt a stab of guilt that she'd guessed right. He wasn't ready for this and she knew it.

"I'm sorry. You shouldn't have to go through this alone."

"I didn't want to go through it at all," Val confessed. "But I'm glad you know. With everything going on, I didn't know how to tell you. And then it seemed like it didn't matter."

Joel raised up on an elbow but could only make out the faint outline of her profile in the dim light from her alarm clock.

"Why would you say it doesn't matter? This changes everything. It's huge."

Val shifted a little, turning her face toward his.

"Nothing's changed. I thought I might be pregnant but I'm not. The test was negative."

"Don't the two lines mean positive?"

"Yeah, but there was no second line."

"There was when I saw it."

"Okay, but the test is hours old. It's only the first five minutes or so that count. After that, you can't trust the results."

"Oh." Joel lay back against the pillow, relief leaking from his body. "You're sure it was negative?"

"I'm sure." Her voice sounded tight.

"Don't take this the wrong way, I just don't think I could handle that right now."

"I know. Me neither." But she didn't sound relieved. Instead, she rolled over onto her side, her back to him.

"Are you...disappointed?"

"Of course not. A baby would be a serious complication, especially now. All I can think about is Abby. It would be shockingly irresponsible to have a baby with you under the circumstances."

Even though Joel had been thinking the same thing, hearing Val say it hurt. A part of his mind warned that he shouldn't be having such an important conversation right now, but he didn't know when he might have another opportunity.

"I agree." His pulse increased with the words that waited on his tongue. "But when the time is right, Val, could we reconsider?"

There was a long pause.

"Consider having a baby? You and me?"

The incredulity in her voice made his cheeks warm.

"I love you, Val. I want to have a real family with you someday."

She rolled over to face him again. Her voice was flat in the darkness. "I had a family once. I had a husband and a daughter who were the center of my universe. But then he left me and I thought I could raise her on my own. I thought I could keep her safe, but I couldn't. I lost her and I may never see her again and my worst fear is that I might never know what happened to her. I could live the rest of my life and never know if she's alive or dead. I'll be looking at every curly-haired blonde I see in case it's my Abby." She was crying now; he could hear it in her voice. "The thought of trying to build another family makes me furious at myself. Because Joel, I want that too. What kind of a selfish mom wants to have another child when she couldn't take care of the perfect one she already had?"

Joel pulled her to him and she curled up against his chest, shaking with silent sobs.

"You're not selfish," he murmured, stroking her back. "Maybe my opinion doesn't count for much, but I think you're the most amazing mom I've ever known. And I promise you, Val, you can count on me. No matter what happens, I'll always be here for you. Now is a terrible time to get pregnant, but a part of me is a little disappointed that we're not. It would be the biggest honor of my life to be a dad, and there's no one else I'd rather do it with."

Val stilled in his arms. Her voice sounded thick and congested. "You know, those tests aren't always accurate."

Joel chuckled nervously. "Now you tell me."

She shifted and her lips brushed his. "Thank you for not freaking out on me."

"I admit I had a little freakout when I saw the stick in the trash."

Val snuggled closer. "I wouldn't call mine little."

Her voice vibrated against his chest and he relaxed, surrendering to the exhaustion sweeping him away. He wasn't sure if he was dreaming or not when he heard himself ask, "Would you marry me if I asked you, Val?"

In the silence that followed, his thoughts became increasingly disconnected and he never heard her answer, if she answered him at all.

27

VAL FELT A SETTLING INSIDE as she closed the stove door on the newly lit fire. Outside, the fog had returned, making it seem as if the world ceased to exist beyond the porch railing of the farmhouse. There was a stillness in the house, apart from the sound of water running through the pipes as Joel showered upstairs and the flexing of the stove as it warmed.

Their conversation last night had been both unexpected and inevitable. Discovering her war room, finding the pregnancy test, and then everything that had released in her. As she'd lain in Joel's arms, it had felt like he'd held all her pain and fears and, for a moment, she'd felt it lift. Just a fraction, the slightest measure of relief, but for the first time all week she didn't feel so alone.

Then he'd asked her...well, she wasn't ready to think about that. And he'd been so tired that before she could even formulate a response, he was breathing the deep cadence of sleep. For all she knew, he wouldn't even remember saying it this morning.

Deciding not to bring it up, she stood and wiped her hands on her jeans. The sound of a wheeled suitcase echoed in the upstairs hallway, a rhythmic thump as it hit each plank of the wooden floor. Gina's flight didn't leave until the afternoon, but it was a four-hour drive to the Portland airport, so she needed to get an early start.

A buzzing sent Val patting her pockets for her phone. But it wasn't her phone ringing.

She followed the sound to the hallway table where Joel's personal phone sat. She picked it up, wondering if it was important, then frowned at the name on the screen.

Maddie Gottschalk.

She answered before she thought twice about it.

"Hi Maddie," she said, returning to the stove with the phone to her ear.

There was a pause.

"Oh. Is this Val?" Maddie asked.

"Yes." Why was Maddie calling Joel? Val was filled with a sudden indignation. Maddie hadn't talked to her for months. Now that Abby was missing she was finally reaching out, but she didn't even have the decency to call Val directly.

"Is Joel there?"

"Not at the moment. What can I do for you, Maddie?"

"I don't—" Maddie began, then stopped. "I'm sorry to hear about Abby. Are you holding up okay?"

But she sounded unsure of herself and Val knew she was scrambling.

"I'm surviving." Val looked up as Gina entered the room, her suitcase next to her and a question in her eyes.

When Val didn't offer anything more, Maddie said, "Well, I hope they find her soon. If you need anything, let me know."

Yeah, right.

"Thanks. Should I tell Joel you called?"

"Uh...no, that's okay. Thanks anyway."

The line went dead and Val frowned as she slipped the phone into her sweatshirt pocket.

"Who was that?" Gina asked as she joined Val at the stove.

"Maddie, if you can believe it."

"Oh that's nice." Gina's expression lightened.

"Maybe. She was calling Joel, not me."

"Oh." Gina held her hands out for warmth. They were tanned and freckled compared to Val's. "Is she still married to Bryson Gottschalk?"

"Yeah. They have a baby. How do you know Bryson?"

"Julie Coolidge dated him our senior year." Gina grimaced. "At the time we all thought he was super cool, but I think of it now and it's kind of gross. He had to have been, what, twenty-three? Twenty-four? What was he doing hanging out with a bunch of seventeen- and eighteen-year-olds?"

Val thought back to the first time she'd met Bryson. "I only met him once but he kind of gave me the creeps. Like he was way too interested in Abby."

A footfall sounded in the hallway and Joel stepped into the light of the living room. He was dressed for work and pulling on his coat.

"Who was interested in Abby?" he asked.

"Bryson Gottschalk," Val answered. "Maddie's husband. Most men don't give your kids a second glance, but he invited us to come over just so he could get to know Abby better."

"Ugh." Gina recoiled next to her.

Joel zipped up his coat slowly. "Did you go?"

"No," Val scoffed. "I don't care how you look at it, that's just weird."

Joel nodded thoughtfully. For a brief second Val thought of the question he'd asked her last night and wondered if he remembered. Watching him now, with his expression closed and who-knew-what going on in that mind of his, she was glad she hadn't answered.

"Have you seen my phone?" he asked.

"Oh yeah." She sheepishly pulled it from her sweat-shirt pocket and handed it over. "Maddie called. Not sure why she called you instead of me. Trying to satisfy her curiosity, I guess."

Joel glanced over it, thumbs moving. "She called my personal phone?"

The way he said it snagged at something in Val's mind.

"Of course. I wouldn't have answered your work phone."

But the suggestion introduced a new thought she hadn't considered. Maybe Maddie hadn't been calling about Val at all. Maybe she was calling Joel for some-thing else entirely. Something work related.

"K, thanks." He turned to leave.

Curiosity welled up in Val. "You didn't ask me what she wanted," she blurted.

Joel looked back over his shoulder. "What did she want?"

"I don't know. Presumably to talk to you."

"I'll give her a call later then. You want coffee?"

Val's dissatisfaction burned stronger than the flames licking the wood behind her. She knew it would be inap-propriate for Joel to share anything about Maddie that was connected to his work, but the mild way he dismissed it made her suspect he knew exactly what it was about.

THE SUN WAS a gray disc through the clouds overhead, visible yet cold. If the fog could burn off, it would be a bright, sunny day—the kind of winter day that held a promise of spring. But as it was, Joel turned his coat collar up against the chill as he leaned against the Charger, watching the members of the local Baptist church file out toward their cars. Their heads were bowed, shoulders slumped, as if the clouds and cold were weighing on them as much as Sophie's death.

Owl Creek was barely a blip of a town, but there were four churches to serve the spiritual needs of residents, with access to more in the surrounding towns. He'd guessed rightly that Maddie still attended the same Baptist church she'd attended when they were young. He wouldn't approach if Bryson were with her, but as luck would have it, she was alone. She held a chubby baby on her hip, bundled up like a sausage in a coat and hat against the cold.

Joel met her at her car. Maddie's eyes narrowed when she saw him, but she didn't acknowledge him in any other way. As she buckled the baby into a car seat, she said, "My parents are expecting me."

"That's fine. I won't take up much of your time."

Maddie started the engine of her car, then shut the door, leaving it running to warm the interior. Joel waited, giving her a chance to find the words she was looking for.

"I wish you'd come to me," she finally settled on. "We've known each other since we were kids. If you had questions about my husband, why not ask me? We've had strangers at our house and coming to the bank and his workplace. It's humiliating."

"I can imagine," Joel said with genuine compassion. "That personal connection is exactly why I couldn't get involved, though. I have to take a step back on this one. The FBI is leading out on this case."

Maddie's brow was furrowed, and with effort she tried to ease it as she waved half-heartedly at a passing vehicle. As soon as the car passed, a weight of worry lined her features again.

"I swear to you that if I'd known…" She gripped her keys, her knuckles white.

"Known what, Maddie? Bryson isn't talking to investigators. If you know something that will help find KJ—"

"It's not about KJ," Maddie said. "At least, I don't

think so. He never..." She pressed her lips together and looked up at the cold sun overhead. "What am I saying? I don't know what he would or wouldn't do."

"What about Abby? Has he had any recent contact with her?" Joel kept his tone neutral but his pulse was stronger, waiting for her answer.

Maddie shook her head. "I don't think so. I want to give you something, but I don't have it with me now. It's at my parents' house."

"What is it?"

"A hard drive?" It sounded like a question and she frowned as if it pained her. "He doesn't know I have it. I'm not supposed to know it exists. We had problems a while back when I thought he was hiding a girlfriend from me." She chuckled darkly. "I only wish it was a girlfriend."

"What's on the hard drive, Maddie?"

"Child porn. Lots of it." Her eyes were bloodshot and she pursed her lips. "I'm so tired of crying. He doesn't deserve my tears. But I think of Rosie and wonder how he could—"

She choked on the words and soon tears were spilling over onto her cheeks. Joel wrapped an arm around her shoulders and she leaned against him, quietly wiping at her eyes. He had so many questions but he held back, giving her a moment to collect herself.

The baby was fussing now and Maddie pulled away, her eyes steely with resolve.

"Can you bring the hard drive to the Grange today?" Joel asked. "Someone can take your statement then."

"Yes. After I put Rosie down for a nap, I'll bring it in. Thank you, Joel."

She climbed into the driver's seat, murmuring soothing reassurances to her baby as she fastened her seatbelt. Joel's phone buzzed as he headed toward his own car.

It was Stacy Porter, and the gravity in his voice pushed thoughts of Maddie out of Joel's mind.

"Joel, we've had a lead come in from a gas station outside of Ontario, Oregon. I'm sending you an image and I want to see if you think it could be Abby."

Joel tried to dampen the excitement that flared in his chest at Stacy's words. They'd had thousands of tips since Abby disappeared, even more since the Fishers had announced the reward money. Most of the tips had amounted to nothing and were screened before they even reached the investigators. If Porter was sending this one directly to Joel, it must be a good one.

"Send it over; I'll take a look."

He slipped into his car and started the ignition as his phone buzzed. He opened the image and stared. It was a zoomed-in still frame from CCTV in a gas station convenience store. A man wearing a bomber jacket and a black beanie held the hand of a little girl. His posture was stiff and guarded.

The girl's face was partially obscured by a baseball cap, and she was wearing an oversized sweatshirt with the hood pulled up over the cap. But she had turned in such a way that the hood had shifted, revealing blond hair—loose and tangled—and a little nose and chin that—

Joel's heart skipped a beat.

"Joel? Did you get it?"

"I've got it Stacy. I think…it could be her." He took a deep breath, his hands suddenly shaking as he stared at the picture. He didn't want to overreact. He didn't want hope to push him to recklessness.

It was hard to judge the girl's size from the angle of the camera, and the hoodie was large and bulky, disguising her shape. He imagined Abby's thin shoulders and bony legs as he picked her up and swung her onto his shoulders.

"You all right, Joel?"

Joel let out a shuddering breath. "Yeah, I'm all right. I can't say with certainty, but we'd better pursue this one hard, Stacy. I'll check with Val and see what she thinks."

The triumph in Stacy's voice was palpable. "Thanks. We're on it."

Joel hung up the phone and gripped the steering wheel, trying to calm himself. Adrenaline rushed through him, giving him a burst of energy stronger than any stimulant. If that was Abby, what was she doing in Ontario?

Who was the man with her?

More importantly, where were they headed?

He checked the clock. He'd promised Maddie he would be waiting for her at the Grange, but he had a stop he needed to make first. This was news he needed to deliver in person.

28

VAL STOKED THE FIRE, noting absently that the stack of wood on the porch was shrinking. She'd gotten used to Joel replenishing the pile, but he hadn't had a day off in two weeks. He was supposed to be working twelve-hour shifts but more often than not they stretched to fifteen, eighteen, even twenty hours.

So when Joel burst through the door as she closed the stove door, Val took one look at his expression and her stomach clenched.

"What's wrong?"

Joel shook his head. "I need to show you something. Tell me what you think."

He thrust his phone her direction and she took it, confused.

A grainy black and white photo looked like it came from a security camera in a convenience store. Her eyes passed over the man with a beard and hitched when she looked at the girl.

"Is that Abby?" she asked breathlessly.

"Do you think it is?"

Val zoomed in and peered closer. "The quality isn't very good, but yes, I think it is. Joel, I think it's her! She's alive!"

Saying the words sounded an alarm in her head. *Don't get too excited. Of course you want it to be her.*

She ignored the warning and focused on the man. "Those aren't her clothes. Who's the man with her?"

"We don't know. He paid in cash. But cameras at the pump gave us a vehicle description and license plate. We're setting up an Amber Alert for all western states. And his picture will go out in a BOLO to law enforcement. Everyone will be looking for them."

"Oh Joel." Val's knees weakened and she gripped his arm. "She's not...she's not like Sophie."

Joel's smile faded. "We can't count on anything yet, Val. But this is a strong lead."

Val texted the photo to herself. "Will you share this with the media?"

"I don't know yet. I'll learn more when I go in. I wanted to show you first. But don't share it with anyone, even Jordan. And especially not Wesley Peters."

"Of course I won't."

"If it's to our advantage, the FBI will share it at the right time."

"Got it. Now get out of here. Bring me more good news."

She kissed him quickly and sent him out the door, but the heady feeling faded almost as soon as Joel left. As the quiet of the house settled around Val she could only think of the man in the photo. The man who had stolen her daughter.

She stared at the picture again. Something about him seemed familiar, but was she just imagining it because she was desperate to make connections? Trying to make sense of something that was completely senseless?

She printed the grainy photo and added it to her research wall in the office. She'd enlarged it, but the quality was so poor she had to stand back in order for the black and white pixels to make any sense. If only this were like the movies when, with a single keystroke, a blurry photo magically became clear. She stared into the man's eyes, wanting to see something that would explain who he was and why he'd taken Abby.

She was tempted to call Wesley Peters, but she stifled that thought. She'd promised Joel, and besides, the FBI had more resources than Wesley. They would figure out who he was. She just hoped it wouldn't be too late for Abby.

―――――

JOEL TURNED off the voice recorder as Maddie stood and buttoned her coat. She looked like she'd aged in the hours he'd been interviewing her. The overhead fluorescent lights accentuated dark shadows under her eyes.

"I don't know how I'm going to get through this, the shame of it. You'd think I would have known what kind of a monster I married."

"Monsters like that are very good at camouflaging. You did the right thing in coming forward."

Maddie took a deep breath and squared her shoulders. "I wish I could run away, but there's nowhere I can go. I'm not naive enough to think that people won't assume the worst."

Like you did with Val? Joel wanted to ask, but he held his tongue. He felt nothing but compassion for Maddie. He just wished she'd done the same for Val when she'd come back to Owl Creek and needed a friend.

Instead he said, "Some will. But most will know you well enough to know better. In spite of how it might seem sometimes, there *are* good people in this town."

She offered a ghost of a smile. "Maybe."

Cooper was waiting for him when he finished.

"Anything tying Gottschalk to KJ Greer?"

Joel shook his head. "Nothing that his wife identified. We'll know more when we hear back from the lab."

"I've got Willis and Keith on surveillance, so if Gottschalk so much as steps out for a smoke we'll know about it. Good work today, Joel."

Joel nodded, but he couldn't help thinking it was a little premature. Maddie stuck to her story that Bryson was home with her the night of the twenty-sixth. She'd been up several times in the night with the baby and each time he was asleep in bed.

If Gottschalk was a dead end, focusing on him wasn't going to get them any closer to finding KJ.

IT WAS hours later when Val was sitting on the couch— waiting for Joel and unable to make herself go to bed— that she finally caught it. That sliver of memory that was connected to the man in the photo.

Once she had it, she reached for her phone and texted Joel.

Adam...I can't remember his last name. Pennington, maybe? He's a longtime friend of Jordan's. That's who the man reminds me of.

Almost immediately, the triumphant feeling faded to ugliness.

Jordan.

She thought of the many phone calls and texts where she'd kept him updated on the investigation. Could he have been mining for information to stay two steps ahead of them all along?

He'd spent a week with Abby before her abduction and likely heard about the planned field trip from her. Could he have orchestrated her kidnapping?

Certainly.

But would he?

During the past harrowing week, she'd begun to see Jordan in a new light. He wasn't the cruel villain anymore. He was a heartbroken father; a grieving, help- less parent who'd lost the person he cared for most in the world.

But now, as she pulled a fleece throw tighter around her shoulders, Val felt like a fool. Anger and shame burned her from the inside out. The thought that Jordan could have arranged to abduct Abby, all while manipulating Val and earning her pity, made her feel like the biggest, most gullible idiot on the planet.

Well, not anymore.

This time she knew what he didn't. Maybe she could use it to her advantage.

She texted Joel again.

Don't let them release it to the press. If Jordan's behind this, it's best he not know what we know.

29

Rain dribbled down the kitchen window, a steady accompaniment to the scraping of a lilac branch against the side of the house. Val picked up her phone—again—and looked at the most recent text from Jordan.

> *I came across this today and about lost it. How can you stand it?*

He'd sent it just this morning. It included a picture drawn by Abby, yet another drawing of Bigfoot.

Val hadn't responded to the text, feeling a surge of anger at the thought that Jordan was using her, getting her to soften up so that he could get insider information on the investigation.

Agent Coleman had advised her to respond to Jordan's texts the way she normally would so that he had no reason to think anything had changed. But she had a hard time making herself type the words.

Finally, she settled on a sad emoji. No text.

She couldn't help thinking back to that day in Chicago. Jordan had been so willing to sign the divorce papers. She should have guessed he'd had something else up his sleeve.

Joel shuffled into the kitchen looking like he'd just rolled out of bed. Unshaven, still wearing his glasses, and dressed in the plaid pajama pants Val had given him for Christmas, he presented such a contrast to the tidy professional law enforcement officer that a thrum of affection stirred in her chest.

"I didn't hear you come in last night," she said as he bent to kiss her neck. "It must have been pretty late."

"I slept in the guest room so I wouldn't wake you."

Val checked the clock. It wouldn't be light for another hour and she wondered how many hours of sleep he'd gotten.

"How long can you go on like this, Joel? You're going to crash and burn if you're not careful."

He poured himself a cup of coffee and leaned against the counter.

"I slept in this morning. I was supposed to be in at six."

"Joel—"

"I know. Trust me, I know. Cooper wasn't too happy about me staying late last night."

"What did you find out about Adam?"

"The plates were lifted off a stolen vehicle in Madison, Wisconsin last year. Have you remembered anything else?"

"No. Jordan would know but I don't dare ask him."

"Would you be willing to talk to him over the phone? We could record it and use it as evidence if it turns out he's behind this."

"Really?" Val set down her mug. "Of course. Yeah, let's do it. Right now."

"Let me call Stacy. They'll want to help you work up a strategy."

"Okay. Will you be here?"

He hesitated only a heartbeat. "Of course. I'll go build a fire to start warming things up."

"Be direct and let him do most of the talking," Rita Coleman instructed after she joined them an hour later. "He'll reveal more than he expects if you give him space to fill. If he uses euphemisms or abstractions, try to pin him down to specifics. But talk to him the way you normally would so he doesn't suspect anything."

Dark shadows under Val's eyes spoke of sleepless nights filled with despair, but she set her jaw and nodded. Joel sat next to her at the kitchen table, one hand resting on her back. Through the soft knit of her sweater, he traced the bony ridge of her spine.

"Are you ready?"

Val nodded and picked up her phone.

The phone rang twice before Jordan picked up.

Joel fit an earpiece into one ear so he could hear. Coleman did the same.

"Val? What's going on?" Jordan's voice was warm

and soothing, as if he'd been born to be a voice actor. But he sounded guarded. On edge.

"Hi. I have news about Abby. She may have been spotted at a gas station outside Ontario."

"Wow. Okay. Um, alive or...?"

"Yes, yes, sorry I didn't say. Yes, alive."

"Oh." Jordan exhaled. "Thank God." It was barely a whisper but loaded with unspoken terror.

Joel had to hand it to him. He was convincing. But again, this was a man who had defrauded hundreds of victims by getting them to trust him. He wielded sincerity like a weapon.

"The thing is, Jordan," Val continued, "I think I recognize her kidnapper."

A pause. "You do?"

"I can't remember his name, but he was an old friend of yours."

Jordan's voice turned insistent. Demanding. "Who is it?"

"Hold on." Val raised an eyebrow at Rita who nodded in return. It was quiet as she texted the image from the gas station.

One beat. Two.

Jordan swore on the other end of the line. "It's Adam Livingston. What the hell is he doing with Abby?"

Val didn't respond right away. When she did, her tone was careful. "You tell me, Jordan."

A sound like a choke of disbelief. "You can't think I had anything to do with this."

"What else am I supposed to think?" Val's voice trembled and Joel rubbed her back for reassurance. "The man who kidnapped our daughter is an old friend of yours."

"I haven't talked to Adam in years. You can't honestly think I would be behind this. I've been going out of my mind with worry."

"Then why else would he kidnap Abby? Have you been playing me this whole time?"

"Val, I would never...how can you think I would put our daughter through that? She's got to be terrified."

Rita made a calming motion with her hands. Val took a shaky breath, her hand seeking Joel's.

"Maybe it's a revenge thing," she suggested. "Any chance he holds a grudge against you? Any reason he would do this to get back at you?"

"I don't...we haven't spoken in years. I can't think of any reason for him to do something like this."

Val slumped a little, bracing herself with an elbow on her knee, her hair falling over one side of her face like a curtain. "Please tell the FBI everything you know. There has to be something that will help."

"Of course I will. You know I would never do anything to endanger Abby."

But the only person who seemed to believe that claim was Jordan. As soon as Val hung up she said, "He's lying."

"Why do you say that?" Rita asked.

"I can just tell."

Joel thought of the catch he'd heard in Jordan's voice. The long pause. The cultivated defensiveness. He was gratified that Val could see through it too.

"I'm sorry I didn't get you what you needed," Val mourned.

"You did great. We got a last name from him, so that's important."

"From now on," Rita said, "we'd like you to limit your communications with Jordan Fisher to telephone calls. We'll record them in case he gives us anything useful. No texts, since we can't prove in court that it's him on the other end. Can you do that?"

"It feels surreal," Val said, tugging at a hair elastic around her wrist.

"What does?"

"That he has the audacity to lie to me after everything that's happened. The weird thing is, I almost believe him. It's like I haven't learned anything."

"Valerie," Rita said kindly, "men like that are drawn to people with big hearts because it's easier to get what they want. That's nothing to be ashamed of."

Val nodded, but she shrank against Joel and he held her for a long moment. Was he just imagining that her shoulders felt sharper than normal? Was he looking for signs that Gina's fears were coming true? He pushed the thought away. He couldn't deal with one more thing. Not now.

They needed to get through this crisis with Abby first. Val would have to be okay until then.

30

JOEL STOOD in front of the screen showing a large topographical map. The longer the investigation progressed without turning up a clear connection between Abby's abduction and that of KJ and Sophie, the more the FBI was stepping back in the Greer-McNamara case and putting it back in the hands of the local agencies. The objective to find Abby Fisher was the FBI's highest priority—not just in the state of Oregon but across the country. They were still being generous with their resources when it came to KJ and Sophie, but much of the investigative work was put squarely back on the sheriff's office.

On the map, the location of Sophie's body had been marked with lines of demarcation suggesting how far she may have walked before succumbing to the cold based on the forensic pathologist's report. The rough terrain, the limited number of roads reaching into the mountains, the condition of her clothing and the contents of her stomach, all were pieces of data pointing them to where Sophie might have escaped from.

Or been dropped off. There was always a chance that her kidnapper had intentionally left her in the wilderness knowing it was unlikely she would survive long enough to make it to civilization.

But the scratch near her left ankle suggested she'd freed herself with a crude instrument and grazed her skin in the process. Sophie—quiet, bookish Sophie—had been a fighter.

Abby, on the other hand, hadn't made any sort of fuss when she was taken. She'd always been too trusting, too willing to assume the best of people. Now she seemed to be complying with her kidnapper, making Joel wonder if Livingston had told her he was taking her to see her dad.

"How's Valerie doing?" Lieutenant Cooper asked as he joined Joel.

"Hanging in there. Sorry I missed the briefing."

"It's fine. Did she get anywhere with the ex?"

"Not yet. But they've got an identity for the suspect and should know more soon." He sipped his coffee and turned back to the map. "So, we're expanding the search?"

"We're waiting on warrants for these properties," Lieutenant Cooper said, pointing to the map. "Not every lot has a residence, but that doesn't mean someone couldn't have staged a camp there for holding the girls. We need to know who has access to each of these properties and determine if they have any connection with our guys." Cooper gestured to another screen where the list of persons of interest was continuing to ebb and flow.

Bryson Gottschalk was on that list now, even though Maddie had given him an alibi for the night of the kidnapping. But until they knew what was on that hard drive, they weren't taking him off the list.

It would be tedious work expanding beyond county property records to look at each of the property owners in detail—cross-checking prior records, work associates, and family members who may have had access. But on a day like today when Joel's head was so full of thoughts of Jordan and Abby that he could barely think straight, tedious was good.

FOR THE FIRST time since that horrible Tuesday almost a week ago, Val was glad to be alone. After Joel and Rita left, she went straight to the office with her laptop. The rain was really coming down now, and the gushing of the gutter on the back side of the house was the only noise breaking the stillness as she opened her browser.

Adam Livingston didn't have a large internet presence. His LinkedIn profile hadn't been updated in over three years and showed a career of business consulting, real estate, and even a stint as a visiting faculty member at a community college in Milwaukee.

What would a man like that want with Val's little girl? He had to be working for Jordan. The more time passed, the more she was convinced.

She couldn't find anything related to Adam's personal life, and after searching on social media for an hour she realized that all the bearded faces were looking the same. It didn't take much to believe that any one of them could be the Adam Livingston she'd met almost ten years ago. But none of them seemed to line up perfectly with the LinkedIn profile, and without knowing anything more about him—where he went to school, where he lived now, whether or not he was married—she couldn't be sure.

Now that Joel knew about her suspect wall, she didn't feel ashamed adding to it. She knew it was embarrassingly amateurish but she'd always been a list-maker and this gave her the feeling—however false—that she was doing something productive.

She moved to a clear portion of wall near the corner and started writing down what she knew.

Adam Livingston
Age 33-37 plus or minus
Childhood friend of Jordan's (school?)
Business consultant
Real estate agent
MATC instructor

It was woefully anemic. There had to be some sort of personal connection with Jordan that would lead him to do this. Was it loyalty or blackmail? Had Jordan threatened him? Made him an offer he couldn't refuse?

If only Val could remember more about him.

The office was growing cold. She would need to stoke the fire before it went out. But first, she went to the boxes piled in the corner. When she'd set up Gina's bedroom as a guest room, she'd moved the last few vestiges of her life with Jordan here. Photo albums and legal documents that she had no current use for but was practical enough not to throw out. Now she was glad she'd kept them. She knew the FBI would have access to way more information about Adam Livingston than she did, but she couldn't sit idly by waiting if there was a chance an answer was in that box.

File folders came out one at a time, and Val sat against the wall and thumbed through each one quickly before discarding it. As the discard pile grew and spread across the hard wooden floor, she stopped and went back to the beginning. She wasn't being careful. She was looking for the name Adam Livingston, but maybe the connection was more subtle than that. Maybe some of these records, receipts, and statements were for entities owned or operated by Livingston.

His name had come up only once during the federal investigation into Jordan's fraudulent activities. Val tried to remember why. Whatever it was, his connection had been dismissed and, as far as she knew, he hadn't been investigated further.

Val closed her eyes and leaned her head back against the wall, trying to think. That had been such a tumultuous time that she couldn't remember much of anything about those days. Whatever it was that had connected him to Jordan, she couldn't recall it now.

She would need to research the business registrations for each entity, and even then it might not tell her anything. With a sigh, she pulled out the photo albums.

Jordan's albums from his youth—the kind with plastic coverings and brackets to hold the photos in place

—weren't here. Val had returned them to Jeanette after Jordan's memorial service. But she'd kept the ones of their life together, not for her sake, but for Abby's.

Val flipped through the pages now, looking for one face. There he was at their wedding, but without any facial hair. Livingston's eyes were bright, and in spite of efforts to eliminate the red eye glare from the flash, a hint of it remained as he and Jordan faced the camera together. The camaraderie of the pose, with Jordan's arm tossed carelessly across Adam's shoulder, made Val angry. Jordan had always been capable of collecting friends who were loyal to a fault. Who would do anything he wanted without thinking twice.

Even commit a felony.

Even kidnap Val's daughter.

She continued thumbing through the photo albums, though it was merely a cursory glance. She couldn't remember another time Adam would have shown up besides the wedding.

Her stomach growled and she ignored it.

A chill bite was forming on the air and she ignored it.

Not until she finished going through this box with a fine tooth comb would she stop looking.

And then, unexpectedly, she saw his face again.

It was a photo album from Christmas of 2008, back when Val was pregnant with Abby. Jordan had taken her on a holiday getaway to Park City, Utah where his parents owned a luxury cabin purchased during the 2002 Olympic Winter Games. Jordan loved skiing, and Park City had once been a favorite winter destination. But Val's visit had been clouded by pregnancy and

Jordan's ever-present memories of a previous girlfriend, so she'd preferred winter vacations at the family's cabin in Minnesota or on the sunny beaches of Costa Rica.

She didn't remember Adam being there on that trip, but there he was, standing with Jordan and Charles on the ski slopes. He sported a five o'clock shadow and his grin was radiant. If he'd traveled with the Fishers, surely she would have remembered. He must have met up with them separately.

If Adam came from a family like the Fishers, it wasn't a stretch to think that he, too, may have had a vacation home there.

Val pulled up Google maps and did a quick search.

Ontario was only six hours from Park City.

JOEL WAS deep into his search through property records when his personal phone buzzed with a text from Val.

A photo, printed on glossy paper that caught the light in a glare, showed three men in ski gear standing at the edge of a breathtaking precipice.

How about Park City, Utah? Fishers have a cabin there. Maybe Livingston does too.

Joel resisted the urge to put aside his own search.

Did you show this to Porter?

LOST IN OWL CREEK

Rita. She said thanks and to let her know if I think of anything else.

Good work.

It's a bit maddening, tbh.

I'm sure Porter will reach out to Salt Lake and get some answers soon.

While Val typed, Joel entered the next property address and hit enter.

His phone buzzed again but he barely registered it, for the name on the display was one he'd seen before.

Bobbie Jones, age 66. Nathan Weiss's mother owned property that bordered the public lands where Sophie's body was found. All at once Joel remembered how much information the hardware store manager had been able to access with Leisa Greer's phone number. She had used her rewards account at the hardware store the day before KJ disappeared, and Nathan had been the clerk. He had access to her personal information, including her address.

"Lieutenant," he called. "I might have something."

31

RITA COLEMAN HAD a careful poker face. Val expected a grin or at least a smile when she and Gretchen showed up at the house later that evening. For hours, Val had allowed herself to daydream that her phone didn't ring only because the FBI was so busy hunting down Livingston that they couldn't take time to call her. She was half convinced that her hunch about Park City had turned into a solid lead and while she sat in her house picking at a hangnail that had turned bloody and sore, they were extracting Abby and preparing to bring her home. As soon as she saw Rita's vehicle approaching, she stepped out onto the porch to greet her.

But Rita's news crushed her.

"Park City is a dead end," Rita said as she climbed the porch steps. "There's no record of Livingston owning property there and the Fisher residence is currently being leased to a family of five from Texas who have no connection with either family."

"That can't be," Val insisted. "Did they check on it in person?"

"They did. The family wasn't present, but the property manager met them there with a contract in hand."

Val's swelling anticipation burst with an ugly pain in her chest.

Gretchen's expression softened. "Do you know of any other locations where Livingston could be taking her?"

"I don't know. You're sure? They didn't...get the wrong address or something?"

"It was the correct address. But there may be other locations like that. Can you remember if he spent any time in Idaho or Montana? Colorado?"

"I really don't know. I only met him a couple of times. He and Jordan weren't that close, I didn't think. Have you learned anything else about him?"

"Livingston is the son of a former business associate of Charles Fisher's," Rita said. "He's a year older than Jordan and they spent summer camps together as young boys. There's no indication that Jordan has contacted him since being in custody, but we're monitoring Jordan's communication just in case."

"So that's it, then? We know he has her but we just have to wait for him to surface?"

"I know it's so hard to be patient," Gretchen said. "But it's only a matter of time until we find him. The word is out and his bank accounts and mobile activity are being closely monitored."

"We'll update you as soon as we know anything more," Rita said. "In the meantime, we'd like you to try

Jordan again. He's clammed up and isn't talking to us, but if you can get him talking, he might tell you something that will help."

Val felt sick at the thought of talking to Jordan again, but she agreed. She led them into the living room and dialed Jordan's number with her heart in her stomach. It rang without answering.

She tried again. And again.

"Apparently he's done talking to me, too."

Rita's expression didn't betray disappointment. She merely promised that she'd check in again first thing in the morning, or sooner if there were new developments.

"I never should have told Jordan about Adam," Val said as she followed them to the door. "Now he knows you're onto him."

"You don't know that. It was a calculated risk and it may force Jordan to communicate with Livingston, which will in turn lead us to Abby."

"Has he?"

A flicker in Rita's eyes was her only hint of frustration. "Not yet."

After she left, Val opened her laptop again to the map in her browser window. If Adam Livingston didn't take Abby to Park City, where else might he be? Salt Lake City or Denver were obvious choices. Jordan had been apprehended in Denver. Maybe he still had connections there who would help him plan a crime like this. But even if Livingston's destination was Denver, he still had to pass through Salt Lake City. Val could only hope that with law enforcement all over the west looking for him, he wouldn't make it any further than that.

JOEL COULDN'T REMEMBER a time he'd felt more pressure writing an affidavit for a search warrant. While a part of him wanted to rush it so they could get out to Bobbie Jones' property as soon as possible, he knew his efforts would be wasted if he cut corners. So he took his time carefully crafting an argument for probable cause that delineated the connection between Nathan Weiss, the Greers' visit to the hardware store, Bobbie Jones, and the location where Sophie's body was found.

In the end, the judge saw Joel's name on the affidavit and barely glanced at it before signing the warrant. "You do your homework, Ramirez. I appreciate that about you."

Joel had never been more grateful for those extra college writing classes.

The steady rain made night descend even earlier than it should have, painting the pavement an opaque black that seemed to swallow any light from streetlights, porch lights, and headlights. Storm drains that couldn't keep up with the flow of rainwater spilled over onto the road, the depth of the standing water deceptive in the darkness. Joel slowed as a wave of water splashed against the Charger's undercarriage, the slight rub of his thumb against the steering wheel the only sign of his impatience at the delay. He followed Marnie out of town and onto the county road that led up into the hills, two units behind him. Rain pounded a chorus against the roof, drowning out the radio chatter of additional units on their way.

He passed the logging road that led to the overlook where Val found Sophie's body. Bobbie Jones' property was accessed from another direction, a private road that wound for miles through the hills. He turned and began the climb up the mountain, listening as another two units reported their arrival at Nathan Weiss's residence—prepared to make an arrest if the search of the Jones property necessitated it.

A blue and red reflector marked the driveway for Bobbie Jones. Ahead of Joel, Marnie's headlights illuminated a double-wide trailer set on concrete blocks with vinyl skirting. The Chevy Impala he'd seen at Weiss's residence was parked out front on a gravel pad. Marnie went there first, shining her flashlight through the glass.

"Circle around back," Joel directed the other two deputies as he joined Marnie.

"Vehicle is clear," she said.

Together they turned toward the mobile home. The front window was covered, and blue light flickered beneath the curtains.

Joel climbed the steps with his weapon in one hand, flashlight in the other.

Rain pattered on the aluminum porch roof, sending a sheet of water directly onto the steps and streaming down his neck as he ducked under it.

Joel pounded on the door. "This is the Wallace County Sheriff's Office. We have a warrant to search these premises."

He waited a breath. Two. Three. Just before he reached for the door, it opened from inside.

Joel's light blinded the man who stood there, old and balding, easily past seventy.

"What's this all about?" he demanded.

"We're looking for Bobbie Jones."

The man glanced to the side of the room. "What do you want with Bobbie?"

"We have a warrant to search this residence and the surrounding property."

The man's jaw dropped. "She under arrest or something?"

"Where is Bobbie Jones?"

The man stumbled away from the door.

"Bobbie wouldn't hurt anyone."

Joel stepped into the house and lowered his light. Marnie followed, weapon drawn as she moved along the perimeter of the room. In the glow of the television screen, an older woman stooped over a quilting frame, needle in hand and glasses perched on the end of her nose. A floor lamp with a bendable arm was directed at the quilt that spanned the width of the room. She was caught frozen in its spotlight.

"Bobbie Jones?" Joel asked.

"Yes?" Speaking seemed to rouse her, and she lowered the needle and removed her glasses.

"You're Nathan Weiss's mother?"

"Yes," she squeaked, "but he doesn't live here."

"What's Nathan done?" the man asked.

"What's your name, sir?"

"Patten Jones," he said. "Bobbie's husband."

"We have a warrant to search this property, including the residence and any outbuildings."

Bobbie pushed herself to her feet slowly and leaned on the chair back for support. "What's this about?"

"Joel." Marnie's voice was sharp. She was standing in a corner of the room where a stack of plastic drawers were labeled in tidy, handwritten script—*Flannel, Calico, Jeans scraps.*

Draped over the top drawer were several long strips of folded flannel in light blue.

32

VAL COULDN'T SLEEP. She didn't even try. Her eyes burned and she yawned with exhaustion, but she knew that as soon as she laid down her brain would go into overdrive and she wouldn't be able to shut off her racing thoughts.

Instead, despite the lateness of the hour, she tried to call Jordan twice more. She even texted him, although Rita had explained that texting was less useful in court since it was impossible to prove who was on the other end. But he hadn't responded to that either.

Finally she went back to the office and added to the growing list of details about Adam Livingston that she'd learned from Rita. His father had died back in 2010. He'd married in 2011 but had separated from his wife last year. She claimed she hadn't heard from him in months, and strain from starting a business had contributed to the separation.

Money trouble could explain how Jordan had convinced him to do this.

"But Jordan doesn't have any assets," Val muttered as she stared at her wall of notes. "How does Adam think Jordan will be able to pay him?"

For a moment she considered the horrible thought that when Adam realized Jordan's duplicity, he would punish Abby for it.

Once again she pulled up the map. If Adam were headed to Salt Lake, he should have reached it by the time Jordan found out he'd been discovered. If he intended to go to Denver, would he risk it now that authorities were on to him?

Val pulled up the address Rita had given her for the Fishers' vacation home. She used Google street view to look at the building and knew immediately that something was wrong. It wasn't just that the photo had been taken in the summer and bright sunlight bathed the row of townhomes, their peaked roofs sharp against a blue sky.

What bothered Val was that it was a row of townhomes at all.

She frowned and peered closer. She'd only visited once, and it had been in winter when the bare trees were lit with holiday lights and cars couldn't be parked on the street overnight to accommodate snow plows. But still... this didn't feel the same.

She remembered driving up a canyon away from town, with a winding road and separate luxury cabins tucked away into the trees. "Cabin" was a misnomer. They were no more cabins than a yacht was a rowboat. She supposed that over the years the area might have been developed so that it didn't have the same remote feel, but her memory wouldn't have turned a townhome unit into a single family dwelling. And surely she would have remembered having to climb all those stairs to reach the front door.

Which left only one other possibility: It wasn't the same house.

Val's heartbeat quickened. She went to the kitchen and heated water for a cup of tea, considering the implications.

Maybe the Fishers had sold the cabin and bought a townhome instead.

Maybe she'd written down the address wrong when Rita gave it to her.

Or...and this made her hands shake...maybe someone was lying.

The property manager, perhaps. Or even someone at the FBI.

Could Jordan have enough connections to influence someone in the Salt Lake field office?

Maybe.

Or maybe Jeanette was helping him.

The thought soured Val's stomach. Would Jeanette stoop to committing a felony in order to help her son get his daughter back?

That was hard to believe. Jeanette was a forceful woman, sure, and she would bend the rules to get her way, but Val had never seen her break them.

Jordan was most likely working alone, which is why

he'd resorted to turning to a childhood friend for help instead of someone with more resources.

It was all conjecture and she knew it might fall apart under close scrutiny in the clear light of day, but she seized on it, desperate to make sense of something. She closed out Google maps and pulled up Google Earth instead. Entering Park City, Utah in the search field, she tried to orient herself from memory. She remembered downtown, with its quaint shops and over-priced restaurants. But the entire city was surrounded by mountains. It was impossible to know which canyon road led to the cabin of her memory. Besides, her visit had occurred eight years ago. Resort towns could change a lot in that amount of time.

As she scanned the area, zooming in and out to aid her search, she realized how pointless this was. She needed to remember more about their trip, to have other points of reference. She didn't have a smartphone back then, but they'd had a digital camera and Jordan had insisted on uploading her old photos to the cloud.

Browsing photos from the year 2008 now made her feel like the world had shifted. Almost all of the photos were of her and Jordan. They looked so young and carefree and she could almost feel what it was like in those days. Those days when they thought they'd grow old together. She pushed the feeling of regret away. It was long past time for what-ifs.

It didn't take long to find the pictures from that Christmas trip. Val examined them, looking for landmarks and other identifiers. Most of the photos were taken on the slopes or in town, but there was one of

Jordan where he was modeling a traditional Andean beanie made of alpaca wool that she'd picked up for him in one of the shops. His pose was clearly meant to inspire laughter, but she barely glanced at him, instead recognizing the surroundings as the bedroom where they'd stayed in the cabin.

In the photo, the blinds covering the window were open and although daylight washed out most of the view, through the trees she could just make out a stately roofline with dormer windows. She scanned the pictures to see if she could get another view. There. The top part of a sign built on thick timbers. Zooming in, she could just make out the words *Alpine Lodge*. That's right. A ski resort had been located across the winding road from the cabin, and she'd used their bathroom once when she didn't have a key to get into the cabin.

Now she knew its name.

With renewed determination, Val stifled a yawn and went back to Google.

Bobbie Jones watched in disbelief as her fabric bins were loaded into Kim's Yukon.

"You can't take that. I need my fabric. I still have to finish the binding!"

Joel and Marnie left her protests behind. There would be time for a more thorough search later, but a quick search of the house hadn't revealed any sign of KJ or Nathan Weiss, so they pulled down pieces of vinyl skirting to search under it. The cement block pillars the house rested on looked ghostly in the sweeping light.

"KJ?" Marnie called. The only motion came from a mouse skittering away from the light.

The flashlight was slick with rain in Joel's hands as he turned toward the surrounding woods. About thirty yards away, a tall shop stood in a clearing with a camper trailer parked beside it. The dirt road leading to the shop was overgrown and Joel's boots sank into unseen puddles as he approached. His waterproof coat kept him dry, and his protective vest added warmth, but rain ran down the back of his neck and dripped from the brim of his cap.

Marnie entered the camper first, weapon and flashlight drawn while Joel held the door. The little table was pulled down and an empty yogurt container lay on the floor. With quick efficiency they opened drawers, cupboard doors, pulled up the mattress and searched every nook and cranny.

Kim was waiting for them when they emerged.

"Nothing?" she asked, her voice raised to be heard above the rain.

Marnie shook her head, wiping rainwater from her eyes.

The roll-up door to the shop wasn't locked, and inside they found a parked Jeep. It was a relief to step out of the driving rain, and Marnie pitched her voice lower as she trained her flashlight on the vehicle.

"He told you his Jeep was in the shop, right?"

Joel scanned the interior of the shop, the light from Kim's flashlight joining his. Tools littered the floor and empty canning jars lined shelves. A broken rocking chair balanced upside down on a workbench and Joel stepped over a metal pail full of stained rags to work his way around the Jeep. The tires were thick with mud, and there were no signs of active repairs. No jack nearby or open hood.

While Marnie stepped around a metal oil barrel to reach the light switch, Joel shone his light through the back windows of the Jeep. A scrap of pale color that may have been a strip of fabric caught his eye, and the rubber sole of a tennis shoe peeked out from under a seat.

Breath streaming out before him, he moved to the driver's side door and raised his flashlight. Through the window, the beam reflected off a pair of eyes staring back at him.

Joel jumped back as the Jeep's engine roared to life.

Light flooded the garage, illuminating Nathan Weiss as he reversed without a backward glance, a pistol firing out the driver's side window.

Joel's ears rang and he scrambled to take cover behind the barrels as bullets pinged against the metal. Heart pounding, he could just make out Marnie calling in the description of the Jeep as it peeled out of the shop and toward the dirt road.

JOEL FOLLOWED the Jeep down the mountain road, his windshield wipers swiping furiously. The rain poured unchecked, forming sheets of light in the beams of his headlamps. The strobing of his light bar cast the thick forest in pulsing shades of red and blue.

Weiss clearly knew this road and drove recklessly, the Jeep's brake lights in danger of disappearing as he edged ahead.

The Charger's engine growled and Joel's tires skidded as he rounded a muddy corner too fast. Built for speed, the car wasn't made for a mountain road, and it bottomed out with every rut. But Joel pushed the Charger faster, trying to catch the glowing red lights that taunted him, never growing nearer. Weiss had gotten too far of a head start.

Over the radio he heard a call for air support. More units were on their way, but they were still ten minutes out.

Weiss reached the bottom of the road and turned onto the asphalt without a moment's hesitation. Joel followed, Kim's lights getting further behind in his rearview.

"Subject is armed and heading north on Glenbrook Loop," Joel said into the radio.

The Jeep swerved as it rounded a sharp corner, and the flash of a muzzle indicated Weiss was firing again, struggling to stay in control of the vehicle at the same time. Joel pushed the accelerator, scanning the road ahead and hoping for no oncoming traffic as the speedometer needle entered triple digits.

Too late, he spied water flowing across the road from a ditch on his right just as he entered a curve. The Charger hit it at full speed and hydroplaned, its tires losing contact with the road as it skidded across the water. Joel swore, gripping the steering wheel and backing off the gas as the Charger headed for the soft shoulder and steep drop on the other side. When the tires gained traction again, Joel reacted in a heartbeat, seizing control before the Charger could skid off the road.

He radioed a warning about the standing water and resumed his pursuit of Weiss, flooring the accelerator as much as he dared, praying there wouldn't be any deer with a death wish on the road tonight. When he caught sight of the Jeep's taillights turning onto the county road, he checked his speed and called it in.

Now that Weiss had reached the county road, Joel's goal wasn't to stop him. It was to drive him toward the barricade that was waiting for Weiss when he got to town. Two minutes later, Joel rounded the sharp corner by Brett Rogers's place and saw lights in the distance. The bridge which marked the entrance to town was blocked with county and federal vehicles, lights flashing red and blue. If Weiss didn't slow down...

The Jeep hit spike strips and lost control, spinning into a white county Yukon and pushing it onto the bridge. The vehicles slid into the railing, which buckled but held. Silhouetted figures scattered, seeking cover.

Joel slammed his brakes, skidding to a stop as Weiss staggered out of the Jeep. Joel exited the Charger in a crouch, gun drawn.

Cooper's voice came over a bullhorn, yelling at Weiss to drop his weapon, but the rain was pouring so hard it distorted the sound.

Joel skirted around the barricade and approached Weiss from behind, keeping a vehicle between him and the suspect. Sheets of blowing rain obscured his vision.

"Nathan!" Joel shouted.

Weiss turned, the gun in his hand shaking like he might drop it. His hair was plastered to his forehead and his mouth was twisted in anguish like he had something to say.

"It's over, Nathan," Cooper said. "Put the weapon down."

In answer, Weiss raised the pistol to his chin.

Only twenty feet and the hood of a black SUV separated Joel from Nathan.

"Wait!" he cried, shouting above the rain, his own firearm trained on Weiss. "We're not going to hurt you. We just want to talk. You don't need to do this. Put the gun down and—"

There was a flash of light and the crack of a shot. Weiss crumpled onto the pavement.

33

VAL DELETED the text and started again.

> *I know you'll think this is a bad idea, but things aren't adding up and I just have to know for myself. I'll explain later. There's a PDX flight to SLC at 9 am. I'll let you know when I land.*

She paused. It was the middle of the night and Joel hadn't come home. He also hadn't responded to her calls or texts, so he must be in the middle of something important. She couldn't wait much longer, but trying to figure out how to tell him her plans without alerting the FBI was proving to be harder than she expected.

She thought about telling Gretchen, but knew she would try to persuade her not to go. And if there was any chance that someone in the Salt Lake FBI office was helping Jordan, Val didn't want to risk letting them know she was coming.

The only person she trusted was Joel. But he wasn't here.

She wouldn't send the text. It made her feel slightly panicked to travel without her phone, but she plugged it into the charger by her bed and slipped the flip phone into her pocket instead. She printed off her boarding pass and screen shots of the location of the Alpine Lodge. It wasn't likely she could shake off the FBI if they decided to follow her, but leaving her phone behind would mean one less way they could track her.

She went to her room to pack a small bag and paused beside the bed. Joel's gun safe sat there under the side table. She knew the code; he'd insisted. He'd also insisted on taking her with him to a private shooting range in Salmon Ridge, wanting Val to be better able to defend herself if she ever found herself threatened again.

She tapped the buttons and opened the safe. Only one handgun rested there, a Glock 9 mm. The other he would be carrying with him. If she brought the 9 mm with her, she would have to check her bag, which would slow her down at the airport. But it would be worth it to have protection.

There was a time it would have been laughable to think she needed to protect herself against Jordan. But she didn't know what he was capable of anymore.

Val felt a twinge of guilt taking the gun without Joel's permission, but he'd wanted her to have access to the safe in case she ever needed to defend herself and Abby. Isn't that what she was doing now?

Her hand closed around the cold grip, and instantly she was reminded of that terrifying night when she'd fought with Hannah Quinton at the trestle bridge. Her heartbeat tripped faster, but her hands were steady as she grabbed a box of ammunition.

JOEL KNELT at the body of Nathan Weiss, hands covered in blood and brains and fragments of skull. Checking against all hope for a pulse. Nathan must have flinched when he fired because the bullet had taken off half his face. Nearby, Willis reached for Weiss's gun, then staggered to the bridge railing to vomit.

"Don't drop it," Joel warned. "You can be as sick as you want after you secure the weapon."

"Sorry." Willis wiped at his mouth.

Joel knew it was pointless, but he went through the motions of trying to save Nathan's life as he bled out on the bridge, his blood mixing with pooling rainwater. Anger heated Joel from the inside out, and when he looked up to see Cooper's face, cold rage reflected in the lieutenant's eyes.

"Did he give you anything?"

Joel shook his head.

Someone handed him a towel for his hands and he backed away as the paramedics approached.

"Are you good here?" Joel asked, looking with disgust at the dead man at his feet. The ultimate cowardice. "I'm going back up there. KJ's body has got to be on that mountain somewhere."

"Go," Cooper answered, bending over Weiss. "We'll send in more teams to help."

Joel dropped the towel on the wet pavement and headed to his car. His pants were soaking wet from where he'd knelt on the bridge, and his hands were still vaguely sticky. Deputies were extending the perimeter, placing flares to divert traffic. It would be miserable work cleaning up this mess.

Joel called Marnie as he drove.

"Weiss is dead. Took a bullet instead of surrendering."

Marnie didn't usually swear, but she made her thoughts clear with a few choice words.

"We found some cigarette packs and shoe prints," she said. "A shovel and pick axe look clean."

"That's twenty acres of rugged terrain to search. Let's make sure we've got a plan for when daylight hits."

Joel listened to the radio as units were dispatched to the mountain property, the bridge, and Nathan's personal residence. He mentally reviewed the past hour of activity, trying to account for how they'd ended up with a dead suspect. One thing was certain, if Bobbie had loaned her car to her son, she surely must have known he'd been on the property.

Did she know what he'd been doing there?

When Joel got back to the house, he found Bobbie sitting at her kitchen table. Patten stood at her side, a hand on her shoulder and a quiet rage in his eyes.

"They're getting everything wet, taking it outside like that," he said. The plastic drawers were gone now, and deputies were continuing to search the house.

"Mrs. Jones," Joel said briskly, "we have reason to believe Nathan Weiss abducted two girls and was keeping them on your property. We need to know where he hid them. This will go much faster if you help us."

She looked up at Patten, her chin quivering.

Joel leaned forward, his hand on the table, forcing himself not to shout at her. He waited until Bobbie looked at him before saying firmly, "Sophie McNamara's family will be able to bury her and say a proper goodbye. Do you want to be the one to tell KJ Greer's mother that she'll have to spend the rest of her life wondering what happened to her little girl? That she won't get the comfort of bringing her home and laying her to rest?"

Bobbie swallowed. "You'd have to check the shop. I haven't been out there in months. It's too hard since my surgery."

"Anywhere else? Any other structures or shelters on your property?"

"There's always the rental," Patten offered, laying a hand on Bobbie's shoulder.

"What rental?" It came out sharp.

"It's an old hunting cabin my dad turned into a rental," Bobbie said, stroking Patten's hand. "It's been years since anyone lived there. Probably full of asbestos and mold."

"Where is it?"

"You go up the road from here, skip the next driveway, 'cause that's the Hardy's place, and then—are you sure? I can't believe Nate would do something like that."

"Please, Mrs. Jones. After the Hardy's driveway, then what?"

She laid one trembling hand over the other "The next driveway after that on the right leads to the back side of our property and the rental. It's not marked, but if you know where to look you can see the ruts."

Joel could have hugged her. "That's good, Mrs. Jones. Thank you. If you think of anything else, let one of the deputies here know. They can reach me on the radio."

"Did you find him?"

Her question stopped Joel at the door.

"Did you find my Nate?"

Joel was conscious of the sticky residue between his fingers. "We found him. But he isn't talking."

He strode out the door before she could ask anything else.

JOEL ALMOST MISSED THE TURNOFF, in spite of Bobbie's directions, because his mind was already skipping ahead to what they might find when they got to the cabin. Evidence that the girls had been kept there? A shallow grave? He thought back to Carter hiding the body of Eliza Bellingham in the old well on Val's property. There were hundreds of acres of rugged forest in these mountains. If they didn't find KJ now, it could be years before a hunter stumbled upon her remains.

He couldn't accept that. They had to find her and give her family closure.

The side road was overgrown and blackberry bushes scraped against either side of the Charger. Joel passed through a set of weathered fence posts, with no fence or gate left standing, then was brought to a halt by a downed tree blocking the road, the spread of its roots shallow and packed with soil. He reached for his flashlight and stepped out of the car, pausing to look at the soft shoulder. Tire tracks indicated someone had been there recently.

Marnie parked behind him.

"Watch the tire tracks," he said, showing her the prints with his flashlight. He stepped around them and crawled over the fallen log, its bark slick with wet moss. The overgrown road made for slow going in the dark. The rain still hadn't let up, and the noise of its persistent drumming was accompanied by the creaking of tall firs in the wind.

Joel swept his light ahead and saw the corner of a structure just visible through the trees. He quickened his pace and drew his sidearm as the cabin came into view. It was little more than a shack, with a sagging roof and slanting porch steps. The windows were dark and the whole thing looked abandoned. As far as they knew, Nathan Weiss didn't have an accomplice, but they needed to be prepared for anything.

"Check out the door," Marnie said at his side, directing her light that way.

Sure enough, the front door looked solid and had an updated lock that didn't fit the age of the rest of the structure.

"How long was he planning this?" Joel murmured.

They circled the structure in opposite directions to identify any other exits. It was slow going, and Joel had to step around blackberry bushes that crawled up one wall and obscured a cracked window. Whatever horrors had taken place here seemed to be reflected in the lifeless despair of the cabin itself. If Joel had been superstitious, he would have guessed it was haunted.

He and Marnie met at the back of the cabin. There they found signs that a rear door and steps had once existed. But the steps were gone now, and the place where the door had once stood was boarded up. That left the front door with the new lock as their only entry point.

They made their way back to the front and carefully climbed the rotting steps to the porch, the wood sighing under their weight.

"Give me your light," Marnie directed as she holstered her weapon and retrieved her pick set.

Joel shone his light on the lock while looking over her head at the surrounding area, peering to see through the driving rain. The yard was overgrown with tall grass and blackberry bushes, and nothing appeared to be freshly disturbed. There was no sign of KJ's final resting place.

The lock gave way and Marnie opened the door. A scent of musty decay wafted out into the night as they stepped into a small hallway with aged, peeling linoleum. The bits of pattern that weren't covered in filth looked to have come straight from the fifties. A small bedroom off to the right showed a bare floor with exposed boards stained black. Water damage streaked the walls where faded wallpaper ripped and bubbled.

The room held no furniture except for a thin mattress. Joel's light rested on a wadded piece of clothing discarded on the floor. From there, he traced a line of rope to a large eye hook drilled into the floor. The scent of urine and feces was strong.

"At least he fed them." Marnie pointed to a brown fast food bag.

A skittering from somewhere down the hall made Joel whirl around and draw his gun, pointing the beam of light behind them.

"Mice?" Marnie asked with a grimace.

Across the hallway was a small living room and it took mere seconds to clear it. Aside from a pile of garbage spreading in the corner, the only occupants were a single bucket chair and a wood stove. A stack of firewood sat against the wall. The newspaper beside it looked fresh. Joel checked the date. January 8, 2017.

Very fresh.

Passing through the living room, Joel glimpsed a gutted kitchen through another doorway where a grocery bag sat on the one remaining cabinet. Above it sat a pane of glass streaked with lichen.

"Wallace County Sheriff," Joel called, his voice loud in the small space. "Is someone there?"

A muffled noise came from the back of the house. Joel exchanged a look with Marnie and stepped back into the hallway to follow the sound. She led the way, gun drawn in one hand and flashlight in the other.

Her light briefly illuminated the boarded up exterior rear door before passing over a door on the right. It was closed and swollen with water damage.

"Wallace County Sheriff's Office," Marnie said as she approached the door. "Identify yourself."

The muffled sound returned, this time accompanied by words. Words that sounded faintly like, "Help me?"

Joel's pulse jumped and he rushed to the room in two long strides. Together he and Marnie burst through the door, sweeping their flashlight beams around the room.

This bedroom was similar to the first, but on the ripped mattress a pale face looked out from beneath a pile of blankets.

The girl raised her hand to shield her eyes against the light. "Are you the police? Can you take me to my mom?"

Marnie made a sound in her throat like a gulp she swallowed down.

Joel's smile cracked through what felt like a lifetime of dread.

"Yes, sweetheart. We're going to take you to your mom."

34

WEISS HAD LEARNED his lesson after Sophie escaped. KJ was tethered with a cable, not a simple rope, and it took the bolt cutters in Joel's trunk to free her. She couldn't stand or walk, but she was anxious to leave the cabin, so Joel carried her. She weighed no more than Abby, diminished as she was by malnutrition and dehydration.

She wrapped her thin arms around Joel's neck and huddled close when he stepped into the rainfall.

"Did Nate get arrested?" she asked, her voice weak against his chest.

Marnie walked at Joel's side, illuminating the path with her flashlight. Before Joel could answer, she said, "Yes, honey. Nate won't be bothering you again."

"Where's Sophie? Is she okay?"

Joel nearly stumbled on the uneven terrain. Marnie glanced at him in concern, but he adjusted KJ's weight and continued walking.

"Right now we're going to make sure you're okay," he said. "There's an ambulance on the way and they're going to take you to the hospital where you can see your mom."

"Okay." KJ's voice was small and Joel couldn't help but think of Abby every time she spoke. Was Abby suffering the way KJ had suffered? Would law enforcement find her in time?

Sirens sounded in the distance, and by the time they reached the downed tree, two other deputies were there to take KJ from Joel. Marnie went with them, promising KJ that she wouldn't leave her side. While Joel went to get his camera out of the trunk, Kim joined him, silhouetted against her Yukon's headlights.

"If Nathan Weiss hadn't blown his brains out himself, I'd be tempted to do it for him," she growled. "Need any help?"

"Grab the lights, would you? You can pass them to me after I get over the tree."

He glanced back at Marnie's car where KJ was sitting in the front seat, the engine running. Marnie was wrapping her in an emergency blanket and handing her a water bottle. It was unreal to see her there, eyes wide and blinking as Marnie talked.

Joel turned away and headed back to the cabin. He found comfort in the routine of setting up the lights and prepping his evidence markers. It helped keep the emotion from rising in his throat as he photographed the scene. A half empty bottle of baby oil. An empty prescription bottle.

He had just finished the first bedroom when Cooper

arrived. He clapped his hand on Joel's shoulder. "It's one in a million to find her alive like this. Good work. You've all earned your shields tonight."

Joel stood aside as deputies approached the cabin with larger lights and a generator. He couldn't shake the image of KJ's eyes peeking out at him from the blankets. It filled him with an overpowering urge to be at Val's side.

"Sir, if you have enough help here, I think I need to go home."

Cooper gave him a searching look. "Give your report and go. But keep your phone close."

When Joel returned to his car, KJ was being loaded onto a stretcher to be transported to the waiting ambulance. Marnie was at her side, but she looked up and caught Joel's eye, giving him a slight nod of satisfaction.

Boxed in with more vehicles arriving, it was another hour before Joel was able to leave. Once he finally made it off the mountain, he barely noticed the drive to Val's. The whole time his mind was full of how he would break the news. She would be thrilled KJ was alive, of course. But would Leisa's miracle only throw into sharp relief Val's loss?

It was hard to be happy for a mom whose child was found when yours was still missing.

The Charger's headlights formed a tunnel up the long dirt road to the farmhouse. He passed the FBI's secondary command post—a large trailer parked on the shoulder on the edge of the property—and as he reached the top of the driveway, he slowed. The tailgate to Val's car was lifted and a boxy shape sat in the back.

A suitcase.

Tired as he was, Joel was gripped with the ugly memory of Lacey calmly standing in the hallway with her mismatched luggage next to her. The tears in her voice when she'd told Joel she needed a break to clear her head. At the time, he'd been flooded with the uncertain feeling that she expected something from him, but he didn't know the script and his lines were coming out wrong.

The feeling passed as quickly as it came. He wasn't thinking straight. Val wouldn't need to leave her own home if she were breaking up with him, and the bag was only a small carry-on size anyway.

He parked next to her car and let himself into the house. Val was coming down the stairs, heavy coat on and purse in hand. She stopped when she saw him and a guilty expression flitted across her face before being replaced with a smile.

"Hey stranger. How did it go?"

"We found her."

Val nodded grimly, and Joel realized she was making the same assumption they all had.

"She's alive."

Val's gasp cut the air. "Alive? Are you serious?"

"I freed her myself." The weight of exhaustion made his voice catch.

"Oh Joel. I can't believe it."

She stepped into his embrace and quickly pulled away again. "You're soaking wet."

"It's been a long night." He wanted to tell her everything, but he couldn't burden her that way. He needed food and a shower. He needed to work through some exercises to clear his mind so he could rest.

But the bulk of her purse reminded him of the suitcase in the car and he asked, "Are you going somewhere?"

Val tried to meet his eyes, but her gaze wouldn't stick.

"Don't be mad. There's a flight to Salt Lake that leaves at nine o'clock."

His brain was too slow. It took him a heartbeat to realize what she meant.

"Val," he said gently, "they already followed up on that lead. She's not there."

Her jaw tensed. "You don't know that. That's what they said, but you don't know that it's true. There's something else going on that doesn't fit."

"Val, it's not—"

"I know you think it's all fine, that everyone's doing their job, but somewhere, something's broken down. I looked up the address and it's not the same place. I remember. I have photos."

"So you're going to fly out there and do what? Go knock on the FBI's door and insist they listen to you?"

The color in Val's cheeks heightened, but her eyes narrowed stubbornly. "Not necessarily. I just want to see it for myself."

"And what will you do when there's nothing there?"

"Then I'll come home."

"Val, at some point you have to trust that—"

"Don't say that. Don't say I have to trust them. I don't have to trust anyone except myself. And you," she added, but it sounded like an afterthought. "I can't sit here and wait anymore. With every day that passes, Abby gets further and further away. I know she's still out there and I want to bring her home. Like KJ." Her eyes were intent, pleading.

Joel sighed. The thoughts flowing through his mind were disjointed. KJ's arms around his neck. Nathan Weiss dead on the bridge. Abby's backpack by the front door. The pregnancy test in the wastebasket. He scratched at the day's stubble lining his jaw. "Can you give me ten minutes to throw a bag together?"

She blinked. "You'll come with me?"

"You think I'm going to sit here waiting for you to come back and just hope everything is okay? No way."

She smiled and kissed him. "You're even worse at sitting around feeling helpless than I am."

Joel started up the stairs, but stopped when she spoke.

"Joel? I have something else to tell you."

He turned back and waited.

"I took your gun from the safe," she said. "I'm sorry. I should have asked. I wanted to bring protection, just in case. I was going to tell you so you didn't worry."

"You thought I would worry *less* that you took my gun?"

She cringed. "I'm sorry."

Joel sighed. They needed to get on the road if they were going to make that flight. "We'll talk about it on the drive. But let's take my truck. The roads are bad tonight."

"That's good. Maybe the FBI won't follow us in your truck."

Joel snorted. "You're trying to evade the FBI now?"

She picked at her thumbnail without meeting his eyes. "If there's any chance someone in Salt Lake is helping Jordan, I don't want to risk him finding out we're coming. I'm leaving my phone behind just in case."

Joel's humor died. "You really *are* trying to evade the FBI? This sort of secrecy isn't going to look good. You'll divert important resources while they try to figure out what you're up to instead of trying to find Abby. You sure you want to do this?"

Her brown eyes were wide and begged for understanding. "I have to try."

He shook his head. "Geez, Val. Promise me you'll never pursue a life of crime. You'd be scary good at it." He smiled to let her know he was kidding, and she smiled back in relief.

Upstairs, he changed his clothes and scrubbed his hands clean, working out the dried blood staining his cuticles. He would have rather taken a shower, but there wasn't time. While he packed an overnight bag he thought of what they would find when they got to Utah. How might Val react when she found an empty vacation home with no sign of Abby?

Val was waiting for him when he came downstairs. She paused to kiss him.

"I do trust you, you know," she said. "Even if I disagree with you."

Joel grunted. He wasn't convinced, but it was something. He took her hand and together they went out to the waiting car.

35

THE SALT LAKE VALLEY stretched as far as the eye
could see from the north to the south, hemmed in by
mountains mostly obscured by clouds. A gray expanse of
nothingness must have been the Great Salt Lake itself.
From Val's viewpoint as the jet descended, roads were
black grids carving out cookie-cutter neighborhoods. Off
in the distance was the murky outline of a city against
the snow-capped mountains. Remnants of snow lined
the roadways and made a patchy design on fields and
buildings. Val hadn't thought to check the weather, but
the sky's underbelly was steel, hinting that more snow
was on the way.

She'd worried all the way on the long drive to
Portland that they wouldn't be allowed through airport
security, even though Joel assured her that the FBI
wouldn't stop them. She hadn't relaxed until the plane
had lifted off from the tarmac.

Joel leaned against the window now, his eyes closed

and breathing slow and steady, fingers around Val's. But as the plane began its descent, he woke with a start and gripped Val's hand.

"You okay?" she asked in a low murmur, her back turned to the middle-aged man in the aisle seat whose head was bent over his phone.

Joel nodded, but his eyes looked troubled. He hadn't told her much about the previous night's events. When she'd asked him if he wanted to talk about it, he'd said, "Not yet."

To be honest, she wasn't sure how much she wanted to hear about KJ's ordeal or Leisa's reunion with her daughter. Not until she had Abby safe in her arms. She didn't need more fodder for her nightmares.

They disembarked and made their way through the Salt Lake International Airport. It was under construction, and their route to baggage claim took so long the luggage was already circling the carousel by the time they arrived.

Val let Joel handle the rental car. She felt so distracted, she had no patience for standing in line working out minutia with a bored service agent who couldn't even be bothered to make eye contact.

At last they found themselves in an SUV that smelled expensive with only four-digit mileage, heading toward the mountains in the east. The air was bitingly cold, and Val turned the heat on full blast as soon as the engine warmed.

She watched out the window as they approached the city. She spotted the Mormon temple in the distance against a backdrop of tall buildings, and the capitol building visible on a hill before her perspective was swallowed up by the sprawling city. The snow lining the road was dirty from car exhaust. Any visible grass was brown and dead. Even the neighborhoods she saw from a distance were varying shades of brown. It was as if the high desert demanded a narrow palette of colors, and survival was contingent on a willingness to comply. Already Val missed the lush greenery of home.

"Thank you for coming with me," she said, resting her hand on Joel's leg.

Joel's expression softened. "I still don't think it's a good idea."

"Which is why I appreciate you even more."

"I get veto power though. If at any point I think it's not safe or I say we need to pull the plug, you'll listen to me?"

Val pursed her lips.

"Val..."

"Okay. But don't rush me. I want to see it for myself."

"That's fine. But I don't know what we'll find when we get there. And if turns out you're right and Abby really is there, we'll need to bring in law enforcement."

"If they'll listen," Val murmured. But the idea of Abby being only an hour away almost took her breath away.

Billboards lined both sides of the highway, their clever quips drawing Val's eye and distracting her from the traffic congestion.

"I forgot what it's like to live in a city."

"Give me the country roads of Wallace County over this traffic any day," Joel grumbled, applying his brakes as someone cut him off without using their turn signal. He checked the rearview mirror and swerved into another lane.

"Actually, I was thinking about the shopping." Val watched in awe as a seemingly endless supply of strip malls and shopping centers passed her window. "Can you imagine having all this in your backyard? No more taking a whole day to go to Eugene or Grants Pass when you need something you can't find at Walmart. And yes, I remember what it was like before Pineview even had a Walmart."

"These big cities have their own problems."

"That's fair," Val said. "But Owl Creek hasn't exactly been the safe haven I was looking for."

Joel checked the rearview mirror again as they passed an exit ramp, then—at the last second—swerved onto it. The tires rattled over debris and chunks of ice collected on the shoulder.

Val gasped. "What was that for?"

Joel checked his mirrors again and accelerated to get around a large semi truck. "Just making sure we don't have company."

Val stared at him, her blood pressure spiking. "Who is it? FBI?"

"That's my guess. They were at the airport in Portland. Probably waiting for us in Salt Lake too."

Val swore. "If Jordan knows we're coming..." She leaned back against the seat in defeat.

"We're not here to stop Jordan. We're here to see if your memory is correct and if the FBI got the address wrong. That's it. If you're right, we go straight to them with our evidence. If Jordan's behind this, you know Abby is safe. There's no reason to risk our lives trying to do the FBI's job for them."

He sounded impatient as he navigated a tricky intersection with more than six lanes going both directions, then flipped a u-turn, cut through a grocery store parking lot, and came out on a narrow side street that ran under a freeway overpass.

Val remained quiet, not wanting to distract him. A couple of minutes later, as they merged onto the freeway in a different location, he released a breath and spoke more calmly.

"Of course, the most likely scenario is that this trip will be a dead end."

"I know," Val said softly. "But at least then I'll know for sure. Thank you."

Joel glanced her direction, then tapped his brakes when the car ahead of them slowed. "For coming along? Or my amazing driving skills back there?"

Val cracked a smile. "Both."

The corner of his mouth twitched. "It doesn't feel right to me, you know. Doing it like this."

"We'll just tell them I forced you into it."

Now he did smile. "I never could resist you, Valerie Rockwell."

Eventually the freeway began climbing toward the mountains, leaving the city behind. Light snow fell as they traveled through Parley's Canyon toward the resort town of Park City. It swirled on the asphalt in front of the car, forecasting even colder temperatures ahead.

Scrub oak stood leafless and forlorn against mountains that looked desolate without a comforting fringe of thick forests. Runty pines fringed bald hillsides like an old man's ring of hair. Here in the foothills the snow lay deeper, wide swaths of white broken by the occasional landslide and dotted with sagebrush. It was hard to tell where the sun should have been in the clouds that hung low and thick, blanketing the mountain peaks.

"I don't like the look of those clouds," Joel said.

"Let's hope the storm holds off until we can get back down to the valley."

As time passed, signs of civilization began sprouting up until they passed whole communities nestled among the hills. At last, ski jumps with the distinctive Olympic logos came into view against the distant mountain.

"Is that it?" Joel asked.

"Not where we're going. It's still a little ways."

When they exited the freeway, Val directed Joel toward the touristy old town, but he pulled into a little sandwich shop instead. It was made of brick and heavy decorative timbers, an aesthetic echoed by other businesses, managing to look both quaint and expensive at the same time.

"What are we doing?"

Joel gazed at her for just a moment too long. "I'm hungry," he said, "and you haven't eaten anything either. Before you argue with me, trust the man who's done more hours of surveillance than he can count. You'll be glad we took the time now."

Val wanted to protest, but she nodded instead. She didn't even argue when he ordered double.

"In case we want something later," he explained in answer to her unasked question.

The smell of the food turned her stomach, but she ate a few bites dutifully, reminding herself she was doing it for Abby.

Joel finished his off and sighed. "All right. Now that I feel a little more human, let's go find this cabin."

Gratitude surged in Val's chest. She didn't know what she would do when they reached the cabin, but she was glad she wouldn't be doing it alone.

THE STREETS of Park City narrowed and sloped sharply as Joel drove through downtown. The mountains were obscured by low-lying clouds, but Joel imagined they would form a dramatic backdrop on a clear day. It was hard to know which was more plentiful—ski resorts or high-end shops. There seemed to be no shortage of both, and he understood why a wealthy family like the Fishers would pick this as a holiday destination.

The main roads were well salted, but packed snow persisted on the less-traveled surface streets. More than once, after coming to a stop on a slope, the SUV slid backward before the tires could get traction. It was stressful, to say the least, and Joel wondered briefly if it would be wise to get a hotel for the night and look for the cabin the next day.

The firm set of Val's profile kept him from suggesting it.

The GPS led them out of town and farther up a

winding canyon road where snow-tipped pines rose on either side, nearly touching overhead. Mounded snow flanked the shoulder, cut with a snowplow's blade. Val became quiet, scanning each driveway with her knee bouncing in agitation.

At last they reached the Alpine Lodge, a historic resort that looked to be straight out of the early twentieth century, with large timbers, steeply sloped gables and a row of cheery dormer windows.

"That's got to be it," Val said excitedly. She wasn't looking at the lodge. Instead, she was leaning forward, pointing to the road on the opposite side. It climbed away from the lodge, and through the trees Joel saw several buildings staggered up the hill. "I swear it's that one closest to the road. Aren't you going to turn?" she asked as Joel passed the turnoff.

"Let's find a more discreet place to watch."

But with snow piled on either side of the road and private residences along every driveway, there was nowhere to park except back at the lodge. The parking lot was less than half full, and Joel had no trouble selecting a location that gave them a view of the properties on the other side of the road. The lot hadn't been recently cleared this far from the lodge, and snow creaked under the tires as he pulled the SUV into place.

"There you go." He shut off the engine, and the cabin began to cool almost immediately. "We're far enough away that no one will notice us."

Val nodded, but said nothing.

"Try to relax if you can. It could be a long wait."

"Relax? Never. What if she's in there right now?"

"And what if she's not? You need to prepare yourself for the strong possibility that there's no one in that cabin except the family of five who are renting it right now."

"The address they went to was wrong," Val snapped. "*This* is where Jordan and I stayed; I know it. But this isn't the address the FBI gave me. So either someone messed up big time or someone is covering for him. "

"Have you heard from Jordan at all?"

"No. I haven't been able to reach him since I told him about Adam Livingston. I think he knows we're on to him."

Joel's phone buzzed with a call from Marnie.

"Hold on, I need to take this."

He stepped outside the car, and the wind cut through him immediately, teasing out every bit of warmth from his neck to his wrists and tossing half-hearted snowflakes onto the driver's seat. There was a stillness on the air, a heavy weight of expectation as if the whole world was waiting for the clouds to release their load.

Marnie wasted no time getting straight to the point. "Hey, just checking in to see how you're doing. I know last night was rough and I wanted to make sure you're okay."

"Thanks. I'm doing all right. Val and I are..." Joel kicked at a mound of packed snow in the rear wheel well of the SUV. "Actually, we're in Utah right now."

Marnie's voice broke up. "What was that?"

"Park City, Utah. She thinks the FBI got the Fishers' address wrong. We're checking things out, just in case."

"Joel. That's not..." The rest was lost in a choppy mess.

"I'm having a hard time hearing you." Joel stepped away from the car and moved closer to the lodge, trying to improve his signal.

"What's that? You're breaking up."

"Look, I really don't think it'll amount to anything, but I need to be here for her no matter what. I'll be back as soon as I can."

Joel hung up before Marnie could argue with him. His phone was already cold against his skin and he'd only been outside for a few minutes.

"Who was that?" Val asked when he got back in the driver's seat.

"Marnie checking in."

"Did you tell her where you are?"

"Yeah, but the signal isn't great. I'm not sure how much she picked up."

Val leaned back against the seat, frowning. "What if she tells Porter where we are? You lost our tail once, but she could send them straight here. What if they try to stop us?"

"As long as we aren't doing anything illegal or inter-fering with an active investigation, there's nothing for them to stop."

Val pondered this, a worry line creasing her brow. "You're sure?"

"I'll bet there's a nice restaurant in that lodge there. If anyone asks, we're on a date."

Val's frown eased and her lips twitched in a smile.

"Unauthorized surveillance in a snowstorm? You sure know how to show a girl a good time."

"Just you wait. If it gets cold enough, we'll need to share body heat."

"Aha. Now your true motivations are coming clear."

Joel snorted. "What are you talking about? I'm only here because of you."

"That's true." Val grew serious. She held his gaze, her expression measuring. "Thank you. It really means a lot."

36

THEY'D BEEN WATCHING the cabin for over an hour before Val caught the first sign of movement. The windshield was beginning to fog up on the inside and she wiped it with her sleeve to get a better look. A man was walking down the dirt road, his coat a splash of red in the trees.

The forest here was so different than at home. There was no thick understory or tangle of blackberry bushes making the view impenetrable. Instead, when Val held Joe's binoculars up to her eyes, she could clearly see through the trunks of the pines and focus on the man's face.

"He's walking a dog," Joel pointed out. "Most likely a local."

"He is?" Val pulled the binoculars away. "Oh, I didn't notice. Well, it's not Jordan anyway."

It was only late afternoon, but the clouds were tinged with the weight of early dusk. A few flakes of snow drifted on the breeze, and Val hoped the rest of the storm would hold off a little longer.

Her eyes followed the man and his dog as they reached the main road, then turned and headed back the way they'd come. She counted at least three homes accessed from the lane, but the man didn't stop at any of them. He continued walking and disappeared around a bend, so there must have been even more homes out of sight.

The one she was most interested in was the one constructed of wood and stone that sat on the lower part of the slope. The outdoor lighting had come on, painting the gables with splashes of warmth. The windows were dark and covered, so it was impossible to know if someone was inside. Joel hadn't said as much, but she worried that once night fell, their surveillance would be over.

"I wish I'd brought a blanket." She shivered. "It's so cold."

Joel leaned over, cupped her hands in his own and blew warm breath into them.

"Better?"

"Not really. But thanks for trying."

He unzipped his jacket and tucked her hands under his arms. His torso radiated warmth. "How's that?"

"Better, except now I can't use the binoculars."

"Field glasses."

"Whatever."

She could just make out his pupils, a differentiation that was hard to spot in his dark eyes unless she was close. Close enough to feel an awakening rippling across her skin, an almost sluggish response to his nearness. A reminder of what else they'd lost these past weeks. Between his absence and her crisis, they hadn't had a tender moment between them since their interrupted dance on New Year's Eve.

His gaze dropped to her lips as if he was thinking the same thing. "I'm sorry I haven't been there for you like you needed me."

"You're here now," she said. "That's all that matters. And you make an excellent hand warmer."

"My hands are cold too, you know," he said impishly as he reached for the zipper on her coat.

Val pulled back, snatching her coat with a laugh. "No way! Stick 'em in your own armpits!"

Joel's chuckle soothed her. How long had it been since they'd laughed together?

She settled back against her seat, watching the road again as she reached for his hand.

"You know," she said seriously, "I've been thinking about what you said about someday having a family together."

"Yeah?"

She could feel his eyes on her. His voice sounded wary.

"I'm sorry I said what I did. I was...it was a rough night."

"You didn't say anything wrong."

"Except I did. I made it sound like my true family was the one with Jordan, not with you. Like I wouldn't want to have a family with you, and that's not what I meant at all. That's not how I feel."

She risked looking at him now. He was staring out the windshield, his expression inscrutable.

"You're giving me the detective face," she said dryly.

"Sorry. It's just my face."

"No. It's the look you get when you don't want me to know what you're thinking. Trust me, I know."

A smile cracked through Joel's veneer. "Okay, maybe I have a detective face. But you still haven't told me how you really feel."

"I guess I'm trying to say that you and Abby *are* my family now. Before all this happened, I was thinking that maybe, if you didn't mind the extra driving, maybe you could...stay more than just on weekends and the occasional day off."

Joel traced the logo on the steering wheel without looking at Val. "And now that everything's happened?"

Val gazed out the window. The snowfall that had teased all day was finally beginning in earnest, thick white flakes that clumped together as they fell.

"Well," she answered carefully. "I figure one of two things will happen. Either we'll find Abby and we can start that new chapter together, or my worst nightmare will come true. In which case, I'll need you more than ever."

After a long moment as Joel took this in, he finally answered. "The drive isn't that bad."

"So...is that a yes? No pressure. You can take some time to think about it."

Joel sighed and leaned forward, resting his forearms on the steering wheel. "The thing you seem to forget, Val, is that I need you too. I know I don't say it enough, but you bring a rightness to my life that just...I don't know, it just works."

"Really?" It wasn't the most romantic thing Val had ever heard, but the sincerity of it touched her.

"Absolutely." He shifted to meet her eyes. "The fact that you're surprised tells me I suck at showing you. The truth is, I thank God every day that you came back to Owl Creek. And I know it sounds like a cheesy country song, but I really do want to be the kind of man who never lets you down. I always want to be there for you."

She smiled. "I believe you. I mean, look at us." She gestured to the interior of the vehicle and the waning daylight outside.

A spark lit his dark eyes. "Well, you are by far the sexiest stakeout partner I've ever had."

"Is that right?" She kissed him then, a real kiss, not just the perfunctory kind that had been sprinkled in their comings and goings of the past week. The kind that raised her pulse and almost made the outside world melt away.

Almost.

Part of her hung back, and she knew that part would always hang back until she had Abby back. In that moment, though, it was enough. And when she pulled away, it felt like the world had righted itself again.

"There's a car," Joel said, nodding out the windshield.

Sure enough, a sporty wagon was making its way slowly up the canyon road. It turned onto the lane across from the lodge and Val's breath caught as it pulled up in front of the first cabin.

Was this the Texan family who were supposed to be renting the cabin? Or was it someone else?

Whoever was driving sat in the vehicle, the taillights on, the engine running and sending a cloud of exhaust into the cold air.

"Look at the plates," she said. "Indiana."

"Which may or may not be significant."

"Still..."

Val waited for the passenger door to open or little kids to come piling out the back. But no one did. It wasn't until the shadows deepened with twilight and the lights in the parking lot came on that the engine finally shut off and the driver's side door opened.

Val grabbed the binoculars. The figure was wearing a black ball cap and a thick jacket over a hooded sweatshirt. He stuffed his hands into his pockets and, with a furtive glance up at the cabin windows, walked to the front door.

A wave of adrenalin washed through Val, leaving her hands tingling.

"It's him," she said. "It's Jordan."

37

WHILE VAL FUMBLED with her flip phone, trying to snap a picture before Jordan stepped inside the cabin, Joel reached for his phone. A single bar.

Val swore. "It's too dark and this phone is garbage. I can't get a clear picture."

Joel switched on the engine of the rental SUV.

"What are you doing?" Val demanded.

"The service is crap here. We need to get somewhere we can call it in."

"We can't leave right now. Someone needs to watch him. You go. I'll stay here."

Joel wavered. He looked at the cabin—only a vague shadow now behind the gathering dusk and falling snow —and back at Val. Her eyes shimmered with fierce determination in the glow from the dashboard. He felt torn between a desire to take her away for her own safety and an instinct to go breach the cabin himself. Most of all, he knew that if his caution led to Jordan getting away, Val would never forgive him.

"Don't leave the car," he said firmly. "Keep the doors locked and don't let him see you. I'll go to the lodge and see if I can get a signal or borrow their phone. I'll be right back."

"I'll be here," she promised. "Hurry. If he's here to get Abby, he's not going to sit around waiting with this storm coming in."

Joel left the engine running to warm the car and jogged across the parking lot to the lodge. The snow was accumulating fast now, and a thin layer clung to his shoes. By the time he reached the lodge, he was warm enough to unzip his jacket.

He checked his phone.

No service.

He got a brief impression of a spacious interior with large timbers supporting an upstairs gallery and a vaulted ceiling overhead. Couples gathered on leather couches near a fire blazing in a massive stone fireplace. Joel headed toward the reception desk where a uniformed employee stood next to a giant grandfather clock.

She was young, college-aged maybe, and smiled in a saccharine way. "Good evening. How can I help you?"

"I need to use your phone."

Her smile stayed pasted in place. "Calls can be charged to your room if needed."

Joel pulled out his shield. "I'm not a guest."

The clerk's smile faltered. She glanced at the guests warming themselves by the fire. "I'm not really supposed to—"

"Fine. Then I need you to call the FBI office in Salt Lake for me."

Her eyes widened. "It's okay. You can use it." She thrust the desk phone toward him. "Dial nine to get out."

VAL'S HEART thumped painfully and she took a deep breath to try and calm its insistence. She reached into the back seat for Joel's suitcase and retrieved the Glock, then loaded it with shaking fingers. She sat watching the cabin with the gun in her lap and the binoculars in her hands. The lot was landscaped with shrubbery and manicured beds near the house where the eaves kept the snow off the decorative bark mulch. From this angle the front entrance was partially obscured by a cluster of aspens that sat at the home's corner. At their base sat a half-buried wagon wheel and a massive longhorn skull next to a decorative boulder, illuminated by landscape lighting that drew the eye and made it even harder to see the entrance. More aspens obscured the rear of the house as well.

Abby was in that house; Val was sure of it. Maybe she was sitting at an upstairs window watching the snow falling right now. As night descended beneath the trees, Val couldn't sit still. She looked back toward the lodge but there was no sign of Joel.

What was Jordan planning? He wouldn't stay put for long, she knew. He'd risked too much by breaking house arrest. He would be on the move soon.

When Jordan appeared on the front porch with a

duffle bag, she was out of the car before she even realized what she was doing, switching off the engine and tucking the gun into her coat pocket. The icy air bit at her exposed skin as she crossed a border of tumbled river rock edging the parking lot to climb the shoulder to the road. The snow dampened all noise, disguising her footfalls as she cut across the main road. Her breathing quickened as she climbed the incline to the cabin, ducking her head against the falling snow.

Jordan was at the back of the car now. He tossed the duffle bag into the cargo area and pushed the button to close the lift. She didn't have time to think of how she would approach him. She just moved, driven to stop him any way possible.

He looked up as she approached, and panic flashed across his face.

"Val, what are you doing here?"

"Where is she?" Val demanded.

Jordan swore and glanced back at the cabin. "You shouldn't be here."

"She's my daughter! You have no right—"

"Yeah, she's my daughter too. I'm trying to keep her safe."

"By kidnapping her? What is wrong with you?"

His eyes were bloodshot and he had several days' worth of stubble on his jaw. He had a wild look in his eye as he grabbed her arm. Val gasped.

"Get out of here, Val. I'll explain when I—"

The front door of the cabin opened and Val looked up expectantly. But it wasn't Abby standing there. Instead, the shape of a man was silhouetted against the interior. A chandelier was visible through a decorative elliptical window above the door, and two narrow windows flanked either side of the entrance, glowing faintly from within.

"Bring her inside," the man said.

Jordan hesitated.

"I want to see my daughter." Val shook her arm from Jordan's grip and walked up the path to the cabin.

She recognized Adam Livingston as he stepped aside to let her in. Only then did she see the handgun in his grip. She balked but continued, thinking of the gun in her own coat pocket. Hoping Jordan wouldn't let Adam hurt her.

She recognized the vaulted entryway with the curving staircase and glimpsed a darkened sitting room off to the side. Abby wasn't anywhere in sight.

"Abby!" she called, heart racing. "Where is she?"

"She's in the basement," Adam said.

Of course. There were bedrooms in the basement where Abby wouldn't be seen like she might from an upstairs window.

"Val, don't do this," Jordan said. "Just go. I promise it's for the best if you leave."

But Val wasn't listening. She knew where the basement was and jogged to the door and down the stairs.

"Abby? I'm here."

The stairs opened onto a lounge space with a mini bar. Built on the slope as it was, the windows here sat at ground level, making the finished basement feel spacious. The room was empty, so Val went to the nearest of the closed bedroom doors. But just as she reached it, hands grabbed her from behind and shoved her against the wall. The cold muzzle of a gun pressed against her jaw.

"Adam!" Jordan cried. "That's enough, she's not—"

But Adam was pushing her toward another door.

"Open it," he directed Jordan.

"This is going too far. She's not going to—"

"Open it or I swear I'll end it right now."

Val tasted fear like metal in her throat. Jordan looked as scared as she felt.

Jordan obeyed, opening a door to a room lined in cement with empty aluminum shelving. Some kind of cellar or cold storage.

"Here," Adam directed, digging thick zip ties out of his pocket. "Tie her hands and feet and secure her to the shelves."

"Jordan, don't—"

"Shut-up," Adam snapped. The gun pushed against her throat and she gasped reflexively.

Jordan approached with thick plastic zip ties, and she wanted to fight him off, but the pressure of the gun made her sweat. Instead, she begged him silently with her eyes, willing him to have compassion.

"It's going to be okay, Val," Jordan said as he bound her wrists. The plastic was tight and cut into her skin. Then he fastened another zip tie to bind her hands to the post of the nearest shelf before binding her feet. "Don't worry. Abby's safe. Everything's going to be fine."

"This isn't fine—" Val began, then cut off when the phone buzzed in her pocket.

"Get her phone," Adam said, stepping back but keeping his gun trained on her.

Val's stomach sank as Jordan reached first for the pocket that held Joel's gun. He took it, slipping it into his own pocket, then found her flip phone and silenced the call.

"I don't think so," Adam said. "Hand it over."

Reluctantly, Jordan gave him Joel's gun and Adam pocketed it, then gestured with his gun to Jordan.

"Who else did you tell?" Adam said.

"No one else," Jordan said calmly. "There's been a change of plans. Abby needs her mom. But Val's not going to tell anyone, I made sure of that."

What was he talking about? Jordan was lying so smoothly that for a minute Val almost believed him herself.

Adam turned to her. "How did you know about this place? He said he would get the property records fixed so if anyone was looking they wouldn't find us."

Val's head spun. What was the right answer? What could she say?

"I've been here before," she said. "A long time ago."

"Who else knows?"

"No one. I came alone, just like Jordan said."

Jordan's eyes flickered to hers, measuring. She wasn't sure if it was the right thing to say or not, but instinct kept her silent. Any advantage Joel had would be lost if they knew he was coming.

"You see?" Jordan asked. "This is unnecessary. We don't need to tie her up."

Adam's frown deepened. "We'll see. It's time you get on the road."

"Jordan, don't leave me here," Val pleaded. "Please."

But it was no use. Jordan turned and left the room. Adam swung the big metal door shut and with the sound of a key turning outside, slid the dead bolt into place. Then, to make matters worse, the lights went out, leaving her in the dark.

38

JOEL'S MIND WAS BUZZING. He'd called 911 first, knowing local law enforcement could respond sooner than any FBI field office in Salt Lake City. But it had taken far too long to explain to the dispatcher what he needed. He confused him further by getting the name of the resort wrong, until the hospitality clerk corrected him and helpfully offered the address.

She stood by with a wrinkle of concern between her brows, now fully engaged in assisting him however she could. When a guest came to ask for more towels for the hot tub, she barely disguised her impatience.

When it was clear there was nothing more Joel could do except wait for the responding units, he left the lodge to go bring Val up to speed. The snow was falling thick now and there was no sign of his earlier footprints as he crossed the parking lot. He'd intentionally chosen a dark corner of the lot, so the interior of the rental SUV was lost in shadow. But as he drew near, an alarm sounded in his mind and he broke into a jog.

He'd left the car running, but there wasn't any exhaust coming from the tailpipe. When he opened the door, Val's seat was empty.

She was gone.

VAL TRIED to guess how much time it would take for the feds to get there. She'd been an idiot to evade them in the first place. Unless Marnie notified them of where she and Joel were, they were at least an hour away.

It was cold in the storage room and she was grateful for her coat, but the concrete floor made her ache after only a few minutes, and her jeans—wet from walking through the snow—chilled her further. Jordan hadn't fastened the zip ties around her wrists as tight as he could have, but they still rubbed painfully. The awkward position pulled on her shoulders, and she tried to shift to relieve the pain, but nothing helped.

Waiting outside had been stressful, but waiting in this concrete box with no phone, no clock, and no daylight was agonizing. Her anxiety was ramping up to panic attack levels. How long would it take Jordan to grab Abby and run? He didn't seem to want to hurt Val, but how long would it be before authorities found her? What was Jordan's plan? He'd fled overseas before; he knew how to disappear, and Val knew with certainty that this time, he wouldn't make the mistake of coming back.

If he made it out of the country, she would never see Abby again.

She wasn't sure how much time had passed when a dull thump sounded overhead. Was it rescue?

Her hips ached and she had a hard time pushing herself to a standing position without the use of her hands. She stared in the direction of the door, willing some shred of light to appear and serve as an anchor. But the door was sealed too tightly.

Like a tomb.

Please, Joel.

Light suddenly flooded the room, making her flinch. Her eyes barely had time to adjust before the door opened and Jordan stumbled inside. Adam stood at the door, his breathing accelerated.

Val gaped.

Jordan's nose was bleeding and his lip was split and swollen. The right side of his face was puffy and an angry gash lined his cheekbone.

"What happened?" she blurted.

"Sit," Adam commanded, "or I shoot her right now." He leveled his gun at Val and she stilled.

Jordan's eyes flashed mutinously, but he obeyed. Adam stuck his gun in his belt while he zip-tied Jordan's hands and feet with quick, practiced movements. He was so close; if only Val were free to grab his gun, she might be able to fight past him to the door. But as it was, with her feet bound, there was no way she could make it up the stairs before he caught her.

Adam left the room but came back again a few minutes later with a damp towel.

"That was a stupid move." He knelt in front of Jordan, wiping the blood from his nose and cheek.

Jordan's muffled obscenity drew a faint smile from Adam.

"I won't take it personally. I get paid either way, and it was an extra bonus seeing you try to take me down. Pitiful."

He dropped the bloody towel at Jordan's bound feet and left the room. This time he left the light on, a small mercy.

"Are you okay?" Val asked as soon as the door latched.

Jordan wiped his bloody nose against his sleeve, leaving a trail across his cheek. "I'm fine," he grumbled. "He went easy on me, all things considered."

"What happened?"

"I tried to get the gun from him. I thought I could get you out of here."

"I don't understand. Isn't he working for you?"

Jordan shook his head. "No. I had nothing to do with this."

"Seriously?" Val's scoff pained her throat. The dry desert air was getting to her and her thirst was acute. "How stupid do you think I am?"

"I don't expect you to believe me." Jordan leaned his head against the rack of empty shelves. "I know it looks really bad, but I swear to you that this wasn't my doing."

"Yet here you are," Val said pointedly, not trusting any word coming out of his mouth. Still, she was grateful he was there. That meant Abby was still there too. She still had reason to hope.

"When you sent me that picture of Adam," Jordan said, "that's when things started to make sense. When Abby was visiting at Christmas, she talked about going on a field trip to the hatchery. You know how she is, she has so much enthusiasm that you don't even care what she's talking about, it's just delightful to watch her getting excited about something."

"So you called up your old buddy and hired him to kidnap her?"

"No! Will you listen to me? I didn't even have a number for Adam. We hadn't been in contact for years. But I wasn't the only one who knew about the field trip."

"What are you saying, Jordan? Did your mother orchestrate this?"

"No. She's stubborn and relentless, but there are lines she won't cross. She would never do that to Abby."

But the only other person that left—

"Not your dad, surely," Val said with a disbelieving chuckle.

Jordan sighed. "Welcome to the dark side of Charles Fisher."

39

VAL COULDN'T BELIEVE IT. It simply wouldn't compute. Not Charles, her kind father-in-law who ran interference for his aggressive wife and made Val feel a part of the family. Not gentle Grandpa Fisher who sent Val a sticker activity to keep Abby entertained on the flight to Chicago.

Jordan's mouth hardened. "I thought my dad was just being a good grandpa and showing interest in Abby's life when he asked questions about the field trip. But when I learned Adam was involved, I knew it had to be my father behind it. He and Adam's dad were always close. Adam and I weren't even that good of friends; it was just one of those things where we were thrown together because our dads were friends and expected us to be by default."

"You're saying your dad hired Adam to kidnap Abby?" Val couldn't keep the incredulity from her voice. Of all the Fishers, Jordan was the one she trusted the least. As far as she knew, he was still trying to manipulate her. But it seemed best to play along for now. Whatever kept Jordan from leaving.

"I confronted him with the picture you sent me. He didn't even break a sweat, just gave me a choice. Tell the police and risk losing Abby for good, or follow through with his plan."

"Have you seen Abby?"

"She's upstairs."

Val's heart tripped. "Is she okay?"

Jordan was sitting close enough that she felt his shrug against her own shoulder. "Mostly. I think he tried not to make it too hard on her. He's been keeping her in the master closet because it's right off the bathroom but has those high windows she can't reach. He hasn't hurt her, I don't think, but she's scared. She clung to me and didn't want me to leave. I was trying to get her away from him when you showed up. And now—"

"Don't you dare blame me."

"Relax, Val." He winced as he said her name, then paused to prod his swollen lip with the tip of his tongue. "I'm not blaming you. If anyone deserves the blame, it's me."

Val's indignation subsided. "You know you're going to jail for breaking your house arrest."

"Do you think I care? My daughter was kidnapped. Nothing else matters."

"How did you do it?"

"Good old Dad again. The plan was always to get me away at some point to join him and Abby in Canada, so he simply put that part in motion sooner than expected."

"Why didn't you tell me this days ago? You went radio silent as soon as I showed you the picture."

"Well, I wasn't exactly going to bring my phone with me and give the marshals an easy chase."

"It's really hard to believe your dad would be capable of something like this."

"You'd be surprised. He can be a force to be reckoned with when he really cares about something. And he really cares about Abby. He was so mad that I didn't fight you for custody. He blamed me for giving her up and being a lousy father. I think that angered him more than the fraud."

Val paused, considering. "Why *did* you decide not to fight?"

Jordan smirked, but it turned into a grimace. "Let's see, I was facing felony charges, prison time, and a wife who wanted me out of her life. I figured I couldn't do anything about the first two, but maybe I could make things better with the third. We're going to have to work together, Val, and I didn't want to give you any more reason to hate me. I figured if I could show you that I was cooperative, you would be more willing to let me in Abby's life."

"Ah. Jordan Fisher the Master Manipulator strikes again."

He let out a breath of frustration. "It's not manipulation. It's called compromise. What judge is going to reward me custody? Cooperating with you is the best shot I have at being a part of Abby's life. And I really, really don't want to go to battle with you."

Val searched for any sign that he might be manipulating her now. But he seemed so sincere, and under the circumstances, she realized a part of her wanted to believe him. Wanted evidence that the man she'd once loved really was a good man after all.

She leaned against his shoulder.

"What about you?" he asked. "How did you get here?"

"When I looked up the address the FBI gave me, I realized it couldn't be the same cabin. I was worried someone was intentionally interfering with the investigation."

"Could be," Jordan said darkly. "My father wouldn't have attempted this without covering all the details."

"I remembered this place, so I came out here to find it for myself. I thought maybe I could talk to you and convince you to give yourself up."

"What about Joel? He's not here with you?"

"No," Val lied. "He's been busy working that other case."

"That's unfortunate. We could use a little hero action right about now."

They grew silent, and after a while Jordan said, "Val, I haven't really apologized for everything. I know it's too little, too late. And I can't really explain why I did what I did. It was...stupid is so inadequate."

"Evil? Monstrous? Cruel?"

"Okay...that's fair. All those words apply. But I didn't feel evil when I was doing it. I can't describe it. When I think about those things I did, it doesn't feel like me."

Val shifted away from him. Her tailbone was losing feeling again. "Are you looking for absolution?"

"Maybe? I know I don't deserve it. But I want you to know that if I could go back in time and do it all over again, I would. Losing you and Abby was the worst part. What it did to us—"

"I've moved on, Jordan," Val snapped. "There is no 'us.'"

Jordan fell silent. After a moment, where Val's barb hung in the air between them, he finally asked, "Does he treat you well?"

Val considered the question. In Jordan's world, the answer to that question would mean something very different. Joel wasn't one for lavish displays or grand gestures. He'd been raised by working class parents who were subdued in their affection and exacting in their expectations.

But when she thought of his gentleness, his unwavering loyalty, and his restrained confession in the car, she knew she would take all that over showy expressions any day.

"He's wonderful. I couldn't be happier."

She felt Jordan's muscles contract against her shoulder.

"Good. I'm so glad."

In the silence that followed, Val's thoughts lingered on Joel. How long before help arrived?

"Mr. Ramirez?"

Joel rubbed a hand over his face. He'd been staring out the lobby's bank of wood-paned windows at the parking lot where snow was accumulating at an alarming rate. What he wouldn't give for a radio to communicate directly with dispatch, though in this storm comms would be a nightmare.

The clerk—McKenna was her name—watched him pensively. She held the black desk phone against her shoulder and mouthed, "There's a policeman on the phone."

Joel crossed the lobby and took the receiver.

"Ramirez here."

"Yeah, this is Sergeant Rice of the Park City PD. I understand you have a situation up there at the Alpine Lodge and need some assistance."

"Yes. I expected support to arrive an hour ago."

"Yeah, that's gonna be a problem. Unfortunately there's a bad pileup at the mouth of the canyon that's tying up all units. We'll get to you as soon as we can, but it might be hours yet."

"Hours." Joel repeated it, unbelieving. "Have you heard from Special Agent Shurtleff of the FBI? They should be on their way."

"I don't know anything about that, but we're working to get this scene cleared and will send units as soon as we have a lane open. I'd advise you in the meantime to sit tight. Don't engage with the subject."

"That's not going to be possible, Sergeant. I have reason to believe the girl's mother has entered the residence and there's likely an imminent threat against her."

There was a pause on the other end of the line. "Well shoot, that does complicate things. You know, I can't advise you to put yourself in harm's way. All I can do is caution you to stay put until our officers arrive."

"Understood."

Joel hung up the phone.

McKenna hovered nearby. "Is there anything I can do to help? Do you need a ride somewhere? Someone else I can call?"

Joel considered. "Are you a praying sort of person?"

She looked taken aback by the question. "Well, yeah. Do you want me to pray for you?"

"That's about all you can do at this point."

McKenna pressed her lips together. "Okay. Good luck."

As Joel zipped up his coat, he took small comfort in the weight of the gun at his hip. If Jordan knew he was coming, he'd need more than luck and a few prayers.

40

IN THE LIGHT from the nearest streetlamp, the snow was blowing almost sideways as Joel made his way across the parking lot. He stopped at the rental car to retrieve a few things—wishing for the full kit from his work car—then crossed the road and approached the luxury cabin from the rear, staying under cover of trees as he scoped out the terrain. Wrought iron fencing bordered the manicured yard, providing a suggestion of security without obstructing the view. On the back side, basement windows sat above-ground, dark and covered with blinds.

Joel assumed the Fishers would have a security system installed for times when the residence was empty, but if he had to guess, Jordan likely deactivated it in order to avoid an accidental alert to police.

The only light on the back side of the residence came from a high window on the upper floor. Small and narrow, it looked like it belonged to a closet or maybe a bathroom, providing light without offering a view.

Hoping he was right and no one was watching him right now, he grabbed the fence and pulled himself over. The iron bars were cold on his hands, and the skin on his back strained painfully, but he managed to get across to the other side. He ran along the fence to the back of the house and approached the nearest window at ground level. It was lit by a fixture recessed into the eave overhead. If someone happened to pass on the road and glance this way, he'd be discovered.

But no one was out in this weather. Crouching next to a thorned barberry bush, he pulled out the screen, leaving it bent on one side as he tossed it to the ground. The window was secure, so he took his multitool and wrapped it in a napkin left over from the diner sandwiches, tapping the window quickly and quietly. The broken glass fell inward and he paused, waiting to hear if anyone came running. No noise came from within the house.

Finding the latch, he opened the window and quietly raised the blinds to give himself room to drop inside to the floor. He was in a bedroom that appeared neat but uninhabited, illuminated faintly by the diffused glow of exterior lighting scattered by snowfall. He moved to the interior door and listened. All was quiet.

Drawing his sidearm, he silently turned the knob and pulled the door open.

He scanned the dark basement room—couches, a wet bar, and a large flat screen television mounted to the wall —and saw at a quick glance that the room was unoccupied. Light emanated from a stairwell, giving him enough visibility to move around the room without a flashlight. Thick carpet dampened his footsteps. Snow clinging to his hair melted and dripped onto his neck. His shoes were soaked through. As he moved toward the stairs he noted bright drops of blood on the carpeted lower step.

Now the flashlight came out, and he examined the blood in its beam. It appeared fresh, and he swung the light around looking for more.

There, in front of a door that had a heavy, insulated look, was another spatter of blood. The door was locked with a simple deadbolt, and he picked it quickly.

Bracing himself for what he might find, he carefully turned the deadbolt and pushed the door open, gun at the ready.

The sight of Val sitting on the floor, arms and hands bound but otherwise unharmed, filled him with relief. Her face was pale and her lips were tinged purple with cold.

Next to her, similarly bound with thick zip ties, was none other than her ex-husband, infamous white-collar criminal Jordan Fisher.

"Joel." Val's voice cracked on the word. Her mouth was so dry and her throat ached for water. But relief flooded her limbs and made her want to weep.

He stepped into the room and dropped to her side, pulling out the blade on his multitool and cutting the zip ties around her ankles.

"What is he doing here?" His gaze flitted to Jordan.

"Good to see you too," Jordan said dryly.

"Did you find her?" Val asked desperately.

"Not yet."

"But the FBI's here? Have they caught Adam Livingston?"

"They're on their way but the storm has thrown a wrench in things." Joel finished freeing her hands and she winced as she flexed her wrists.

"You mean...it's just you?"

His mouth twitched in an almost-smile. "Don't sound so disappointed."

"Jordan said Abby is being held in the master bedroom closet. It's a big walk-in style off the bathroom on the second floor."

"Let's get you out of here first." He pulled her to her feet.

"Believe it or not, this isn't my idea of a good time." Jordan raised his bound wrists.

"I don't really care," Joel replied. "I'm here for Val and Abby."

"Joel," Val said. "We can't leave him here. Adam tied him up too. Jordan tried to free me. Adam's not working for him after all."

Joel took a closer look at Jordan. Val could see his quick assessment and the hardening in his eyes. He wasn't impressed.

"Look, I know you think I'm one of the bad guys, but I swear this time it really isn't my fault," Jordan said.

"It was Charles," Val said. Why was she feeling so defensive on Jordan's behalf? Why did she want Joel to trust him? "Adam was hired by Charles. Jordan was trying to get Abby away from them both."

Joel's closed expression told her he wasn't buying it, but he didn't argue with her. Instead, he said, "I'll free him as soon as you and Abby are safe."

A door closing overhead made Val's heart stop.

Jordan straightened. "He's coming back."

Joel scanned the room and kicked the broken zip ties under the nearest bank of shelves. "Val, you sit by Jordan. Tuck your hands and feet out of sight so he thinks you're still restrained."

Then Joel left the room and Val watched the deadbolt turn. She waited, scarcely breathing.

"Would it have killed him to cut me free?" Jordan whispered, his lips near her forehead as Val tried to angle her body to disguise that she'd been freed.

"Shh."

A key sounded in the lock and Adam opened the door, his heavy eyebrows drawn together in a scowl. "There's been a change of plans. Jordan, you're coming with me. This storm is—"

Before he could finish what he was saying, Joel appeared behind him in the doorway.

"It's over, Mr. Livingston. Drop your weapon."

Adam froze, unblinking.

"I'd prefer that no one gets hurt, but if you insist, you won't be the first scumbag whose brains come home with me today."

Val recoiled. She'd never heard Joel talk so brutally.

Adam smirked. "It's Ramirez, right? Where's your backup? I don't hear any sirens."

"Gun on the floor. Hands on your head. I swear to you there isn't a court in this country that will rule against me. And even if they do, that won't do you any good with your brains painting the ceiling."

Finally, Adam bent to lower his gun.

"Smart man. Now, hands on your head."

As soon as Adam's weapon left his hand, Val jumped up and rushed to Joel's side.

"I'm going to go find Abby."

"That won't be necessary," a voice said from the darkness behind Joel.

Val turned, taking in the muzzle of a gun before she saw the reflection of glasses and distinguished white hair.

JOEL'S MIND SPUN, scanning for any possible way to escape, while cursing himself for a rookie mistake. He should have secured the location first, but he'd been so desperate to get to Val when he saw her that he'd gone against his training. Now they were both captives.

Charles Fisher was dressed like he belonged in an ad for a travel magazine selling timeshares to retirees. Dressed in slacks and a layered v-neck sweater, he would easily fit among the wealthy tourists Joel had seen heading toward the bar in the lodge.

Next to him was a man who gave off serious ex-military vibes from his hard expression to his ramrod-straight posture. The Sig he held looked like an extension of himself, a suppressor nearly doubling the length.

"You don't need to worry about Abby," Charles said

genially. "She's safe and happy and everything will be taken care of soon. Now, I'm sure you can guess that I'll need you to lower your gun, Mr. Ramirez. I'd hate for Abby to hear anything that might upset her, wouldn't you?"

Joel's eyes were fixed on Charles' bodyguard. He crouched and lowered his gun gently to the floor. He might as well have been stripped naked for how vulnerable he felt surrendering his weapon.

Adam immediately retrieved his own gun as well as Joel's and trained them on both Val and Joel.

"That's better," Charles said. "Valerie, my dear, why don't you do the honors for Mr. Ramirez?"

"Can't we talk about this?" Val asked, blotchy pink spots appearing in her cheeks. "Please, Charles, I don't know what you think—"

"No, no time for that. The storm won't wait. But if you want to speed things up, Robert will be happy to accommodate." He smiled, showing teeth that were too perfect, too white.

Robert, the ex-military grunt, did not.

"It's all right, Val," Joel said gently. "Do what he says."

Her eyes were red as she searched his, and he could almost smell her fear. But he saw a flicker of acceptance and she obeyed.

He crossed his wrists as she wrapped the zip tie, keeping his gaze on Charles. The feeling of being restrained made his temperature rise.

When she finished, Charles said, "Good. Now it's your turn. Robert, check the cop."

"Father, is this really necessary?" Jordan objected. "You got what you wanted. Let's take Abby and go."

Charles gave his son a steely glare. "Your opinion is neither welcome nor helpful, Jordan. May I remind you that it is your shortsightedness that put us in this situation to begin with?"

Joel wondered if Charles was referring to the shortsightedness of agreeing to Val's divorce terms or his criminal past that led her to divorce him in the first place. Watching Adam bind Val filled Joel with a terrifying helplessness. Robert patted him down, removing his phone, multitool, flashlight, pick set, and extra cartridge of ammunition. Joel forced himself to hold still even as his pulse accelerated.

Adam freed Jordan next, and the younger Fisher jumped to his feet, raking a hand through his hair in agitation. But his father's expression was unperturbed, as if Val meant nothing to him. Joel tried to read Charles Fisher, the quiet, mild-mannered man who had seemed like the honey to his wife's vinegar when Joel had met them at the Grange. He couldn't reconcile Charles's previous kindness with the cold disinterest he saw now.

But Jordan's own dual nature was a little easier to understand.

"I want you to know how sorry I am that things turned out like this, Valerie," Charles said. "I never intended for you to get hurt. You were supposed to stay out of it entirely. We were supposed to be long gone by now, but Adam had a bit of weather trouble getting Abby out of Oregon."

"Please let me see her?" Val begged, her voice cracking.

"Not like this." Charles shook his head. "I don't think that's a good idea. This is going to be hard enough for her as it is. The sooner she can forget you the better."

"Please, she's my daughter."

"Yes, and you've had a good year of her all to yourself. Things didn't go so well, did they? We'll take much better care of her. She'll want for nothing and will have opportunities you could only dream of."

"Dad, come on," Jordan pleaded. "Let her at least say goodbye."

Charles narrowed his eyes at his son. "This is for you. You signed away all your rights even though I warned you not to."

"I was trying to do what's best for Abby."

"By leaving her in this woman's care? My granddaughter deserves so much better."

"How dare you treat me this way?" Val hissed. "I'm a good mom. I've sacrificed everything I could to give Abby a good life."

"Not quite everything. But you will. Come on, Jordan. Let's go see my Abby."

41

VAL COULDN'T PROPERLY BREATHE. Her lungs felt closed and tight, and her heart pounded erratically. It didn't help that with her hands tied to the shelf support, her lungs felt compressed. Her shoulders ached, and her thirst was almost unbearable. She closed her eyes, trying to push away the panic. Abby was going to be lost forever.

"Hey," Joel said from across the room. "Val, look at me."

She opened her eyes reluctantly and saw that Joel's were creased with pain.

He was twisting his wrists in the zip ties and had somehow managed to gain some space. How had he done it? Then she remembered the way he'd held his wrists when she'd put on the restraint. He'd already planned for this.

"It's okay. We're going to get out of here." He winced as the zip tie tore against his skin, but his thumb came free and the rest of his hand followed.

Val barely registered it. "I can't..." She tried to breathe through her nose and out her mouth, but her chest was seizing on its own, making it impossible for her to draw breath.

Then, impossibly, Joel was there. Using his discarded zip tie, he shimmied the long end through the lock of her own.

"Slow down. Match your breathing to mine," he said calmly as he worked. He took a long, deep breath and she tried to mimic it. Hers felt shallow and wheezing. "You're doing great," he said. "Let's try again."

The zip tie binding her to the shelving unit came free and her hands dropped. It was a relief to breathe without her hands over her head. Within seconds he'd freed her wrists as well.

"Put your hand on my chest. Feel my breath. Just like that. In and out."

She closed her eyes, trying to focus on his lungs expanding and envisioning her own expanding as well. Eventually, her breathing slowed and her racing heart calmed.

"I'm so sorry," she said. "You said not to leave the car, but Jordan was leaving and I had to try to stop him."

"Don't worry about that now. We have to leave before they come back."

"What about Abby?"

"We'll find her. But first we have to get to safety."

She pulled herself up to her feet. "Do you think they'll kill us?"

Joel paused, and in the silence she heard the truth he

wouldn't say aloud. "I don't think they'll do anything while Abby is here. But we need to be gone before they get back."

He moved to the door and held very still, listening. At last he turned the dead bolt and opened it so carefully Val didn't hear even the slightest scrape of the door latch as he turned the knob. Light from the stairwell painted a distorted rectangle on the carpet.

Joel slipped out the door and held it as Val followed, then he paused to close the door again just as quietly as before.

He reached for Val's hand and she gripped his as he pulled her toward the nearest bedroom. When she entered, she understood why. The basement window was broken.

"Watch out for the broken glass," Joel said as Val quietly closed the door. She didn't turn on the light; enough light came through the window that she could pick a path to the windowsill.

"Do you think you can pull yourself up?" Joel asked.

The bottom of the window was at chest height, and without leverage for her feet, Val knew immediately that she didn't have the upper body strength.

"I'll need your help. You go first and pull me up."

Joel hefted himself easily to the sill and crawled outside. But as he turned around and reached a hand back for Val, a noise sounded outside the room.

Val's eyes shot to the door in a panic and back to Joel.

"Quick!" he urged.

She grabbed his forearms and tried to scrabble up the wall as he pulled, but it was too late. The bedroom door flew open and the overhead light turned on, filling the room with blinding light.

Shouts of alarm and heavy footsteps sounded behind her just as her knee reached the sill. She rocked forward, but before she could gain her feet, rough arms grabbed her and pulled her back into the room.

Val screamed and Joel shouted and grasped for her, but Adam's grip was firm and he pulled her back with such force, she toppled onto him.

She caught a glimpse of Robert running toward the window with his gun drawn and had a fleeting desperate hope that Joel would get away before a bullet reached him. She thrashed, trying to gain her feet and aimed for tender parts, throat or eyeball, but Adam held fast, keeping her pinned.

She whipped her head back and felt a satisfying thunk, then swiveled and brought an elbow hard below his belt. It was clumsy, but his grip loosened and she scrambled to her feet and tore to the door.

Robert had disappeared through the window in hot pursuit of Joel, which meant she had only one hope of escape. She ran as fast as she could to the stairs.

JOEL STAGGERED BACK as Val's hands were ripped from his own. He dove away from the window just as Robert raised his weapon. The gun's silenced report sounded wrong in the night, further muffled by the falling snow.

Joel crouched low against the house and ran toward a group of aspens near the corner, feeling completely exposed. To avoid footprints, he stayed under the eaves where snow hadn't yet accumulated on the bark mulch. His gun and radio were his lifeline, and now he didn't have either.

Val's panicked scream was cut off and his heart raced, but he was listening for other noises. The sound of footsteps creaking in the snow. The drag of a barberry bush against a pant leg. The scrape of tread against a concrete edge. If this were rain falling, it would impede his hearing. But this was snow, and even though it was falling so thick now he couldn't see the lodge across the road, it was as silent as the grave.

He looked around desperately for something he could use as a weapon to disarm the gunman, but there was nothing but bark dust under his feet and snow piling across the grass.

For a moment, he worried that his pursuer had returned inside. He had to draw him away from the residence if Val was going to have any chance of fighting off her attacker.

She had to stay alive. He couldn't consider the alternative.

A flash of light was accompanied by a pop as Robert fired at Joel, the bullet biting the bark of the nearest aspen as Joel ducked out of sight around the corner.

Nineteen.

Twenty.

He couldn't help counting the seconds since he'd left Val.

A lot could happen in twenty seconds.

Joel ran the length of the house and paused beside

another grouping of three aspens, their pale bark scarred with gray striations like ghostly apparitions. There was the longhorn skull, just as he remembered it, next to a half-buried wagon wheel. The points looked wicked sharp, and when he lifted it, the whole thing weighed more than he expected. It would be awkward, but it was all he had.

Robert would be around the corner in seconds. The only way to gain the upper hand would be to surprise him and put him on the defensive.

Joel crouched down beside the dual air conditioning units just as Robert's light rounded the corner of the house. He needed room to maneuver the skull if this was going to work, but he also needed to stay hidden as long as possible.

Robert was moving cautiously, his sweeping beam just visible beyond the air conditioning units. Joel sank lower against the ground, assessing his enemy.

Robert was right-handed, which would bring his gun arm close to Joel. Perfect.

How many minutes had passed? Joel couldn't be sure. It felt like far too many. But he hadn't heard a gunshot from inside the house so he had to hope Val was okay. Adam didn't seem like the kind of guy who would do his killing up close and personal.

Joel, however, had no other choice.

VAL'S BREATHING was ragged as she tore up the stairs, fueled by pure terror that she would get a bullet in her back before she made it. The door at the top was closed and she worried it would be locked, but she threw herself against it and yanked the handle with a sweaty palm. It opened easily, dumping her into the hallway off the kitchen.

She slammed the door closed and looked for a lock, but there was none. She had to get to an exit. But what if Charles' gunman was waiting for her outside?

Making a blind choice, she rounded the kitchen and barreled toward the front door.

All at once, she lurched to a stop, chest heaving.

In the grand entryway, next to the wide, sweeping staircase, she was there.

Abby.

Val let out a choked cry.

Jordan was zipping Abby's coat, and they both turned as Val ran forward.

"Mommy!" Abby cried.

She hadn't called Val 'Mommy' in years. Val's laugh was part sob as she crouched to scoop her into her arms. She was vaguely aware of Charles standing at the outer door and held Abby tighter.

Abby smelled like urine and unwashed hair, and Val felt a rush of anger at the signs of neglect. Unshed tears burned the back of her throat.

"Are you coming with us?" Abby asked. "Grandpa says we're going on a trip."

Val's throat closed as she glanced back over her shoulder. Adam had entered the room and paused, his hand behind his back. Jordan noticed too and moved to stand protectively between her and Adam.

"I'm afraid not, my little darling," Charles said in the gentle voice Val had trusted for years. In the face of Jeanette's intensity, Charles' voice had represented safety and acceptance. Now, it filled her with dread. "Your mom can't come this time. It's just going to be you and your dad."

Abby's eyes widened. "But I miss her. Please, can't she come?" She touched Val's cheek, and her hand was so small and warm Val almost lost it, but the sight of Adam in her periphery and Charles lurking behind her dried her tears.

Whatever happened in the next few minutes, Val had to limit the harm it would cause Abby.

"I wish I could," she said, forcing a smile to disguise the tremor in her voice. "I can't go this time, but maybe next time."

Adam took a step forward and Abby's gaze snapped to him. She clenched Val's arms and shrank against her, trembling. She didn't speak, she just stared.

"It's okay, he's not going with you," Val said reassuringly. "That man, that bad man, the police are coming to get him. You're going to be safe and Daddy will take good care of you. I promise I'll see you again soon."

The lies kept coming, fueled by a wish that they could be true. She had to give her daughter this last gift. Hope.

"Come on, pumpkin." Charles pulled Abby gently away by the shoulder. "It's time to go."

Val stood and felt Jordan's hand at her waist. Instinctively she sidled away, then realized he didn't mean it as a threat when he said to Charles, "Val should come. Abby needs her mom."

Charles' eyes sparked like flint. "She'll see her again soon. Just like she said."

"But I want her to come. It will be like old times. We could be a family again." Jordan's voice was taking on an edge of hysteria.

Charles took a step forward and leaned in close to Jordan where Abby wouldn't hear.

"Either you come with me now, or you stay behind with Valerie. You choose." Charles' voice was iron as he issued the ultimatum.

In that moment, Val realized Charles hadn't done this for Jordan at all. It had only ever been about Abby. Jordan was expendable too.

"It's okay," Val said for Abby's sake. "I'll be fine and I'll see you all soon."

Charles nodded and pulled Abby toward the door. Abby burst into tears. "But I don't want to go. I just want my mom!"

Val's eyes stung as she lunged for Abby. But Charles swept her up into his arms and strode out the door before Val could reach her.

Abby's cries could be heard all the way to the car.

As soon as she was gone, Adam stepped forward, gun drawn.

Oh Joel, where are you?

Jordan whirled around. "I won't leave you, Val."

"You have to," she said desperately. "For Abby's sake. She needs you."

"But he'll kill you. I can't let that happen."

"If you stay, he'll kill us both. And then who will watch out for Abby? She'll be entirely in his control. You have to get her away from him."

Jordan's fair cheeks were pink with agitation. "I can't leave you."

Val swallowed. "Please. One of us needs to be there for Abby."

Jordan's forehead was creased with pain. He flexed his fingers in agitation.

"Get her away from him, somehow. Then you two can start a new life. Just please don't let her forget me. Make sure she knows how much I loved her." She choked on the words and hot tears spilled onto her cheeks.

Jordan seized her by the shoulders and enveloped her in an embrace. She leaned against him, the feel of him so different than Joel yet so familiar all the same.

"I can't do this," he gasped, and she knew from the shudder in his chest that he was fighting back tears.

Somehow that gave her the strength to pull away and look him in the eyes. "Yes, you can. You can do this for Abby. Do it for me."

Jordan's eyes hardened and he glared at Adam. Val waited for a toothless threat, but all he said was, "Wait until we're gone."

With that, he kissed Val on the forehead and walked out into the darkness.

42

THE DUAL AIR conditioning units formed a pocket of shadow, and there, Joel waited, pressed against the house and gripping one of the skull horns with both hands like a baseball bat.

The sound of a crying child drifted across the snow from the front of the house. A sound that sent chills down Joel's spine.

Abby.

He couldn't see Robert, and he couldn't hear his approach with the blood pounding in his ears.

But he didn't have to wait long.

Robert passed at a brisk pace, and Joel sprang to his feet, swinging the skull hard toward Robert's head. Robert swiveled and ducked as the skull connected, so his shoulder took the brunt of the hit. He staggered to the side, firing a round as he tried to recover. The skull split from the impact, leaving Joel's hands stinging. He dropped it and tackled Robert, knocking him to the ground and reaching for his gun arm.

Robert twisted on his side and bucked, and Joel's hands slipped as he tried to wrestle the gun away. Powder flew in his face, cold and wet and blinding as they grappled in the snow. He trapped Robert's trigger finger and wrenched the gun back, twisting it out of his hand.

Robert grunted in pain and reared back, connecting a fist with Joel's head. The gun went flying into the snow, skidding across the crust. Robert scrabbled on his knees toward the fallen gun, and Joel barreled into him, flattening him to the ground. The broken horn was close but when Joel tried to reach for it, Robert drove his elbow into the soft part of Joel's inner thigh above the knee. A shooting pain shot through Joel's leg and he cried out, his hold slackening.

Robert twisted free and swung a fist wide at Joel before lunging forward after the gun. Joel's hand closed on the broken horn and he dove for Robert, aiming the sharp end at his back.

His strike hit bone and the horn bounced off, tearing through clothes and skin. Robert yelled and swung around, raising the gun. But Joel was close enough to duck into his reach, close enough to avoid the firing muzzle, and close enough to feel Robert's breath as Joel thrust the horn into his abdomen, forcing it upward behind his ribs. Hooking his foot behind Robert's, Joel pushed him to the ground, driving the point further with all his weight.

Robert bellowed with pain and Joel—fingers slick

with warm blood—wrested the gun from his grasp. Robert's hand slackened and he slumped against the ground, crying out in agony. Falling snow speckled his black clothes and the blood spilling onto the frozen earth as Joel scrambled to his feet, panting from the fight.

He glanced back once to make sure Robert wasn't going anywhere, then tightened his grip on the gun and ran back toward the house.

———

A RAPID SERIES of dull shots sounded outside, making Val jump. Joel was unarmed so only one person could have fired the shots. A wave of nausea washed over her.

Adam closed the door gently behind Jordan, as if welcoming a guest. Val's view of the outside was limited to the narrow windows flanking the door, but it was enough. Through one she saw the glow of headlights as a vehicle started in the driveway.

"We'll wait until they're gone," Adam said. "Robert has taken care of your cop friend, and now it's your turn."

Val vaguely realized she was shaking. She wondered if Adam knew something she didn't. Had Robert texted him a picture of Joel's body bleeding out in the snow? She closed her eyes against the gruesome thought. If she were going to die now, she wouldn't die with that image in her mind.

"I'm going to need you to put this over your head," Adam said, holding out a stained pillowcase.

Val recoiled. "Suffocation?"

"It'll make it a little easier to clean up the mess. A tarp would be better, but I don't have time to prepare. This should at least help with the walls."

How could he be so matter-of-fact about taking a life? Val took the pillowcase with trembling fingers. Her throat was raw from thirst and crying, her cheeks chapped from dried tears.

"You don't have to do this," Val implored. "You could let me go. Charles would never have to know. You always seemed like such a nice guy. You don't really want to do this, do you?" She was babbling, trying to find the right words that would get through to him.

Adam was unmoved. "It's just a formality at this point. Now, put it on and get on your knees."

Val's lungs contracted as she slipped the pillowcase over her head. She couldn't breathe. She thought of Joel helping her calm down and the memory of his soft voice and his dark eyes that seemed to see right through to her soul made her crumple to her knees.

She thought of Abby—not unkempt, unwashed, and uncared for, but Abby smiling with reckless abandon, innocent and unafraid and exuberant with life. She thought of Joel's smile and his laugh and the gentle way he held her and the warmth of his sincerity when he told her he thanked God every day that she'd come back into his life.

She cradled either side of her head with her hands and folded, her inner strength gone. She had nothing left to fight for. She'd lost everything. *I'll see you soon, Joel,* she thought. But even that failed to give her comfort as she awaited the bullet that would end it all.

———

Joel's chest ached from the high altitude, the cold burning his lungs. He stumbled up the snowy slope—limping from the pain in his leg—and rounded the front of the house as red taillights turned onto the main road. He paused, winded.

Abby was gone.

Pain and anger combusted with a white heat in his vision as he turned back to the house. He had to find Val. Even if the unthinkable had happened, he wouldn't leave her. And then he would hunt Charles Fisher until his dying day to find Abby and bring Charles to justice.

He ran toward the front walk. Two narrow windows on either side of the door gave him a glimpse into the house. Within a breath Joel absorbed the sight of Val on her knees on the tile floor. A bag over her head. Adam Livingston standing behind her with his gun raised to her skull.

The shot rang out before Joel made the decision to act.

Four rounds.

The window shattered.

Adam jerked like a puppet.

Blood sprayed the opposite wall.

And Joel was standing there with Robert's gun in his hand and the smell of gunpowder on the air.

43

Stunned, Joel leaped into action, racing up the porch steps. He threw open the door, gun at the ready.

Val was on her feet, throwing the hood off her head and whirling around as he entered the house.

She gasped, and it choked off with a sob as she rushed for him. He caught her with one arm, but didn't take his eyes off the body on the floor, holding Robert's gun steady.

A pool of blood was spreading across the tiles from under Adam's skull. Joel didn't check for a pulse. With one arm still clutching Val, he stepped forward and slid Adam's gun away from his limp fingers.

"I thought you were dead." Val trembled, burying her face against his chest. "I heard gunshots and I thought..."

"It's all right. I'm here. I'm here." He kissed her forehead and rested his cheek against her hair, his heart thumping painfully. The image of her kneeling before Adam was seared into his brain, and he couldn't form any other words. He gripped her so hard he worried she wouldn't be able to breathe, horrified at the risk he'd taken. Relieved that she was okay. Furious that he'd had no other choice.

They held each other for a moment or an eternity, he wasn't sure, until his pulse calmed and Val's shaking stilled.

"Abby's gone," Val said when she finally pulled away.

"I know. We need to get back to the lodge." Joel engaged the safety on Robert's gun before laying it on a bench near the door. He bent over Adam and dug through his pockets until he found his own guns, including the Glock Val had taken. Val's burner phone was there too. "There was an accident at the mouth of the canyon, so Charles might not be able to get through. We need to tell them to set up a checkpoint. Did you see what he was driving?"

"Joel."

He straightened and turned to see Val watching him with wide eyes.

"Are you hurt?" She glanced at her jacket where Robert's blood had smeared from Joel to her.

Joel looked down, taking in his blood-stained clothes and hands. "It's not mine."

She nodded once. Didn't say anything else. Just gripped his hand and together they walked out into the night.

Snow swirled in the beams from the headlights as Grandpa drove down the mountain. Abby snuggled against Daddy, his arms tight around her. He smelled different than she was used to, but his arms around her felt the same. Like he was trying to help her feel safe.

But Abby didn't feel safe. The bad man hadn't come with them, but he'd stayed behind with Mom. Would he tie her up with those plastic wires? Would he slap her face and lock her in the closet upstairs like he'd locked up Abby?

Hot tears leaked out of her eyes. She thought she didn't have any tears left, but thinking of Mom somehow made more squeeze out.

Dad was watching the white road with a heavy frown. He looked mad and Abby wondered if he was mad at her. But when she sniffed her stuffy nose, he looked at her and his expression softened.

"Hey, Gabby-girl," he murmured, wiping the fresh tears from her cheeks. "It's okay. You're safe now. Everything's going to be okay."

"What about Mom?" Abby whispered so Grandpa wouldn't hear from the driver's seat. She didn't know why Grandpa didn't want Mom to come with them, but a feeling deep inside told her to keep her voice quiet. "That man is mean. What if he hurts her? He said he would if I didn't do everything he said."

Dad's arms tightened around her. Apparently she'd whispered too loud because Grandpa's eyes in the rear view mirror flickered to Abby's.

"Your mom will be fine, sweetheart," Grandpa said. "Don't worry about her. She'll come see you soon."

But Dad's mad frown had returned and all he said was, "Your mom loves you very much. She would do anything for you—" He broke off and Abby worried that she'd said something wrong.

Grandpa's hands gripped the steering wheel as the car rounded a corner and slipped a little to the right.

"We shouldn't be out in this," Dad said. His voice was tense.

"It'll be better once we get out of this canyon," Grandpa said.

They came around another corner and red and blue lights shone in the distance, blurred by snow. Grandpa swore and Abby sat up straighter. She'd never heard him use those words before. He braked and the back of the car swished a little.

Dad leaned forward. "It looks like an accident." He sounded...relieved?

They joined a line of cars waiting to pass the accident, and Abby could just make out figures moving in front of the headlights. Bulky shapes looked like a fire truck and a tow truck with a bashed up car on its trailer. Firemen had stripes on their clothes that shone in the darkness, and Abby read the words Sheriff's Office on the back of someone's coat.

She poked Dad's arm.

"That's like Joel. He works for the Sheriff's Office too."

Dad glanced up at the front where Grandpa was fiercely pushing buttons on the GPS screen.

"There's not an alternate route," Grandpa muttered. The car crawled forward. Snow had settled on the taillights of the car ahead, muting the red glow.

Dad kept his eyes on the rear view mirror and bent low to whisper in Abby's ear. "When I say, I want you to unbuckle your seatbelt. Quietly, okay?"

Abby gasped. She was never supposed to unbuckle her seatbelt.

"It's okay. I'll keep you safe. But wait until I say."

Sirens wailed and Abby looked up to see a couple of police trucks making their way around the tow truck and the smashed up cars. Dad tensed beside her, watching the cars pass.

"They're letting cars through now," Grandpa said with relief.

The car started moving and Dad reached for the door handle. Abby felt a spike of fear, but didn't know what to do. Should she try and stop him? Dad, too, seemed uncertain. He glanced at Grandpa, then at Abby, an expression on his face that made him not look like himself.

They were passing the tow truck now, a policeman waving them through, his arm circling like he wanted them to hurry. Dad let go of the door and slumped back against the seat. Abby sighed. She didn't want to go out in the snow, especially while the car was moving.

Abby whispered to Dad, but he seemed distracted.

"What was that?" He shook himself and leaned closer to her.

She lifted her chin to try and reach his ear. "We should have told that policeman to help Mom."

Dad didn't reply. He patted her knee and looked out as the road opened before them, twin tire tracks cutting through the snow from the cars ahead, leading the way off the mountain.

44

VAL STOOD over the bathroom sink, scrubbing the blood from her fingers. How was there so much blood? She'd handed over her jacket to be bagged as evidence, and now she wore an oversized sweatshirt from the Alpine Lodge gift shop, sleeves pulled up to her elbows as she tried to wash away Adam's blood.

Suddenly she understood why he'd wanted her to wear the pillowcase over her head. The memory made her shudder.

The bathroom sink was porcelain, and the countertop was a cream-colored granite, which emphasized the brown water running down the drain as she washed for a second time.

She used paper towels to wipe up as much of the spray as possible, wondering what the custodial staff would think. Hoping they used disinfectant. Her reflection in the gilded mirror looked ten years older.

She and Joel had arrived at the lodge at the same

time as the first deputies responding to Joel's call. Joel had coached her on what to expect, but the deputies' aggressive attitudes had still made her feel threatened, her heart pounding even as she reminded herself they were the good guys and were there to help. Joel seemed to know exactly what to say, though, and soon their attention was directed away from Val and toward the crime scene at the cabin.

Now she returned to the spacious lobby and discovered that more law enforcement had arrived. She couldn't find Joel in the midst of Summit County deputies and Salt Lake FBI agents and felt momentarily panicked. She knew they were all working together to coordinate a response to stop Charles, but a part of her—ridiculous though it was—couldn't help but think they wouldn't succeed unless Joel was involved.

It was Joel who had supported her by coming to Utah even when he thought it was a pointless trip. It was Joel who had helped her escape when she'd been captured by Adam Livingston. It was Joel who had stopped Adam before he could pull the trigger. If Val had any hope of seeing Abby again, the only person she trusted to make it happen was Joel.

Val moved to stand in front of the massive stone fireplace, warming herself by the crackling flames. She felt jittery and restless. Useless. Exhaustion threatened at the edges of her mind and she suspected if she sat down, she might not get up again. So she didn't sit down. Because she wouldn't rest until her little girl was in her arms again.

A coat caught her attention, the reflective letters

claiming US Marshal. She felt a sudden surge of sympathy for Jordan. He would be going back to prison after this. It wasn't that long ago that the thought would have given her a perverse sense of satisfaction. But now, she felt only sad.

The outer doors opened and Joel stepped inside, his black hair dusted white with snow. He scanned the room and made a beeline toward her, his eyes red but intent. He was walking with a slight limp and she wondered what had transpired during the fight with the gunman. He'd shed his jacket too and replaced it with an Alpine Lodge hoodie, but in spite of his efforts to clean up, she could still see blood on his pants and boots.

It was strange how such a gruesome sight could fill her with such relief. She didn't know many details about the bodyguard's death, except bits and pieces she'd over-heard from officers who'd visited the scene, but she was grateful for it all the same. Did that make her a monster? There would be time to unpack all that later. What mattered now was that she and Joel were alive.

"The checkpoint was too late and it looks like they already made it through," he said. "The storm is bad enough that UDOT is closing the freeway through Parley's Canyon, but it's not as bad going south through Provo Canyon, so they're putting out APBs in both directions."

"But she was so close!"

"I know." He rubbed her arm gently. "The good news is the storm will slow him down, too. It'll be a lot harder to get out of the state now that everyone's looking for them. I'm going to see if there are any rooms available here at the lodge. It might be a while before they have any word. We should try and get some rest."

A young clerk—the same one who had found them the sweatshirts—perked up as Joel approached. She reached out and touched his elbow as she handed him a packet of key cards.

Did everyone in the resort know what had happened?

A deputy dressed in jeans and a sweater, who looked like she wasn't any older than Val, approached. "It's Valerie, isn't it? I'm Detective Rylie Harris of Summit County Sheriff's Major Crimes Unit. Can I ask you some questions about what happened tonight?"

Val sighed inwardly. They'd been searched, questioned, photographed, questioned, separated, and questioned some more. But she followed the detective to a distant corner of the lobby and sat in a deep leather sofa next to a towering grandfather clock that looked to be original to the hundred-year-old building.

The questions proved to be a distraction, which she appreciated. But she didn't appreciate the direction the questions took after a while. Specifically the questions about Joel. Their relationship, what they were doing there together, his state of mind, and his service record. Val felt indignant and made sure to mention how he'd saved KJ Greer just twenty-four hours earlier.

Detective Harris seemed to run out of steam at that point. "Thank you. That's enough for tonight. I'll be in touch if I have more questions."

Val nodded and left the young detective to her notes. She knew better than to think that was the last of the interviews she would have to give, but she would answer the same questions a million times if that's what it took to stop Charles and bring Abby back.

Joel was waiting for her near the reception desk, their bags at his feet. The elevator was deafeningly quiet as they rode to their floor.

There was so much to say and yet no words to say it. They settled on a squeeze of the hand, a searching look. When they got to their room, Val sidled past the four-poster bed that stretched almost wall-to-wall and looked out the pair of dormer windows. Dozens of emergency vehicles filled the parking lot, and red and blue lights flashed through the trees in the distance where the Fisher's cabin stood.

She glanced at the clock on the bedside table. It read 2:16 a.m.

"Is that time right?" she asked, surprised.

"Yeah. Do you mind if I take the bathroom?"

"Please. You earned it." She meant it as a joke, but thinking of Adam's blood pooled against the tile floor and sprayed across the wall, it suddenly sounded macabre. She couldn't muster a smile and regretted the poor quip.

When the shower started a few minutes later, Val changed into dry clothes. The falling snow was already covering the flashing lights from the sheriff's vehicles, muting everything even as it scattered the light so that it almost seemed like daylight outside.

Abby was out there somewhere. Would Jordan keep her safe? Would Charles surrender peacefully? Would they find them before it was too late?

The activity outside was a comfort to her, a reminder

that Abby had been so close and a whole host of trained professionals were searching for her. Similarly, Val drew comfort from the sound of the water running long in the bathroom. It was a reminder that Joel was there for her. That no matter how long the night lasted while she waited for word about Abby, she wouldn't have to face it alone.

WHEN RED AND blue lights started flashing behind Grandpa's car, Abby swiveled, thinking there had been another accident. She counted at least four big SUVs, two of them black with bright headlights that made her duck down against the seat to escape their blinding lights.

Grandpa swore and the car started to speed up, but more black vehicles moved in front of them and to the sides, blocking them. They slowed to a stop right in the middle of the empty freeway. People were shouting outside and Abby stared, wide-eyed, at the nearest silhouette holding a big rifle. It reminded her of the ones used to kill the cougar on their hill.

Were they going to shoot them?

Grandpa raised his hands above the steering wheel. A bright light shone through his window and he winced. Dad raised his hands too, but as he did he murmured, "It's going to be okay. Don't worry. Everything's going to be fine."

There was more shouting—were they shouting at

Grandpa?—and then Grandpa looked back at Abby, his eyes sad.

"I did it for you, Abby. Don't forget that."

Then he opened the door and stepped out, his hands on his head.

Figures in black rushed forward and grabbed Grandpa. Abby made a small noise of fear, but before she could ask what was happening, the door next to Dad was flung open and a big man was pulling him out of the car.

Why were they getting arrested? Were they not supposed to be driving in the snow? Dad said they weren't but Grandpa had said it was fine.

Abby shrank away as a man dressed in a black coat reached for her too. She raised her hands like Dad and Grandpa, terrified, but not able to find the words.

The man lifted her up out of the back seat. "Are you Abigail Fisher?" he demanded.

She didn't answer. She stared at the ground where Dad was on his knees, his hands behind his head. What was going on? What had they done wrong?

"Daddy?" she managed to choke out.

He raised his head and the expression on his face sent panic through her. She twisted, trying to fight her way out of the man's grip.

"Daddy!"

But the man was too strong, and in a few short strides he was placing her in the back of a black SUV and closing the door. It was hard to see past the swirling snow, but she could just make out Grandpa getting to his feet, his hands behind his back like he'd been handcuffed.

The door wouldn't budge and she was filled with a sudden desperation, like being trapped in the bad man's car. When the opposite door opened, she thought for a second that it was the bad man coming to get her, and she almost screamed, but then she realized it was a woman and she was smiling.

"Miss Abigail Fisher? Boy howdy, am I glad to see you."

45

THE PHONE RANG, its shrill cry startling Val. She barely registered crossing the quaint guest room at the Alpine Lodge and reaching for the receiver before she answered it, her heart in her throat.

"Yes?"

"Ms. Rockwell, you may not remember me," the voice on the other end of the line began. "I'm Deputy US Marshal Wendy Bines—"

"Bines!" Val interrupted. "Yes, I remember you."

"Well, it just so happens that I've been stationed out of Salt Lake for the past three months and I was working a case here in Ogden when I got the call that Jordan Fisher was on the run and presumed to be making his way to the border, and I thought, 'that snake isn't slipping away again.' And I'm happy to say, Ms. Rockwell, that we've recovered both Jordan Fisher and his less-than-squeaky-clean father, Charles Fisher, as well."

"And Abby? What about my daughter?"

"Fine as frog's hair, Ms. Rockwell. In fact, she's sitting right here with me and wants to say hello."

Val's breath stilled. "She's there? Yes, put her on!"

There was a rustling as the phone receiver shifted, and then Abby's small voice asked uncertainly, "Mommy?"

Val's knees went weak, and she sank onto the edge of the bed. "Abby, yes! Hi, it's me! Where are you?" She didn't want to miss even a single sound from the other end of the phone, so she bit back the relieved laugh that bubbled in her throat.

Time stopped for a long moment as she waited for Abby's answer.

"I'm in a big black car. They took Daddy and Grandpa away and won't tell me where they're going." Abby's fear was palpable over the line.

"That must have been really scary. But I promise that they're going to take good care of you."

"Where are you? Are you going to come get me?"

"Yes! Yes I will, very soon."

The sound on the other end shifted and Deputy Marshal Bines came back on the line.

"If you and Detective Ramirez could make your way down to the local station in Park City in the morning, she'll be waiting for you there."

Val released a shaky exhale. "Not until morning?"

"Parley's Canyon is closed so we can't get up there until it reopens. They're going to get her checked out here and then we should have her up there as soon as the freeway opens."

Val checked the clock again. So many hours. "We'll be there," she said firmly. "Thank you."

After she hung up, she moved to the dormer window and closed the curtain against the red lights of the emergency vehicles outside.

"Did they find her?"

Val hadn't heard Joel come out of the bathroom, but he was standing there with a towel around his hips. Water beaded on his shoulders and chest.

"You're all wet." The observation felt out of place somehow, like her mind was split in too many directions.

"I heard the phone. Any news?"

"She's safe." She repeated it again, marveling at the words. "She's safe and they're bringing her back to Park City in the morning. I even got to talk to her for a few seconds."

Joel ran his hands over his eyes and down his face, letting out a sigh. "Thank God." He looked at the bedside clock. "Three a.m. is morning, right?"

Val managed her first smile in hours. "It is to me. But the freeway's closed. They won't be able to get through until the storm passes."

She had a strange feeling of being disconnected from her body, the marshal's words repeating in her head. Like a ship unmoored and seeking an anchor, she went to Joel and slipped her arms around his waist, not caring about the chill wetness against her face as she leaned against his bare chest.

"I don't know how I'll wait until morning."

"Do you think you'll be able to get any sleep?" Joel asked.

"I don't know. Will you?"

"As long as I can hold you like this." His arms tightened around her.

"I wouldn't have it any other way."

The moment stretched long as they stood in silence, her fingers tracing the fresh scars pocking his back, raising goose bumps on his skin. The scars were a vivid reminder of how close she'd come to losing him in the bombing.

Just as she'd almost lost him tonight.

She wanted to tell him how terrified she'd been, how certain that she would never feel his arms around her again. She wanted to tell him how grateful she was that he was there with her, that he had joined her in coming to Utah, and also how grateful she was that he was in her life and Abby's. She wanted to express the hope stirring in her heart that now—with Abby safe and on her way back to them—they could look forward to being a real family.

Words felt inadequate, so instead she lifted her face to his, meeting his lips with hers. He cradled her skull and kissed her gently, not asking for more. Giving her space to pull away. He hadn't shaved and his whiskers were sharp against her lips, but she didn't care. She felt truly alive for the first time in days, relief purging the despair that had been her companion for the longest week of her life.

Her mouth grew more insistent, exploring his with a kindling desire that went beyond physical hunger. She was filled with a fierce urge to peel off all her layers, like shedding an outer skin that had been so damaged it was trapping her in brokenness. She wanted to let it all go, to feel stripped to her core so there was nothing standing between the two of them. No anxiety, no fear, no uncertainty for the future.

She sensed the same intensity building in Joel, the same need to push back against the darkness and find comfort together. And this time, she didn't pull away. His hands were cold as he slid them under her sweatshirt, but she welcomed him, pulling him toward the bed.

They wouldn't stay cold for long.

THERE WERE SO many things Joel loved about his job. The thrill of the hunt. The satisfaction of fitting a crucial piece into the puzzle so the answer was revealed. The unexpected discovery that KJ Greer was still alive—had that really been less than forty-eight hours earlier?

But this. Nothing compared to this.

Seeing Abby run into Val's arms at the Summit County Justice Center—with a teddy bear and fleece blanket in her arms—made Joel's heart swell like nothing else he'd ever experienced on the job. He had to turn away as tears burned his eyes, and he pressed his lips together to hold back the pressure in his throat.

Abby buried her face in Val's neck.

"Don't leave me," she begged. "Please don't leave me."

"Oh, baby." Val's voice cracked. "I'll never leave you. I promise. I had to say those things to keep you safe. But I will never, ever leave you again."

Lines of old tears had dried channels through the dirt on Abby's cheeks.

"They arrested Daddy and Grandpa. I thought they were arresting me too and I was so scared. They weren't like you, Joel. These police were mean."

Joel crouched down by her side and rubbed her back. "They were just doing their job. I'm sure they're nice enough when they aren't chasing bad guys."

Abby cocked her head. "But Daddy and Grandpa aren't bad guys."

Val winced. "I'm sorry you had to see that. Your dad was trying to help you, but Grandpa did some bad things when he took you away from me. No one has a right to take you. Not Grandpa. Not even Daddy."

Confusion creased Abby's brow and she clung to Val again. Val staggered to her feet under the burden of Abby's weight.

"Here, I'll take her," Joel offered.

Val looked as if she wanted to say no, but she passed Abby off reluctantly.

Abby wrapped her legs around Joel's waist and clung to his neck, her head resting against his shoulder as they walked out to the parking lot.

"I tried to call you from the motel," she murmured.

"You did?" He looked down at her in surprise. Did Abby even know his phone number?

"He unplugged the phone or else I would have called 911."

"Ah." He didn't correct her. Instead, he said, "If you had called me, I would have jumped in my car, turned on my siren, and raced to find you as fast as I could."

"I knew it," she said, sounding satisfied.

Then she kissed him on the cheek, a clumsy, light peck.

Joel blinked, surprised. Speechless. Emotion rose in his throat as he caught Val's eye. The way she smiled told him she'd seen it too. She squeezed his arm, her eyes shining, and in her touch he felt he belonged.

You have a family now, Marnie had told him. This was the first time Joel believed it for himself.

46

"I wish it would snow here," Abby said from the back seat of Joel's truck as they approached Owl Creek. She'd been quiet these past few days, her carefree personality subdued. Now she leaned against the window, watching as the pale wintry light filtered through low-lying fog. Grass, trees, fence posts and roofs were covered in a thick frost. Almost like snow.

"It's cold enough for it," Val said. "But we need both the cold and the moisture at the same time to get snow. And look, you can see blue sky through the fog. Hopefully it'll clear and we'll get some sunshine today."

"I, for one, have had enough snow to last me a lifetime," Joel said.

"You and me both. I've never been so grateful for the rain." Val watched out the window, noting that not all of the missing posters had yet been removed from telephone poles.

She'd taken a break from the news since Abby had

been found, not wanting to hear what was being said about the Fishers. She didn't want to hear how Jeanette was trying to spin Charles' involvement, or how the press was vilifying Jordan. But she'd needed to know about KJ.

"He targeted her," Joel had told her the morning after Abby's rescue, while they'd waited at the Alpine Lodge for word that Abby had arrived in Park City. "Nathan Weiss obsessed over KJ for months, following Leisa on social media and spying on their residence. We don't know what tipped him over the edge, why he decided to take KJ that night. But KJ confirmed that he wasn't expecting to take Sophie and had to improvise when he found another girl with his intended target."

The truck slowed as they drove past the Owl Creek Elementary School where children on the playground were blobs of shadow in the fog, formless shapes behind the chain link fence. As they neared the front, Val saw a large banner made of butcher paper and painted letters spanning the brick above the entrance.

WELCOME HOME KJ AND ABBY

Sophie's name was conspicuously absent, and Val felt a wrenching pang of sympathy for Faye McNamara.

She forced a brightness into her voice. "Look at the sign!" She pointed out the window and Abby shifted, craning her neck to see. "They're welcoming you home." Her voice squeaked a little on that last word, her throat closing with emotion. Joel's hand closed over hers, warm and reassuring.

Abby didn't say anything, but she watched the sign recede in the distance until it was swallowed up by fog.

Would Abby ever feel safe again? Val wondered as

they passed the lot where the new bank was under construction. Her eyes went, as they always did, to the empty lot behind City Hall. Would Abby grow to hate this town for the terror she'd experienced, or would she learn how many people were praying for her and find her place in the community?

They passed a truck heading the opposite way on Main Street. Its headlights were on and flashed as it passed, the rapid beep of a lightly-tapped horn accompanying it. Joel lifted his hand in greeting.

"Who was that?" Val asked.

"Either Luke or Angie, I didn't see who was driving."

Val hadn't lived in Owl Creek long enough to recognize their old high school classmates' vehicles, but it gave her an unexpected feeling of pride to think that someday she would. Living in a small town had its downsides, for sure. But there were some real blessings too, and for the first time she felt like maybe Owl Creek could be a destination after all, not just a stop along the way to something bigger.

As they took the county road out of town and drove past the Greer home, her thoughts sobered. Had KJ been able to return to her house and sleep in her bed? Or would Leisa move away so KJ didn't have to live with constant reminders of the nightmare she'd been through?

Recovery would be a long, slow road, and KJ's life would forever be changed by her traumatic ordeal. But, Val knew from the countless hours of research she'd done in the past week, there were many survivors out there doing amazing work to help others heal. She wouldn't have to do it alone.

Val's thoughts were interrupted by Joel's phone buzzing. He handed it over, but she didn't recognize the number. When she answered it to hear, "Mrs. Fisher, this is—" she immediately hung up.

"I think it's time for you to get a new phone number," she said with a sigh.

"Again?" Joel asked.

Requests for interviews were coming in from news agencies all over the country. She might have taken a break from the news, but the news hadn't taken a break from her. And this time she wasn't the only one on their radar.

Val silenced his phone. "I think I'll go ahead and meet with Wesley Peters, though. I feel like I owe him that much."

"You don't owe him anything."

"He didn't have to help me," Val argued, "but he did, without any promise of getting anything in return. He's a decent guy, I think."

Joel grunted his disapproval.

She smirked. "Besides, there's something satisfying about talking to a local journalist instead of one of these big syndicates. Let them be jealous of the little guy for once."

Joel gave a begrudging chuckle as he slowed to turn onto Alderbrook Lane leading to the Rockwell property. The black SUV that had been parked there for a week was gone. Val breathed a sigh of relief. The FBI wasn't finished with them, she was sure, but there was no longer any immediate threat or need for constant surveillance.

With the change in elevation, the fog cleared as if by

magic. It still clung to the valley like static holding Abby's socks to the inside of the dryer, but up in the hills the sun shone brightly through the windshield, causing Joel to grab his sunglasses. The cab of the truck warmed and Val reached for Joel's hand, feeling the closest thing to contentment she'd felt in a long time.

There would still be lots of healing to do. Even though Abby had been abducted in what basically amounted to a twisted custody dispute, the trauma of being taken against her will would shape her for years to come.

And Abby wasn't the only one.

"I'm thinking of calling that therapist," Val said. "The one in Medford who specializes in eating disorders. If you think...would you be willing to watch Abby for me?"

The only sign acknowledging the gravity of her request was a small tic in Joel's cheek. "I'd like that."

Up ahead, half a dozen news vans lined the road. Val straightened, alert. Further up the road, two county vehicles formed a barricade, blocking the vans from continuing.

"Hey Gabby-girl, why don't you put your hood on for a bit while we pass these cameras."

They'd had to buy Abby clothes before they left Park City, and her new coat had a generous hood lined with thick fur. Val offered a reassuring smile as Abby obeyed, but inwardly she cringed as the truck slowed for the barricade, wishing the fog had lingered. She tried to avoid looking directly at the cameras pointed their way.

They reached the barricade, and Joel rolled down his

window as Kim approached. She leaned an elbow on his door and grinned.

"Hello there! Glad you made it back."

"Glad to be back. What's up?" Joel asked.

"Willis and I are protecting your arrival from the lookie-loos, if you will. I can't promise they'll stay away for good, but this should give you a bit of peace while you get your little girl home and settled. Meg and Nicole were here earlier checking on the place, but they cleared out a bit ago so you'll have it all to yourselves."

"Thanks, Kim," Joel said warmly. "Tell Willis we appreciate you both."

Kim gestured to the other SUV and it moved onto the shoulder, making room for Joel's truck to pass. Val breathed a sigh of relief as the news vans disappeared behind them.

"Sounds like it's time to go into hibernation mode. Too bad I haven't been grocery shopping since before New Year's."

"We'll figure it out," Joel replied. "Besides, Nicole texted last night. She didn't come right out and say it, but I think 'checking on the place' was code for 'cleaning up and stocking the refrigerator' before we arrived. I think she and Meg guessed we'd need a little time to ourselves."

The use of the word "we" soothed her.

It would be at least a few more days before he returned to work, and Val knew the time together would pass all too quickly. There was still so much they hadn't talked about: they simply hadn't had the time or the privacy. Once they'd been reunited with Abby, she hadn't been out of Val's sight. Val had even relinquished her insistence on Abby closing the bathroom door.

Abby was having regular potty accidents, but a nice woman at the Justice Center had assured Val that it was most likely a temporary challenge that would resolve over time.

All this focus on Abby meant Val hadn't yet found a good time to tell Joel about that excruciating moment in the cabin when—with Abby in her arms—she'd realized that fighting would only hurt Abby and for her sake, Val had to let her go. She also hadn't yet heard the full story from Joel about making the impossible decision to shoot Adam even though that put Val at enormous risk.

There would be time for all that in the coming days.

But there was one conversation they'd made sure to have with Abby present.

As they rounded the final corner of the lane and the farmhouse came into view—water dripping like jewels from the porch roof where the frost had thawed—Val's gaze went to the real estate sign planted in her yard.

"You want me to take that down tomorrow?" Joel asked.

"You're sure about this?"

"Stop trying to give me an out. I've never been more sure of anything, Valerie Rockwell." He flashed her a smile that made her heart soar.

When Val had called her mom to tell her about Abby's rescue, she'd asked if it would be all right to take the house off the market, at least for the time being. Her mom had readily agreed, citing the importance of having stability for Abby during this crucial time and how upsetting a move would be right now.

Val hadn't mentioned that someone *would* be moving, just not her and Abby.

She did a quick self check-in for any sign of the hesitation and second-guessing she'd felt earlier whenever she thought of Joel moving in permanently. But it was gone. Instead, she felt a reassuring rightness.

The question he'd asked the night he'd found out about the pregnancy test—was it really only a week ago? —came back to her now.

Would you marry me if I asked you, Val?

There were a lot of things Val wasn't sure about. The route to Abby's healing, her future plans for schooling, how her relationship with Jordan would change and what legal recourse she had to protect Abby against his parents. But the past few days had cemented one irrefutable truth: the one thing in her life that she could absolutely count on was Joel, and if he'd asked her that question now, her answer would have been as easy as it was sincere.

"Look, there's Creampuff," Abby said from the backseat as Joel parked and shut off the engine, interrupting Val's reverie. Abby opened her door and jumped down, letting in an icy blast of air.

The cat was sitting on the porch, and as Abby approached she leaped to the ground and headed toward the shop as if to escape. But she didn't seem that committed to it, and Abby caught her before she made it far, making Val wonder if Creampuff had missed Abby too.

Val exited the truck and breathed in the fresh January air, the sunlight warm on her back. The smell of woodsmoke drew her attention to the brick chimney and she noticed a shimmer of heat where it met blue sky.

"They built a fire," she realized with delight. "They thought of everything. Maybe we can hibernate after all."

"Sounds good to me."

They climbed the porch steps and Abby joined them, Creampuff draped over one arm.

"You happy to be home, kiddo?" Joel asked while Val unlocked the door.

She nodded and a ghost of a smile flitted across her lips, a hint of the old Abby.

"I'm happy you're home, too," Val said, pausing to give Abby a squeeze before she pushed open the door.

"Me too," Joel added, but he was looking at Val when he said it. The glint in his eye warmed her more thoroughly than the sun and gave her the assurance that she could face the long road to healing that lay ahead of them.

With Joel and Abby by her side, she could face anything.

THE END

THANK YOU FOR READING!

Ending this series fills me with a range of emotions. I've been looking forward to this day for a long time—the day when I could share Val and Joel's final story with you—because the only thing better than writing stories is sharing them with readers who love them as much as I do.

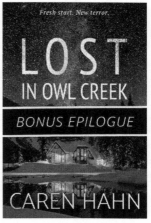

Because I'm a relatively unknown author without the backing of a large publisher and expensive marketing department, every reader is priceless to me. If you've enjoyed *Lost in Owl Creek*, I hope you'll consider helping other readers discover it by leaving a review on Amazon, BookBub, or Goodreads. (While you're at it, don't forget to leave reviews for the other books in the series too!)

I have to confess that in addition to being excited, I'm also mourning a little bit. (Or a lot.) I've grown to love these characters so much—even as I put them through some truly horrific things in this last book—and it's so hard to say goodbye. But I think they've earned their happily ever after and don't want me meddling in their lives anymore, don't you?

If you are mourning the end of the Owl Creek series with me, I have a gift for you: a bonus epilogue that takes place nearly a year after the events in this book. I wrote the first draft of this story for fun during the lockdown of 2020, before I ever knew there would be a book two or three. In fact, this epilogue is one of the reasons I could begin to imagine more to Val and Joel's story, sparking the idea for a series instead of ending with book one.

It's exclusively available when you sign up for my monthly newsletter, giving us a way to stay in touch beyond the last page.

Here's an excerpt:

> *Joel rested a hand gently on Abby's head and kissed her forehead. Every so often it struck him how lucky he was in his new life, and he was left almost breathless. He was glad Abby had shared her worries and hoped that whatever he'd said had comforted her. Val always seemed to know the right thing to say, but parenting was still so new for him. Now he'd be alone for a whole week with Abby. What if she was bored? What if she didn't like him as much by the end of the week?*
>
> *Yawning, he went to his own room, intending to go*

straight to bed. But his packed suitcase was waiting for him on the bed, an expectant reminder that filled him with disappointment. With a sigh, he started putting away his clothes, his thoughts on Abby.

He was glad she'd shared her fears for her friend, Kara. It was a heart-breaking accident and the poor little girl's life would never be the same. By the time Joel had arrived, Kara's brother had already been rushed by ambulance to the hospital, and the responding deputies had their hands full trying to keep the parents from the scene.

Not that it had done much good. From the time Kara's screams alerted them to the accident in the woods until the first responders arrived on the scene, her parents had already tampered with so much evidence that Joel could only reconstruct what happened from eyewitness accounts.

It was the kind of senseless tragedy that made Joel angry with no one to blame. The Simpsons kept their guns locked up and the key hidden. They just hadn't counted on a curious fourteen-year-old finding the key and getting a crazy idea to take his sister plinking unsupervised in the woods.

It still bothered him that they hadn't been able to recover the slug from the shooting. They'd spent the rest of the day combing through the undergrowth and long grass, and inspecting surrounding trees, but to no avail. They found bullets and casings connected to the targets, but none that could have been the one which blew through Steven's chest. It was a small thing, but Joel hated loose ends.

Speaking of loose ends...

At the bottom of his suitcase, tucked inside a pair of running socks, Joel found the little box he'd been looking for. He snapped the velvet lid open to make sure the ring was still there, snuggled into its cushion.

He was reasonably sure Val wasn't expecting a proposal to come out of this trip. She could be surprisingly adept at guessing his thoughts sometimes, but he was very good at obfuscating if he wanted to. He'd made a concerted effort to talk about their future in uncertain terms of "who knows where we'll be in five years," and "there's no rush, we've got lots of time."

In recent months, her relief at his neutral position had subtly shifted to disappointment. She'd tried to hide it, but he could read her like a book.

Little did she know he'd already been ring shopping.

Find out how Abby helps Joel solve the case and how Joel puts the ring to use by downloading the full epilogue at carenhahn.com/lostbonus (or use the QR code below).

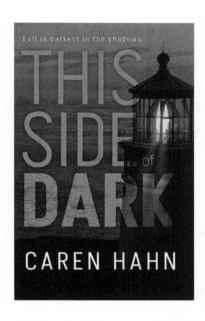

EVIL IS DARKEST IN THE SHADOWS

"...a page-turner that you better not start at bedtime..."

"...a rollercoaster mystery that keeps you guessing at every turn and leaves you wanting to ride it again!"

"...an engaging and suspenseful story that will keep readers hooked until the very last page."

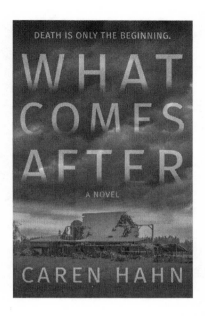

DEATH IS ONLY THE BEGINNING.

WHAT COMES AFTER

A NOVEL

CAREN HAHN

CAN JUSTICE BE SERVED FROM BEYOND THE GRAVE?

"deliciously suspenseful"

"had me hooked from the beginning"

"a few twists to keep the reader on their toes and a final chapter that brought me to tears"

What do a high-octane mommy blogger, a Wild West romance, and a [possibly] possessed antique doll have in common?

You can find them all in my FREE collection of short stories. Visit carenhahn.com to download your copy!

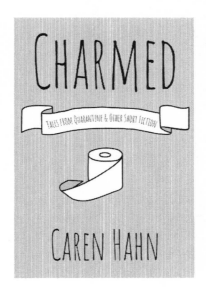

ACKNOWLEDGMENTS

Finishing a series well requires a special touch. The stakes need to be the highest yet, and the relationship growth needs to be rich and satisfying. The ending needs to serve as a conclusion not just for that book, but for the entire series as we say goodbye to characters we've grown to love.

My goal is to give you the kind of book hangover that lasts for days, with an immersive experience that lingers. That can only happen if the story resonates in a way that's relatable and realistic. So what does that mean for me?

Research.

Lots and lots of research.

This book required more research than any other in the series. While there are many wonderful resources online, I'm especially grateful to law enforcement partners who made themselves available to answer my many questions.

B. Adam Richardson of the Writer's Detective Bureau once again deserves credit for helping me get details as realistic as possible, as well as Bob Schofield whose insights on FBI procedure prompted some important rewrites at a critical time. They don't deserve the blame for my mistakes, but they deserve a big thank you for the things I got right!

I also want to thank the Clark County Sheriff's Office in Washington state for putting together a phenomenal Citizens' Academy. I learned so much from each of the presentations; I couldn't take notes fast enough. Even better were the stories told by individual deputies and detectives who gave me a peek behind the shield to see the humanity beneath. They probably had no idea that our casual conversations were helping me shape this story, but they did all the same.

The town of Owl Creek is fictional, but it's inspired by my own hometown in rural Oregon. While there are many heart-warming aspects of life in a small community, it can also be a setting for our worst nightmares. Tragic drunk-driving deaths, sexual assaults, and domestic violence often mar the sleepy tranquility of small town life.

Then there are the unthinkable horrors that leave a community forever scarred.

This book is dedicated to the memory of two girls from my hometown who—in separate circumstances several years apart—left their homes for the kind of ordinary activities that children do every day, but tragically, never returned. In one instance, the murderer was apprehended soon after. In the other, he has yet to face justice.

I think we as a public—with our crime dramas and fictional entertainment—can forget that true life investigations don't include a script with foreshadowing and the relevant evidence skimmed off the top to guide the reader to a well-crafted solution. The dedication to carefully collecting and analyzing evidence, waiting on lab results which can take weeks or months to receive, and observing all necessary protocols so that facts, not theories, can be upheld in a court of law—it's nothing like television. And it can be excruciating when a case falls apart in court and a perpetrator walks free.

So I want to give a shout-out to all the men and women who face the worst of humanity every day, but continue to show up with clear heads and dedicated hearts to protect and serve their communities. I'm especially grateful that there are more mental health initiatives in place to support law enforcement and other first responders so that they can better keep the darkness at bay for the rest of us. These are the quiet, unsung heroes in our communities who show up in the worst moments of our lives and, in the best of cases, do so with grace and compassion.

Beta readers on this manuscript included Cori Hatch, Jenny Hahn, and Andrew Hahn. Their insights were invaluable and their enthusiasm was contagious. I also want to thank Camdon Hatch who helped me work out details in the final fight scene, fleshing it out while preserving realism.

Many thanks to my editor, Rachel Pickett of Polished Copy Editing Services. When I make a manuscript the best I can on my own, it's always gratifying to discover that, with her help, it can get even better.

I also give heartfelt thanks to members of my small yet mighty ARC team who went the extra mile in ferreting out those last pesky typos which persisted through multiple rounds of editing and proofreading.

Nicolette Reite, Kristi Perkins, Amanda Fallows, Ashley Brown, Laurie Boyes, Janelle Mackowiak, Cori Hatch, Arlyse DeLoyola, Michelle Weber, and Penny Romensas —thanks for helping put the final polish on this manuscript. Your love for this series brings a smile on otherwise dark days.

No book I ever write would be possible without the support of my husband. I couldn't ask for a more steady, encouraging partner (or a more supportive cover designer). Building a relationship that lasts a lifetime requires a willingness to take stock and do the work to level up. That's why writing loyal, committed character relationships is my favorite, because—thanks to Andrew and our marriage of twenty-five years—I know for a fact that they're worth the effort.

ABOUT THE AUTHOR

CAREN HAHN is a Suspense and Fantasy author of stories featuring empathetic characters who are exquisitely flawed. She grew up in a tiny logging community with more than its fair share of tragedy and violent crime, giving her early exposure to the dark side of life. Caren graduated from  Brigham Young University where—between courses on Humanities, English Lit, and Biblical Hebrew—she squeezed in as many Creative Writing classes as she could. She lives in the Pacific Northwest with her family.

Receive a free collection of short stories when you sign up to get updates at carenhahn.com.

Follow Caren on Amazon or BookBub to learn about new releases, and connect with her on social media to learn about all the bits that come in between.

Made in United States
Troutdale, OR
11/24/2024

25255268R00296